ENDLESS

MANHATTAN KNIGHTS 3

EVA HAINING

COPYRIGHT

TO MY BEAUTIFUL GOLDILOCKS

You know who you are.
I love you.

PROLOGUE

LOGAN

I love the familiar scent of this room. Leather. I find it comforting. The walls are a dark sumptuous purple, the lighting muted, highlighting the various features it has to offer. There's a black leather chaise in one corner, with metal restraints at the top and bottom. The center of the room boasts an ornate oversized table, perfect for bending a woman over and spanking her until her cheeks are a stunning shade of red. This is my room. Everything is just the way I like it.

My latest submissive in training is standing flush against the wooden cross adorning the wall at the far end of the room. Her legs spread wide, her arms outstretched and ready to be restrained. She is completely naked, vulnerable, and waiting for my command.

"Well done, angel. You are displayed exactly as I requested. You will be rewarded for that."

I watch as a shiver runs through her body at my words, causing her to shake against the harsh wooden beams. I stride forward, unbuttoning my shirt and dropping it to the floor before I reach her.

I slowly run my hand down her spine, her alabaster skin reacting to the lightest touch. I enjoy her sharp intake of breath as I continue to run my fingers down over her tight little ass, before making my way lower until I reach her ankle. I quickly fasten the brown leather cuffs rendering her helpless to escape. First one and then the other, before standing to repeat the process for her wrists.

When I'm satisfied she is completely at my mercy, I stand back to admire the view.

I love the freedom I have in here. To be myself. To cast off the shackles and restrictions of my life outside of this club.

"You look stunning tonight, angel. Are you ready for me?"

Her gaze remains firmly fixed on the wall in front of her.

"Yes, Master Fitzgerald."

"Good girl."

I slip my hand between her legs, firmly grasping her pussy, feeling the evidence of her arousal dripping onto my palm.

"You certainly are. I'm going to taste you now, but do not come without my permission. Understood?"

"Yes, Master."

I drop to my knees, nestling myself between her legs before taking a long, languorous lick from the tip of her clit down through her folds and around her entrance. Dipping my tongue in for a proper taste, her pussy clenches around me.

I continue my ministrations, my tongue sweeping circles over and around her clit. Feeling her thighs trying to tighten around my face. She is helpless to curb her own desire. Spread open for my pleasure alone. I can feel her orgasm building, the sheen of sweat on her naked flesh, the almost imperceptible shaking of her limbs against the restraints. It's a glorious feeling, pushing her to the edge of ecstasy before reeling her back in.

A whimper escapes her at the loss of my warm tongue against her sex.

"Please, Master."

"Did I give you permission to speak?"

"No."

I slap her ass, hard.

"You will address me properly."

"Yes, Master."

I leave her smarting from my hand and make my way over to the door, to the cabinet containing everything I need. I enjoy the sting of my palm from a single hit, but tonight I am in the mood for something… harder. I search until I find my black riding crop. Perfect. It has just the right tension, just enough bite to make her nerve endings sing with every lash, enhancing the euphoria that will inevitably follow.

"You will receive ten lashes of this crop, angel, and maybe you will remember to address me appropriately in future. You will stay silent throughout. If you make a single noise, you will get ten more. Do you understand me?"

She is quick to answer me, her vulnerability and arousal evident in the quiver of her voice.

"Yes, Master Fitzgerald."

I love the feel of the crop connecting with her skin. The sharp sound as it whips through the air and lands across her ass. My dick is getting harder with every hit, straining against my pants, aching to be inside of her, but the growing anticipation is what really turns me on. Knowing I can't chase my own release until I have seen to her every need and desire.

With the last lash, I stand back and admire the imprint of my crop, a crimson flush on her skin, stunning in its simplicity.

"Good girl. You did as you were told and remained quiet. Now you will be rewarded."

I tilt her chin around to face me, but her gaze is lowered.

"You may look at me."

When our eyes connect, the lust I see reflected back at me is absolutely breathtaking. I dip two fingers into her pussy, drenched from the arousal of her lashes, before lifting them to her lips and spreading her juices for her to taste.

"Oh you liked that, angel. You're more than ready for me now."

Our lips meet in a deliberately torturous kiss, our tongues twisting and tangling, her sweet juices mingling with the taste of mint on her breath, and when I step back she is breathless with anticipation.

I slowly unzip my pants, letting my erection spring free, watching as her eyes widen at the sight of my impressive length. I take myself in hand and start pumping my fist. She loves to watch, and I love to see the desire spiral out of control in her eyes.

"You've seen enough. Eyes back on the wall." She's a compliant little sub in training. I might keep this one for myself, for a while at least.

I love the way her body trembles at the sound of me ripping open the foil packet with my teeth, her anticipation growing as she waits for me to slowly roll the condom over my now rock-solid cock.

I position myself behind her, still shackled to the cross, and thrust just the tip inside. Her satisfied moan is so sexy, spurring me on to give her more of what she craves. My dick pounding into her, driving her toward an explosive release.

"That's it, angel. Let me hear how much you want me."

I seat myself to the hilt, filling her, stretching her, enjoying the clench of her muscles around me.

"Oh God... yes... Master... yes!"

I snake my hands around to cup her pert voluptuous breasts, her nipples tight and puckered, desperate for my attention. I knead them, flick them, pull them, rocking into her in measured strokes, nibbling on her neck as she struggles against the restraints, against the intense onslaught of sensations bombarding her body. I circle her clit with my thumb, taking her to the brink and holding her there until I'm ready to let her come.

As I hammer into her over and over, I can feel my own release building, a warmth spreading throughout my body, and with one last brush of my finger, I send her over the edge.

"Come for me, angel." I feel the tension leave her body as she gives in to the euphoria, letting the restraints hold her as I set a punishing rhythm to find my own release. I come hard and long, thrusting into her over and over again as I ride out the waves of ecstasy coursing through my body.

When I'm fully sated, I take the time to dress before loosening her restraints and lifting her languid, exhausted body over to the chaise, laying her down gently, kissing her with a tenderness they all crave after such an intense session.

"You did well tonight. I think your training is almost complete." I turn to grab her clothes from the back of the door when she speaks.

"May I ask you a question, Master Fitzgerald?" I return to her side, wrapping her in a black silk robe.

"Of course. You can ask me anything."

Her voice is quiet and reserved as she speaks.

"Would you consider... keeping me... after my training is finished?" I cup her face in my hands, pressing a tender kiss to her sexy red lips.

"I will be honest with you. It's something I've considered, but I have not yet come to a decision. We will discuss the matter further at a later date."

I stand to leave, her eyes begging me to stay.

"Be here on Sunday at 5 p.m. I want you naked, blindfolded, and sitting on this chaise with your legs spread wide for me. Understand?"

She nods her head, before remembering her training.

"Yes, Master Fitzgerald."

"Good girl. Now get cleaned up and go straight home. I need to go, I have an appointment I can't miss. I've arranged for a car to take you back to your apartment. I'll see you on Sunday."

I turn and leave, eager not to miss my prior engagement.

As I walk through the club, the sights and sounds surrounding me are so familiar, tantalizing my senses as I make my way to the exit, but when I step out into the night air, a weight descends on me. My public persona needs to be firmly in place, the uninhibited freedom I just experienced locked tightly away. I hail a cab and focus on my destination.

I'm going to see a performance of *Swan Lake* at Lincoln Center tonight.

I'm going to see Vittoria...

PROLOGUE

VITTORIA

I've always loved when I truly lose myself in the music, when I let my body take over and my heart soar. It's so exhilarating. It doesn't matter whether I'm in a theatre full of people, or whether I'm alone and rehearsing. When I give myself over completely to the music, it takes me to a different planet, another dimension. I can let go of everything I am, and just... be.

There has never been a better feeling on earth... until tonight.

Tonight was different.

The moment I saw him in the crowd beside my family, something inside of me ignited in a way it never has before. The look in his eyes as he took in the sight of me. I felt naked, exposed, and completely turned on by the heat behind his dark and brooding gaze. Logan Fitzgerald sets my body on fire.

Every move I made was for him, and only him. When I dance, I dance for me, but the elation I felt tonight, was unlike anything I've ever experienced. By the time the show finished and the curtain dropped, I found myself panting. Not from physical exertion, but a reaction to his eyes on me.

It takes me longer than usual to shower and get ready to meet my family for dinner. When I do a show here in New York, at least one of them tries to come, and afterwards we go for dinner and catch up. Tonight, my parents, Carter, and Logan, are waiting for me outside of my dressing room. I can hear them talking, but as I stare at myself in the mirror, I don't know how I'm going to hide the flush in my cheeks, and the arousal I feel when he looks at me.

I've been hiding it for years, since the day Carter brought him home for Thanksgiving all those years ago, but the way I feel right now, I don't know if I'll be able to play the friendly little sister role. I want him, and if I open this door and he looks at me the same way he did from the crowd tonight, I might just crack. Carter would kill me if I ever pursued his best friend, but God, he does something to me. Something I can't control, ignore, or temper.

I smooth my hair down my back, fix my dress, and take one last look in the mirror before I finally work up the courage to open the door. I slowly turn the lock and twist the handle, the rush of cold air from the hallway causing goose bumps on my flesh.

I can't speak. I can't breathe. I can't think. My heart hammers in my chest, slamming against my ribcage, fighting to burst free.

"Hey, sis. You were amazing!" Carter pulls me into his arms, lifting me off the ground, twirling me around as if we were kids again. "I've missed you."

I hold him tight, his familiar scent making me feel safe and loved. "I've missed you, too, Carter. It's been too long."

As my parents congratulate me on my performance, and smother me with affection, their words are lost on me. All I can focus on is the man standing before me. I can't take my eyes off him.

His blond hair is messed to perfection. His stunning blue eyes are smoldering. His hands are firmly in his pockets, which only draws my attention. He's trying to hide his arousal, but I can see how he's straining against his pants, and it sends a jolt straight to my core. His eyes find mine, a moment of recognition passing between us, and when my mom lets go of me, I watch, in what feels like slow motion, as he takes his hands out of his pockets, runs them though his hair and lets out a long, drawn out breath as he strides toward me.

"Hello, Vittoria. You were... phenomenal, tonight. Truly inspiring." He runs the pad of his thumb over his bottom lip, his eyes trained on me, dark and dangerous, before pulling me into his arms. "It's good to see you again."

The warmth of his chest against mine, and the press of his crotch against my thigh, has me struggling to catch a breath. His strong masculine frame enveloping me as his delicious scent invades my senses. Logan is the one to break our embrace, pulling away without taking his eyes off me.

Oh my God.

He feels it, too. Not just a physical reaction, but a connection that can't be ignored. I watch his breath hitch, the rise and fall of his broad, firm chest quicken, and I know he feels it, too.

He closes his eyes for a split second, before leaning down and giving me a chaste kiss on my cheek, lingering a little longer than he should. His hand resting on the small of my back, burns my skin, fanning the flame inside of me that I've tried for so long to extinguish.

"Mmm." I bite down on my lip to stop myself from groaning again.

He pulls away, his gaze holding mine, as if he's trying to tell me something with this one look. I feel like he's staring into my soul and I'm fighting the urge to bridge the gap. The spark between us is a tangible entity, and I want so badly to feel his lips on mine. It could be hours or seconds, I'm not sure, but when he breaks the connection, I'm disappointed. His eyes drop to the floor before glancing in Carter's direction to see him studying us with a frown on his face.

"You done?" There's a hint of annoyance in Carter's voice, but I just ignore it.

"I'm not allowed to say hello to your friends anymore?"

"Of course. Just make it brief!"

"Shut up, Carter!"

My mom saves me any further embarrassment, and suggests we make our way back to the house for a late dinner together. Her knowing look telling me she didn't miss a moment of my interaction with Logan.

"I'll get going and leave you all to catch up. It was lovely seeing you again, Vittoria, Mr. and Mrs. de Rossi." My stomach churns at the thought of him leaving, but thankfully my mom isn't taking no for an answer.

"Don't be so silly, Logan. You're family. I insist you join us for dinner." My mom has this way about her. She's impossible to resist, and she always gets her own way.

"Well, how can I say no? I would love to join you, as long as you're sure I won't be imposing."

She pulls him into her arms, a true Italian mama at work. "My dear sweet boy. You are never an imposition. You know I love you like you're one of my own. Now let's get back to the house so I can feed you properly. You all look like you could use a good meal."

Logan laughs at my mom's never-ending mission to feed us all into an early grave, while Carter and I roll our eyes at each other. He gives me a wink before kissing mom on the cheek. "I need to go and check on a few things at Cube. I'll meet you guys at the house in an hour."

"I'll just ride with you. I don't mind hanging around for a while." Logan's looking for an out, and I don't like the way it makes me feel.

My mom speaks up, irritated that the boys seem to be abandoning her. "You will do no such thing. You can ride with us. Vittoria can keep you company until he arrives. An hour is all you get, Carter. You make sure you're at the house and ready to eat by then. No excuses."

He nods and laughs before slapping Logan on the shoulder. "Sorry, bro. My mother is the one woman I don't mess with. You're on your own."

Logan looks in my direction, and my heart stops. "I'll survive." There's a deeper meaning to his words. An unsettling truth. "Don't be late though, or your mom will make me eat your dinner, too."

"Deal." Carter leans in and gives me a kiss on the cheek. "You really were fantastic tonight, sis. I'll be as quick as I can and then I'm all yours. You can fill me in on what you've been up to for the past three months."

As we all make our way outside, I can feel the tension building. Carter leaves in a cab to check on one of his clubs, mom and dad go to pick up the car, and I'm left with Logan. It's cold tonight, and I didn't anticipate having to wait on the sidewalk for any length of time.

"Are you cold?" He takes off his jacket, wrapping it around my shoulders. "Here, this should heat you up." His scent surrounds me like a warm blanket, enveloping me, his hands resting on my arms, causing my stomach to somersault. "Better?"

I can barely manage to speak, taking a deep breath to try and calm myself. "Much... b... better." We stand, drinking in our proximity to one another, until the moment is broken by my parents' car pulling up beside us.

He opens the door, helping me climb into the backseat before closing the door and making his way round to the other side. As soon as he sits next to me, my whole body begins to buzz, the car seeming claustrophobic all of a sudden.

My mom and dad start grilling Logan about what he's been doing since they saw him last—what band is he working with—is he dating anyone? He's so polite, answering every question they throw at him, and I wait with bated breath to hear if he's seeing someone.

He turns to me as he gives them an answer. "No, I'm not dating anyone." My heart skips a beat and I find myself relaxing back into the seat, resting my hands on the warm leather. When I feel Logan's hand resting beside mine, barely touching, but just enough to make me painfully aware of him, a jolt of electricity coursing from my fingertips to my toes. I daren't move. I don't want to lose this feeling. So I sit, completely still, my gaze occasionally finding his for a split second every so often, before I can't take it any longer and I have to look away.

I've been in love with Logan since the moment I met him, but I've never once gotten the impression he was interested in me in any way, other than as his best friend's little sister. Until now. I know I can't act on whatever this is... a fleeting moment shared in the back of a car. Carter would never let it happen, but I can dream, just for a little while. I can let myself imagine what it would be like to lose myself in Logan Fitzgerald, to give myself over to him completely, and let him take me wherever he wants to go.

But, like Cinderella at midnight, the spell will be broken. As soon as my big brother sets foot in my parents' living room, the reality of our situation will come crashing down on me. It doesn't matter how I feel. Logan is the one man I can never have…

CHAPTER 1

LOGAN

Three Years Later

Fuck. I have the worst hangover. Last night was my friend Xander's "bachelor party." I use the term loosely because he wimped out on having a real, traditional, strippers and ending up naked tied to a pole kind of party. Instead, Xander, Carter and I ended up playing pool, and drinking our own body weight in alcohol.

I met both of them during freshman year at Columbia and we've been thick as thieves ever since. Carter in particular, is like a brother to me. I've spent most of the major holidays with him and his family over the years and they have become the closest thing I have to a family. I would do anything for them, and therein lies the problem. I could never hurt them, and if I acted on my feelings for Vittoria, it would be catastrophic, so I do what I do best. I compartmentalize my life... and their family.

The predicament I find myself in, has become increasingly more difficult over the past seven months. Xander found the love of his life and is getting married, and Carter, who I thought would be my eternal wingman, has gone and fallen for Addi—ball buster and best friend of Xander's wife-to-be, Lily. They are all deliriously happy, most of the time, and Addison has become close with Carter's sister, Vittoria. This is where my life becomes complicated. Up until now I've successfully avoided hearing about any boyfriends she's had—I find it, unsettling—it angers me. These days, Lily and Addi have other ideas. Anytime Vittoria's in town, they want to invite her out with us. Addi also likes to update us all on the ins and outs of her love life at every opportunity, which is slowly leading to me losing my mind, and an unnerving increase in the number of subs I've been training lately. It's getting ridiculous.

I don't keep subs for myself. Not because I don't want to be with just one woman, but because I've always known no one could measure up to Vittoria. It wouldn't be fair to take on a sub, knowing I can't put her needs above all others. The truth is they would always pale in comparison to her. Don't get me wrong, I care about the women I train, and occasionally, if I have a strong enough bond with one of them, it has crossed my mind to keep them. I'm not completely dead inside. I crave connection to another human being, an intimate bond for us, but I decided a very long time ago I would channel my energy into becoming a Master.

I train submissives and get them ready to find a suitable Dom. I teach them every conceivable way to derive pleasure from pain, to please their Master, to understand their own body and how far it can be pushed in the pursuit of sexual gratification. It has always given me great satisfaction to see the transformation in a woman under my tutelage. To see her flourish as she embraces her primal instinct to submit.

Last night I became painfully aware of what I'm missing out on, so I got crazy drunk and seduced the hot bartender at Carter's club. It's not like me, but hearing them talking about the wedding sent me over the edge. I'm going to be staying at the same hotel as Vittoria for five days in one of the most romantic cities on earth, surrounded by people in love. I doubt I could have told you my own name last night. I don't even remember how I got back to my apartment.

I remember vague images of the bartender. There was a backroom at the club—my belt wrapped around her wrists—a cab back to her place. I'm pretty sure we didn't make it to the bedroom. I can picture her face as she came, but my own release was a blur. Unsatisfying and unfulfilling. She seemed like a nice girl, but the one-night stand isn't really my scene. I like to get to know a woman's body, to play it with expert precision. Anything less just doesn't give me the release I'm looking for.

I've known for years that a normal relationship—boy meets girl, falls in love, and lives a cookie cutter life—wasn't going to be for me. I'm not that guy. I can give any woman pleasure beyond anything she could ever imagine. I can make her body tremble with a single word, make her climax with a single touch, and make her beg to be tied up, flogged and spanked. What I can't do, is offer a woman the white picket fence, two-point-four children and an SUV.

They say my sexual preferences aren't for everyone, and they're right in some respects. Not all men want to be a Dominant, and some men just don't have it in them to take charge of a woman's body, mind, and soul. However, I believe on some level, every woman is curious to experience my lifestyle, even if it's only once.

Bring me a bored housewife, an innocent virgin, an experienced vixen, and I can make each and every one of their bodies sing. I can spark a fire inside them so intense, they would literally do anything I asked of them, just for one more kiss, one more caress of my hand over their breasts and their aching clit. They would sell their soul to the devil himself to feel my cock pounding into their slick wet pussy.

It gets me off.

I love the power, the ultimate control watching a woman give herself over to me completely. It's an honor and a privilege to have a woman put absolute faith in me, and I don't take it lightly. I cherish it and nurture it where I can, in the only way I know how.

I got my first taste for it seven years ago when a one-night stand asked me to tie her up and spank her. I was up for anything and readily agreed, but I wasn't prepared for the rush that coursed through my body when my hand made contact with her tight little ass. It was unlike anything I'd ever experienced, and when I came—

fuck me—it was so damn intense. I couldn't get enough. I took her on every surface of her apartment, in every position I could, binding her hands and feet, holding her down, totally at my mercy. The sight of her, bound with black ropes against alabaster skin, her reddened ass in the air, awaiting my attention. I had never seen a woman so completely satisfied. It was so beautiful to me, and I never looked back.

I did some research into places I could go to learn more about the lifestyle, and to learn how to correctly execute the scenes I wanted to create. I found the best club in New York, Andromeda, and it opened up a whole new world for me. A side of myself I didn't know was there. It let me focus the darkest parts of myself, and use it to straddle the fine line between pleasure and pain. It was only after the first year, I realized just how unfulfilling my encounters had been up until then.

Unfortunately for me, as I honed my skills, reveling in the pleasure I could wring from a woman's body, I also became painfully aware of every intriguing facet of Vittoria de Rossi. Whenever I was in her presence, I became more and more drawn to the way her body moved, knowing how pliant she would be under my touch. I was acutely attuned to her personality, her moods, what I could see she needed. Everything about her body language screamed submissive, but there was, and is, something inside of her that will never submit to any man. I would never crush her spirit. It is a beautiful sight to behold, but it's a double-edged sword. It's a trait I admire and adore, but it also means we would never work. I could never be the man she needs me to be, so I started avoiding her wherever possible. Making excuses not to attend family events with Carter, and as my business took off, the excuses became legitimate reasons, and by the time Vittoria graduated Julliard and started touring the world, there was no longer any occasion for us to be in the same vicinity.

It got easier over time, but a twisted part of me could never truly let her go. Whenever she performs in New York, I can't help myself. I always go. I sit in the dark and lose myself in her, if only for a few stolen hours. She is an exquisite dancer, every movement so precise and seemingly effortless. She was born to dance. It's who she is, and

I'm in awe of how consumed she becomes by the music when she's on stage. It's transcendent.

The last time I saw her perform was about five months ago, when Addi and Carter spied me outside the theatre and dragged me to dinner with them and Vittoria. I could barely breathe around her. The gentle scent of her perfume, tantalizing my senses. The brush of her leg against mine under the table causing my chest to tighten and my cock to harden in my pants. It was a sweet agony I would gladly endure day after day after day if I thought I could win her heart, her body, and her soul. If I could possess her in every way possible.

Just the memory of her makes me hard.

I need to call Liam later and get him to arrange a meeting with a few prospective submissives tomorrow night. It'll be a welcome distraction from my upcoming trip to Verona. But for now, I'll have to make do with grabbing a shower and heading into the office to work on the contracts for my latest signing.

LIAM HAS THREE POTENTIAL SUBS FOR ME TO TRAIN. I'M GOING TO THE club to meet with each of them tonight, to see if we connect. I don't train just anyone. I'm very selective. It's one of the great perks of being a Master. I have my choice of willing new submissives, eager for me to teach them how to please their future Dominant, to help them discover what they like and what is a hard limit for them.

I never have sex with a submissive before I've gone through the process of sitting down with them and discussing every aspect of what they expect from me, what training they require, and to gauge what I feel they could benefit from in terms of my expertise. I need to know I can relate to a woman on an intellectual level. The physical side of it isn't a worry for me. As long as I find her attractive, the rest will follow. It's a myth that some people just aren't compatible. If you are physically attracted to another person, then your "compatibility" comes down to a willingness to learn how to please each other.

The club is busy tonight. There are demonstrations in the main room, all private rooms are occupied, and the bars and the dance floor are packed with writhing bodies. Even the VIP lounges are too busy for me to conduct my interviews, so I decide to take a different approach, and meet each of the girls in my playroom. It definitely gives me an added edge, as if I needed one, inviting them into my domain.

The first girl has the intelligence and maturity level of a five-year-old. I can't tolerate her high-pitched giggling and hair twirling for more than three minutes before I have the bouncer outside of my room escort her off the premises.

Girl number two is hot—long legs, a perfect ass, and gorgeous long blonde hair I could wrap around my arm as I hold her down and fuck her. Unfortunately, her looks are her only redeeming quality. In the thirty minutes she spends in my playroom, she tries to undress for me at least three times, offers to give me head twice, and repeatedly tells me how much she likes anal. She has zero class, and I don't think she fully understands the lifestyle she's trying to get into.

If I wanted her naked, she'd be spread on my table already. If I wanted her to give me head, she would be on her knees with her mouth full. And, if I wanted to take her up the ass, she would be up on all fours, screaming my name as I ride her. I breathe a sigh of relief when she leaves and put some music on my iPod through the speakers in the room, to alleviate my agitation before the last woman of the evening arrives.

When I hear the knock on the door, I can barely muster the enthusiasm to open it, but the girl standing behind it, is breathtaking. I open the door wide and invite her in. Everything about her is delicious. She has the physique of a dancer, toned, slender and petite. She has stunning caramel skin and lush black hair falling down her back in a sea of waves.

My heart slams into my chest at the sight of her.

She looks like… Vittoria.

My dick twitches in my pants, and I find myself drawn to this girl without even hearing her speak.

"It's nice to meet you. My name is Master Fitzgerald, but I'm sure you already know that."

She takes my proffered hand giving it a firm shake. The sweet smell of her perfume beginning to fill the room.

"The pleasure is all mine, Master Fitzgerald. My name is..." I cut her off.

"No need for names tonight, angel." I place my hand at the small of her back and lead her over to the couch. "Please, sit."

We discuss her likes and dislikes, her expectations and why she wants to be trained by me. She knows how to flatter a guy. "You are without a doubt the best, and the hottest Master in New York. Every submissive who knows the lifestyle, knows you are *the* expert in shibari, which is something I've wanted to try for a long time now."

"It's obvious to me you aren't new to the scene, or to being a submissive, so my question is why do you feel the need to go back into training?"

Her gaze drops to the floor, her discomfort apparent in the shifting of her feet.

"I need full disclosure. I can't be your Master if you don't trust me. I realize you don't know me yet, but unfortunately, in my position as a trainer rather than a long-term Dominant, I need my submissives to open up to me immediately. I know it's a huge leap of faith at this stage, but I won't be able to make an informed decision as to whether or not I can help you. I need you to understand you have the power here. It's your choice entirely. You don't have to tell me anything, and you can leave at any time with no hard feelings."

Her demeanor softens at my final words, and I can see the moment she decides to confide in me.

"I had a bad experience with my previous Dominant. He made the decision for me that I no longer needed a safe word. He..." I can see this is difficult for her. "He took too much pleasure in punishing me... a long way past my hard limits."

I feel so angry for this girl. Men like him give BDSM a bad name. A Dominant's sole purpose is to ensure his submissive is happy and healthy, satisfied and *never* pushed beyond what she can handle. She should have absolute control when it comes to her hard limits. Any man who doesn't respect and honor the strength it takes for a woman to submit herself completely, is *not* a true Dom.

As a rule, I don't train subs who look anything like Vittoria. I've always felt it would be disrespectful to the woman in question and would feel like I was betraying Vittoria somehow. A pale imitation would never satisfy me.

I really want to help this girl get past what happened with her previous Dom, and restore her faith in our lifestyle, but she looks so much like Vittoria, it's almost eerie.

"I'm so sorry you had to live through that. I can assure you, a true Dominant would never treat you that way." Her small smile is so endearing. I wonder if I could get past the physical similarity and train her.

"I know, Master Fitzgerald. That's why I'm here. I don't want to let him win. I believe I can still find happiness with a Dom who treats me properly. I just think I need the safety of some training to restore my confidence before I try to find a suitable long-term match."

"You're a very sensible woman. I think you're doing the right thing, and I would love to help you."

I see the spark in her eyes at my words, and I feel my cock hardening as I drink in the sight of her.

"I would like to know a little more about you before we take this any further."

"Anything."

"What do you do for a living?"

"I'm a ballerina. I'm in my final year at Julliard and I'm hoping to find a ballet company to tour with after I graduate. It's been my dream since I was five years old."

My stomach drops. I know I can't do this. I was kidding myself to think I could. The similarities are just too much for me to get over. I scrub my hands up over my face, annoyed at myself for being so pathetic.

"Is something wrong, Master Fitzgerald? Have I said something to upset you?"

I stare up into her questioning eyes as I answer, hoping she understands this is in no way a reflection on her.

"I'm so sorry. I can't train you. I would love to. You are extremely beautiful and any man in his right mind would want to explore every last inch of your gorgeous body."

"But...?"

"But, you remind me too much of someone I know."

"Someone you loved?"

"Something like that. Trust me when I tell you this is all *my* issue. You are a lovely girl, and I know when you find the right Dom, he will worship the ground you walk on." I watch as her cheeks begin to blush. "I would still like to help, and if it's okay with you, I'd like to speak with some of the other Masters, discuss your situation and choose a trainer for you who I feel would be a good match. You deserve someone who can give you the training and attention you need to regain confidence in yourself, and in our lifestyle. Will you let me do that for you?"

"It's true what they say about you, Master Fitzgerald. You really are a gentleman. Stunningly handsome, with a beautiful soul. I would be honored if you could choose a Master to train me. I won't lie and say I'm not disappointed. You really are even more gorgeous in the flesh. I would have relished the opportunity to submit to you."

"Thank you for the compliment. I don't take any woman's willingness to submit to me, lightly. I'm humbled. I'll make the necessary arrangements and be in touch when I've found someone for you to come and meet with."

As she stands to leave, I offer her my hand, which she grasps with both of hers, holding my gaze. "Whoever it is I remind you of, she's a very lucky woman. I hope she appreciates it someday."

"Thank you."

She lets go of my hand and strides out the room, turning to give me one last smile before she leaves.

How did I get here?

Three women who could have been a great distraction for me—three women who offered themselves willingly to me—and I sent all of them away. Increasingly, it's becoming more and more difficult for me to switch off and repress the feelings I have for Vittoria.

She's not a part of my everyday life, and yet she *is*.

Ever since the last time I saw her, I haven't been able to stop thinking about her. The way her body moves on stage, her smile when I make her laugh, and so many little things, too numerous to count.

I don't know how to get past this. The one-night stand didn't help in the slightest. Work is a fantastic distraction, but only while I'm working. Training submissives has been my way of coping for years now, and it has served me very well up until recently. But lately, it just doesn't hold the same satisfaction, and if I needed any more proof then tonight has confirmed it.

I need to find a way to get Vittoria de Rossi out of my system for good. I know I have to cut ties with her altogether, but first, I need to get through this wedding. It's not going to be easy knowing she's sleeping in a hotel room down the hall from me, and I can't do a damn thing about it. It's going to be fucking torture.

I leave Andromeda feeling worse than when I arrived. I don't think this has ever happened to me before, so from now until the wedding, I'm going to throw myself into work, teach some Master classes, and do some shibari demonstrations.

It's a sad realization for me. There are two things I'm passionate about in my life, both of which I've had to sacrifice and make do with an alternative. My dream was to be a musician, to sing, play guitar and write songs. My own stupidity and anger made sure it will never happen, and so I became an agent. I started my own label and I make my dream come true for other people. I love what I do, but there will always be a part of me that wants more.

I found BDSM and it let me channel all of my conflicting feelings and become a Master of my craft. I'll never regret it, but I will also *never* be able to share it with the one person who truly means something to me. I will never achieve complete satisfaction as a Master. I love what I do, but a part of me will always want more.

My life will always be a series of second choices.

Bands, bondage, music and Master classes.

CHAPTER 2

LOGAN

I HATE WEDDINGS. SINGLE WOMEN ARE ALWAYS DESPERATE TO HOOK UP and tie you down, and not in a good way. I know the ladies love me. I'm not an ugly guy, I work out, take care of myself, and I dress well. Women are drawn to my dominant nature without realizing it, and even when I try to disguise it, it's still there. It speaks to them on a molecular level—a deep unspoken desire to submit to a strong confident man.

I will have no shortage of willing victims this weekend, easy girls who just want me to make them feel better about their single status. And that's the problem, it's *too* easy. I like my women compliant, but I don't want them to just give it up for nothing. I relish the seduction. I thrive on it. The thrill of anticipation. Making a woman so hot for me she would do anything for my touch, my kiss, and my lips against her quivering naked flesh. I want a woman to give herself over to me completely, to do with as I please.

It's Xander's wedding this weekend and we're in Verona, Italy. The past three days have been a killer and I really need to just get the hell out of dodge already. It's been great spending time with everyone, but it gets tiring having to put on a front for them all the time. No one knows about my… lifestyle, and it can be difficult to rein in my dark side at times, especially around Vittoria, but people wouldn't understand. They wouldn't accept it.

I met Vittoria about eight years ago when Carter invited me to spend Thanksgiving at his parent's house, and from the moment I first laid eyes on her, I've wanted her. I want to fuck her, to own her, to dominate her. I want her complete and total submission to my deepest, darkest desires, and I'm also completely in love with her. It's why I can't be with her. She is so good and pure and innocent, and what I want from her... well, I'm aware a girl like her *does not* need what I have to offer. She deserves better. She deserves the best of everything, and if I thought for a second I could give it to her, I would have made her mine a long time ago.

I'm not into corrupting shy inexperienced girls. I need a woman who knows her own mind and *wants* to submit to my command. Vittoria could never be that woman, she's too... perfect.

I don't think Carter knows how I feel about her. I'm certain if he did, I'd be buried in the woods somewhere by now. I've done my best to avoid her over the past few days, but it's getting increasingly more difficult. I'm drawn to her like a moth to a flame. We hadn't seen each other in months before she arrived in Verona. She's been out of the country touring with a top ballet company so it's been easy to avoid her.

Vittoria de Rossi is an angel, sent from heaven to torment what's left of my soul. She is perfection personified. A single, exquisite rose among a bed of thorns. A beacon of light in the darkness. The only woman I've ever loved, and the only one I can never have. She is also my best friend's younger sister, and the reason I feel like a meteor has rocketed straight into my chest, obliterating my heart into a million fragments, scattering them across the solar system.

I've been standing watching her float across the dance floor with her father, her brother, and even Xander at the reception tonight. She is awe-inspiring to watch. She lives and breathes the music, letting it flow through her, bending to its will. I don't think I could ever tire of watching her. She looks so carefree and happy, and unbelievably beautiful. She's enchanting.

I've fought every urge I have, staying fixed to this spot, but I know I'm fighting a losing battle. Every time she glances in my direction, she calls to me like a siren, tempting me, and I don't want to fight it anymore—just one dance. To hold her in my arms and feel the warmth of her body against mine, if only for a few minutes. To feel her sweet breath on my neck as we sway to the music. It's all I can ever have from her, but I'm selfish and I want it, no matter how badly my body will ache when I have to let her go.

As Vittoria takes her seat, our eyes connect and I feel like my insides are on fire, adrenaline pumping hard through my veins. The DJ starts playing *Just the Way You Are* by Bruno Mars and before I can stop myself, I'm standing in front her transfixed as she takes a sip of her wine, her eyes on mine as she darts the tip of her tongue out into the glass. It is so damn sexy I feel my dick hardening. Without a word, I hold my hand out to her. As soon as her skin comes into contact with mine, the spark I felt from across the room becomes a blazing inferno of desire.

I lead her onto the dance floor, lights twinkling all around us, the rest of the guests a distant blip on my radar. All I see is her. As we begin to move, she snakes her arms around my neck and I feel goose-bumps appear on her skin. I wrap my arms around her waist and pull her body flush against mine. It's as if she was made for me, our bodies fitting together perfectly. Every move she makes is like the sweetest form or torture I could ever endure.

I look into her eyes as we move in time to the music, hoping she can sense just how much this song conveys my feelings for her. I can see the lust in her eyes as she presses against the evidence of my arousal, her tight body gently grinding on me. It feels phenomenal, but as I realize this moment is about to end, along with the song, I can't fight it anymore. I give in to every urge I've repressed for the past eight years.

We stop moving, our eyes fixed on one another. I gently slide my arms up from her tiny waist, grazing the side of her breasts as I move my hands up to cup her angelic face in my palms, her arms sliding down my back. I savor the moment, rubbing my thumbs over her cheeks and onto her lips. Her tongue darts out to lick the tip of my thumb, the same way she did with her glass, and it's my undoing. All control is gone as I pull her lips to mine, colliding in a cataclysmic event that will alter my heart and soul forevermore.

Our tongues devour and explore, both rough and tender at the same time. It is everything I've ever imagined and more. The taste of her is like a hit of the finest heroine, a sip of the finest champagne. We lose ourselves in the moment, enjoying every intense and explosive second of it. My dominant nature replaced by something even more pressing, more primitive. I need her touch, her taste, more than my next breath. Nipping at her lips I trace the lines of her mouth with my tongue, savoring every electrically charged flick, suck, and caress.

When the music fades and the atmosphere in the room changes, I know I have to let her go, but I take one last kiss, one last chance to feel her warmth, to smell her intoxicating scent before I walk away. Breathless, I lean my forehead against hers and try to compose myself.

"I'm sorry. I shouldn't have done that."

I quickly make my way off the dance floor and away from her, putting as much distance as I can between us, a hole forming in my chest with every step. I stride out of the marquee, but there's nowhere to go. L'Arena is dark and deserted as I stand in the moonlight, looking at the stars, breathing the cool night air into my lungs, contemplating all the ways I want to dominate the sweetest girl I've ever met. The feel of her skin is seared into my brain until the end of time. I think of how amazing her elegant limbs would look spread wide on my St. Andrew's cross, her pussy wet in anticipation of all the delights I could inflict on her. I need to get the hell out of here before I go back inside, drag her to my hotel suite and act out every last one of my fantasies with her.

I take a moment to admire the night sky, but it pales in comparison to the sight that greets me when I look back toward the marquee. She's standing in the entrance staring at me, the twinkling lights dancing across her flawless features, and everything else around me becomes inconsequential.

"You need to go back inside, Vittoria. I've apologized for my mistake. I just need a few moments alone."

She ignores my request, gliding toward me, an ethereal enchantress.

"We need to talk. We've needed to talk for a long time now."

"No, we don't. What happened back there… it can't happen again. It was wrong of me to take advantage of the moment. Again, I apologize."

"You didn't take advantage of anything." She takes a step closer, forcing me to step back. "Why? Why can't it happen again? I want it to happen."

The plea in her voice is killing me. My inherent nature is to give her whatever she wants, whatever she needs. I want to give her this so badly, but I can't.

"Because you don't *really* know me. This… us… we could never work. We want very different things. I would *never* ask you to change for me. You are… perfection. I would only mar you with my desires. There's a side to me you do *not* want to be a part of."

She closes the distance between us, placing her hand over my hammering chest, her eyes locked on mine. "I know exactly who and *what* you are. I *want* what you are, I *crave* what you are. It's *my* deepest desire."

I grip her hand, desperate to claim her as my own.

"You don't know what you're asking for, and I won't tell you. I couldn't stand for you to look at me differently if you knew the real me. It would break the only morsel of hope left in my jaded heart."

She removes her hand from my grasp, a permanent mark etched on my chest where her warm tender hand had been. "I think the problem here isn't *me* knowing you, but *you* not knowing me."

I cut her off. "I know you. I see you in all your beauty. I see all of the intricacies that form to make you who you are, and it's resplendent."

Her face looks pained as she replies. "There are things you don't know about me. Things no one knows. But you… I know you can see it. You just don't want to admit it to yourself. If you did, there would be no reason for us to be apart. I'm not afraid of what you try to hide from everyone else. I'm not afraid of you."

I close the gap between us, my lips brushing against hers as I whisper my response.

"You should be."

Her lips crash down on mine, unleashing all of the pent-up desire we've been holding back. I lift her off the ground, running my hands down her toned, slender legs, wrapping them around my waist. Her fingers twist in my hair, pulling me closer, begging me for more. I can't get enough. I want to taste every inch of her body.

"Oh God, Logan. I've wanted this for so long. Please. I want you."

Hearing those words tripping off her sweet pouty lips just fuels my desire even more. She starts ripping at my suit jacket, discarding it on the ground as I hitch up her dress to pull her tighter against my body. Her ass feels amazing, covered in the smallest scrap of lace, torturing my senses. My hands roam her body, memorizing every line and gentle curve.

It's not until she starts grappling with my belt buckle that my brain kicks in, and I'm horrified by my behavior. I seem to lack any level of control around her now. I've had a taste and I want more. It's not in my nature to lose control. I don't like it. I need to stop this… now.

"I can't. I'm sorry. This isn't right."

I allow myself one last longing kiss before gently lowering her to her feet. Picking up my jacket, I smooth out my shirt, turn, and walk, forcing every step that takes me further away from her, but her low husky voice stops me in my tracks.

"Please…"

She closes the distance between us, taking my hand in hers, leading me back into the marquee through the crowd and out into the seclusion of the bridal dressing room. I didn't even know this was here. I quickly scan the room, taking in every possible surface I could use to take what I want in this moment. To have Vittoria sprawled naked for my perusal, for my pleasure. The tension in the room is electrifying and I find myself unable to turn and look at her, knowing that if I do, I will have no control over my actions.

"Look at me, Logan." I run my hand over my face, trying to sober my riotous emotions. "Please. Look at me."

I reluctantly turn my gaze to the woman I so desperately crave with every fiber of my being, but what I find when I do absolutely floors me. I am dumbstruck and completely aroused. Her dress is pooled at her feet, along with her bra, her stunningly unblemished skin covered only by a scrap of black lace. Her body is everything I ever fantasized about and more. Small pert breasts, the sweetest nipples I've ever seen, lithe limbs and a sexy as hell piercing through her belly button. She is an Italian goddess.

My breathing is labored as I take in ever last inch of her, my cock aching, straining against my pants.

"Vittoria…" My hands are fisted at my sides as I fight desperately to remain fixed to the spot. Struggling against her magnetic pull and the all-consuming need to have her. "You need to put your clothes back on before I do something you'll regret."

She makes a move toward me, stepping out of her dress, her slender legs stunning in high heels. I have never seen any woman look as sexy as she does right now.

"Really look at me, Logan. Tell me what you see. I need you to *see* me for who I really am."

I grab her shoulders, relishing the warmth of her skin, her scent invading my senses. My hands buzzing at this small touch, her naked body crying out for me to lavish it with my caress.

"I *do* see you. You are… exquisite. I want you so badly it's a physical ache coursing through every inch of my body."

"Then take me. I *want* you to take me." As she speaks she lifts her elegant fingers and begins to caress her breasts, kneading them, flicking her thumbs over tightly budded nipples. My dick feels like granite—almost painful.

"I only have so much control, Vittoria, and you're testing it to its limits."

She lets out a sexy as hell moan with a sly grin on her face, before licking her lips as she moves her hand down her stomach and under the tiny scrap of lace hiding her from me. I am entranced by her every move. My desire for her is at a fever pitch as she removes her hand and slowly lifts her fingers to my mouth, holding them just shy of my lips.

I can hear my heartbeat hammering in my ears. My dick is throbbing with the need to claim her.

"Goddammit!"

I grab her wrist, holding her tighter than I should, before taking her fingers wet with her own arousal into my mouth. I can't hold in the groan of satisfaction that escapes me as I suck her dry. "You taste so good. Do you have *any* idea how badly I want to fuck you right now?"

Her breath is shallow but fast, the rise and fall of her chest quickening as she offers up her breasts to me, calling for my attention. Her voice is a breathless rasp. "If it's half as much as I want you, then I don't see how you could possibly fight it."

"It's for your own good. Trust me." Everything inside me is at war, and she knows it. She grabs my hand guiding it down her body, sliding it underneath the lace of her panties and letting it rest on the warmth of her pussy, wet and ready for me.

"I trust you. I trust you to do... *anything* to me. I'm not beneath begging to get what I want. I want you. I always have, and I'm tired of having to hide it and pretend I don't know you want me, too." She moves my hand with her own, tracing circles around her swollen clit. "I won't offer myself to you in this way again. This is your chance to have me, exactly the way you want me. I am completely at your command."

Master Dom or not, I am under her spell and helpless to deny her. The feel of her swollen flesh against my fingers is too much. I rip her hand off of mine and pin both of hers behind her back. She winces as I remove my hand from her panties, just long enough to tear them off and leave her completely exposed to me. She is stunning, absolutely breathtaking.

"I'm going to make you come with my fingers since you were so intent on forcing them down your panties. I'll give you what you want, and then I'm taking what I want." I thrust my fingers inside her tight little pussy, pressing the palm of my hand against her clit, letting her writhe in pleasure. She doesn't disappoint, riding my hand and fingers with wild abandon, moaning her desire, driving me to the edge. I quicken the pace, thrusting a third finger inside, curling them forward at just the right angle to make her fall apart.

"Oh God, Logan… Fuck!" I immediately stop, leaving her helpless and desperate for release.

"You will not curse when any part of me is inside you. Do you understand? And don't call me Logan." I realize I can't finish the sentence. "Don't make a sound. You are going to come in silence, and only when I let you. Understood?" She doesn't speak. God, she would make a perfect sub. "You may nod your understanding of my command." She does as I ask and my dick is about to burst out of my pants. I am so turned on by her whole demeanor.

I take her mouth in a fierce kiss, my hands exploring her naked flesh, memorizing every delectable inch, making my way back down toward heaven. As soon as my thumb flicks over her clit, she's struggling for control, trying not to come until I tell her. She bites down on my shoulder sending a deliciously torturous pain through my system. Normally I would punish a sub for biting me without permission, but it feels so damn good.

"That's it, little one. Hold on until I tell you." I work her with my hand, ghosting kisses along her neck, over her shoulder and onto her breasts. She tastes amazing, a mixture of perfume and her natural scent. It's a heady cocktail. When I feel her pussy start to tighten around my fingers I know she can't hold back much longer. "Now, Vittoria. Let go and feel it." One last flick of my thumb over her clit and my teeth clamp down on her nipple, sends her spiraling over the edge. Her hand flies up to her mouth and I watch as she bites down hard on her fist, forcing the screams into silence as I requested. I let her ride out the aftershocks of her orgasm, relishing the feel of her juices dripping down my fingers.

She is perfect.

"You've had what you want, little one, now it's time for me to take what I want. Lie on the table. I want your hands above your head and your legs spread as wide as you can."

Without question or hesitation, she moves to the table, her gaze lowered to the floor, and I know in this moment I can't fuck her. If I claim her in this way, she'll be mine, and I will never let her go. No matter how broken and twisted my soul is, I would be making love to her, and I can't come back from that. The mere thought of it devastates me.

I strip off my suit jacket, shirt and tie, loosening the buckle on my belt without taking my pants off. "You have permission to make noise as I make you come... over and over again. Let me hear how much you love it. Understood?"

"Yes..."

"You will call me Mr. Fitzgerald."

"Yes, Mr. Fitzgerald."

She looks divine, stretched out on the table, her hands above her head, clasped together. I take my time, pacing around the table in quiet, measured movements, slowly drinking in the sight of her, watching her flesh start to quiver in anticipation as I gently run a single finger down the side of her body from her hands all the way down to her pretty, painted toes. She doesn't flinch, she simply gives herself over to the sensation, her legs remaining spread wide for me, her pussy glistening with arousal.

"Now I'm curious. Is this how you react to every man who kisses you? Do you give yourself over so freely to others?"

I dip my head down between her legs and take one long, luscious lick, reveling in the sweetness of her taste. Her back arches off the table and a low moan escapes her, making my cock twitch, aching to be inside her.

"Do other men make you this wet, little one? Do you cream at the sound of their voice, the way you do for me?"

"No, Mr. Fitzgerald. Only you. It's always been you." My heart breaks at her words, and I fight the voice inside of me telling me to walk away and save us both.

"You've said quite enough." I can't bear to hear such tender words pass her succulent lips. I need her to stop. I pick my tie up off the floor and wrap it around her mouth, just tight enough so she can't speak, but not so tight as to hinder her breathing.

She never once makes eye contact with me, and I don't know whether it's complete submission, or fear. I hesitate for a fleeting moment before my desire takes over. She looks so... flawless. She is completely at my mercy and it makes me so hard I can barely stand it.

I push my pants and my boxers just low enough to free my throbbing erection and fist it in my hand. "Look at me, Vittoria. Take a good, long, *hard* look at what you do to me."

When her eyes take in the sight of me working my cock with my hand, she bites down on my tie, fighting the urge to clench her thighs together and alleviate the pressure I know is building. She is fixated, mesmerized by every movement of my fist. I close my eyes and let myself imagine being inside her, hammering into her over and over again, feeling her hot, wet walls tightening around me. I let myself go almost to the edge of release and then pull back. I'm not ready to have this moment, this tryst, this scene, end.

There's hunger in her eyes, and all I want is to feed her desire, and feast on her arousal.

"You like watching me touch myself. You're a very dirty girl. I should punish you for that, but it's so goddamn sexy, and right now I need to taste you. I want to feel your clit writhing against my tongue. I'm going to wring as much pleasure from you as you can stand, and then, if you're a good girl and manage not to move while you orgasm, time after time, after time, I will reward you."

I give a sharp pull on her legs, bringing her ass to the edge of the table. I drop to my knees, spreading her thighs as wide as they can go before my tongue descends on her folds, licking her from her entrance, slowly up, until I reach her clit, circling it, flicking it with the tip of my tongue before drawing it in and sucking on her. My satisfied groans reverberate against her skin causing her to convulse beneath me, her muffled cries of pleasure spurring me on. I could do this for hours and not tire of her taste. It's sweet and sensual and better than any woman I've ever tasted. I lap up every last drop of her arousal before giving one last flick of my tongue against her clit, sending her crashing over the edge, spiraling out of control, screaming against the silk of my tie as I continue to kiss her, throwing her straight into a second mind-blowing orgasm.

Her breathing is heavy, her body glistening with a sheen of sweat from the intensity of her release.

I don't give her long to recover before I'm thrusting my fingers inside her. She's so wet for me and it's making me question my restraint. Every cell in my body is willing me to fuck her, right here, right now, and as I battle against the war waged on my cognitive thought, I quicken my pace, pumping in and out of her, brushing my thumb over her clit until she explodes around me again, her body going limp as she lets the myriad of sensations wash over her. Her hands are still outstretched above her head, hands clasped together and her legs spread wide. She is divine.

"You've done well, little one, and now you can have your reward." I gently loosen my tie and remove it from her mouth. "Open wide." Her eyes are alight with anticipation, greedy for what I have to give.

I drop my pants and boxers to the floor, completely naked as I crawl up onto the table, straddling her body, skin to skin, stalking her like a panther stalks its prey. I'm ready to take what's mine. I fist my hand around the base of my cock, watching her hungry gaze take in the sight of me above her. A sultry grin spreads across her face, her eyes filled with lust.

"Do you have something you want to say, little one? I want to know what that sexy look on your face is for."

Her soft, gravelly voice is a sweet caress. "You are so much more than I expected. Your body is male perfection. Sculpted and strong. Muscular but lean. You have the most beautiful cock, and my entire body is aching with the need to feel you inside me. I want to taste you, to feel your hard length pulse and thrust against my tongue, letting my mouth envelop you in a sensual caress."

I need to stop her saying these things that both arouse me, and touch something deeper inside of me, but I'm greedy and I want to hear every last torturous word.

"I want to feel your large, warm, callused hands, fisting in my hair as you take control, fucking my mouth, taking what you want from me. I want you to watch as I give it to you freely. I want to see you spiral out of control as you fall apart above me, your cock pulsing as you release each delicious, hot spurt of your come down my throat. I want to lap up every last drop of you, Mr. Fitzgerald. And after you wring every drop of pleasure from my mouth, I want to feel you inside me. Hammering every hard, thick inch of your cock into my wet, warm pussy."

"Enough." My body aches for her, my heart heavy knowing I can't give her everything she desires. I want to, more than I've ever wanted anything in my life, but it will cross a line I can't cross. "Stop talking and open your mouth, little one. Let me give you what you so desperately crave."

She does as I ask without hesitation, and the moment I lean over letting the engorged head of my dick touch her pouty lips, I'm lost. Her tongue swirls around the tip before she takes me fully into her mouth, her arms still outstretched above her head. Holy Shit! I don't think anything has ever felt this good. I brace my arms above her head, taking her hands in mine, entwining our fingers together in a slow, tender gesture. A stark juxtaposition to the harsh thrusting of my hips, my cock claiming her pretty, little mouth. The combination of sweet and animalistic is so intense. She's everything I imagined her to be.

"Vittoria. You feel so fucking good." I drop my head, letting wave after wave of pleasure wash over me, letting it control me. I don't have a conscious thought in my head, only a feeling. A need and an overwhelming desire for the woman beneath me.

She begins to groan against my dick, her tongue licking from root to tip, up and down, her lips clamping around me, sucking me until I can't hold back any longer. As I let go, my release courses up the length of me and spills out into her mouth, a satisfied hum reverberating from her throat, catapulting me deeper into the most intense orgasm I've ever had. I shout her name in a plea for more.

She continues to milk every last drop from me, all the while tracing soft sensual circles with her thumbs on the back of my hands. I reluctantly pull out of her sweet little mouth and move to down take her lips in a fierce kiss, pouring all of my love and regret into this one moment. I so desperately want to stay here with her and make love to her, but as the mist in my mind clears, I know what I have to do.

I extricate myself from her grasp, leaving her dazed and confused. I grab my clothes and start getting dressed when she speaks up. "What are you doing?" It physically hurts me to hear the pain in her voice, and when it turns to anger, it hurts even more. "Don't you want to fuck me... Mr. Fitzgerald?" Her words are dripping with disdain, but I can see the vulnerability in her eyes. She is naked before me, both physically and emotionally. She doesn't move, laid bare on the table, her legs still wide open for me, exactly as I commanded.

"Jesus Christ." I run my fingers through my hair, trying to temper my arousal. "You need to get dressed." She stays completely still, staring me down, unshed tears evident in the shimmer clouding her deep brown gaze. I turn away, buttoning my shirt and restoring myself to some semblance of a calm exterior.

"You wanted me like this, Mr. Fitzgerald. Why won't you fuck me? I know you want to. I can see how hard you still are for me." I stride over to the table, taking in the sight of her gloriously naked form one last time. Leaning down, I brush my mouth against hers, letting her lick the seam of my lips as I savor my scent mingled with hers.

"I can't fuck you, Vittoria. If you let me inside you, if I slide every achingly hard inch of my cock inside your sweet cunt, I wouldn't be able to stop. I couldn't walk away. No matter how rough I would take you, how hard you'd be screaming my name and begging for the depraved pleasure I could give you... I would always be making love to you. You would be mine. Forever, completely, irrevocably... mine. You're not ready for that. You never will be."

I can't stop myself from feathering kisses over every inch of her body, her back arching to get closer, offering herself to me even now.

"I'm ready. Please... don't do this. Don't go. Make love to me. Make me yours."

I trail my hands up her body, coming to rest on either side of her beautiful face. I allow myself one last, deep, soul destroying kiss, letting her know just how hard this is for me. When I break away breathless and desperate for more, I hold her gaze as I speak my final words to her. "I want to make you mine so badly. I always have and I always will, and that's why I need to walk away. I will *always* protect you... from me. Even if it leaves me a hollow shell of a man in the process. Goodbye, little one."

I watch as a single tear escapes her stunning eyes, rolling down her cheek, and I wipe it with my thumb before forcing myself to turn around and leave the woman I love, naked, vulnerable, confused and heartbroken, more beautiful than she's ever been. This is the hardest thing I've ever had to do. Each step toward the door, feels like I'm being dragged down by quicksand. Every moment I feel her gaze burning into my back, fighting the urge not to turn and take one last look at her naked beauty, is sheer agony. A hot poker staked through my heart. My hand trembles as I reach for the door handle, slowly twisting it, wishing I didn't have to walk through the door and leave this moment with her behind.

A strangled sob escapes her. A single word. A plea. "Logan..."

As I close the door behind me, the darkness descends and a coldness spreads, enveloping me as I mourn the loss of her. Tonight was the most alive and exhilarated I've ever felt. Watching her come apart beneath me will always be my greatest pleasure and my biggest regret, because I know in my very core, I will never be able to fill the void she has created in me. Nothing and no one will ever compare to the exquisite beauty of Vittoria de Rossi, lost in a moment of sexual ecstasy. She has left an imprint on my soul, and it's a heavy burden to bear. A permanent scar that will stay with me until I take my last breath.

CHAPTER 3

LOGAN

I THOUGHT IT WAS HARD TO LEAVE VITTORIA WHENEVER I SPENT THE holidays at her parents' house, giving her a chaste kiss on the cheek and saying goodbye. The softness of her skin against my lips, the delicate scent of her intoxicating me as I lingered for a moment longer than I should have. The look in her eyes as I pulled away—bereft and wanting. That agony was a drop in the ocean compared to the way I felt when I left her in Italy. Ever since I got back from Verona, ever since I walked out of that room in L'Arena, ever since I walked away from *her...* life has seemed so bland and colorless and one dimensional.

For eight years, it has been there simmering in the background, tainting whatever small connections I've made with the subs I've trained. But now I've tasted her, felt her writhing beneath me and seen her laid bare, vulnerable and desperate for my touch. She's all I can think about. I've tried to suppress it with work, but everything just feels empty and lackluster.

It's been two weeks since I got back, but it feels like forever. Carter and Addi stayed behind for a few weeks, Xander and Lily are off on their honeymoon, and I'm right back where I started, except now, I know what I'm missing out on. It's a brutal form of torture, but I derive a twisted pleasure from it. At least now when I lie awake at night tormenting myself with visions of Vittoria, they are memories rather than fantasies. It's a small consolation, but I need to cling to something. My world feels like it's out of sync, and for a man like me, it's so far out of my comfort zone. I detest not being in control of every aspect of my life.

I'm just about to head out to Andromeda for the first time since I got back, when my phone beeps. It's a message from Vittoria. I know I should ignore it and continue with my plans for the evening, but even as I think it, I'm opening her message.

Vittoria: *We need to talk.*

Me: *There's nothing to say.*

Vittoria: *Bullshit, and you know it.*

Me: *Why now?*

Vittoria: *Because I haven't been able to think about anything else for two weeks. If not for you, then for me. Please. I need to get this off my chest.*

There's something so wrong with me. Just the mention of her chest has me sporting a semi.

Me: *Give me five mins. I'll call you.*

I put in a quick call to the club to cancel the demonstration I had planned for this evening—flogging for pleasure over pain. I was looking forward to working off some of this frustration, but I can't ignore her need to move on. If talking about it is the only way, then I guess I need to suck it up and tell her once and for all that it was a mistake, no matter how good it felt.

I hear the foreign dial tone, and a part of me is upset, knowing she's so far away from where I am. When she answers, the sound of her sweet, sultry voice causes a physical pain inside of me.

"Hi, Logan. Thanks for calling."

"What is it that you feel needs to be said?"

"I… I'm angry with you for what you did in Verona."

I take a deep breath, my heart heavy from her revelation. "You have every right to be. I'm sorry. It was a mistake, I should never have taken advantage of you. It was wrong of me."

"I'm not angry because of what we did. It was amazing. It was everything I've ever wanted. I'm angry because you left without asking me how I felt about it. You made the decision, disregarding anything I might have to say on the matter."

"Vittoria…"

"No. You didn't want to talk. I do. So, you get to listen." She fucking slays me from half the world away.

"Okay. I apologize. By all means, continue."

I can hear her breathing, slightly labored, with a small waver of nerves.

"You didn't take advantage of me. I'm not a child. I knew what I wanted, and I pursued you. You may have initiated that first kiss, but don't kid yourself that I didn't want it. I came after you. I'm the one who stripped. I'm the one who offered myself to you willingly and without expectation. You threw it back in my face." There's a pause, but I know I need to let her finish. "You hurt me, Logan. You made me question myself, and why you don't want me. You confirmed what I already knew, I'm not good enough for you."

"Stop right there. That never has and never will be true. I'm the one who's not good enough."

She swears under her breath before continuing. "Shouldn't it be *my* decision to make? Why do you get to take the choice away from me? What gives you the right?"

"I only want what's best for you."

"So why did you kiss me? Why did you touch me, caress me, and push me over the edge into the most amazing orgasm of my life? Why did you thrust your dick into my mouth and fuck it hard?"

"Stop talking. I can't take it anymore. You want to know the truth?"

"Yes!"

"Walking away from you was the hardest thing I've ever done. I've *never* wanted a woman so badly in all my life. You were everything I ever fantasized and so much more. It took all of my strength not to make love to you."

"But I never asked you to stop. I wanted you to do it. I still do."

"You don't know what you're saying. I can't."

"I know exactly what I'm saying. I'm fully aware of who and what you are. I want you, every part of you."

"We're just going to go around in circles. We can't be together for a lot of reasons, one of which is your brother. He would never understand. You're his sister. His *little* sister. He knows me better than you do, and he knows I'm not boyfriend material. I'm not the guy a woman takes home to meet the family. I love your parents like they were my own, and I would hate to see the disappointment on their faces if we got together. They love me as their son's best friend, not as a potential partner for their daughter."

"Fuck what any of them think. This is my life! This has nothing to do with any of them. This is about what *we* want."

"And I've already told you. This can't happen. I don't want this."

"Oh… well… you're right then. There's nothing left to say. I have my answer. You really don't want me. Goodbye, Logan." I can hear the unshed tears, thick in her voice.

"Vittoria, wait. That's not what I…"

The line goes dead.

I'm such a fucking idiot. I'm an educated man, but when I'm around her, or talking to her, I become an imbecile. I can't string a coherent thought together without making things worse.

Fuck!

I'm left with no resolution to this situation. I can't go to the club now, I'm too amped up to exercise control, and I can't stomach the idea of touching another woman when I am consumed with thoughts of Vittoria.

I don't know how, but I need to fix this.

I'VE PICKED UP THE PHONE SO MANY TIMES OVER THE PAST MONTH, I'VE almost hit the call button, I've typed out messages and emails and talked myself out of pressing send more times than I can count. I can never find the right words to explain. I'm not great with vocalizing how I feel. I'm great at demanding and commanding a woman to do what I want, but when it comes to me I'm all about keeping it inside.

Vittoria has an effect on me, something I can't explain or rationalize.

I know it's for the best.

Right after our conversation last month, Addi broke up with Carter and left New York without so much as a word to anyone. He's been a complete mess ever since. I've tried to be there for him when I can. Mostly, he just wanted a wingman to party harder, drink more, and forget about her. None of it has worked, but I've done anything he asked of me, supporting him until he's ready to face the reality of what's going on. Truth be told, it's been good to have him around. It's selfish, I know, but it's helped me forget for a few hours here and there. Focusing on him lets me *stop* focusing on myself, and my problems.

Xander called me today and told me he knows where Addison is, and he thinks it's time to tell Carter before he's too far gone. He said something about having to bail him out of jail, and I'm sure he mentioned the office at Cube being trashed, but it all became insignificant the moment he told me Vittoria is in town and planning to be there when Carter finds out about Addi. He asked me to be there too, but I didn't think it would be helpful to have an atmosphere between her and I when the focus should be on Carter. I told him I had a meeting I couldn't reschedule and I'd check in with them all tomorrow and do anything I can to help. I feel like a dick after everything he's done for me, but I just couldn't sit in a room with her right now without acting on it.

I try to distract myself the best way I know how, and decide a trip to Andromeda is in order, but she invades my thoughts the entire day.

By the time I reach the door of the club, she is *all* I can think about. I walk through the bar, across the dance floor and upstairs to my room. Nothing piques my interest—nothing and no one. I could have my choice of women in here, ready and willing to submit, but it holds no appeal to me right now. Not when I know she's in the city. She's within my reach.

I'm out the door and back into a cab before I've even formulated a plan.

"Where to?" The taxi driver turns and stares at me.

"Good question." I give him Xander's address and decide no matter what I'm going to be there for my friend, but as I pull up in front his building, I see Vittoria in the lobby.

She looks breathtaking.

I throw money at the driver and quickly make my way to the entrance to open the door for her. She's looking down at her phone, so it's not until she can physically feel me just inches from her that I hear her sharp intake of breath and watch as her eyes slowly lift to meet mine.

"Hello, Vittoria."

"Fuck!" Her cheeks immediately flush with embarrassment, and it's so fucking cute.

"Please, don't swear at me. Your lips are far too beautiful for profanity."

"Don't say things like that to me, Logan. It's not fair. You don't get to say nice things to me." She moves to walk past me, but I block the door. "You came to see Carter, so go and see him. I need to go."

"I came for selfish reasons. I wanted to see you. I needed to see you."

The look of defeat in her eyes tells me she'll hear me out... reluctantly. "You made your feelings quite clear the last time we spoke."

"No, I didn't. As usual, when I'm talking to you, I made a complete mess of what I was trying to say."

She places her hand on my cheek, caressing the scruff on my jaw with her thumb. "Then tell me now."

Her proximity clouds my judgement. I hate it and love it in equal measure. I'm drawn to her by an invisible force pulling me into her orbit and holding me captive.

Words escape me. I'm mesmerized by her lips, her smile, and the intensity of her gaze. I lean in, silently asking her permission before my mouth comes crashing down on hers. It's the only way I can convey how much she means to me without screwing it up.

She tastes amazingly sweet and so much better than my memories. Her hands fist in my hair, tugging me closer as she gives me everything she has. I wrap my arms around her waist and pull her through the door and out onto the street, never letting her lips break contact with my own. I push her up against the wall of the building, without a care for who's watching. I lose all sense of right and wrong around her. All I feel is desire, want, and above all else, *need*.

Her hands travel up and down my back, clawing at me, and it drives me wild. I grind against her, my tongue tangling with hers in a frenzy, and I'm lost in the moment until I hear a familiar voice.

"What the fuck?"

I pull away, the loss of her taste, her smell and her body tight against mine making me ache. I stand in front of her in a defensive stance, my instinct, to shield her from the abuse I'm about to hear.

"It's not what it looks like."

"The fuck it isn't. It looks like you're groping your best friend's little sister against a wall. Am I wrong?"

"Xander..." I hate the way he describes us, like it's something dirty. "You're so fucking wrong I don't know where to start."

"How about starting at the beginning? How about telling me what the fuck is going on in your head? You know Carter, you know he's having a really hard time right now, and if he finds out about this, all the rage he's feeling will be getting channeled into beating you to death. You know that, right?"

I turn to Vittoria. Her head is lowered to the ground in shame. I close the gap between us and lift her chin to look at me before I whisper in her ear. "I'll deal with this. Go home and I'll call you later."

She throws her arms around me. "I don't want you getting into trouble for me. I'm not worth it."

I cup her face in my hands, forcing her to look at me and hear every word I say. "You *are* worth it. Don't ever think otherwise." I give her one last kiss before hailing her a cab and watching her get further and further away from me... again.

Xander is still standing on the sidewalk with a look of disgust on his face. "What the fuck are you doing, man?"

The tone in his voice really pisses me off. I know they all think I'm some kinky sex pervert who can't commit, but they don't really know anything about me. "It's none of your business, Xander. She's not *your* sister."

I'm caught off guard when he grabs my shirt and slams me back against the wall. "I've known her my whole fucking life. She's as much a sister to me as she is to Carter, so don't fuck with me. She's been through more than you could ever comprehend, and she doesn't need a guy like you to fuck with her head. She's not the type you have a one-night stand with, or a few weeks of fun. She's the forever girl, Logan."

I push him off of me. "Don't you think I know that? I've known it since the moment I met her. Why do you think I've never settled down with anyone?" Understanding dawns on him, his face softening as he realizes what I've been carrying around all these years. "I love her, Xander. I've always loved her. She's… everything."

"Holy Fuck!" He rubs his hands over his face. "How long has this been going on?"

"I kissed her at your wedding. I thought I could handle letting myself have just one kiss, but it wasn't enough. I didn't anticipate she would feel something for me in return. She wanted more, but I walked away and it just about killed me. We've spoken since, but it ended in disaster and tonight is the first I've seen her. I didn't mean to maul her in the middle of the street, but I seem to lose all control around her."

"Well, shit. Who knew Logan Fitzgerald could fall in love? You poor bastard. Carter's going to kill you."

"I know. That's why I walked away in Verona, but I can't ignore it anymore. This could be my one chance to be happy, to have what you have with Lily. I owe it to myself to at least try."

"I understand. I became a demanding dick when I met Lily, but she got past it and saw the real me. I want to punch you in the face right now because Tori is family to me, but I can't fault you for wanting what I have. Lily is my world. She's everything I didn't know I needed. If you truly believe Vittoria could be the one for you, then you have to go for it. But, you need to be absolutely certain. If you're not, then walk away. You could lose Carter's friendship over this, and you need to know it's worth it."

"She's worth it. She's so fucking worth it. I can't even look at another woman now."

"Then you need to tell Carter."

"I will. I don't even know if she still wants to try. I caught her off guard tonight. She's angry with me for walking out. She's out of the country most of the time, and I travel a lot, so before I tell him, I need to know she feels the same way. I need to know I can make this work. She deserves so much better than me, and if I was less selfish, I would let her go and find someone else."

"You're a good guy, Logan. I always thought you just couldn't commit to one woman. Now that I know how you've felt about Vittoria all this time, it makes sense. You were trying to be the good guy and sacrifice your own happiness. You coped the best you could. You deserve her, man. She'd be a lucky girl to have you, and I don't say those words lightly. I love her."

"Thank you."

"But know this. If you ever hurt her, you won't just have Carter to deal with, I'll be right there with him, ready to dig your shallow grave. Got it?"

"I wouldn't expect anything less."

"Go and talk to her. I told Carter and Lily I'd be back in ten minutes with Chinese food. They've probably starved to death by now." He gives me a slap on the back and a smile. "I won't say anything to anyone. It's yours to share, when you're ready."

"Thanks, man. You're a good friend."

"I know. I'm fucking amazing."

"And so modest."

I hear him laughing as he heads down the street, flipping me the bird.

I stand outside his building for a moment longer, staring at my phone. I pull up her number and wait for a few minutes. What I'm about to do could change everything. When I finally hit the call button, she answers on the first ring.

"Logan?"

"We need to talk."

"You're sending me so many mixed signals. I don't know which way is up anymore."

"I know, and I'm sorry. I need to see you, I need to explain. Can I come over?"

"I... I need to be at the airport in an hour. That's why I was leaving Xander's earlier. I won't be back for a while. I'm sorry."

Fuck.

"Don't apologize. I just wish we hadn't been interrupted."

"What happened with Xander? He's a little protective of me."

"That's an understatement. We talked, he slammed me into a wall. I shouted at him in the street, I explained how I feel, and he told me to treat you right."

"Well, at least *he* knows how you feel about me, because I sure as hell don't."

"Fuck! I wish I could come and see you."

"I know. Me too. I'm going to Prague and then Vienna. I think they're adding a few other cities onto the tour, so I'm not sure when I'll be back. Maybe we could talk while I'm gone?"

"Okay. It might be good if we talk when we're on different continents. I seem to lose my head around you. I shouldn't have kissed you tonight. You were angry with me, and for good reason. I should have respected that."

"Logan. I get it. Whatever this is between us, it takes over when we're within two feet of each other. I can't speak for you, but for me it's been a long time coming. I know how it feels to kiss you, to watch you come, and I want it so bad it hurts."

"Fuck me."

"I want to, but you won't let me."

"You're killing me here, Tori."

Her laughter is so melodic, like music to my ears. "I'm not going to make it easy on you after you left me naked and frustrated at the wedding."

"Frustrated? I'm pretty sure I watched you come, more than once."

"You did, but it still wasn't enough. I wanted to feel you inside me."

My heart is racing as she speaks, her sexy voice telling me what she wants from me.

"You need to stop talking. I'm rock-hard and alone."

"I need to go now, I'm already running late, but I'll call you when I get settled at the hotel. You can go and deal with your rock-hard situation. I'm just hoping you'll be thinking of me. Remember how I taste, what I sound like when I come and how I look naked and spread wide for you. Do you remember, Logan?"

She knows exactly what she's doing to me. She's feisty, and she doesn't play fair.

"Every single night since it happened. I'm consumed by the memory of you laid bare for me. It haunts my dreams." I can hear her gasp on the other end of the phone, causing a jolt of desire to course through me. "Travel safely. I'll speak to you soon."

"Bye, Logan."

I put my phone in my pocket and hail a cab. I started tonight with the idea of going to Andromeda and losing myself in another woman's pleasure, but instead, I find myself embarking on a long-distance relationship with a woman I've never had sex with. The woman I've been in love with for as long as I can remember.

I'm so far out of my comfort zone.

CHAPTER 4

LOGAN

Two Months Later

TRAVELING USED TO BE ONE OF MY FAVORITE THINGS, BUT NOW, I HATE it. Every time Vittoria has been in New York over the past few months, I've been out of the country.

She was true to her word. The night she left to go on tour, she called me the moment she got to her hotel room, and we talked for hours. We talked about Verona, we talked about the kiss, and we decided to keep talking. To see where this takes us. To give ourselves a chance to see if we can be together. It's been difficult being so far apart all the time, but it's letting us get to know each other outside of our normal roles of best friend and little sister. We've not told anyone, and that's the way it needs to stay for now. Until I know if I can make this work, I don't want to cause a fight with Carter, or between him and Vittoria.

I made the decision not to tell her I'm a Dominant. I don't want to bring that into her life, or make her feel like she needs to be a part of it to make me happy. It's easy to make the choice when I'm not on the same continent as her. I'm not sure how it's going to feel when she's here, in my arms, and I can't act on instinct, but I need to try. That's why we have to take it slow.

We may not be able to have the type of relationship I want, but I would sacrifice the lifestyle to be with her. I just hope I'm strong enough to do it. I would never forgive myself if I brought her into my world. No one should go into this lifestyle to please someone else. It must be a choice you make for yourself, because it's what you want. If I asked her to do this for me, she'd probably say yes and she might even like it for a while, but there would come a point when she'd resent me, and I couldn't deal with that. I made the decision to be a part of this lifestyle, and for her, I can make the decision to leave it. She's worth it.

With every day that passes, and every call, text or email we exchange, I find myself falling even harder for her, which I didn't think was possible. Talking with her for hours, unable to act on any physical chemistry we have, my desire for her body has become secondary to my desire to really *know* her. Not the girl I've been in love with for years, but the real down to earth beauty inside. Her hopes and fears for the future. What she loves to do with her time off. How she feels when she dances in front of thousands every night.

Last week she made me download the Snapchat app onto my phone. If Xander and Carter ever find out, I'm never going to hear the end of it. They would ridicule me until the end of time! I find myself doing and saying things that are so unlike me when it comes to her. She's so funny, sending me crazy selfies from every city she visits, hot as hell videos that leave me more than a little frustrated, and some of the stuff she says in emails cracks me up.

FaceTime has become our favorite way to keep in touch. Last night Vittoria called me wearing a sexy black negligée, making out like it was nothing, talking to me about her day with mischief clear in her eyes. I played along, but by the time we said goodnight I was in physical pain.

This morning I'm getting ready to head to Berlin via London. I would normally relish the chance to spend a few days in a great city, but last night I found out Vittoria is flying back to New York for the weekend, and I'm not going to be here. I would have rescheduled my trip if she'd told me sooner, but she was trying to surprise me. To say I'm disappointed would be the understatement of the year.

As I pack my bag and get ready to head to the airport, my phone beeps with a message from her.

Vittoria: *I have a surprise for you.*

Me: *You're going to Berlin instead of New York? ;o)*

Vittoria: *I wish. If I could I would, but I have to be in New York. I promised my mom I would be there for my dad's birthday party.*

Me: *I know. I just can't believe I'm going to miss seeing you.*

Vittoria: *I'll send you pictures.*

Me: *Naked pictures?*

Vittoria: *Naughty boy.*

Me: *I've got to go. My cab is here to take me to the airport. Text me when you land. I need to know you're safe.*

Vittoria: *Will do.*

Then I remember her saying she had a surprise for me. I fire out a text as I throw my bag into the trunk of the cab.

Me: *What's my surprise?*

Vittoria: *Wait and see. X*

Me: *Tease.*

I can't stop thinking about her—in the cab, through security, at the gate and as I take my seat on the plane. I should have been coming to pick her up at the airport tonight, bringing her home with me, and finally getting to taste the sweetness of her lips again. I shouldn't be getting on a plane and heading thousands of miles away from where she'll be. Since I lost my virginity at sixteen years old, I've never gone this long without sex, and I've never wanted anyone as much as I want Vittoria. Life can be a cruel son of a bitch sometimes!

As the plane takes off, I sit back and replay every moment of our encounter in Verona, recalling every line and curve of her body and the way she fell apart at my touch. I can almost smell her seductive scent as I lose myself in the memory.

THE FLIGHT DIDN'T SEEM LONG TODAY. IN FACT, IT FELT LIKE I WAS being dragged away from Vittoria at lightning speed. Every moment taking me further and further away from where she is.

As soon as we land, I pull out my phone to see if she's messaged to say she landed safely in New York. By my calculations, we must have passed each other in the air around three hours into my flight. Sure enough, my phone beeps with a text, but it's not to say she landed. All it says is *Text me when you land.* I type out a quick message and wait for her reply, grabbing my bag from the overhead locker and making my way off the plane to navigate Heathrow Airport for a few hours.

My phone chimes with a Snapchat picture. It's of Vittoria. It looks like she's at the airport. She should have landed hours ago. I quickly reply.

Me: *Was your flight delayed? Why are you still at the airport?*

Vittoria: *You didn't look closely at the background, did you?*

Me: *I was too busy looking at the gorgeous girl in the picture.*

My phone chimes with another picture. I take a moment to really look at the backdrop. It can't be... surely not. My phone beeps again.

Vittoria: *Look up*

I scan the crowd in front of me, my pulse racing when I see her. She's here. In London. My phone goes off again and I look down, reluctant to pull my gaze from her in case she disappears.

Vittoria: *Surprise*

I shove my phone into my pocket and stride toward her, oblivious to anything and anyone around me. I can't believe she's here, a hundred yards in front of me. I close the distance between us, never taking my eyes off her, watching her sexy grin as she begins to move, almost running toward me.

I drop my bags as our bodies collide and she throws herself into my arms. I spin her around with a blatant disregard for the crowd surrounding us, trying to make their way through the airport to wherever they're going.

"What the hell are you doing here? Shouldn't you be in New York by now?"

"I..." She begins to answer, but I'm too impatient. I swallow her words with my mouth, my lips crashing down on hers in a fierce kiss. Her arms snake around my neck, her legs wrapping around my waist as I hold her tight, our tongues exploring each other. She tastes amazing, and her smell... it's divine.

We're breathless and blissful, and achingly bereft as we break our kiss, our eyes locking as I slowly set her down on the ground.

"How are you standing here with me?"

She gives me a sly grin. "I changed my flight. Instead of a two-hour wait, I now have a twelve-hour wait, but it means I get to spend two hours with you before your next flight. I figured it was worth the trade-off."

"You're incredible. I can't believe you did this for me."

"You're worth the wait." I can see in her eyes she doesn't just mean today, and it slays me. I've wanted her for so long, I have to pinch myself to believe this is real, that she's real, and she wants to be with me.

I sling my arm around her shoulder, pick up both of our bags, and pull her into my side. "Let's make the most of our two hours then. Would you like to go for coffee with me, Miss de Rossi?"

A mischievous grin creeps across her face. "I'd love to, Mr. Fitzgerald. Lead the way. I'm yours to command."

Fuck me! I'm hard from hearing her say those four little words, *I'm yours to command.* If I didn't know better, I'd worry that she knew about me. She couldn't have picked a sexier phrase to say to me if she tried. I caress my hand down her side and give her ass a sharp, short, smack. "Be careful what you say, little one, I might just take you up on it."

We weave our way through the crowds, the tension between us a palpable force, every nerve ending in my body alight with desire for her.

I find a quiet corner for us to sit in, set down our bags and head up to order us some drinks. An uneasy feeling settles in my stomach as I walk away from her. She's no more than twenty feet away, but I feel the distance and I don't like it. I only have two hours with her. I haven't seen her in months, and our last encounter was a brief tryst outside Xander's apartment building. I want to be touching her every moment we have together, even if it's only holding her hand. Being around her makes me feel… whole. I don't know how to explain it. I've never felt like this around another person before. She causes a physical reaction inside of me, like she's altering my very DNA when I'm in her presence. It's both disconcerting and completely electrifying.

As I wait in line, I can't take my eyes off her. The woman behind me attempts to strike up a conversation with some flirtatious innuendo, but she's not even on my radar. I drag my gaze from Vittoria just long enough to politely decline the woman next to me, and when I find her again, she's smiling at me, shaking her head in mock disappointment.

When I finally return with coffee and croissants, her first words are, "I can't take you anywhere without women throwing themselves at you." She's mocking me, but I detect a hint of possessiveness. "How do you ever get anything done? You can't even buy a coffee without being accosted by hot women. It must be so difficult looking like you do. A true hardship."

I let her ramble, making herself blush with embarrassment in the process, while I set down our coffee and plates and discard the tray on the empty table beside us. I take a moment to enjoy her small show of jealousy, taking a sip of my coffee before I put her mind at rest.

"Firstly, you're right, it's a curse being this hot. You understand why women want me so badly, though, you're one of them!" She leans across the table to slap me on the arm, which is totally adorable. "Secondly, it's easy to fend them off these days, I just tell them I have a girlfriend. End of story."

She almost chokes on her coffee, spraying it all over me. "Oh God, Logan, I'm so sorry. She immediately jumps out of her seat and starts trying to clean me up with napkins, but I'm too busy laughing to care.

"You are so cute when you're worked up. I didn't realize calling you my girlfriend would get such a reaction from you. Is it really such a big a shock?" Her hands stop dead on my chest, the napkin scrunched into a ball in her fist. I pull her down onto my lap, wrapping my arms around her. "Don't you want me to call you that?"

"I... I like it. I just didn't know what we were. We've not really defined it, and..." She hesitates.

"And what?"

"I didn't think you were a girlfriend kind of guy."

"I'm not. But I'll make an exception for you. I'm breaking all my own rules with you already, one more won't make a difference."

She extricates herself from my arms, smoothing her hair and adjusting her top as she sits back down across from me. She grasps her coffee in both hands, staring into its depths as if it will give her some answers before she opens her mouth to speak.

"What do you mean, you're breaking all your own rules with me?"

Her gaze is hesitant, her demeanor wary.

"I didn't mean it in a bad way. I guess I'm just doing things differently with you than I have with anyone in the past. It's not important."

"It is if you're not happy. I don't want you to feel like you can't be yourself with me. I don't want you to change because of me. I like you the way you are."

I reach across and take both of her hands in mine, caressing my thumbs over her knuckles. "Vittoria, I want to change for you. I want to be better. I want to treat you the way you deserve. The guy I've been up until now wasn't good enough for you, and I intend to be a man who is worthy of you... someday. Trust me when I tell you that you would not want to be with the guy I was before." A part of me craves the opportunity to make her a part of the lifestyle. She would be an exquisite submissive. But a better part of me, the part that's winning out right now, wants to protect her from it, and never let her see the darker, hidden side of myself.

"I would want to be with you no matter what. I long to be with the man you are, the man you were, every part of you. The parts of yourself you think aren't worthy of me, are the parts that draw me to you, the parts I want you to share with me." She holds my gaze, as if she's trying to convey some unspoken understanding to me.

I need to change the subject before I confess everything to her and watch what we have fall apart before my eyes. "You better drink your coffee before it gets cold. So, when are you going to be in New York again after this weekend? I want to make sure I'm not on another business trip when you fly in."

"Two weeks." Her gaze drops, disappointment evident at my change of subject. "I'll be back in two weeks and I'll be staying for close to three weeks before I have to fly back out to Europe."

"I get you all to myself for almost three weeks? You've made my year with that little tidbit of information. The things I could do to you in that time." I wink at her, and watch as she melts, her annoyance forgotten, excitement at the prospect of our time together taking over.

"Promises, promises."

"I always keep my promises, Vittoria."

"Well then, I look forward to it."

We fall into an easy conversation, flirting and chatting, and enjoying each other's company while we can. Our legs tangle together under the table, maintaining some sort of physical contact until the announcement for my flight to board comes over the PA system. I'm devastated that our two hours are gone already, a pain taking up residence in my chest as Vittoria disentangles her legs and stands from the table.

"Guess it's time to turn back into a pumpkin."

I stand and pull her into my arms, resting my chin on her head. "You'll always be a princess to me." I kiss her hair, inhaling her scent, needing my fix before I have to leave her again. She holds onto me as if her life depends on it, and I can't make my feet move. I can't bring myself to let go and leave her behind.

She's the one who finally breaks free, putting some distance between us. "You better go. You don't want to miss your flight."

I take her hand in mine as I lift our bags. "I want to miss my flight more than anything in the world right now. I can't stand the thought of leaving you."

She takes her bag from my hand, a resigned look on her face, her eyes glassy with unshed tears. "Come on. I'll walk with you as far as I can. I actually need to go in the opposite direction for my flight."

"How long do you have left to wait?"

"Six hours."

"Fuck! I feel terrible that you've done all this just for two hours with me."

She stops me in my tracks, turns to face me, rising onto her tiptoes, and plants the softest kiss on my lips. Her sweet taste, mixed with the bitterness of her coffee, is a delightful combination. "I would have waited twice as long, just for a glimpse of you."

I rest my forehead against hers, trying to calm the storm raging inside me. "Don't say things like that to me. I'm already fighting everything inside me that's screaming at me to stay here with you, telling me that where you are is where I'm supposed to be." Her breath quickens and I'm lost in her. Nothing else matters in this moment...only her.

I'm pulled from my reverie by a voice over the PA system.

"Could Mr. Logan Fitzgerald please make his way to Gate 16? The gate is ready to close. Passenger Logan Fitzgerald on flight 168 to Berlin, please make your way to Gate 16."

"Shit!"

"You need to go, Logan, now! Go, I'll be fine." I pull her into my arms, unwilling to let her go, but she pushes me away. "Go!"

She gives me a chaste kiss, turns, and strides away. I can see in her movements that she's fighting every step she takes in the opposite direction from me, quickening her pace to stop herself from looking back. I can't leave her without a proper goodbye. I won't see her again for two weeks.

I take off in her direction, grabbing her hand in mine, spinning her round to see the tears streaming down her beautiful cheeks. My bag drops to the floor as my hands reach up to clasp her face, my lips descending on hers in a ferocious kiss, claiming her as mine, devouring her tongue with my own. I bite and suck, nibble and lick her, savoring every delicate flick of her tongue. She submits to me, her body going limp against me as she gives herself over to me, to our intense chemistry.

"Don't ever walk away from me without saying a proper goodbye." She's breathless and flushed as I pick up my bag, giving her one last kiss before I have to leave. "Goodbye, little one. I'll see you soon."

She's practically panting as I turn to leave. "I can't wait."

"Me either. Now, I've got to go and catch my flight." I give her a quick slap on the ass, much to her delight, before breaking out in a sprint to my gate.

I make it to the gate just as the flight attendant is about to close the door, her disapproving look doing nothing to lessen the high I feel with the sweet taste of Vittoria fresh on my lips. She hands me my boarding pass and wishes me a pleasant flight. When I thank her for waiting for me, and flash her my best dimpled smile, her stern exterior crumbles and she blushes like a giddy schoolgirl. It makes me laugh, only because it makes me think of Vittoria. Her feisty little jealous streak, and her jibes at me for being attractive to another woman.

As I settle down into my seat for the short flight to Berlin, I find myself lost in thoughts of her, but unlike my flight to London, I have new memories to keep me going, the taste of her on my lips, and the smell of her perfume on my clothes. I still can't wrap my head around the fact that she changed her flight and waited at the airport all this time just to see me for two hours.

She really is amazing. Far too good for me… but I'm selfish. I need her, and I'll be counting the days until she's in my arms again.

CHAPTER 5

LOGAN

Carter just messaged me to go to dinner at his place tonight, saying that Xander, Lily, and Vittoria would be there. I feel terrible that I already knew I was being invited. I was sitting next to Vittoria when he called her twenty minutes ago and asked her to go. She didn't mention me, she gave nothing away when he said he was going to ask me to come along. I feel like the worst kind of friend. Not only have we lied by omission, but the last thing I want to do is go to his place tonight.

It's been two long weeks since I left Vittoria at Heathrow Airport, and I've been counting the days, the hours, and the minutes until I picked her up at the airport an hour ago. We've been sitting in traffic, the tension building between us, making it almost impossible to breathe. The air is thick with anticipation, the knowledge that tonight is the night we'll finally be together, in every way possible. It's a physical presence in the space between us.

I was going to take her straight to my place, but the current twist of events has thrown a wrench in the works. Instead, I find myself taking a detour and heading toward her apartment, where I'm going to have to leave her, again, even if only for a couple of hours. We've arranged to meet at Carter's place. It's for the best. If we turn up together, the night will be ruined before it begins.

As I drop her off and watch her enter the building, disappearing from sight, a strange feeling of dread descends upon me. I thought tonight was going to be all about us. The beginning of three glorious weeks of exploring each other, learning and loving each other's bodies, and finding out if what we have is the real thing. I already know the answer, but I need her to be sure. Suddenly, I feel uneasy about what this time together will bring us. I know that I have to come clean with Carter before we can move forward. If I lie to his face tonight, it'll eat away at me, and I know it will make it harder for Vittoria to focus on us if she feels that she's somehow deceived her older brother.

I need to approach this the right way if I want to convince him that I'm not going to hurt his little sister. I know that tonight, something is going to go down between us. I'm hoping beyond hope that he'll see how serious I am about her, that he will see past his preconceptions about the way I treat women and give me a chance to prove him wrong.

As I head back to my apartment alone, I can't shake the feeling that something bad is coming my way. I hope I'm just overreacting. I'm just upset that our plans for the night have been derailed after two weeks of waiting and wanting.

WHEN MY CAB PULLS UP OUTSIDE OF CARTER'S BUILDING, I CAN FEEL the tension in my shoulders. I didn't even notice my hands balled tightly into fists, my knuckles white with the strain. I tell myself that when he sees how I feel about her, he'll understand.

I ring the doorbell and wait... Addi answers the door, looking radiant at six months pregnant, searching the hallway for, I don't know what.

"Well hello, sexy. Where is the latest drone? I know you have one!"

As I step inside, I can feel her before I see her. Vittoria's already here. She's chatting with Lily, laughing and smiling, but I see the almost imperceptible tremor of her lips and the narrowing of her eyes at Addi's words. Our eyes connect for the briefest of moments before she turns her head, her body language screaming her discomfort.

I lean in to kiss Addi on the cheek and hand her the flowers I brought for her. "No drones. There is a new lady in the picture, but I'm not ready to share her with you yet. She's… important."

"OMG! Lily, Vittoria, did you just hear this? New York's very own Casanova has found a special someone! Hearts will be breaking all over town tonight."

"Oh shut up! You and Carter weren't exactly monks before you got together and look at you now!" I brush my hand against her growing belly, her cheeks blushing with pride. "Give me a break, will you? I don't want to mess this one up."

"Okay. Just this once, but I expect details later though."

I say hello to Lily and Vittoria, but it feels strange not to touch her. I want to pull her into my arms and feel her heartbeat against my chest. Instead, she hands me a beer, her fingertips brushing mine as she tells me the boys are in the den. My dick twitches at even this smallest of interactions.

I leave the ladies to their chat, a smile pulling at the corner of my lips as I hear Lily talking. "What do they put in the water around here? All three of those boys are super-freaking-H-O-T! You should have snatched that up, Tori!"

"I'm pretty sure he's the one who makes those kinds of decisions. I don't think any woman would be able to snag Logan Fitzgerald. Not really. Like Addi said, who will the next drone be?"

My heart sinks. Is she playing a part? Trying not to give anything away about us? Or is that what she believes? That she's just the next in line.

I open the door to the den to find Carter and Xander having a heart-to-heart. I can't take anymore 'feelings' tonight so I decide to lighten the mood.

"I knew it. I leave you two alone for a few months and you're butt buddies."

"Hey, dickhead! How the hell are you? Long time no see!" The guilt washes over me. I've been avoiding him like the plague since the wedding.

"I'm good. Your sister's here and colluding with your women while you guys have been busy having your lovefest in here."

Carter's face lights up. "Vittoria's here? When did she arrive?"

"What am I, her damn keeper? I don't know. I just got here." That came out so defensive. Could I be any more obvious?

"It was a simple question. You need to get laid, loosen up a bit." He has no idea how fucking true that is. I'm going to explode if I don't get inside of Vittoria soon. My dick is hard just at the thought of it. "Where's your latest victim? She out talking to the girls?" I stiffen. He's so close to the truth, and yet a million miles off the mark.

"No. I didn't bring her. It's... complicated."

"Complicated? Does she actually have opinions, instead of blindly doing whatever you ask?" I can't help but laugh. He hit the nail right on the head without even knowing it.

"You have no fucking idea!"

I can always count on Xander to offer his support. "Have you met my wife and his girlfriend? Opinionated, bullheaded, and complicated as hell. Welcome to the club!"

His revelation hits me square in the chest. I'm in exactly the same position as these two idiots. I thought I was all about being in control, keeping my relationships neat and tidy, but I've ended up in the same place anyway. Hopelessly in love with a girl who is far too good for me.

Addi offers a reprieve, interrupting to let us know that dinner's ready. Now all I have to do is get through dinner without declaring my undying love for Vittoria in front of everyone and I can call the night a success.

Dinner is amazing. The food, the wine, and the company are fantastic. I find myself unable to go five minutes without at least a glance in her direction. It's so nice to see her having fun and laughing with her friends. She must be able to sense when my eyes are on her, because every time, her eyes find mine. Stolen glances that say a thousand words.

My ears prick up when the girls start grilling her about her new 'boyfriend.' I'm intrigued. I didn't know she had been in touch with Addi while we've been... seeing each other. Vittoria plays it down, blaming schedules, saying they haven't spent much time together, which is true for the most part. Ever the wallflower, Addi won't let her off that easily. "Oh come on, you can do better than that. You told me last week that he gave you, and I quote, 'the most phenomenal orgasm you've ever had.'"

Holy. Fucking. Christ!

There is no way I'm getting out of this alive.

"What the fuck, Addi? Brother in the room here. I don't want to hear shit like that. Lucky the son of a bitch couldn't make it tonight."

He turns and stares right at me. "Any man who lays a finger on my sister, better be prepared to take a severe beating from me." I hold his gaze. He knows. It's now or never.

Vittoria stands up for herself but Carter isn't interested in what she has to say.

I need to step in before she says the words that need to come from me.

"If Vittoria's happy, surely that's what matters?"

The table is silent. Everyone is staring at me... waiting. Xander gives me a knowing look, a flash of sympathy in his eyes.

"No. What matters is that this new guy is *clearly* not good enough for her. He couldn't even be bothered to show his face tonight." So, this is how he wants to play it, forcing me into admitting it.

"Or maybe, he's trying to respect her wishes." This just angers him further.

"And why are you such an expert on the guy, Logan? Do fucking tell!"

"Goddammit!" I stand from the table and make my way round to where Vittoria is sitting. "Because it's me, but you already worked that out, so let's not play games."

Vittoria stands, wrapping her arms around me, and Carter looks about ready to rip my throat out. She pleads with him to give us his blessing, to be happy for us, but it's a red rag to a bull at this stage.

"Happy? One of my closest friends has been fucking my little sister behind my back, and I'm supposed to be happy about it?"

Now, I'm angry. I don't give a shit what he thinks of me, but he's disrespecting her now. He knows she wouldn't just go around 'fucking' anyone. She's not that kind of girl. I step in front of her, my instinct to protect, on high alert. "Don't talk about her like that, Carter. You know this is about more than fucking or I would never have let anything happen. We both travel all the time, but we've kept in touch since the wedding, and we've only seen each other twice since then." He needs time to process this. "There are no guarantees we can make this... arrangement... work..." That was the wrong thing to say. I'm so used to using the terminology with my subs, it just sort of slipped out. "But, I want to give it a chance. I would never do anything to intentionally hurt you, you're like a brother to me. And I would *never* hurt Vittoria."

He is seething with rage. I haven't seen him this upset in a long time. "Well if I'm your brother, that would make her your sister, which makes your 'arrangement' just fucking sick." I knew he would jump on my inept word choice, but this is out of fucking order.

I move Vittoria out of the way before squaring up to him. He has every right to be angry, but he's taking it too far. I'm not the fucking devil. I'm his best friend. "Say one more word like that, Carter, and I won't be responsible for my actions." Adrenaline courses through my body, my anger reaching boiling point. How dare he talk about her like this. She's fucking perfect and he shouldn't be judging anyone. I wouldn't treat a dog the way he treated women when Addi was gone.

"Get the fuck out of my house... NOW!"

I grab Vittoria's hand and make my way to the door. She doesn't give any resistance, and I know, she's *with* me.

"Vittoria. Don't you dare walk out of here right now, especially not with *him*." I knew he would take it badly, but I wasn't prepared for how devastated I feel by his disdain for me right now.

She holds her head high, her voice even and assured as she delivers her parting words. "I have to go with him, Carter. If you can't at least try to be happy for me, then I guess we won't be seeing each other much for a while. Please... don't make me choose."

Xander and Lily look shell-shocked, and Addi looks sympathetic to both Carter, *and,* Vittoria and me. I give Carter one last glance as I walk out the door. This is exactly what I didn't want to happen. He's my family, and the look in his eyes as I leave tells me he feels betrayed.

I feel so many emotions as I stride down the hallway with Vittoria by my side. I'm so angry I could punch through the walls of this place until my hands can't take it anymore. The way he spoke about her. He had no right to do that, and I don't care who he is, he doesn't get to talk about the woman I love that way.

I'm worried about her. What this will do to her if we continue on this path. I can't ask her to choose between her family and me. It would be selfish and wrong. But if I walk away from her, how will it affect her?

I'm sad that I almost came to blows with my oldest friend. I don't know how to make things right with him, and until I do, there will be a gaping hole in my life. I know I shouldn't be, but I'm also fighting to curb my own arousal in this moment, waiting on the elevator to arrive. Thinking of Vittoria, and how she stood her ground... for me. No one has ever done anything like that for me before. Her hand is tight in mine as we stand in silence, the gravity of what has just happened weighing heavily between us.

She's the one to break the silence.

"He needed to know. I can't live my life for him, Logan. I won't. I want to be with you. I *am* yours. I always have been. From the moment we met, I was yours whether you knew it or not, ready and waiting for the day we would find our way to each other." Her voice becomes quiet, a hint of insecurity as she continues. "I know I made a fool of myself to begin with, that I threw myself at you, but I've been waiting since the day I met you to kiss you, to touch you, to feel you inside of me. To be... yours, in every possible way."

I can't believe how vulnerable she looks in this moment. Fragile and unsure of herself. How does she not know that I feel the same way? Didn't I just prove it? I just gave up the closest thing I have to a brother, to be with her. I've obviously not shown her enough, if she doesn't have faith in the depth of my feelings for her.

My disappointment in myself is overshadowed only by my overwhelming desire to let her know, in the only way I feel she'll understand. I can't hold back any longer. It's hurting her more than it's helping, and every moment that I'm not kissing her feels like an eternity.

I grab her with both hands, hoist her up into my arms and wrap her legs around my waist. I take in our surroundings and spy the door to the stairwell. I'm there in two strides, opening the door with one hand, grasping her with the other as I hold her gaze, inches from mine. She coils her hands up around my neck and into my hair, tugging ever so slightly. It drives me wild, and I can feel my control slipping.

I press her back up against the cold, hard stone walls, encasing her, trapping her. My breathing labored as I struggle to find the words.

"Vittoria... Nyx... I... need you more than my next breath."

"I'm right here."

My lips find hers in an instant. The feel of her soft, full lips on mine is a taste of paradise. I've been a man lost in the desert these past few weeks, thirsty and desperate for the smallest drop to keep me going. She is my oasis. Her tongue tangles with mine and I can feel her need. It fuels my own as I run my hand down her side, finding the space between us, cupping her breast and squeezing it in my palm.

"I've wanted this for so long." Her words are a strangled plea for more, and in answer, I start grinding my cock against her sweet spot, eliciting a sexy as hell groan from her. I swallow it, thrusting faster, feeling myself getting harder and harder until I feel like I'm going to burst out of my pants.

I break our kiss, gasping for air. "I want to be inside of you so badly right now. But I'm not going to do that to you, to us." I continue to thrust against her slowly, unable to stop myself from trying to alleviate some of my discomfort.

She shows her appreciation with a sharp thrust of her hips against my cock, sending a jolt of pleasure straight to my core. I know I can't make love to her tonight. She's too vulnerable after what just happened, and I don't want our first time to be fueled by anger and hurt. I want her to remember it as a moment that is ours and ours alone, not marred by an ugly fight with her brother. My balls ache as I pull back, putting the smallest of spaces between our bodies, and yet it feels like miles. I'm trying so hard to focus on getting her home before I fuck her right here, right now, and to hell with good intentions.

CHAPTER 6

LOGAN

I CAN'T DO THIS TO HER.

I know she thought she could walk away from her brother and be okay with it, but she's falling apart. It's been almost three weeks since our run in at dinner, and Vittoria just isn't the same. The sparkle in her eyes has faded, she doesn't look at me the same way. I feel like every time I look in her eyes, all she sees is the reason that her brother won't take her calls. We were supposed to spend this time together, exploring our new relationship, but we've barely seen each other, and when we have, it's been... different. She's different. She's due to fly back out on tour tomorrow, and if I don't let her go now, I won't be able to.

I need to fix this. For her. For them. I should never have kissed her. I should never have let myself believe I could have it all. A best friend who is like a brother, *and* a woman to love, and who loves me back. It's just not in the cards for me. There are millions of women in New York, and I had to fall in love with Carter's younger sister. It really is true what they say—you can't choose who you love. But, you can choose whether or not to act on it, and I made the selfish choice, and now Vittoria is paying the price.

She's going to hate me, but I hope that in the long run, she can forgive me, and see that what I'm about to do is *because* I love her. She should be here any minute, and I know I'm going to want to cling to her with everything that I am, and never let her go, but I have to do this. If I don't do it now, I never will. I couldn't bear to have her resent me in a year or five years' time, when she realizes that I'm the reason her relationship with her brother will never be the same. Maybe this way, someday, she'll forgive me, and I won't have lost her from my life completely, and maybe I can repair the damage I've done to my friendship with Carter.

The doorbell rings and my heart lurches up into my throat. I take a deep breath, steeling myself for the vision of beauty I know is waiting behind the door. How can I look her in the eyes, her stunning brown eyes, and tell her we can't be together? That I can't give her all of the things in life that I want to.

A knock at the door, forces me to face my darkest fear.

She throws herself into my arms, kissing me with a vulnerable passion. She tastes like coffee and Vittoria. Bittersweet in more ways than one. The painful duality of it isn't lost on me, and she senses my dilemma, pulling back, breaking what will probably be our final kiss, and staring up into my eyes with... love.

"I missed you. Are you okay? You seem... I don't know. Don't get me wrong, you're an amazing kisser, Mr. Fitzgerald." It makes me hard hearing her say my name like that, even if she's being playful. "But, you seem a little lackluster today. Do I smell bad, or do I look a mess?"

How could she ever think she's anything less than perfect? I pull her back into my arms, selfish enough to want our last kiss to be something for her to remember me by. A kiss that conveys how deeply I feel for her. "You're perfect, baby. Always perfect." She flinches, but quickly melts into my arms when I close the door and press her gently against the cold, hard wood, and pour my soul into this kiss. I savor the smell of her perfume, the feel of her lips against my own, and the taste of her tongue as it strokes mine. I love how her body molds to mine, as if she were the other half of me. I ache at the feel of her breasts pressed tightly against my chest, and how her hair feels as I tangle my fists into it, pulling her as close as possible. My heart beating in time with hers.

I never want to let go, but I know I have to.

I break our kiss, leaving us both breathless and desperate for more.

"I want you to make love to me, Logan."

Her words cut me like a knife. "I can't." Resting my forehead against hers, I repeat the words over and over in a mantra, trying to convince myself to stay strong. I need to do the right thing by her. "I can't... I can't."

"Why? I don't understand. You have feelings for me. I want to be with you. I know I turn you on, I can feel you right now, hard and big, and ready for me. Why won't you let this happen?" She slides her hand between our bodies, rubbing her hand over my erection, clouding my judgement, and making me want her so badly I feel like I might die if I don't make love to her.

"You need to stop. I... I can't think straight when your hand is on my cock."

"Then stop thinking and *feel* it. I want you to make love to me before I have to leave you to go back out on tour tomorrow."

I want to do that for her. I want to do it for me. But, what kind of man would I be if I chose my own pleasure over her relationship with her family? I would be a bastard, and a hypocrite. It goes against everything I believe as a Master. Her needs come before my own, even when she doesn't see it. Even when she doesn't understand that's what I'm doing.

I find the strength to step back, to take her hand, and lead her to the couch. "Sit with me. We need to talk."

"Nothing good ever came from that phrase. What's wrong? You're scaring me."

I sit for a moment, trying to figure out how to say this. To speak the words I never want to say. To break her heart, and my own.

"These past few months, the wedding, talking with you, and getting the rare chance to see you a couple of times, has been the most amazing time of my life."

Her face looks tortured. She knows what's coming. "Don't do this, Logan. Please. Don't."

"Tori, if I thought it could be different, trust me, I would be doing everything in my power to keep you by my side. I've waited so long... to touch you, to taste you, to give you everything I have."

"Then why do I feel like you're throwing me away, casting me aside because it's too difficult."

I grab her face in my hands, wiping the tears that mar her beautiful cheeks with my thumbs. "Please don't think that. If it was only difficult for me, I would fight until my dying breath to be with you, but it's not. I can't be the reason you and Carter don't talk to each other."

"He'll come around. He's a pigheaded asshole sometimes, but he'll come around."

"I broke his trust. I was his best friend, and I broke his trust. He loves you more than life itself. I understand where he's coming from, and yeah, maybe he'll come around, but it'll never be the same, as long as you're with me. I can't shoulder that burden. You have a family I would kill for, and I can't come between you. I can't do that to you. I care too much."

She turns her face, pulling away from me, standing to put some distance between us. "That's bullshit! You don't care *enough*. If I was worth it, you wouldn't let Carter or anyone else stand in the way."

I can't breathe.

"You're not hearing me. This isn't about me, or the way I feel. It's about you and what's best for you. Your family, your brother. You need them, and I would never forgive myself if I took them away from you, if you had to give them up to be with me."

I try to comfort her, to hold her, but she pushes me away. "Don't! You can't have it all, Logan. You don't get to touch me and kiss me, and then discard me. Don't fool yourself that this is about me, about protecting me. It's about you. You thought you wanted me, and now that you realize you don't, that reality isn't as good as the fantasy, you want out. Fine. I'm out. Don't speak to me, don't look at me, and don't come to my parents' house. I don't want to see you ever again."

I try to stop her from walking out, "Please, Vittoria. That's not true. Let me explain," but as soon as my hand find hers, she whips round and slaps me in the face.

"Fuck you! I thought you were different. I thought I meant something to you."

"You do. You mean everything to me."

She slaps me again. "Don't you *dare* say that to me. I know you, Logan. Better than you know yourself. You want to be in control of everything? Fine. Enjoy controlling all of the *nothing* and *no one* in your life."

She slams the door behind her, and the walls start closing in on me. I can't speak. I can't feel. It's too painful. Knowing that she hates me, that she thinks I don't care enough—will haunt me for the rest of my life.

I need to respect her wishes. She doesn't want to see me again, and I need to find a way to come to terms with it.

I will never see Vittoria again... never hear her laugh... never see her smile... never watch her come apart under my touch.

I did the right thing for her. She needs her family, more than she needs me. I couldn't be the man she needed me to be. I could have given up the lifestyle for her, but how long would it have lasted? Eventually I would have dragged her down with me, because I'm weak when it comes to her. I'm selfish. I want all of her, in every way possible. Her pleasure, her pain, her trust, her obedience. I want her love and her submission. If Carter couldn't accept us as a 'normal' couple, he never would have forgiven me for making her my submissive. It would have changed her irrevocably, and I love her too much to do that to her.

Hell, is this moment, this feeling. Nothing but darkness, and despair.

It's been five weeks since Vittoria walked out of my apartment and out of my life, and it's still as raw and painful as it was then.

Carter still won't speak to me. Now I'm the asshole who not only had the audacity to try to date his sister, but I'm also the bastard who broke her heart. I can't win either way. Xander told me that they're talking to each other again. She gave him a hard time for a while there, but now they're slowly beginning to rebuild their relationship. It's what I was hoping for, but hearing it didn't seem like much of a consolation in the face of losing her. Strange I know—I broke up with her so she could fix her relationship with her brother, but I never could have anticipated the hole that's been left inside of me.

I'm going to meet Xander for lunch today, to try and take my mind off of everything. I haven't set foot inside Andromeda for months, but I'm scheduled to do a Master class on punishment tomorrow night, and I can't muster any enthusiasm for it. I figured if I go out and interact with a friend then it might get me out of the funk I've been in. At least a little. I've been avoiding everyone lately. Xander is so happy with Lily, Carter won't speak to me, and I just couldn't be bothered hanging out with anyone else and being completely fake. I'm tired of being fake with everyone, all the fucking time.

I can't tell people I'm a Master Dominant. I can't tell anyone at Andromeda that I've been in love with the same girl for over eight years and would have tried to give up the lifestyle to be with her. They wouldn't understand. I can't tell the bands I work with, how badly I wish I had everything that I strive to get them on a daily basis. I feel like I'm so busy being what everyone else wants me to be, I don't really know who I am anymore. I'm lost in my own web of deceit.

Xander arrives with a grin on his face and a slap on the back, dragging me from my self-pity.

"How the fuck are you? I haven't seen you since the dinner party horror."

"Hey, man. Things are… fine."

"Wow. Don't give up the day job to become an actor. You suck at it. How are you really?"

We're seated straight away. It always helps when you're eating with the restaurant owner. I swear he owns half of Manhattan! We order some food and drinks, and then the inquisition begins.

"What the hell happened, Logan? You told me you loved her. You finally tell Carter, and then you walk away. I don't get it. Why didn't you fight for her? What changed?"

So much for forgetting my troubles for a few hours.

"She did. She changed. After dinner, everything changed. She didn't look at me the same way, she was always sad. Carter kept rejecting her calls, and I just couldn't be the reason for that. I let her go *because* I love her. That will never change."

"Look, I know he can be an insufferable asshole at times, but he would have come around eventually. For her, he would have. You? He might have cut your balls off, but he would've gotten there in the end."

"No, he wouldn't. I get it. She's amazing and beautiful and it's impossible not to love her with a real intensity and a need to protect her. Whether you love her, or you're in love with her, it's the same. She inspires that in people. Look how you reacted when you first found out. You were ready to smear me across the wall of your building. Carter feels that tenfold, and I can't hold it against him. He wants the best for her, and I'm not it."

He scrubs his hand over his jaw before downing the Scotch in front of him. "Fucking hell. I was expecting a laid-back lunch, some laughs and some sports talk. This is some heavy shit you're laying on me right now."

"I know. I'm sorry. I'm just really fucking fed up with my life at the moment."

"Can I ask you a question? And I want an honest answer."

"Go for it."

"Why do you believe that you're not what's best for Vittoria. Carter's reaction aside. If she loves you and you love her, why wouldn't you be good for her?"

"It's complicated."

"So, un-fucking-complicate it for me. Whatever it is, it's obviously eating away at you, so tell me."

He's right. I feel like I'm going to drown if I don't just level with one person in my life. One person who can know who I am—all of me.

"I'm a Dominant."

"Yeah. So? I already suspected."

I'm floored by his reaction. "What?"

"Come on, Logan. The way you are with women, it's not a giant leap to connect the dots. You cover it well, but I've known you for a long fucking time. What I don't understand is, why this is a problem?"

"Go say that to Carter and see if he thinks it's a problem." Why is he so okay with this? I've never told anyone because I was concerned they'd judge me, that they wouldn't understand, and here I sit with one of my closest friends, and he's acting like I just told him the most normal thing in the world. It's a huge weight off my shoulders.

"You know I would do anything for him, but you can't live your life based on his opinion. If it's what Vittoria wants, what you both want, then it's none of his business. He doesn't exactly have a fantastic track record in the way he's treated women. He's made choices I don't agree with, but it's his life. You make choices that I wouldn't, but I don't need to live your life. I do what I want with Lily, and it's no one's business but ours. Our relationship, physical and emotional, is only between us. I don't give a flying fuck what anyone else thinks, and neither should you."

"That's just it though. I don't know if it's what she wanted. I never told her."

"What the fuck?"

"We only saw each other a few times before I ended things. I never slept with her. I never told her, because I didn't want to risk losing her. I lost her anyway in the end, so I guess I'll never know."

"I'm sorry man. I just assumed... when I saw you two together at dinner. She seems... I don't know what the right terminology is... submissive, to you. You seem like a good match for each other, and Vittoria craves structure. She needs it in her life."

"The way you speak about her, you mentioned it before... did something happen to her that I don't know about?"

"I can't answer that, Logan. It's not my place. Just know that she's been through a lot, she came out the other side, and that I think you could have been good for her."

"Maybe. I don't know. I guess I'll never know."

Xander's phone starts to ring. "Speak of the devil himself."

It's Carter. "Take it. I'll grab the waiter and get the check."

As he holds the phone to his ear, the color drains from his face.

"We're on our way now. What hospital?"

Shit.

He ends the call and immediately dials Lily, arranging to pick her up in a few minutes. "I'll explain when I get there. Just be ready. I'm coming for you now."

He shoves his phone in his pocket. Agitation and fear, clear on his face.

"What's wrong?"

"It's Addi. She's in the hospital. It's bad. I need to go."

"I'll come with you."

His face drops, his expression grave as he replies. "I don't think it's a good idea right now. He's a mess. Addi is... the baby... it's bad. Really bad. I think it would be too much for him. I'll keep you posted."

He stands from the table and reaches for his wallet.

"Don't even think about it. I got this. You go. Look after him, he's like a brother to me, you both are."

He gives me a hug. Not something we do often, but I think we both need it.

"Tell him I'm here, and that I care. If he needs anything at all, just let me know."

"I will."

He leaves in a hurry and I'm left alone, terrified for my friend and the loss he's facing. If I was a praying man, I would be on my knees, begging for Addi to pull through this. It kills me that I can't go and be there for him, and for Addi, but I won't be selfish. I won't add to his problems.

She has to be okay.

He needs her to be okay.

Fuck. Vittoria. What will this do to her? They've become so close. Losing Addison would be devastating to her. It would destroy her to see Carter broken by such a loss.

All I want to do is go to her. To comfort her, to tell her it will be okay.

I want to reassure myself that *she's* safe and healthy.

What kind of man does that make me?

I CALLED AND LEFT A MESSAGE FOR VITTORIA, BUT SHE'S EITHER ignoring it, or she hasn't gotten it yet. I don't want to bother her, so I haven't tried to call back, but I need to know she's okay. I don't have the right to know, but I love her, and the thought of her dealing with this, is painful.

I left the restaurant and came to my office, but I haven't been able to concentrate. I haven't heard any news from Xander yet, but I'm hoping that's a good thing. I hate feeling helpless. I wish there was something I could do to help my friends, to help Vittoria.

When my phone beeps, I grab it like it's my lifeline. It's her.

Vittoria: *My plane just landed. Going to the hospital now. Xander will call with news. Please don't call me again.*

Me: *I'm so sorry. If there is anything you need. I'm here.*

Vittoria: *You don't get to be that guy for me. You made your choice. Don't call me, don't text me.*

I stare at my phone for the longest time. Devastated by her words. Horrified that I've made this situation even harder on her.

It's late by the time I hear from Xander. Addi is going to pull through. Carter is holding it together by a thread, and now, he's a daddy. Vittoria is an aunt. I'm so relieved for all of them. I can't even begin to imagine how terrifying today must have been.

I'm on the outside, looking in, and I don't know if they will ever forgive me—if they will ever let me be there for them—if *she* will ever let me be a part of her life again.

VIENNA

VITTORIA

Eight Months Later

I miss him.

Every minute of every day, since I walked out of his apartment, since he broke my heart into a thousand shattered pieces, I miss him. I miss the little things. His voice on the phone, low and sexy with a rasp that would melt even the coldest heart. His sweet text messages to say he was thinking of me, or to check that I'd arrived in the next city on tour safely. I miss the way he looked at me, as if I was the most beautiful creature he'd ever laid eyes on. And, most of all, I miss his touch. I never had much time to be with him, and we never made love. But in every way that mattered, he made love to me with every touch of his hand and every kiss. He devoured me, claiming me as his, ruining me for any other man. I lie awake at night, remembering his smile, and the dimples that could disintegrate any woman's panties. Everything about him haunts me, and it's impossible for me to move on. It's been almost nine months since he ended things between us, and I just can't let go: I can't stop loving him.

Logically, I can understand why he did what he did. He knows how much Carter means to me, and he didn't want to come between us. I hate him and love him in equal measure for his decision. He was trying to do what he thought was best for me, and it took me a long time to forgive him for that, and even longer to realize he did it from a place of caring for me, rather than a lack of it. There's also a part of me, that will never understand or forgive the fact that he gave me no option but to walk away. He didn't care if I wanted to choose him over family, if I thought he was worth the risk. If he'd taken even a moment to consider that, and ask me what I wanted, I would have told him, without hesitation—I chose him. Even now, I would choose him.

Carter and I have managed to find our way back to the close relationship we shared before all of this happened. It took me months to get over the fact that he's the reason Logan and I aren't together. For the first month, I wouldn't even speak to him, but slowly, we started talking again, and he apologized for causing me so much pain. I don't think he really understood what his reaction would do that night. It was a shock, and he handled it badly. When he finally admitted it to me, my heart thawed, and little by little I felt like I got my brother back.

These days, on the rare occasions when I'm in New York, I try to spend as much time as possible with him and Addi, and little V. She's the light in the darkness for me. An innocent blessing, who gives unconditional love and expects nothing in return. She gives me hope for the future, that maybe, someday it won't hurt as much. Maybe at some point the future, I won't love him as much, and hopefully I'll find someone to love me the same way I love him.

Love unrequited, is life's cruelest form of torture.

It's tough to hear Lily and Addi mention Logan. They don't mean to upset me, and I hide it as best I can, but hearing about what he's doing, where he is, and how him and Carter are back to being the best of friends, is difficult for me.

I spoke to Carter about it a few months ago, pleading with him not to throw away his relationship with Logan over something as trivial as a few stolen kisses. I played it down, telling him it was a fleeting attraction on my part, and how I would hate for it to ruin a great friendship. Eventually, he listened, but not before giving Logan a black eye, and coming home with a few bruised ribs. When Addi called me to tell me that they had sorted it out like cavemen, all I wanted to do was go to Logan's apartment. To kiss his eye and tell him how much I love him. Instead, I punched Carter in the face, which did nothing, it didn't even leave a mark, and it didn't make me feel any better.

I'm happy they're friends again, but it's almost as if what I had with Logan never happened. There is no evidence that we were ever together, that we ever meant anything to one another. The only way I know I didn't dream it, is the invisible scars I carry with me. There's a gaping hole in my heart telling me it was real, that it mattered, if only to me.

A month ago, I tried to get back on the horse, as they say, but I couldn't do it. I sat across from a very handsome gentleman, strong and sexy, commanding and considerate, but I felt... nothing. No butterflies, no excitement at the prospect of something new... nothing. I hate to admit it, but I think Logan might have been right. If he had made love to me like I begged him to, I would never recover. I'm lost and ruined by the memory of his tongue and his lips all over my body. To have felt him inside me, to be completely possessed by him, would have killed me.

I want to hate him so badly, to be consumed by rage until it obliterates all traces of the love I feel. And more than anything, I hate myself—for knowing that I would run into his arms tomorrow if he turned up at my door and told me he wanted me. How pathetic does that make me? The weak girl who forgives a man for breaking her heart, repeatedly, and welcomes him back with open arms, always surprised when he does it again.

I guess the question is moot. Logan's not coming back for me, and I need to come to terms with it... one day... I hope.

CHAPTER 7

LOGAN

THREE MONTHS LATER

I'M WORKING ON THE BIGGEST DEAL OF MY CAREER RIGHT NOW. THE band I'm bringing over from Scotland, Flaming Embers, are about to cut their first record and go on tour around the U.S. It's a huge find for my label, and if I pull this off, it is going to mean big things for my company, and for the bands I represent.

I've been in and out of the country over the past few months, never staying in one place too long, setting up the tour, meeting with promoters, finding support acts, and getting the boys in as a support act for some of the hottest names in music at the moment. In some ways, it has been a good distraction, but being on the road doesn't really afford me the freedom to indulge in my... particular pleasures. I know a few BDSM clubs in the bigger cities I visit on a regular basis and have taken to giving demonstrations on some very lovely subs in training. It lacks the satisfaction I used to gain from my lifestyle, but it's all I can bear. I haven't taken on a new submissive to train in the twelve months since Vittoria walked out of my life. The thought of being a Master to anyone but her just doesn't sit well with me. I tolerated it in the past, knowing that none of them could live up to the fantasy I had of her, but now that I know what I'm missing, it's incomprehensible to me to claim any other woman as my own.

I deal with my physical needs and my urge to dominate by conducting Master classes, and teaching others to be Dominants, using faceless submissives in cities that aren't my own. It's a fleeting pleasure, a moment of relief from the blackness that burdens my soul. A quick release to quench my carnal desire, leaving me empty and alone, craving a real connection to another human being, to feel that I'm not alone in this world.

If I had the chance to go back and change that night in Verona, to stop everything that ever happened with Vittoria de Rossi... I couldn't. I know it would be easier if it never happened, if I had never felt the sheer euphoria of her falling apart beneath me, but I would *never* trade that night for anything, *ever*. I wouldn't trade a single second of our time together. The torture, night after night, when I lie awake, reliving every second with her, is worth it. It's the only way I know that I still have the ability to feel—to love—that I still have a soul.

My world is black and gray, and she is the glorious splash of crimson making the rest of my dull existence worthwhile.

As I load my bags into the cab idling at the curb outside my building, I'm happy to be getting out of New York for a few days. I'm heading to Edinburgh to bring the band to the States. Their Visa applications have been approved, and I have an apartment set up for them here in Manhattan, in one of Xander's many buildings. I could only afford to get them the smallest place, but it's in a great location, and like everything that Xander does in business, it's sleek, elegant and cutting-edge. They're going to love it.

I can feel myself relax as we pull into traffic, heading over the bridge, and out of Manhattan. My home has become oppressive of late, and I'm eager to get some distance. I'm also mildly excited to visit a great BDSM club in the Scottish capital city. Steeped in history with a dark underbelly, Edinburgh is an exciting place to be long after the tourists have gone to bed. I've made plans to meet an associate of mine and give a demonstration to a small group of Dominants who are training as Masters. I'm told there are several new submissives who are desperate to be my subject, and anything else that I might want them for afterwards. Sounds like exactly what I need right now. It's the first time in a long time that I feel anything other than indifference.

When the driver pulls up outside La Guardia, I'm excited, and as I grab my case and head inside to check in, I'm feeling optimistic for the first time in months. The queue is non-existent and the stewardess takes her time checking me in, flirting outrageously with me. I indulge her, flashing her my killer smile, darting my tongue out to wet my lip, and watch as her gaze travels to my mouth. Her pupils dilate, her nipples becoming tight under her blouse, on display through the thin white silk. I had almost forgotten how much I love the effect I have on women, and I can't help but enjoy it just a little.

"Keep looking at me like that, and I'll take you over my knee, darling." Her breath hitches, her cheeks flush, and a seductive grin spreads across her pretty red lips as I turn to leave. As I walk away, she's almost panting in response.

"Anytime, Mr. Fitzgerald. My number's on your boarding pass." I'm never going to call this girl, but the shit-eating grin on my face right now makes me feel alive again with the possibilities. Maybe, just maybe, I will be able to forget for a minute, an hour, maybe even a day. I look over my shoulder and give her a wink, visibly turning her into a quivering mess before my eyes. I'm a dick for reveling in it, but today, I'm going to let myself enjoy it.

My mind wanders to the pretty blonde stewardess as I stand, scanning the departures board to find my gate, when a familiar voice sends a shudder through my body, rocking me to my core.

"Logan. What are you doing here?" I slowly turn my head, knowing that the calm, carefree feeling of just moments ago is going to be obliterated the moment I set eyes on her.

I'm not wrong.

My reaction to her is visceral. I can't believe how badly she affects me.

"Mother." I give her a tight grin. It's all I can manage. "Whose dime are you traveling on this week?"

I can feel her disdain for me, dripping from every pore.

"I see you're still your usual judgmental self, Logan. But since you asked, I'm going to Paris with Guillaume for a few weeks. He has some business to attend to and thought I would enjoy it."

"What happened to Roger?"

She simply sneers at me. "Roger was six months ago, darling. He wasn't the man for me, but I think Guillaume could be." I won't hold my breath. The last ten boyfriends have been 'the one.'

"I'll keep an eye out for the wedding invite in the mail."

"You're always so negative about my relationships. No wonder they never last." Seriously?

"Yes, Mother. I'm the problem. I don't have time for you to rehash how I've sabotaged all of your relationships over the years. I have a plane to catch. Have a safe flight and enjoy Paris." I give her a strained kiss on her overly plumped, botoxed cheek before turning on my heels and striding away from her poisonous mouth.

"Goodbye, Logan. Remember to control that temper of yours!"

She knows exactly how to bait me, but not today. I'm not letting her drag me down. I was feeling good for the first time in months. I know, even as I try to talk myself out of it, that she's already succeeded. I'm angry, edgy, and pissed off by the time I reach the departure lounge.

I work my way through the crowd and board the plane ahead of time. One of the perks of first-class. It's not long before the other passengers start filtering through, jostling with their bags and making their way to their seats. I'm about to close my eyes and block out everyone around me when I'm frozen to the spot.

It can't be.

I can't speak. I want to, but the words won't come.

I reach out and grab her wrist, holding her in place. Her gaze flying down to meet mine.

My heart is pounding so hard, and so fast, I feel like it is going to burst at any second. I'm mesmerized by the exquisite beauty before me, roaming every inch of her like a man starved for the past twelve months. Her scent invades my senses, soft and demure, subtle and fresh... and... Vittoria. She's dressed in faded blue jeans, a baggy green sweater and a pair of old Adidas high-tops. Her hair is tied in a messy bun, small strands escaping, caressing her face and neck. She's wearing a pair of deep purple framed glasses, and she looks just as stunning as she did in a ball gown, standing in L'Arena, so long ago.

"Vittoria. Why... what... how are you here?" She gives me a satisfied grin. She knows she's affecting me, and she loves it. Her eyes travel down to confirm her suspicion, coming to rest on the sight of my dick straining against my pants. She licks her lips, causing me to harden even further.

"I'm heading to London on tour. What about you?"

I know I'm holding up the passengers waiting impatiently behind her, but I just don't give a damn about them!

It takes me a moment to stop staring at her lips and force my brain to remember that I'm not a babbling idiot, and that I am in fact a grown man, a businessman, and a Master.

"I'm flying through London to Edinburgh to finalize the contracts with Flaming Embers and bring them back to the States to start work on their first album for my label."

"Wow. That's great, Logan. The label seems to be doing well. I've followed the artists you've signed so far, and I'm impressed. I've heard great things about this new band from Lily, so I'll look forward to my advanced, signed copy of the album!"

She makes me laugh.

I can see the line behind her growing restless, grumbles and stares that are obviously making her uncomfortable, and ready to walk away, but I can't let that happen.

"Your wish is my command, Miss de Rossi." Her face sobers at my words. Any discomfort has been replaced with anger.

"I won't hold my breath for it then. You tend to leave me hanging when it comes to what I want from you. I learn from my mistakes. It was nice to see you, Logan. Safe travels and I hope it all goes well with the band."

She turns to leave and I feel like I've been kicked in the gut, winded and wounded. Instinctively, I tighten my grip on her arm, to stop her from walking away. I don't know what to say. Everything she said is true. I left her in L'Arena, naked and wanting, offering herself to me in the most vulnerable and beautiful of ways, then I sent her away in New York. She gave me a second chance, and I blew it. A decision I've regretted every minute of every day since.

We're both instantly aware of where our skin touches. Adrenaline courses through me, stemming from this one point of contact, my body vibrating with lust and desire.

The guy behind her starts mumbling under his breath. "I'll just stand here all fucking day, shall I, while you fucking first-class assholes catch up?" He picked the wrong day to annoy me. I'm up in an instant, pulling Vittoria behind me before I square my shoulders and stare him down.

"A simple 'excuse me,' would have sufficed." He's about to give me some verbal abuse when I move closer, invading his space, towering over his small, plump frame.

"I... I..."

"You... you... were just about to apologize to the lady for your unnecessary cursing." He's about to protest but thinks better of it when he looks up at my face, my anger evident in the furrow of my brow. He looks to Vittoria.

"I'm sorry, miss. Please, forgive my outburst." She is gracious as always.

"Thank you. It was my fault. I'm sorry I held you up. I haven't seen my angry friend here in a long time. Enjoy your flight, sir." Now I really want to punch someone. I don't like hearing her calling someone else 'Sir,' even if it's in a different context.

"Sit down." Without hesitation she responds, making my dick twitch at her willingness to obey me.

I give the asshole in front of me one last look of disdain before I move out of his way, letting him, and the rest of the passengers pass. We sit in silence for a moment, allowing the situation to sink in. We're going to be on this flight for the next seven hours together, and I know she's pissed at me. That was evident right before the *prick* started cursing and I missed my moment to apologize. To explain. I don't even know how to explain. Maybe he did me a favor, buying me more time to decide what to say to her.

When the first-class cabin settles down and everyone is seated, a stewardess appears, giving me a sickly sweet, completely fake smile before turning her attention to Vittoria, her smile transforming into a sneer.

"You can't be in here. Your seat is in coach. You need to move... now." What the hell is wrong with people today? Is it me? I have zero tolerance for this passive-aggressive bullshit right now. I reach into my jacket, pull out my bank card and hand it to her.

"Upgrade her."

"It doesn't work like that, sir."

"It does now. She won't be moving from my side, so you can either charge me for the upgrade, or let her sit here on her coach ticket. It's your choice."

I watch, irritated, as she takes in the sight of the breathtaking beauty beside me. The over primped, heavily made up, average looking stewardess looks confused, unable to comprehend that less is more. Vittoria would outshine her in every way, any day. She could be wearing a burlap sack and look better than any woman I have ever met.

"You can go now. Are you taking the card or not?" She snatches it from my hand and stalks down the aisle toward the front cabin. I know I have a satisfied smile on my face, when I feel a tiny but strong punch to my arm.

"What the hell, Logan? You can't just be a dick to people whenever you feel like it, and you don't get to decide where I sit. You gave up that opportunity long ago. I offered myself to you... naked. I've offered myself to you clothed. I offered my body, and I offered my heart, but you didn't want me, so you don't get to order me around. I'm going to go and sit with the other dancers in the seat I was assigned." I run my hands through my hair, frustrated, and lost for words.

She moves to stand.

"Sit. Down. Little one." I know her brain is screaming at her to walk away, to defy me, I can see it written all over her face. But her body can't deny me, and I take the opportunity to study her demeanor. Her breathing is shallow but labored, her hands are clasped and wedged between her knees. She drops her head, unable to look at me. I can tell she's at war with herself. She doesn't want to submit to me... and I hate it.

"Vittoria. Please look at me." I don't push her, even though it's killing me. I wait... for what feels like an eternity before she turns her head, a tear rolling down her face. It causes me physical pain to see her upset like this. I reach out to stroke my hand down her cheek, feeling the wet warmth of her tears as she lets herself relax into my touch for mere seconds before shirking away.

"Why did you make me leave, Logan?" The hurt in her voice is too much for me.

"This is exactly why I've stayed away from you for all these years. I never wanted to hurt you. To see the look in your eyes right now."

"That's not an answer." She turns in her seat, her body facing away from me.

"I can't give you the answers you really want."

"Give me something at least. I need... something. Do you have any idea how much you hurt me? I felt so ashamed of myself for the way I acted when we were together. That's not me. I don't throw myself at men. I don't open myself up to getting hurt emotionally. I've always avoided those things at all costs. You made me give you a second chance after Verona. You pursued me. You made me let my guard down, and then you tore my heart out. How could you do that?" I can't bear to hear how badly I hurt her. I reach out and take her hand in mine, brushing my thumb in circles over her delicate skin. It feels so good to touch her, even in the smallest way.

"You have *nothing* to be ashamed of. I can't believe you would ever think that, even for a second. I'm the one who should be ashamed of myself."

"How was I supposed to feel? Cherished? Used? Desired? Discarded? I felt worthless when you ended things between us. Like I didn't matter enough for you to fight for me, for us." A knife cuts deep into my soul at her words. I need to focus, before I fall apart and tell her everything.

"Don't *ever* say that again. Do you understand?" I can't contain the anger in my voice.

"Fuck you, Logan. You don't get to throw demands at me. You made me feel like shit. At least fucking man up and own it." She pushes my legs out of the way, quickly moving past me and out into the aisle as I sit, eviscerated by her declaration. She's right. I know I should let her go to her seat, far away from me, and get on with her life, but even as I think it, my body has other ideas. I'm out of my seat, striding toward her as she speeds up, her hand on the curtain between first and business-class when I catch hold of her. I spin her round, pushing her into the small space between the curtains. It's dark and private and her body is flush against mine, not out of choice, but by necessity.

I press her against the wall, her arms wedged between us. Her breathing harsh and warm against my skin. The darkness envelops us, our lips almost touching as I fight the urge to take her. She lets her guard down for just a moment before shoving me as hard as she can, lashing out, beating her fists against my chest.

"How *dare* you! You don't get to do this to me. You don't want me, then *fine*, but it's not fair of you to act this way. You want to tell me what to do, how to feel, where to sit? Then earn it! I'm so angry with you for getting me all twisted up over you. I was fine before you decided to *let* yourself have just a taste. You got what you wanted and I was left... broken. It wasn't enough for me. Just a taste. I wanted more. I needed more." Her words are a strangled plea, full of hurt and regret.

"Vittoria." I let her punch and smack me for a moment, getting out some of her anger and frustration before I grab her hands, stopping her from lashing out anymore. I can't take it. I hate that I make her this upset. I pin her hands by her sides, pressing her back against the wall and forcing her to feel the length of my body against hers. Her breasts pressed against the hard muscle of my chest, her heart racing in time with my own.

"Don't, Logan. It hurts." I loosen my grip. "I don't mean you holding me. I mean… this. You're a breath away from kissing me. I know you want to, but you won't. I want you more than anything, and it… hurts. You want me, but not enough. You don't need me. I never thought you were capable of hurting me, but I'm wrecked… because of you."

I drop my head, horrified that she believes I don't want her as much as she wants me. I *know* I will always want her more than she could ever comprehend.

"I…"

"Don't. Just let me go."

I take a deep breath.

"I can't. I know it's selfish, but I need you to stay with me just now. I need to explain. Will you let me do that?" My voice is barely a whisper, unrecognizable to me in the darkness.

"Yes." It's one small word, with such great depth behind it. A lifeline. I wrap my arms around her, holding her tight, just for a moment before leading her back to our seats. All eyes are on us, but I couldn't give a fuck what any of these first-class morons think of me. The only person whose opinion matters to me, is Vittoria's.

I can't take my eyes off her as she sits, elegant and dignified as she gives me yet another chance I don't deserve. I'm a dick. I can't even tell her the whole truth, and yet I still couldn't let her go.

"You need to understand. It's not that I didn't *want* to be with you. I wanted you so badly, every step away from you in Verona was a physical ache, and every step you took as you left my apartment in New York was sheer and utter hell. I've wanted you since the moment I met you. I thought that time and space between us would help, but it never has. My feelings for you have never diminished. It has been the polar opposite. Every moment I spent with you only intensified what I felt, and now that I haven't been a part of your life for the past year, those feelings have magnified tenfold. I'll never get over you."

Her eyes fly up to meet mine. "Then why, Logan? You know how I feel about you. I lo...."

I press my finger to her lips. "Don't. Please don't say it. I can't... we can't. You're too good for me. You always have been. I will never be worthy of you, and if I hear you say the words, I don't know if I could survive it. I'm trying not to be selfish with you, to be a better man, so that maybe *one* day I might be even halfway worthy of you."

She cups my face in her hands, my heart fighting to burst through my ribcage as she forces me to look at her. "But I want... I need... I." She searches my face for permission that I can't give.

I place my hands over hers. "Don't make me hate myself more than I already do." I pull her hands from their sweet caress of my tense jaw and watch her as she crumples into her seat, trying to calm herself, fighting the tears that are threatening to fall.

An unwelcome interruption comes in the form of the stewardess hovering by my side.

"Can I get you something to drink, Mr. Fitzgerald?"

"Yes. A Scotch neat." She turns to leave and it exasperates me even further. "Miss de Rossi would like a glass of Prosecco. Thank you for asking. Your customer service skills are somewhat lacking." She shoots me daggers before scurrying off to get our drinks. Why would she think it's okay not to offer Vittoria a drink? It's her fucking job. Just because she thought she was going to get the pleasure of sucking my cock on this flight, doesn't mean she gets to treat my impromptu traveling companion with disdain. I could see it in her eyes the moment I set foot inside the cabin. She devoured every inch of me with her greedy little eyes, licking her lips suggestively as her eyes came to rest on my crotch. Truth be told, after the run in with my mother I might have given her a second glance if Vittoria hadn't shown up, if for no other reason than to take my mind off of my pathetic life.

The reality of my situation is that Vittoria *is* here, and no other woman on earth even registers on my radar. There is only her. She is my Eve. The first and only woman in my world. I try so hard to forget her, but it's impossible. She has infiltrated every fiber of my being, and I'll be damned if I'm going to let anyone treat her badly. It's hard enough to watch her hurting because of my actions.

She lets out a small sob, and without a thought for the consequences I lift her up out of her seat, and into my lap, where she breaks down, quietly letting out all of the hurt and confusion that *I* caused. She feels so small and fragile, curled up like a frightened kitten, and all I want to do... is love her.

"Please, don't cry. My heart can't take it. I'm doing this for you. Trust me. You're too good for me, and I only want what's best for you."

"You're what's best for me. I feel it in every touch of your hand, in the way you speak and the way you look at me. I feel it in the way my body responds to you. You are exactly what I need. Everything about you calls to me. Why can't you see that?" Her voice is no more than a whisper.

I pull her closer, hold her tighter, trying like hell to calm the tirade of emotions raging inside of me.

When our drinks arrive, I down my Scotch and request another, but before I finish my sentence, Vittoria hands her empty glass to the stewardess and moves back down to rest her head on my chest. Under normal circumstances I would chastise her for drinking so quickly, but I have no right to ask anything of her. I just thank my lucky stars that she remains in my lap, letting me soothe her. I slowly trace the lines of her back, listening to her breathing as it evens out and she drifts off. I think it's probably a mixture of emotional exhaustion and alcohol rather than her being physically tired. Whatever the reason, I revel in it.

I sit for hours, a continuous stream of Scotch being brought to me as I sit clinging to Vittoria. Listening to her shallow breaths, I love the warmth of her body against my own. I've been rock-hard in my pants for the past three hours while she's slept soundly, but I don't care. The physical discomfort is nothing in comparison to the elation her presence sparks in me. For the first time in a year, I *feel*.

I can't resist her, and gently slip my hand underneath her sweater, my palm pressed against the naked flesh of her back, causing a shiver to run down my spine as I feel hers flex beneath my fingers. She lifts her sleepy eyes to mine, her lips full and sleep swollen. She is breathtaking. I can only imagine what she'd look like first thing in the morning with sex-mussed hair, naked and tangled in the sheets. My dick twitches beneath her and I know she feels it. Her gaze darts between my eyes and my lips as she licks her own, making them even more enticing. Just one kiss, one lick, one nibble of her perfect pout. I want it so badly, I would sell my soul for one more taste, but I've already caused her so much pain through my own selfish desires. She is a shell of the woman who offered herself to me in Verona, who fought for me in her brother's living room. A shadow of the woman who walked out of my apartment a year ago.

Her scent surrounds me, her breath warm and sweet on my face as she moves closer, our lips just millimeters apart when I speak. "I want to kiss you so badly, Vittoria. Every inch of my body is screaming at me to do it."

Her words are a sweet caress. "Then do it."

I cup her face in my hands. "I can't." I rest my forehead against hers in defeat. "I just can't. Ending things with you was the hardest thing I've ever done. I was doing the right thing for you, but the worst thing imaginable for me. I couldn't do it again."

"Then don't. Be with me." My body sags under the intense pressure I feel in this moment to do the right thing by her. I know she feels it, because she pulls away from me, extricating herself from my lap and moving back into her seat.

"Maybe I should go and find my seat back in coach."

I grasp her hand firmly in mine. "Don't. I want you here. I don't know when I'll see you again. Stay. Tell me about your life, work, anything. I just want to hear your voice."

She gives me a small, but genuine smile. "Okay."

We spend the rest of the flight talking about our lives and it feels so normal. The tension between us is still thick in the air, but I'd tolerate any level of discomfort just to be around her, to hear her sultry voice caress my senses. I'm transfixed, enthralled, obsessed with every detail she offers.

I in turn tell her about the band that I'm working with, what it means for my company, what I aspire to in the future. It's uncharacteristic for me to open up, but with her it just feels natural, and I find myself telling her about my run in with my mom in the airport.

"God, Logan. No wonder you were on edge when I first saw you. I don't know the ins and outs of it, but Carter told me your relationship with her is tumultuous at best. I figured it made sense, considering that you've spent almost every family holiday at our house since I met you." She gives me a sympathetic smile, which I would curse from anyone else, but from her it's a comfort I've never felt before.

"Your powers of deduction are spot on, Sherlock. I won't bore you with the details, but a summation of my relationship with my mother would be that she blames me for loving her too much. All I ever tried to do was protect her, from herself, from her decisions. She blames me for her life not turning out the way she wanted, and she never lets me forget it. These days, we tolerate each other when we have to, which isn't very often."

"I'm so sorry. That must be hard. I know you would only ever have been looking out for her. It's who you are. What about your dad?"

"The less said about that deadbeat, the better."

"When was the last time you saw him?"

"We're done talking about him. I mean it. I'm not going to waste any more time and energy on him in this lifetime." She slinks into my side, resting her head on my shoulder, giving me solace in the silence between us. We stay like this for the remainder of the flight, Vittoria drifting in and out of sleep as our time together fades away. Our approach to Heathrow Airport is getting closer with every minute.

As we touch down in London and disembark, I feel my chest tighten. My time with her has been so fleeting. I don't want to leave her.

We work our way through security and toward the departure

gates, relishing each moment we have together. Our imminent departure to connecting flights is hanging heavy in the air between us. I guide her toward the international departure gates, my hand on the base of her back, my skin burning from the contact. I can't even wait with her. I need to go to the domestic flights departure lounge. I should have been there ten minutes ago, but I just can't tear myself away from her.

When I can't go any further I stop dead, unable to let go of her hand. We haven't spoken since we stepped off the plane, but it doesn't seem necessary. The draw I feel in her proximity is crackling between us, a physical force we can't ignore. Electricity courses through every cell in my body as she turns to face me.

"I guess this is where we say goodbye then. Prague awaits." I have no words. I just stand and stare at her, entranced by her effortless beauty. "When will you be back in New York?" She says, snaps me out of my reverie.

"A week. I'm only in Edinburgh for a week. You? How long is this tour?" I don't know why I'm desperate to hear her answer. I know I need to stay away from her, but I also need to know that she's close by. To know where she is in the world.

"Three weeks. I'll be back in New York for a week before I set off again. Doing a stint around the States, so at least I won't be halfway across the planet. Maybe we could meet up when I'm back in town?" She looks at me expectantly.

"I don't know if that's a good idea."

She steps closer, her breasts brushing against me as she drops my hand and snakes her arms around my neck. This is the Vittoria from Verona, the girl I fell even more deeply in love with. Her quiet confidence has returned. She stands on her tiptoes, her lips almost touching mine, tormenting me as her breath caresses me. "Tell me it's not a good idea. Tell me you don't feel this, that you don't feel how explosive it is between us when we're together. Tell me you don't want me and that you don't feel anything more than friendship for me and I'll never bring it up again. But don't lie to me, Logan. I can feel your heartbeat against my breasts. It's racing, just like mine. I can feel your dick straining against your pants, hard against my thigh… go on… tell me you don't want me."

"Jesus Christ. Why do you push me?" I bite down hard on my lip, tasting blood, trying to no avail to hold in the words I know are about to trip out of my mouth. "You already know."

"Know what? Tell me." I grab her face in my hands, searching it for a way out, for a reason *not* to say it, but I have to. I can't keep it in any longer. I've waited nine years to say it.

"I'm in love with you, Vittoria. Never doubt it." I crash my lips down on hers, exploring, pillaging, taking, giving, wanting. She tastes even better than I remember. She gives me everything, melting into my arms, her hands fisting in my hair, pulling me closer. Her tongue strokes mine, teasing me, torturing me. It's a sweet kind of agony.

It takes every ounce of strength I have to break this kiss, this connection between us.

"I need to go. You need to go. This has to end here, Vittoria. It's what's best for you, and I will *always* do what is best for you." I steal one last kiss. "I love you. You are my Nyx. No one will ever compare to you."

It breaks my heart as I turn and walk away from her, forcing myself not to look back, and that's when I hear it. It's barely a whisper through the crowded airport, but it hits me like a freight train.

"I love you, too… Master Fitzgerald."

I whip my head around to see her striding through the gate, her back to me. "Vittoria…" She doesn't falter. She simply turns her head and locks her gaze with mine, placing her hands behind her back, clasped at the wrist in a submissive position. She nods her head in acknowledgement, before dropping her gaze to the floor and walking out of my line of sight.

"Fuck!" She knows about me. What have I done?

My mind is reeling as I'm left standing, staring at the spot where she stood. My world has just shifted on its axis… completely fucking stopped.

Why do I feel like my life is becoming a series of moments where I find myself walking away from Vittoria de Rossi?

PRAGUE

VITTORIA

I HATE THAT I SHOW WEAKNESS AROUND HIM. I'VE *NEVER* SHOWN THIS side of myself to anyone before. I shut that part off so many years ago, I didn't even know I was capable of it. He brings something to the surface, a vulnerability that I have long suppressed. I can't explain it or rationalize it. I simply have to survive it.

Logan has made it clear in his words that we can never be together... but his body tells an altogether different story. I'm not usually the predator when it comes to men, I'm the exact opposite. I'm a submissive for God's sake. I know everything there is to know about Logan Fitzgerald. Music mogul, best friend to my big brother, man of honor, and a Master Dominant. He is everything I crave in a partner, and yet I find myself going against everything I stand for when it comes to him.

I have thrown myself at him, forced him into a position where he can't ignore me, which I know is not something he finds attractive, but I can't help myself. I want him. He makes me feel and act in ways that I've never even contemplated before, that I don't understand. When I'm around him I don't *think*, I only *feel*.

When he told me he loved me at the airport, I snapped. I hadn't planned on letting him know that I'm aware of his... extracurricular activities. I had a plan for talking to him about it, for telling him about my own predisposition, and now I've really thrown the cat amongst the pigeons. There was a reason he never told me when we were together, and I respected his decision. I wanted to carefully broach the subject with him when the time was right, but I never got the chance. The look on his face when I called him Master, was so pained, so wounded. I wish I could take it back.

Now, I'm in Prague, he's in Edinburgh, and it's been three days since I left him in London.

I've replayed all of our interactions over and over in my mind, looking for a hint... anything that could help me figure out my next move. I can't sleep and I can't concentrate. The only time I can ever really block him out is when I'm on stage. It's the only time I can truly let go of everything in my life and in my head. I can escape. I can be free of the shackles that bind me. I can... fly... soar... be anything I want to be. Even rehearsals have been a bust these past few days. My dance partner Luca has been on my back about my lack of focus.

I sprained my ankle today and with a performance tonight, it's something I could have done without. They wanted to put my under-study on, but I got the doctor who travels with us to give me an injection and strap it well enough for me to power through. Being a ballet dancer is all about dancing through the pain, and this is no different. I'm just annoyed at myself for letting Logan get to me so badly. It's affecting the one thing that has grounded me all these years.

When everything happened with Marcus, I never thought I would feel again. I shut down completely. Carter was the only person I could let in. I don't know if it's because he found me that day, or because he was already the person I trusted most in the world. Whatever the reason, he was my lifeline. He sat with me night after night, holding me, protecting me, telling me it was going to get better, and little by little, it did.

I began to channel all of the feelings I couldn't deal with, focusing them on a single task—to become a prima ballerina. I started dancing when I was four years old. It was always inside of me—that desire to dance. But when I truly focused all my energy, it transformed into something different. Something that went far beyond a love of dance, or a yearning to succeed. It became the air in my lungs and the blood pumping through my veins, the very reason for my existence.

IT'S A TRADITION, OR MAYBE A SUPERSTITION OF MINE BEFORE A performance, to have a long hot bath in my hotel room. I let the steam rise around me, the bubbles surround me, and I let myself drift off into a calm space, where I can mentally run through all the choreography for the evening ahead.

Tonight, as I lie naked in the burning hot water, my ankle is soothed, but my mind is still unsettled, filled with thoughts of my last encounter with Logan.

He said he loves me.

That *has* to mean something. Surely. But, why did he say it when he doesn't want to be with me?

I'm going to drive myself crazy if I keep playing these questions on a loop in my head, and so I do the only thing that seems to be a solution to my problem in this moment. I pick up my phone from the side of the bath, shut off the music I have playing, and pull up Logan's contact details. My finger hovers over the call button for what feels like an eternity before I chicken out and open the message app. I think better of it at least five times before I finally type a short message.

Me: *Why did you say you love me?*

The moment I hit send, I regret it, but I don't have long to ponder my mistake. I'm startled by the sound of my phone beeping with an incoming message within seconds.

Logan: *Because I do.*

My heart soars and crashes inside of my chest as I quickly type my reply.

Me: *Then why don't you want to be with me?*

Logan: *I do want to be with you...*

Me: *Why do you keep pushing me away?*

Logan: *It's better this way.*

Me: *For who? You?*

Logan: *For you. Always for you.*

I don't know how to respond , and I don't have to when my phone beeps again.

Logan: *How do you know about me?*

Me: *We have mutual friends.*

Logan: *My friends would never divulge my private business to anyone outside the lifestyle.*

Me: *Exactly.*

It takes him a few minutes to respond as I wait impatiently, tapping my fingers on the side of the bathtub.

Logan: *What are you saying?*

Me: *You know what I'm saying. You just don't want to admit it.*

Logan: *It can't be true. I would know.*

Me: *I've gone to great lengths to keep this a secret.*

Logan: *Then why are you telling me? Why now?*

Me: *Because you said you love me. That you want me.*

It's an agonizing wait for his reply. What can only be minutes, feels like hours.

Logan: *Don't you have a show tonight?*

I can't believe that's his response.

Me: *Yes.*

I'm hurt that yet again I'm putting myself out there, and he's pulling away from me.

Me: *Forget I said anything. You're right. I have a performance to focus on.*

How many times am I going to throw myself at Logan Fitzgerald and have him turn me down, all the while telling me that he wants me? It's confusing, and I can't keep feeling like this. My life is regimented and simple. I know where I stand in all things. I need to let this go and move past it. I switch my phone onto silent, place it back on the side of the bath and slowly immerse myself under the water for as long as my lungs will allow. When I emerge, I try my best to leave behind the sadness, and the negativity I feel. I don't even glance at my phone as I grab a towel and head for the bedroom.

~

TWO HOURS, AND A LOT OF MAKEUP AND HAIRSPRAY LATER, I FIND myself dressed and ready to do my final warm-ups before the curtain call. Luca is hounding me about my mood, and I know he means well, but I just want him to let me get through tonight and go to bed. My ankle is still hurting and my heart is heavy as the music begins.

There is an electricity backstage in the minutes before a performance begins. A mixture of nerves and excitement, fear and anticipation. It's what fuels each and every dancer to give their all, to dance every night and every show as if it is the most important of their lives. Tonight, I can't feel it. For the first time in my career, I feel flat, and Luca can see it. He can sense it.

"Vittoria... bella. What's wrong? I've never seen you like this at show time. Talk to me." I rub my hand reassuringly over his bicep.

"I'm fine. Sorry. Just a little tired tonight, and my ankle is a little sore, but nothing I can't handle. I'll be fine when the curtain goes up. You know me..." I don't have the words to end that sentence, so I leave it hanging in the air. No one really knows me. I let them see what I want them to see.

For Luca, he sees a calm, confident dancer, who thrives under pressure. The reality is that I don't feel pressure when it comes to dancing. It doesn't matter if I dance for a room of thousands, or no one at all. I dance for me. I would rather not have the attention that comes from being on stage, but it comes with the territory, so I deal with it.

My parents see a daughter who was broken but has faced adversity head on and pieced herself back together. They think I've moved on with my life. They see what they can bear to see. If they really looked, really *saw* me, they would see just how broken I still am. They ignore the signs and cling to the positives. I don't blame them. Sometimes I almost convince myself that I'm okay.

Carter will always see me as his kid sister, who needs protecting. What I love about him, is that he's always been this way. He didn't change the way he treated me because of what happened, it's just who he is, but I've always felt so guilty when it comes to my big brother. He may not have changed the way he is with me, but the way he's treated women over the years has everything to do with what happened. He kept his distance, not getting emotionally involved, he guarded his heart against the bad, but it also stopped him from letting someone really love him. That was, until he met Addi. She has transformed him and she's had an impact on *my* relationship with him. I don't need to carry around the burden I once felt, the guilt of him missing out because of me. The moment I saw them together, I could see it. The look in his eyes, the way his demeanor changed only for her. They've had a really rough time in their relationship, but I know they'll get through whatever life throws at them. They are perfectly imperfect for each other. So alike and yet so complementary. They just... work. And they give me hope that I can find love someday.

When it comes to Logan, I have no idea how he sees me, or what he thinks of me. He says he loves me, but he can't see the part of me that's screaming out to him, calling to the Dominant inside of him, and begging for him to claim me as his own. He thinks I'm his best friend's perfect little sister, innocent and unmarred by the evils of the world. If he only knew...

I don't want him to know. I hope he never finds out. But, I want him to see me for who and what I really am—a submissive who so desperately wants to be his. He challenges me in ways I both love and hate in equal measure, and I think I challenge him, too. I've forced his hand more than once now, and I can see that it unsettles him.

I'm brought back to the present by Luca's voice in the distance, and yet, he's standing right beside me. "Showtime. Get your head straight."

The music begins, heralding my entrance, and Luca sweeps me into the air and out onto the stage.

My concentration dances between the ballet I'm performing, and Logan, swinging back and forth like a pendulum. The fanciful stage that I'm gliding across, and the departure gate at Heathrow Airport. My heart just isn't in it tonight, and as I perform a basic pirouette, my footing falters and I land awkwardly on my already sprained ankle.

The crowd gasps, and Luca rushes to my side before the other dancers on stage improvise for a moment until my understudy takes to the stage. He lifts me into the wings, setting me down gently, and returns to finish the show.

I can't put any weight on my ankle, and I know my own body so well, I can tell that I've torn the ligaments before the company doctor even looks at me. I lie heartbroken when he confirms my worst fear. I'm looking at up to three months of recovery time, six weeks without any form of training whatsoever. I've *never* gone so long without dancing. I don't know how I'll survive it.

LUCA STAYED WITH ME WHILE THEY WRAPPED MY ANKLE AND SET ME UP with a set of rather cumbersome crutches. Then, he helped me back to the hotel where we booked my flight back to New York. I shouldn't have travelled on my own, but I couldn't face staying in Prague and watching everyone perform while I sat on the sidelines.

Now I'm back in New York, in my apartment, and I haven't told a single soul that I'm here. I've spent the last twenty-four hours sleeping thanks to some very heavy painkillers. When I finally come around long enough to be aware of my surroundings, I grab my phone off the nightstand to check the time. I forgot that I'd switched it off after texting Logan… it must be three days ago now.

I slump back down onto my pillow and power it up, watching as it immediately starts beeping and chiming. Emails, texts, missed calls and voicemails. Half of them from Luca wondering if I got home safely, a handful from my mom asking how the tour is going and if I'm eating enough! And then there's the name that catches my eye. I have a message from Logan and a single missed call from his number.

I throw the phone down on the bed, unable to face whatever he has to say to me. I didn't exactly leave things on a friendly note with the last text I sent. I'm so frustrated by how crazy I am over him. We've shared one very hot, very intense night which ended too quickly, a handful of kisses, and a few intense moments when I thought we were really connecting. I'm not this girl. The one who goes gaga over a guy from the get-go, but I know it's different with Logan. We've known each other for nine years, and I've been aware of my feelings for him since the beginning, but I still hate what he turns me into. A silly schoolgirl who can't concentrate on her own life, obsessing over what a boy thinks of her. It's everything I hate. Everything I've never let myself be. I never give second chances, but with him, I seem to give them unconditionally.

Maybe he's right, maybe I should stay away from him. But I can't. Something inside of me keeps telling me, over and over again, that if I just break through his exterior, and he understands what I want in a relationship, then we could be *amazing* together.

I decide to call Luca and my mom before I brave looking at the text from Logan. I spend thirty minutes listening to my mom going on about Prague and all the things I need to see while I'm there, and I can't bring myself to tell her I'm back in New York. She would fuss and worry and smother me for the next six weeks. Luca gives me an earful for not calling sooner, and then he talks about everything *except* the show. He knows that I live and breathe dance, and how much it will kill me to be away from it for so long, but *not* talking about it feels so fake, I can't stand it.

When I hang up the phone, my stomach starts to churn as I open the message from Logan. I look at the time it was sent, realizing it was three hours after I had sent my last text to him. It said only two words.

Logan: *I'm Sorry*

Tears well in my eyes at the simplicity of his message.

I quickly dial my voicemail and brace myself to hear his low rasping voice in my ear, and a chill runs through me at the sound of my name on his lips.

Vittoria. Fuck. I don't even know why I'm calling. We've said everything that needs to be said. I'm so sorry for hurting you. If I could take it back... I'd love to tell you that I would... but it wouldn't be the truth. It's selfish and wrong, but I wouldn't give up a single second I've had with you. The feel of you coming apart beneath me has ruined me for anyone else. I know this isn't what you want to hear, and it wasn't really my intention to say any of that. Fuck! This is what you're doing to me, Tori. You have me twisted and conflicted, and I want you so badly my body burns every minute of every day. I need to put the phone down before I beg you to tell me where you are so I can come and get you. It was never meant to turn out this way. You're my Nyx. You always have been. You are beautiful inside and out. You excite me and terrify me in the same breath. Take care of yourself. I promise that if we see each other again, I will keep my hands to myself, and I won't make this any harder on either of us. I'm so sorry.

I'm calling his number before I even know what it is I want to say.

"Vittoria?"

"Hi, Logan. I just got your message." The silence on the other end of the phone is deafening, but I can hear his breathing, labored and erratic. "I know it was a goodbye speech, but when you said that you were close to begging to come and get me… Logan… I need you right now."

"I… I can't."

"I'm not asking for love, or forever, or even sex. I'm…" I don't know why I'm telling him this. "I'm back in New York."

"What happened? I thought you were in Prague for three weeks."

I can feel my voice thick with tears as I say it out loud. "I got injured. I can't dance for at least six weeks." I breakdown into a flood of tears as I let myself feel the weight of it all bearing down on me.

"Oh shit. Tell me exactly what's going on."

I take a deep breath before I continue. "I've torn the ligaments in my right ankle. I'm pretty swollen, strapped up, and on crutches for the next few weeks. I won't be able to even *begin* training again for six weeks or I risk permanent damage. I can barely walk right now, and the thought of not dancing for so long… destroys me."

"I'm so sorry. What can I do to help? Who's with you?" I hesitate, knowing he'll be annoyed. "Vittoria. Who. Is. With. You?"

My voice is a whisper. "No one knows I'm here, or that I'm hurt. I can't face them. They would be all over me, wanting to talk it to death. I just can't deal with it. I'm holding it together by a thread as it is."

"Not even Carter?"

"Especially not him. He would have me moved into his apartment immediately and I would be on bed rest with him fussing over me. He might even be worse than my mom."

That makes him laugh. "Well, I don't feel good about hiding this from him. It took me a long time to earn back his trust." Pangs of guilt strangle my insides, but I just can't face him right now.

"Please, don't tell him. He's done enough worrying about me to last a lifetime. He has enough going on with Addi and Verona, and work. I am *not* adding to that. Please."

"Fine. But I'm coming over to look after you. My flight gets in late tonight, so let your doorman know I'm coming."

My heart skips a beat. "You don't have to do that. You said you didn't want to be around me."

"I know what I said, Vittoria. Don't argue with me. I'll be there around eleven. You shouldn't wait up for me, you need your rest, but I'll be there when you wake up."

I pause for a moment. Letting his commanding voice wash over me. "Okay. Thank you."

"Now go and rest. I'll see you soon. Bye." He hangs up the phone before I have a chance to say goodbye. My head is spinning as I lie back down on the bed. Logan is coming here, tonight. He wants to look after me. I feel terrible for imposing on him, but more so, I'm elated that I'm going to see him again.

I spend the day drifting in and out of a drug induced slumber, dreams and visions of Logan dancing in my head. I don't even get out of bed to eat. I simply take the painkillers the doctor gave me with a sip of water and let myself be pulled back into the darkness. I feel comfortable there. *He's* there. My dark defender.

CHAPTER 8

LOGAN

I FEEL LIKE MY FLIGHT TOOK TWICE AS LONG AS IT SHOULD HAVE. Normally I can sleep from takeoff to landing without a problem, but today was different. Not only do I have the boys from Flaming Embers flying back with me, high on the anticipation of their future success in the USA., but my mind is racing with the knowledge that I'll be seeing Vittoria tonight. My focus should be solely on the band. I've worked so hard to get this deal together, and it will be huge for them, and for the label. I need to give them my full attention, and yet, I'm already preoccupied.

I couldn't let her stay in that apartment alone, not telling anyone she's injured, or even that she's in the country. Dancing is everything to her, and if she made her ankle worse by struggling through without help, I could never forgive myself for knowing and not doing anything. I should have called Carter, but the pleading tone in her voice stopped me, and she was right when she said that his plate is full with all things Addi. Those two are the perfect storm. So good together, and yet toxic in their own self-sabotage.

Once I get the guys settled in their new apartment, I stop at my own to drop off my luggage and grab a quick shower, before packing an overnight bag and heading to Vittoria's apartment.

When I arrive in the lobby, the doorman is waiting with a key and a smile, telling me to let him know if Miss de Rossi needs anything else. I thank him and make my way to the elevators. I've never actually been inside Vittoria's apartment in all the years I've known her, and I'm curious to see her little piece of Manhattan, but when the elevator stops on the twenty-fifth floor, I'm reluctant to step out. I know that I must exercise complete control while I'm here. I can't give in to the way I feel when I'm around her. She needs me to be strong enough for both of us.

I quietly turn the key in the lock, trying not to alert her to my arrival. It's well after midnight now. The apartment is silent and dark except for a small lamp in the corner of the living room, which she must have left on for me. Her small gesture isn't lost on me, and I take a moment to take in my surroundings.

The air is infused with the light aroma of her perfume, tantalizing my senses, intoxicating me.

I'm torn from my reverie when I hear muffled noises coming from down the hall, and my body reacts in an instant. I'm drawn to her. My heartbeat races and my pace quickens. A tiny sliver of light creeps out from under the door, lighting my way as her noises become louder and more urgent. She sounds pained. I don't want to scare her, so I slowly open the door and slip into the room.

She is a vision of beauty in the center of the bed, but she's restless and unsettled.

I'm reluctant to wake her in case it makes the nightmare she is obviously having, any worse. Instead, I make my way over and slowly sit on the edge of the bed beside her. I can't make out what she's saying, it's too jumbled and frantic, so I gently reach out and stroke her hair, hoping it will calm her down. She reacts to my touch almost immediately. Within minutes and without waking, her body relaxes, her rambling stops and her breathing evens out. It's only then that I realize I was holding my breath. I take a moment to relax, rolling my shoulders to relieve the tension, before kicking off my shoes and lying down beside her. For someone so small, she manages to take up a lot of space in a king size bed! I find myself balancing on the edge, certain that I'm going to fall on my ass at some point during the night, but I don't want to leave her here alone. I can't.

I lie on my side, staring at her for the longest time, wondering what terrorizes her in her sleep. I think about how much pain she must be in both physically and emotionally right now with her injury. The crutches by the side of the bed are a devastating sight. My mind is racing with thoughts of our time together, and the last time I saw her. I still don't know how she found out about me, or exactly what she knows. Her texts hinted that she runs in the same circles as me, but if that was the case... I just can't believe she's a Dominatrix or even a submissive, and I've never seen her in the clubs. I would have figured it out.

Then it hits me—what if she's a Dominatrix? Surely not. She is so submissive with me, but she is strong and assertive. She was the one who pushed in Verona. Maybe she was giving me what she thought I wanted. If she is, then we are even more incompatible than I thought. I need to believe that isn't the case. I told her we can never be together, but the moment she said those words, when she called me Master, I let a small part of myself hope.

I have talked myself out of being with her for so many reasons, so many times. She's Carter's sister, and it's taken me a long time to regain his trust after last year. He's never going to accept me as the guy for her. I still believe she's too sweet and innocent to be open to what I have to offer. I know that what I do isn't wrong, but I know I'm not good enough for her. I can't be everything that she needs. But ever since the airport, I keep coming back to the same thought, over and over again until it drives me crazy.

I crave her with every fiber of my being, and if there is even a chance that she's a submissive, then I *will* make her mine at any cost.

Consequences be damned.

The thought of her with any man makes my blood boil—but with another Dom—that makes me feel downright homicidal. I feel so conflicted that it's a physical pain in my body. I throw my hand up over my face, lying flat on my back as I struggle with the images that plague my mind. I must have disturbed Vittoria, because she moves toward me, her arm sliding across my abs as her head finds the spot between my chest and my arm where she fits perfectly, as if she were made for me—the missing piece. I slide my arm around her, pulling her closer. If I were exercising complete control, like I told myself I should, I would extricate myself and go to the guest bedroom, but it feels so fucking good to have her in my arms. I'm selfish and greedy for anything and everything I can get when it comes to her.

I don't know if she's awake or sleeping, but she murmurs my name as her body settles against mine and I love the way it sounds. I let all the shit that's going around and around in my head just fade away. I savor this moment and the girl I'm lying next to, and I let myself drift into a deep and contented sleep with her nestled at my side.

"Logan... Logan..." I can hear Vittoria's voice whispering in my ear as I wake, and without opening my eyes I know it's morning. The sun is streaming in through the curtains as I open my eyes and find her staring back at me. "Hey, stalker. What do you think you're playing at creeping into my bedroom and sleeping with me? I thought you were all about the distance." She has the cutest smirk on her face as she says it. Playful and sexy in one look. I don't know how she pulls it off, but I love it.

"I was... I am. You confuse me. I can't think straight when I'm around you. I only came in to check on you last night and, well, you can see it didn't quite work out that way." I'm painfully aware of the morning situation going on in my pants, as is Vittoria. I quickly adjust myself and put some distance between us. The smile on her face fades, and I desperately want to fix it. "How about I make us some breakfast? What's your favorite?" That distracts her.

"Mmm. Pancakes with fresh cream and blueberries on top, but I rarely have them. Too many calories to burn off."

"There isn't an ounce of fat anywhere on your body. I think we can make an exception this one time, don't you?"

"Well... I shouldn't. I won't be able to dance it off later. Or any time soon." The pain I see flash in her eyes is soul destroying. "Fuck it! Let's go to IHOP." She attempts to get out of bed, but I can tell she's in agony.

"Get back in bed. You're not going anywhere. I'm going to make you pancakes, and they're going to be much better than anything you'd get at IHOP. Trust me!"

"I do." Those two words and the sultry tone of her voice slay me.

"I'm going to go to the store and get what I need. Is there anything else you would like while I'm out?" She shakes her head, reaching for the tablets and water on her nightstand. "How often do you need to take those?"

"Every six hours, at least for a few days and then I can take them less often, I hope. I hate taking tablets. They make me gag." I can't help the small grin on my lips. "Why are you smiling? You like that I'm in pain?"

"No. God no. I *hate* that you're in pain. I was just making a mental note that you have an active gag reflex!"

She sprays water all over the bed as she laughs. "What the hell, Logan? You can't just say stuff like that! I don't know where I am with you from one minute to the next."

I hang my head in shame, knowing she's right. I've given her so many mixed signals it's ridiculous. "I need to go and make you something to eat if you have those tablets in your stomach. We'll talk properly later. Do *not* get up or try to do anything while I'm gone. Understand?"

"Yes, Sir." She gives me a mocking salute as I leave the room. How does she do that? She can be so real and raw and vulnerable in one moment, and then she's making fun of me and joking the next. And she says I make *her* head spin!

I go to the closest store I can find, grab what I need, and while I'm at the counter waiting to pay, I remember that she loves Milk Duds, so I throw three boxes in the basket, hoping they'll make her smile.

When I get back to the apartment it doesn't take me long to whip up a batch of pancakes and get everything else ready, just the way she wants it. I head to her room to tell her that breakfast is ready when I hear cursing in the bathroom.

"Shit! Vafanculo!" [*What the fuck!*]

"Are you okay in there?"

"No, I'm *not* okay! I can't even get in the damn shower."

"Open the door." I hear the small click and her face appears with tears in her eyes.

"I hate this. I hate not being able to do things. I…"

I pull her into my arms and hold her tight as she breaks down. "It's okay. It's only been a few days. I'm here to help now, and soon you won't need me for anything. You'll be back training in no time. But for now, can I get you fed and then we'll worry about getting you clean?"

"Okay," she says in a whisper.

I scoop her up into my arms, careful not to hurt her ankle in the process, and carry her through onto the sofa in the living room. "I'll bring it over."

"I can sit at the table."

"Humor me. I want you as comfortable as possible, and you need to keep your ankle elevated."

"God! You're as bad as Carter. If I wanted to be fussed over, I would have called my family."

"If you wanted to be left alone, you wouldn't have told me, so just get over it and let me help you."

We eat in companionable silence, but as soon as she finishes her last bite, she's questioning me.

"Thank you. They were yummy, and you were right, they were better than IHOP. I'd love to find out where you learned to cook like that, but I'm too impatient, and I want to know why you're here."

"You need help."

"Okay, Professor Obvious, but you could have called Carter or my mom and told them what's going on. Why are *you* here?"

I scrub my hand over my face, two days of stubble scratching at my palms as I try to come up with an answer. "You asked me not to tell them, and I wasn't going to let you stay here alone, so here I am. You're my best friend's sister and I've known you forever. If something happened to you and I could have prevented it, I would never forgive myself."

"Wow! You're really playing the 'best friend's little sister' card right now?"

"It's not a card. It's a fact."

"One of which I'm painfully aware." She shifts uncomfortably in her seat, unable to get up and walk away from me. "Well, you've done your duty, I'm not going to starve to death. You can go. I'm not a charity case, and I don't need your pity."

I grab her face in my hands. "This isn't goddamn charity, or pity. You already know the answer, so spare me the dramatics."

"Do I? I don't know which way is up with you. I'm a friend, I'm your friend's sister, and then I'm sprawled on a table with your cock in my mouth. You want me. You don't want me. You love me, but you want to stay away from me. You kiss me in the airport and then you freak out when you realize I know about you. Now you're here, apparently against your will, but I woke up with you in my bed this morning. What the hell is going on, Logan?"

Hearing it coming from her, I sound like even more of an asshole than I already feel. I let her go and slump back on the couch.

"I'm so sorry."

"I don't want your apologies. I want an explanation. It's driving me nuts."

"Okay, okay. First, you wanted to have a shower. How about I run you a bath so you don't have to put any weight on your ankle, and then we can continue this conversation?"

She throws her head back and covers her face with her arm. "This is exactly what I'm talking about! Are you going to run me a bath, help me completely naked into the tub, and then act like there is nothing between us? I don't generally go around letting guys see me naked or let them get me off when we're 'just friends.'"

"Stop. I told you we will continue this, after. Don't make me repeat myself." My tone leaves no room for question or a smartass reply. I lift her into my arms and stride down the hallway and into the bathroom, where I set her down on the countertop. She pouts as I start the water running and pour some bubble bath into the stream, but when I turn around she's not playing fair.

I watch, mesmerized as she pulls her t-shirt over her head and discards it. Next, she tugs at her pajama bottoms, shimmying her butt on the counter until she gets them loose and lets them drop to the floor. She is completely naked except for the bandage around her ankle, and I'm fighting every urge in my body right now, but I can't ignore the tight, uncomfortable feeling in my pants as my dick strains against the denim. She looks incredible. Every inch of her body is perfection. You can tell she's a dancer, a vessel who moves with effortless grace as the music flows through her.

I don't say a word. I simply walk over to her, lift her foot and place it gently against my chest, caressing her slender calves as I slowly and carefully remove the bandage. Her skin is bruised and swollen, and I can see that even this small movement is painful for her. Holding her foot for a moment, I'm aware that she can feel how fast my heart is beating under her toes.

I carry her over to the tub, her arms holding tight around my neck as I try not to react to the exquisite feel of her naked flesh against my fingertips. She scents me as I lower her into the water, our eyes locking as we acknowledge the current passing between us, flowing from her skin to mine. I place a chaste kiss on her forehead before letting her go, sitting with my back against the tub, my arms resting on my knees and my head resting on edge of the tub.

Vittoria starts running her wet fingers through my hair, simultaneously arousing me and relaxing me. I close my eyes and give in to the conflicting sensations.

"Talk to me. Tell me what's going on. Why do you keep pushing me away?"

"There is no simple answer to that."

"Well, answer me this. Why did you sleep with me last night?"

I take a deep breath, her fingers still tangled in my hair as I begin to speak. "Honestly? Because I couldn't have left you lying there alone, looking so fucking beautiful, even if I wanted to. Whenever I'm around you... I can't explain it. I *need* to be near you, to touch you, feel you, even if it's just my arm around you as you sleep. *That's* why I tried to stay away."

"I don't get it. Why do we need to stay away from each other? Because of the way Carter reacted? Even he admitted that he blew the whole thing way out of proportion. You feel the same way as I do, so why can't we give this a try?"

"You know why. You know what I'm into, what I want in a relationship. We..." She cuts me off.

"We're perfect for each other. I *do* know exactly what you want, and I can give it to you. You have to have figured it out by now... that I'm a..."

"Don't say it, Vittoria. Please, for fuck's sake, don't say it."

"Why?"

I turn to face her, distress evident on her delicate features. "Because, I've known you forever. I've been in love with you from the moment we met. You're Carter's sister, and I'm pretty sure he has an idea that I'm into 'kinky shit' as he would call it. If we were together for real, eventually he would do the math and murder me for corrupting you. It doesn't matter if you want it, he wouldn't see it that way. You guys are my only real family, and when I fuck things up between us again, which I would because you're far too good for me, I would be left with nothing. No family, no best friend, and *most* importantly, you wouldn't be in my life anymore. I've been there before, and it tore me apart. I don't think they would afford me anymore chances."

"That won't happen."

"You say that now, but I don't exactly have a great track record with the people who are supposed to love me more than anything in the world. I can't risk it. I can't risk hurting you again or losing you for good. This past year has been the worst of my life. Please, don't make this harder than it needs to be. I'm trying to be the good guy here. I'm trying to do what's best for you, and what I can live with. Don't think for a second that this is the easy way for me. The easy way would be if I didn't give a shit about how badly I could hurt you in the long run. The easiest thing would be for me to take you to bed, tie you down, and fuck you until your voice is hoarse from screaming my name and begging for more."

"Then take the easy way, Logan. It's what I want."

"Aren't you listening? If I do that, then you're mine. I won't let you go. You'd be my sub, and I'd be your Master. You would have all the power in our relationship, and when the day came, and it would come, when you decided to walk away, I would be left an empty husk. A shell of a man. I would lose everything, and I can't live through that again."

"But..."

"Enough! You asked, I answered. I'm sorry that I've given you mixed signals, that's my own weakness at work. I won't let it happen again." I get up off the floor. "I'll leave you to your bath. Call me when you need help getting out. I'll be in the bedroom." I walk out, hearing her quietly cursing under her breath as I close the door behind me.

I have so much pent up energy and anger as I pace her room. My whole body is vibrating. The smell of her perfume lingers in the air, taunting me as I fight to be the good guy... for her. I ball my fists at my sides, singing the lyrics to the first song that comes to mind, to try and distract myself, but I end up grabbing one of the pillows off the bed and beating the shit out of it. As if that's going to make me feel better in any way, shape, or form! What *would* make this all better, is if I could shackle Vittoria to my St. Andrew's Cross, spank her for pushing me almost to my breaking point, and then fuck her into next week.

"Ouch... Shit... Logan... I need help getting out the tub." I can hear the reluctance in her voice, but I can't blame her. I take a few deep breaths and try to prepare myself for dealing with a hot, wet, and very naked Vittoria, but it doesn't matter worth a shit. When I open the door I see her lying there, the bubbles all but gone, her body on display.

"Fuck." I scrub my hands over my face before grabbing a towel and making my way over to her. "Hold on tight, I don't want to drop you." As I lift her out of the water, the tiny, sexy little groan that escapes her is too much. I pull the towel around her and take her into the bedroom. Once she's safely on the bed, I quickly search her drawers to find something for her to wear. She'll look sexy as hell in everything she owns, so I pick the first top and shorts I can get my hands on and give them to her, before striding out of the room. I can't even steal a look at her, or I'll crack.

"I'll check on you in a little while."

After finding my overnight bag still in the living room, I retreat to the guest room for an hour, spending half of that time in the shower, shamelessly taking myself in hand, over and over again. It's not something I do very often. I prefer to get my subs to do that for me, but today is different. No matter how many times I jerk off to the image of Vittoria naked in the tub, or laid out on that table in Verona, it isn't enough. I'm still rock-hard and desperate for her. Eventually, I give up and give in to the fact that I'll be spending the next few days uncomfortably hard, with no real way to relieve the tension.

Lying on the bed, I wonder when I became such a pussy. I'm a Master for God's sake! Yet here I am, hiding from a woman I want to fuck more than anything in the world, jerking off like a teenager and sulking because she's mad at me for trying to do the right thing. It's pathetic! I would tear Xander and Carter to shreds for this kind of behavior, and I'm the worst offender by far. I purport to exercise complete control, and it's a joke. From the moment I stepped over that line with her, my life has been in utter disarray. Whichever way I turn and whatever I do, I'm making a mess of this… whatever *this* is.

I decide to catch up on some emails and call the boys to see how they're settling in at the new apartment before I check on Tori. They really lighten my mood, going crazy over every little thing about their new place and New York. I don't think they've even been to bed since I left them yesterday, too pumped to calm the hell down and get some rest. I try to convince them that they have a huge week ahead at the studio, and that they absolutely need to have some downtime, but I can hear a few of them in the background, arranging the rest of their day in the city that never sleeps! It makes me laugh, but it also reminds me I have other responsibilities, and I need to get my head back in the game.

An hour later, I think I've composed myself enough to go and see if I'm still public enemy number one. I don't hear any noise in the living room or coming from her bedroom, so I figure she's sleeping, until I push open the door. I couldn't have been more wrong.

Holy fuck!

Her eyes meet mine. She doesn't speak. She doesn't stop.

I'm hypnotized by the sight of her. Her cheeks flushed, her breathing labored, her hand moving beneath the sheets, her legs parted.

"Logan."

CHAPTER 9

LOGAN

"Fuck!"

I know I should walk out and close the door behind me. But instead, I'm standing at the foot of the bed, tearing the sheets off so that I can see her properly and watch her as she touches herself. She doesn't take her eyes off me, and I can't bring myself to leave. My faltering control is becoming a problem, but I manage not to touch her. I want to crawl onto the bed between her legs and bury my head at the apex, delighting in the taste of her. Instead I remain fixed to the spot, admiring the breathtaking sight of her writhing under her own hand. I unbutton my pants and lower them just enough to free my rock-hard erection, wrapping my fist around the base and pumping up and down. I watch as her eyes devour me, her hand quickening as she flicks her clit, pushing herself higher, getting closer to orgasm. I relish the excitement in her eyes as I chase my own release.

The distance between us is charged with an intensity and a need that I've never experienced outside of an elaborate scene in my playroom at the club. The fact that she can do this to me without us touching, without so much as a kiss, is incredible and terrifying, and it doesn't take long until I'm on the edge.

"Come with me, Vittoria."

I can see that she's been holding back, waiting for me to say the word, and the moment she lets go and allows her orgasm to wash over her, is fucking resplendent. Her back arches off the bed, one hand brutally grasping at her breast, pinching her nipple to a hardened point. Her other hand works frantically, her fingers drenched in her own juices as she palms her clit and thrusts three fingers inside herself. It's fucking beautiful. I let myself join her, my hand fisting tighter around my cock, my movements quick and precise, my legs trembling beneath me. The look in her eyes as she watches my come spurting into my other hand is one of complete female satisfaction.

She loves that she has this effect on me.

I take a moment to compose myself, taking off my shirt and wiping my hands clean, before buttoning up my pants, grabbing the sheet off the floor and covering her with it. I turn and walk out the room without a word. I know she's expecting something from me, but I need to do this my way now.

I find a length of rope in my overnight bag and head back to her room. I don't know why I brought it from my apartment, or maybe I just don't want to admit the reason, even to myself. I talk a good game of being the nice guy when it comes to Vittoria, but I'm not. Deep down, I knew I wouldn't be able to resist her for long.

Her eyes light up at the sight of the pretty purple rope in my hands as I make my way over to the bed. I crawl up the length of her, the smell of her arousal thick in the air, enticing me. When I'm happy with my position, I slowly unravel the rope before grabbing her wrists and binding them together. Her headboard is perfect for a playroom—hardwood spindles that could act as strong tethers for any form of restraints. I wonder if it's intentional, but the thought that she's had other men in here tying her up, makes me want to break something. I push the thought aside and focus on weaving the ropes through the headboard, securing her hands in place.

She doesn't say a word, simply watching me as I work, a contented look on her face. I can see that she feels comfortable with this, with me, and it makes my dick throb in my pants. I ignore it, telling myself to remember the bigger picture.

I can't bind her ankles, so I decide on some shibari knots around her knees. I feel a calm serenity wash over me as I work the ropes around her skin. I realize that this is the moment when everything changes. I can't ignore my feelings for her anymore, and I can't keep losing control around her. It's not who I am. If I change for her, if I let her keep pushing me, pushing for us to be together—if I pander to her —I'll become a man I don't recognize, a man I don't respect, and at some point she would lose respect for me, too. She was drawn to me *because* of the man I am. I control everything around me, I command it. If I lose that, I lose myself.

When I'm happy with my handiwork, I get up off the bed and take a step back to admire her. Even this small amount of rope on her looks so fucking hot. The purple is perfect against the warm hue of her skin, highlighting just how stunning her body really is. I could turn her into a work of art if I bound her full body using shibari.

I cross my arms over my chest, feeling my rapid heartbeat thundering against my forearms. Every muscle in my body is tense, adrenaline coursing through me as I fight my instincts, my desperation to be inside of her. I pull a chair from the corner of the room and place it at the end of the bed, sitting down to collect my thoughts.

"Logan. What are you doing?"

I take a few minutes before I answer, letting my pulse return to normal and my inner calm wash over me until I feel like myself again.

"You will refer to me as Master Fitzgerald from now on, unless I tell you otherwise. I've earned it."

She stares at me, lust and desire evident in her eyes.

"Do you understand?"

She's quick to answer. "Yes, Master Fitzgerald."

"I'm going to talk, and you're going to listen. You will speak only when I ask you a question. Understood?"

"Yes, Master Fitzgerald."

"Good. Firstly, let me tell you how absolutely stunning your little show was. You are breathtaking when you touch yourself, Vittoria. I assume you already know that, or you wouldn't have tried to entice me with it." Her gaze drops to the bed. "Look at me when I'm speaking to you." She does as I ask, but I can tell that she's starting to feel uncomfortable. This isn't what she was expecting. "I can see in your eyes that you thought I was going to give in to you. That I wouldn't be able to control myself. You are stunning, but know this… everything that's happened up until this point and every bit of control you have felt over me… is because I *let* you. I chose to discard my own self-imposed rules. I *chose* to let you suck my cock. I *chose* to lick your sweet little pussy. I also made the decision to kiss you in the airport and tell you that I'm in love with you."

She's squirming now.

"I've been going over and over every one of our interactions last year, and there are three possible explanations. So I'm going to lay them out for you, and maybe we can figure out which is correct."

I stand from the chair, walking around the bed, trailing my hands from her toes, up the length of her legs.

"The first possibility is that you're a spoiled brat who likes to get her own way no matter what anyone else says or thinks. That would explain you pushing me, even after I told you we couldn't be together."

"That's not it at all…" I flip her onto her side and slap her naked ass, hard. The sound reverberates around the room.

"Do *not* speak until I tell you to, or your ass will be the same color as a pretty red rose. Understand?"

"Yes… Master Fitzgerald."

"The second option is that you are most definitely involved in my lifestyle, but you're a Dominatrix. In that case, I could only hazard a guess that you had some silly notion of turning me from a Dom into your submissive. Playing on the fact that you know I've been in love with you for years." I continue to trail my fingers over her soft, supple skin. "I *know* that can't be the right answer, because you wouldn't be so naïve! The reason you are so attracted to me is because of how controlling I am in all aspects of my life…" I slip my hand between her legs. She's wet and warm, and oh so ready for me. I lean down to whisper in her ear. "…especially in the bedroom."

I relish the sound of her breath catching at my words, her flesh trembling under my touch, but I leave her bereft and make my way back over to the chair at the end of the bed. Her gaze follows my every move.

"The final option, and the one I'm really rooting for, is that you are an extremely feisty submissive in need of some training from a real Master. That maybe you've forgotten exactly what it is that you 'love' about me. You were drawn to my dominance. You crave it. You thrive under it. It's why you excel as a dancer. The discipline, the pain, the pleasure of it all. The euphoria that comes as the music flows through you. You give yourself over to dance completely, and in return it rewards you. This is the same. If you gave yourself over to me completely, I would play your body with such utter precision. I would walk the fine line between pleasure and pain with such effortless ease, that you couldn't help but feel the same euphoria when you come for me."

The groan that escapes her lips is raw and sexy and filled with desire.

"I think that you haven't found a Dom who can satisfy your needs. You have Italian fire inside you, and it tears you apart sometimes. I've seen your submissive side, and it is… exquisite. But, there is a side to you that doesn't want to give complete control over to me. Maybe not to any man. I don't know what fuels it, but I want to find out. You seem to be at war with those opposing sides to your personality. I can understand that. I tried to be someone I wasn't last year. I tried to hide my true dominance from you, prepared to leave it all behind to be with you. In the end, that's part of the reason it didn't work between us. I was unable to exercise my nature to its fullest extent in my pursuit of you. It almost broke me. So, until you decide what you want, I can't help you. After a long year of soul searching, I know exactly what I want. Do you know what you want, Vittoria?"

Her voice is a low whisper, but full of the fire I was talking about. "I want to be yours. I want to give myself over to you completely, Master Fitzgerald."

"I want to believe you. So badly. But, I can't shake the feeling that you're not ready to submit. You see my love for you as a weakness.

One that you can exploit. That couldn't be further from the truth. The fact that I've been in love with you for so long, is my strength. It is the reason I will *never* exercise anything other than complete control with you. You're too important to me. I have stayed away from you all these years because I felt it was best for you. Now, I'm not so sure."

I hold her gaze for what seems like hours, searching for the answer I need.

"So... which is it? Are you spoiled, a Dominatrix who thinks she can change me, or are you an unruly submissive?"

"The last one. I want to submit to you, Logan..."

"Logan? That has just earned you ten spanks."

I stand from the chair and flip her onto her stomach, careful not to aggravate her injury.

"Present your ass to me, Vittoria." She lifts herself onto her knees, pushing her ass into the air, her head resting on the bed. "Good girl."

I gently rub each cheek before I administer the first blow. "I don't punish for no reason, and I never punish excessively, but you need some basic training. After every slap, I want you to say "Thank you, Master Fitzgerald. It will remind you to address me appropriately."

The first slap is always the sweetest. The feel of her soft, naked flesh connecting with the warmth of my palm, the crisp sound and the tingling sensation that radiates across my palm. "One."

Her anticipation followed by surprise, is so fucking satisfying. "Thank you, Master Fitzgerald."

The second hit has the blood rising to the surface below her skin, a sexy blush spreading over her cheeks. "Two."

Her body shivers. "Thank you, Master Fitzgerald."

With each slap her ass grows redder, her breath quickening, and my dick hardens to steel in my pants. I can tell she's enjoying this, but there is just enough bite to remind her why I'm doing it. As soon as my hand connects with her firm, supple skin for the last time, she lets out a satisfied groan followed by her almost screaming the words I commanded. "Thank you, Master Fitzgerald."

I slide my hand between her legs, the evidence of her arousal dripping down the inside of her thighs. She tries to writhe against my hand, her frustration evident as I leave her wanting. She watches as I lower my head and lap up every last drop. Her moans of pleasure set my blood on fire, but I don't reward her with my tongue where she needs it most. "You taste like heaven. Remember this frustrated feeling. Every time you defy me, I will punish you. You enjoy the punishment more than you should, so I will also withhold your orgasms."

She slumps down onto the bed, squirming to try and alleviate the pressure that's building to a fever pitch between her legs, but to no avail. I flip her over onto her back and wait, giving her time to slow her breathing and regain her composure before I speak.

"This is my proposal to you. I will *not* take you as my 24/7 submissive, and not as my sexual sub, *until...*" I can see her eyes light up at that one little word. "Until... you can prove yourself. *If* you comply and adhere to my training over the next month, then and only then will I even *consider* taking this further." I start to untie her, loosening the knots and massaging the skin underneath. When her hands are free, I sit down on the bed beside her and pull her into my lap.

"I need to know that you're serious about this. If you're not, if you just want me to fuck you and move on, then I need you to tell me. If we do this, I'm risking losing everything for you. The only real family I've ever had... and you. If you don't think you can do this, then you need to tell me and we can both walk away from this right now."

She places her small warm hand on my cheek, pulling my face down toward hers, forcing me to look at her. "May I speak freely, Master Fitzgerald?"

"Yes, and you can call me Logan."

Her other hand moves up to cup my face. "Logan... I am all in. I'm *very* serious about this. I've never been more serious about anything, other than ballet. I want to be with you. I want to be yours. I know what you're risking if you choose to go down this road with me. I don't take it lightly. I can't promise it will be easy, or that I won't mess up. There are... things... that you don't know about me, that I'm not ready to share with you yet, and I may never be ready. I don't want you to see me differently. I love the way you look at me, and to risk that changing is something I can't live with. Can you understand that?

Can you deal with there being some things I can't tell you right now, things that might affect the way I respond to situations, or the way I act at times?"

Her eyes are thick with unshed tears.

"What happened to you?" Her gaze drops, and I pull her hands from my face, grasping them tight. "Look at me." She does as I ask, a single tear rolling down her cheek, breaking my heart. "I can deal with it, for you, but only if you promise you'll try to work on it and tell me when you're ready. I need you to trust me, otherwise this isn't going to work. I'm not asking for immediate one hundred percent trust. I know I need to earn it, as do you. Can you promise that you will try to work toward telling me at some point?" She nods her head, defeated. "I need to hear you say it."

"Yes. I will do my best to get there and to tell you someday. But, please don't stop looking at me the way you do. Don't stop loving me. Don't give up on me." I search her face, wondering who hurt her. What happened to make her so insecure? It's a rare moment to see her show any vulnerability, and it humbles me.

"I promise you now, I will *never* give up on you, Vittoria. Cling to that in your darkest moments, when I can't be by your side, *know* that I could never give up." I claim her lips, pouring every ounce of raw emotion that I feel into this intense connection. Her body relaxes against mine, her lips parting, inviting me in. I dart my tongue into her mouth, exploring, caressing, tasting her sweet lips. The feel of her tongue stroking mine is divinity in motion. I fist my hands in her hair, holding her where I need her, forcing her to take more of me, and taking everything she offers me in return.

Her hands are clawing at my back when I break our kiss, resting my forehead against hers. I breathe her in, letting my pulse return to some semblance of normality. "You're mine now. My submissive in training. I will not make love to you for the next four weeks. It might kill me, but if we have any chance of this working, I need to separate how fucking turned on I feel when I'm around you, from how we interact as Dom/sub. There are no guarantees that we can make this work, and even if we do, we have so many hurdles to get over." I pull away, letting her see how serious I am. "I won't lie to Carter. At the end of the month, if I decide that I can be the Master you need me to be, then I'm going to tell him. No secrets, no lies. If we do this, it's all or nothing. I can't risk fucking this up again, and I promise that I won't leave if he doesn't accept it. I will walk away... with you. It's you and me now, for as long as you'll have me."

"I don't want to hide anymore, either. I will do whatever you feel is best. I want this." She gives me a slow, sensual but chaste kiss. "How will this work for the next four weeks?"

"Let me worry about that. You just relax and get some rest. It's been a tiring afternoon and you need to get your strength up." I lay her down on the bed, pulling the sheets up to cover her. "Do you need anything?"

"A glass of water and my painkillers."

I fetch a bottle of water from the fridge and return to find her eyes heavy, almost asleep. "Here you go. Now rest, my beautiful Nyx."

She pops two tablets on her tongue and takes a sip of water. Her voice is sleepy and sexy as hell as she speaks. "Why do you call me Nyx? You've called me that before."

I run my hand over her sleek, dark hair. "I'll explain later. Get some rest. I have some work to do. I'll be back in a few hours with dinner." I kiss her forehead, draw the curtains, and close the door gently behind me.

"THIS PLACE IS SO FUCKIN' AMAZIN', LOGAN! WE CANNAE GET O'ER HOW fan-fucking-tastic it is! The boys are goin' mental for it. I dinnae think they've slept more than two hours since we got here."

I can barely understand Campbell when he's excited. He's the lead singer of Flaming Embers, and he has a thick Glasgow accent. Usually he remembers to slow down and not use as much slang around me, but on days like today, he's too excited and he's talking at rapid speed. It almost sounds like he's speaking a completely different language.

"Remember, you've got to learn to calm the accent down a bit here.

Otherwise, *Rolling Stone* won't be able to get any quotes for an interview!"

"Shut the fuck up, man! You serious? You think a bunch o' twats like us could make it that big here in the U.S. of A?"

I really like this guy. He's only twenty-one, but he's lived a tough life in a rough part of Glasgow. He's fought for everything he has, and he appreciates every good thing that comes his way. He's genuine, and in this business it's a rare commodity. "Only if you stop referring to the band as 'a bunch of twats!'"

"Ha-fuckin'-ha! Duly noted!"

"Okay. So, we need to get the rest of the guys rounded up and have a talk about what I have planned for you over the next few weeks. Are they all here?"

"Sure. Hang on." He disappears, but I can hear his low, strong rolling brogue from here. "Get yer arses out here, lads. Logan's wantin' to talk shop. This ain't a free ride, ya losers!"

They all come tumbling into the kitchen and I take a moment to look them over. Every teenage girl in America is going to swoon over these guys. They're all so different in personality and appearance, but each has a charm and sex appeal that's a prerequisite if you want to be successful in the music business these days. It's a sad fact, but it's not all about talent, which these boys also have in spades.

Campbell's songwriting skills blew me away the first time I saw them in action, and his voice is... haunting. His low rasp loses the harsh accent and transforms into something truly spectacular. He is an artist in his own right, but he would never sellout his friends for a solo deal, even if it meant never getting to live out his dream. The band as a whole have a great energy on stage, and they have a strong indie following already, including Lily!

When I arranged for the boys to perform in London so Xander and Lily could see them perform, Xander called me the next day, completely blown away by how good they were. I knew then that I was onto a game changer for my label. He was eager to help bring them to the U.S. and endorse their first album. He's been a great help with the business side of things, and I'm certain I can use my experience to take them to the next level.

"How the fuck are you, Logan? Thought you were goin' tae party wi' us last night, brother!" The other boys seem to speak in unison, and it makes me laugh. "It was fuckin' epic."

"I had… a prior engagement. I'm not here to get drunk with you. I'm here to turn you into rock stars. You ready for that?"

As one, all five guys shout, "HELL FUCKIN' YAS!"

"First thing's first, calm down the cursing. I can't market you to the screaming high school girls of America with every second word out of your mouth being 'fuck.'"

Campbell is the natural leader of the group being the front man, and he takes his roll seriously.

"Sorry, Logan. We'll keep the swearin' tae a minimum, at least in public. This actually *is* the lads holdin' back. You should try holdin' a conversation wi' any one o' their da's. They'd make a sailor blush."

"I'm not saying cut it out, girls love a bad boy, just rein it in a little for the press and when you're working with people. You want to put your best foot forward and make people *want* to work with you. I have you scheduled to start laying down tracks in the studio in two days. I want you to get some rest and some actual sleep. Sober up at least a little, and be ready for the car to pick you up at 10 a.m. on Monday."

"I'm ready, man. I was born ready for this shit! I promise we won't let you down."

"I know you won't. I wouldn't have brought you here if I didn't think you could cut it. Just try to keep each other grounded, and don't get carried away with all the trappings. It's about the music, and if you stay true to that, everything else will follow. I'll make sure of it."

"We cannae thank you enough. Seriously. None of us thought for a second that we'd ever get out o' Glasgow. Meeting wi' you in Edinburgh was a reprieve from our sad fuckin' lives. This… this is… I dinnae even have the words tae thank you enough."

I stand from the table and give him a slap on the shoulder. "Don't thank me yet. You have a long road ahead of you, but you deserve this,

Campbell. You're a talented son of a bitch. Now, I have to go to the office and make sure everything's in place for Monday."

All of the guys are shouting goodbye as I make my way out to the lobby. Campbell follows me out.

"You okay, big man? You seem a bit off today. Everything okay wi' the deal?"

"It's all good, Cam. Personal stuff. You wouldn't believe me even if I told you!"

"Woman trouble?"

"Isn't it always?" He's a perceptive guy. Wise beyond his years. "I'll see you Monday."

"Later, man."

I close the door behind me and head to my office. It's a reprieve before heading back to Vittoria's apartment. I could do what I need to get done on my laptop, but I need some time to clear my head, to grasp the gravity of what I've agreed to with her.

As I sit in my office, quiet and deserted, I contemplate my after-noon—Vittoria, Carter, and what this all means. Their parents have practically adopted me as one of their own over the past nine years. Losing them would be hard. As if he knows I'm thinking about him, my phone lights up with a message from Carter.

Carter: *Drinks? Cube 8 p.m.*

Me: *Can't tonight, bro.*

Carter: *Stop banging your latest sex slave and come have a drink with me and Xander.*

Me: *You're a dick. Working. Maybe this week sometime?*

Carter: *I have a HUGE dick! You're a loser. Will text you this week. Blow me off again and I'll beat the shit out of you.*

Me: *You wish! Fuck off! Tell Xander I said hi.*

I hate lying to him, even if it's in a text. This is exactly what I told Vittoria I didn't want to happen. If I'm going to make it work with her, I need to be honest with him. The reality is that he's going to freak out and try to kill me rather than let me date her. We've been down this road once before, and it didn't end well for us.

I think my days as his friend are numbered, but she's worth it.

CHAPTER 10

LOGAN

THE PAST THREE WEEKS HAVE BEEN AMAZING AND TORTUROUS AT THE same time. I've spent most nights with Vittoria at her apartment, sleeping next to her, but not *with* her. I had planned on staying in the guest room, but I'm too drawn to her, and when we realized that her nightmares stop when I'm beside her, I couldn't refuse her request as her Dom. It's what's best for her right now, even though it's the hardest thing I've ever done. My level of self-control has been tested to its limit. Night after night with her curled up in my arms, her breasts pressed against my chest, her leg thrown over my thighs. It's a beautiful kind of agony. Every minute of every day, I ache to be inside her.

The first week, I kissed her, licked her, made her come with my fingers, but I never let her touch me. Even then, it was too difficult. Trying to train her without being able to really take her, is new territory for me. I may be a Master, but I usually have all my... skills, at my disposal. Sex is a powerful incentive, and a strong bonding mechanism between a Dom and his sub. Taking that deepest of connections out of the equation has forced me to employ other tactics.

After that first week, I had to stop even the foreplay, it was too confusing for her. She kept expecting more, and when I didn't give it to her, she got frustrated and lashed out at me. It made her insecure, questioning my attraction to her. I felt like I was punishing her for my own shortcomings. In the end, I discussed it with her and told her that until the four weeks were up, there would be no orgasms, other than the ones I allow her to give herself while I watch. No kissing. She pleaded with me, begging me to touch her, but that just showed me she needs the training more than ever. She needs to respect my decisions and trust that I know what to do for the best. She doesn't understand that it's just as difficult for me. Every inch of her body was made for me, calling to me like a siren, whether she's sitting across from me at the dinner table, watching TV on the couch with her legs in my lap, or tucked against my side in her sleep. I *want* her.

She still won't talk to me about what terrorizes her during the night, but I think she's beginning to trust me more. She seems more rested and happier in herself these days, and I would like to think that our burgeoning relationship has something to do with it. The fact that I can see a difference in her at night, is what I cling to. It's what's keeping me sane.

I feel like I'm slowly losing my mind. I've always been a very sexually aware kind of guy, but this is getting ridiculous. I can barely function! When I'm at the studio with the band, I find myself getting lost in fantasies of having Vittoria in my playroom and the things I plan to do to her. I think I spend more than half my time trying to hide a semi.

Punishment has been almost a daily occurrence. She has such a fiery personality. I like to change things up, and I now know that the best way to punish her, is to deny her. Last week, I cuffed her to the dining chair and made her watch as I pleasured myself. She couldn't touch herself, and her legs were also cuffed, so she couldn't even press her legs together to alleviate the pressure. By the time I came all over her pretty blue skirt, she was promising me anything I asked if I would just let her come. I didn't. It was hell for me, and for her. I wanted to drop to my knees and lap at her glistening folds, to feel her come apart beneath the flick of my tongue.

Thankfully, I think we're getting somewhere now. It's a fine line training her to submit, without breaking the spirit in her that I fell in love with. As a Master, I must learn the limits of my sub. People have preconceived ideas about BDSM. They think it's a purely sexual thing, but it goes so much deeper than that. My main concern is always for her wellbeing, And that pertains to every aspect of her life, not just her orgasms. I need to know that I am doing everything in my power to make sure she is safe, happy and healthy.

Our situation has been further complicated by the fact that we have known each other for such a long time, and the intense emotion between us has been there from the start. Usually that depth of feeling grows over time. In reality, I have never felt this way about any of my subs. These are unchartered waters for me.

Vittoria's injury is getting better every day. I've been careful not to let her push herself back to dancing too soon, because I know that she misses it, and that's precisely why she needs to take her time, to avoid any long-term damage. She's off her crutches, with a light bandage still in place, and her pain meds are down to a minimum.

Last week we were invited to Verona's first birthday party, which was interesting. Vittoria made me promise not to speak to Carter about us because she was worried he would react badly, and unintentionally ruin his little girl's birthday. It didn't sit well with me, but I respected her wishes. To be honest, I've been avoiding Carter, and even at the party, I kept my interaction with him to a minimum. A lie of omission still feels like a lie, and until I knew for sure that she really wanted this, I didn't want to cause another family feud, but D-Day has arrived.

My thoughts are interrupted by Vittoria at my back. She wraps her arms around my neck. "What's got that frown line working overtime on your forehead?"

I take her hands in mine, lacing our fingers. "I need to talk to Carter. I need to tell him that we're seeing each other."

"I thought you wanted to wait until the four weeks are up? Until you decide where we go from here?"

"I think we both know where this is headed, don't you? I need to be honest with him before we move forward."

She practically chokes me to death trying to hug me. "Does that mean we don't have to wait until next week for the sex?"

"No. It means that when next week comes around, and we reach the date I set, I am going to split you in two. You won't be able to walk properly for days when I'm done with you."

"Promises, promises, Master Fitzgerald."

I pull her down over my shoulder, lift her skirt, and give her a sharp spank. "Keep that up and I'll make you wait another week."

"You wouldn't?"

"Wouldn't I?"

"Aren't you even a little frustrated?" Frustrated does not even come close to describing how badly I want to be inside her.

"That's not your concern. Let's just get through this week."

She twists her body over and down into my lap, her lips just millimeters from my own. It's been two weeks since I felt those plush lips against my own, since I felt her tongue perform a sensual dance with mine. Her eyes switch between holding my gaze and devouring my lips with her penetrating stare. She darts her tongue out to wet her lips, making them all the more inviting. I want to kiss her so badly, but I know that kissing will turn into touching, and touching will turn into me ripping her clothes off and making love to her right here on my desk. I don't know how much longer I can hold back. I let myself breathe her in for a brief moment, letting her see the desire in my eyes, before I gently remove her from my lap and sit her on top of the desk.

"You better be prepared for me in seven days' time." My voice is laced with promise and a hint of menace. I can see the excitement spark in her eyes, and I know that when I finally take her, I won't be the one who owns her... *she will own me*. I will never get enough of her.

Vittoria has a doctor's appointment this afternoon, and she insisted that I go to my office for a while. She thinks I've been neglecting my work for her over the past few weeks. She's not wrong, but she's my priority, and with that in mind I message her brother.

Me: *Got time to meet up? Need to talk.*

Carter: *Cube, in an hour?*
Me: *See you there.*
I guess it's now or never.

~

CUBE IS EERIE DURING THE DAY. THE SMELL OF STALE BEER FROM YEARS of people having a good time, night after night, clings to every surface. It's like a ghost town, except for a few members of staff who are in setting up for the night ahead. One of them nods at me to go to the back office, and I can't help feeling like I'm walking the green mile as I slowly make my way to the end of the hall.

I knock the door before opening it to find Carter engrossed in some boring looking paperwork.

"Hey, man. Is this a bad time?"

He looks up, somewhat relieved. "This is perfect timing. I need a break from all this shit. I fucking hate the paper trail that comes with running clubs. Even though I hired a manager to oversee everything, I like to come in occasionally and get myself up to speed."

I take a seat across from him. "How's the family?"

He sits back with a smug, satisfied grin on his face. "They are fucking amazing. I never thought I would be this guy. Happy as a pig in shit, with an amazing girlfriend and a kid. I fucking love it."

"I'm really happy for you, bro. You deserve it. You and Xander really hit the jackpot."

"Yeah. He'll never let me forget that he's the reason I met Addison, though. Smug bastard!"

We share a few laughs and catch up. I get shown at least thirty pictures of baby Verona on his phone, but I'm happy to see them. She's adorable, and she's a de Rossi woman. I know how irresistible they can be.

Finally, he remembers that I asked to come and talk with him. "So, what's going on? What do you need to talk about?"

I pause for a moment, wondering how to phrase this, how best to soften the blow and minimize the fallout that will inevitably follow. In the end, I figure, direct and to the point is all I can do.

"I'm in love with Vittoria."

"What the fuck?" I can see his anger building as he stares me down, his hands balling into fists on the table.

"Hear me out."

"You have exactly five minutes to convince me why I shouldn't beat the shit out of you right now."

"Fine. If that's what you need to do, then so be it. But, it won't change the fact that I'm in love with her." I can hear him grinding his teeth, fighting to stay in his seat.

"I wasn't lying when I came to you last year and told you that I broke it off with her after the dinner at your apartment. I didn't want to come between the two of you. You know I consider you family, and your parents feel like my own. I would have been lost all these years without you guys. But... and it's a big but... Vittoria has always been special to me. I've been in love with her forever. I stayed away as long as I could, because I never wanted to lose you as a friend, and when I walked away from her last year, it just about killed me. I've been fucking miserable without her."

I watch his face soften ever so slightly, knowing he's experienced that level of loss and misery.

"We met by chance on a flight to London last month and we started talking again. My feelings for her haven't changed, Carter. If anything, I'm more in love with her than I've ever been."

"So, you've been fucking her for a month behind my back? What's this then, a fucking courtesy call?" And then it dawns on him. "You two were together at Verona's party last week? You were sneaking around at my daughter's first fucking birthday party?"

He stands from the table

"Sit the fuck down, Carter. I haven't 'fucked' her, and if you *ever* speak about her like that again, I will fucking end you."

"I'd like to see you try."

"Just sit down and shut the fuck up until I'm done."

He grabs a bottle of Jack from the cabinet behind his desk and pours himself a glass before sitting back down. "Talk. Fast."

"Firstly, yes, we were together last week, but Vittoria didn't want to take any of the focus away from Verona's day. She adores that little girl and wouldn't do anything to jeopardize her happiness. Secondly, I've never slept with her. Not when we were together a year ago, and not now. Not that it's any of your fucking business. I'm serious about her. She's it for me. I wanted to be sure that I could be the man she needs me to be before we take the next step. I know that if I cross that line with her, there will be no going back. If I lost her after that, I would never recover. Surely, you can understand, after everything that happened when you and Addi were trying to figure things out."

"Don't compare this to me and Addi. You want to fuck my sister. *My sister!*"

"For fuck's sake! I want to *be* with her, build a life with her, and protect her from anything that could ever hurt her. She's my fucking world! If I never have sex with her, she'll still be the fucking *one!*"

"But…"

"No fucking buts. I love her. She loves me back. I want what you and Xander have. Someone to share my life with. I've denied myself that for so long, because no one has ever measured up to her."

"You've not denied yourself anything. You've been a fucking controlling man-whore for years."

I can't disagree with him.

"You've fucked more women than I ever will, but here you are with an amazing girlfriend and the cutest kid on the planet. The reason I acted the way I did, was because I was trying to get over Vittoria. But it never happened. She's always been the one, she's always going to *be* the one. I don't want to lose you as a friend, and I really don't want to cause a fallout between you and Tori again, but I can't give up this chance for you. I did it a year ago, and it was the wrong decision. I know the risk I'm taking here, but she's worth it."

He scrubs his hands over his face. A look of defeat in his eyes.

"Fucking, Fuck! You're such a dick, Logan. Of all the women in Manhattan, why the fuck did you have to fall for my little sister?"

"Trust me, if I could have clicked my fingers and been in love with someone else, I would have done it years ago. She's amazing. You know that. I would do anything for her, and I will *never* hurt her or betray her. There is no one else on earth for me. I need you to be okay with this, because Vittoria will never be truly happy if you're not."

"That's a low blow. You know I would do anything to see her happy." He swallows his drink in one gulp before slamming the glass down on the table. "I fucking hate you right now, but… if she wants to be with you, then I won't stand in your way."

I let out the breath I've been holding for the past five minutes. "Thanks, man."

"But, remember this. If you ever so much as make her cry, I will hunt you down and cut your balls off."

"Fair enough." It's better than I expected from this discussion. "Are we good?"

"No! But we will be. I need some time to wrap my head around this and try to curb my instinct to beat the shit out of you for laying so much as a finger on her. I'll get there, eventually. I want Vittoria to be happy, and despite my aversion to you dating her, I want you to be happy, too. I'd just rather it was with someone else's sister."

I can't help but laugh. He's an arrogant fucker sometimes, but he loves Vittoria, and the fact that he can put aside his own feelings and give us a chance, shows how much Addi and Verona have changed him.

"I appreciate that. I'm sure I'd feel the same way if I had a sister. Thank you, though. This will mean a lot to Vittoria, and it means a lot to me."

He pours another drink, except this time he grabs a second glass and pours one for me.

"Here's to us." He hands me the glass. "To you not fucking up, and to me not killing you."

"Cheers."

We share a few drinks and manage to steer the conversation back to lighter topics, but I don't want to overstay my welcome. I know this is hard for him.

When I stand to leave, he asks me when I'm seeing her again.

"I'm seeing her tonight, actually."

"Tell her to come and see me while she's still in town. I need to talk to her about her appalling taste in men."

"You're a dick."

"Yeah, well now I have good reason to be a dick to you."

"Touché. I'll tell her to swing by. I'll talk to you soon. Thanks again."

"Fuck off before you start crying like a girl."

I walk out with renewed purpose. There's nothing standing in the way now. Vittoria and I can be together, for real, in public, and she doesn't have to choose between me and her relationship with her brother.

Her happiness and wellbeing will always be my number one priority, and this is a huge step in the right direction for us as we move forward.

VITTORIA WAS SO HAPPY WHEN I TOLD HER ABOUT MY CONVERSATION with Carter today, and so relieved. In truth, so was I. I relayed our conversation, leaving out all of his crass insinuations. I think we both felt like a weight had been lifted, and in the end, I just couldn't stand not to touch her anymore, to feel her come apart for me.

Hours later and too many orgasms to count, I lie awake next to her, content to watch the rise and fall of her chest. The peaceful sleep of a satisfied submissive. I've missed seeing the beautiful flush of her cheeks after I've taken her to the edge and let her bask in wave after wave of ecstasy. There were no punishments tonight, no bondage, and no toys, only us. Two people exploring each other's bodies, giving and receiving pleasure, over and over again until we collapsed in a heap of sweaty, sated limbs.

I trace the lines of her face with my fingers, her stunning cheekbones and her perfectly pouty lips. She has long, lush eyelashes that kiss her cheeks. She looks so angelic—like a goddess.

"I'm glad you sorted things out with Carter."

"I thought you were asleep. Did I wake you?"

"No. I'm just resting. A devil of a man wore me out." She keeps her eyes closed, a mischievous grin spreading across her face.

"A devil, you say?" My hand trails down her neck, edging beneath the sheet that covers her sweet, sexy curves.

"I do."

"You have no idea just how devilish I can be, Nyx. Just you wait."

"Why do you call me Nyx? You never did get around to telling me."

I prop my head up on my hand. "Nyx was the goddess of the night. Of darkness. She was the mother of creation, said to be so powerful and her beauty so exquisite, that even Zeus himself feared her. She was only ever seen in glimpses, found in the shadows."

"Am I the darkness?" She looks pained.

"No, Vittoria. You are *not* the darkness. Why would you think that?"

"Because I'm not good enough for you. I'm damaged goods. The things you don't know about me… there's a darkness inside me that eats away at any good there is."

I take her face in my hand. "I wish you would trust me. I wish you would tell me why you feel this way about yourself." Her gaze drops to the bed. She can't even look at me. "The truth is, I call you Nyx because you are the most enchanting beauty I've ever seen in my life. A goddess sent to torment my tarnished soul. You have so much power over me. Can't you see that? The way I feel about you terrifies me. I feel like I'm at war with myself on a daily basis, fighting to control the urge to make you mine no matter what the consequences are." She finally meets my gaze. "Don't you see? I'm a man who controls everything in my life. You throw that into chaos, while at the same time, craving my control. You need it, and I need to be sure I can provide it. That I can be the Master you so desperately need. I don't know if I'm what's best for you, but the thought of another man being your Dominant…" I fist my hand in the sheets, "it makes my blood boil. I see bloody, murderous red at the very thought of it."

She silences me with a gentle kiss. "*You* are the only man I want.

It's your dominance I crave, no one else's. I'm so in love with you that I can't even see straight. The reason I've never said anything to you over the years, is because I didn't want to bring my darkness into your life. You're a good man, and I don't want to taint you."

"Don't ever think that." I sit up, pulling her into my arms. "From now on, when we are in a scene, or when I am referring to you as my submissive, I will call you Nyx. This will remind you that you're beautiful to me, inside and out. It will remind you that you hold all the power in our Master/submissive relationship. It will serve to remind you that you're a goddess in my eyes, and my sole purpose is to see that your needs are met, emotionally, physically, and sexually. Do you understand me... Nyx?"

"Yes, Master Fitzgerald."

"Good. Then as of now, you are my 24/7 submissive. You will meet me on our agreed date in a week's time, at the club. I will send you details of which room, and how I want you to present yourself when I arrive. After I claim your body as my own for the first time, you will be mine. Body, mind and soul. There is no going back from that."

"I know."

"I need to be certain that you do. Tomorrow I'm going to go back to my apartment, and I'm going to give you this week to think it over. If you change your mind, I won't hold it against you, and I'll let you walk away without any reprisal from me."

"I don't want to be away from you for the whole week."

"Neither do I, but things between us are so intense. I want to give you time to think, to breathe, to consider the line we are about to cross together. I don't want you to worry, baby. We'll talk this week, and before you know it, we'll be together again... if that's what you choose." I slide us down the bed and under the covers. "I don't want you worrying about this. You need your rest, and tonight, I'm not going anywhere. I'm right here, where I want to be. Now get some sleep."

I wrap my arms around her and pull her body flush against my own. A perfect fit. I listen as her breathing evens out, and her body relaxes in slumber. I on the other hand, find myself restless, wondering if time apart is a good idea. It will be so hard to be away from her. I've gotten so used to having her around, even if it's just knowing that she's in the apartment, sharing the same space. I've never done that before. I've always kept the club and my home life separate. She's already changing me in ways that can never be undone.

If she does change her mind, and I need to let her walk away, it will destroy me. But in the end, it's not about me or what I want. As a Dominant, my priority will always be her needs over my own. Her desires ahead of mine. Her pleasure in all things.

It's 4 a.m. by the time I finally fall asleep, but even then, I'm plagued by my own nightmares.

CHAPTER 11

LOGAN

"Your new submissive is waiting, Master Fitzgerald. The room has been set up as per your requests."

It's been a long time since I was last here. The familiar sounds, the energy vibrating off the walls, the music pulsing through everything, and everyone in the building. Rihanna blares through the sound system, singing of chains and whips. It's an obvious choice for a club like this, but it sets the mood perfectly. I've missed this.

"Thank you." Every nerve ending in my body is alive tonight, adrenaline pumping hard in my veins. I'm too distracted to even bother with the usual small talk on the way up to my room.

"Is everything okay? If she's not to your liking I can have someone else train her." My fists tighten at my sides. Rage clouding my vision.

"Listen carefully. *No one* will ever touch her. Do you understand me? If anyone lays so much as a finger on her, I will make sure that they leave this place on a gurney. *No one* but me even *speaks* to her. Got it?"

"Understood, Master Fitzgerald. I'll make sure of it."

"Good." I run my hand over my face, scratching my palm over the scruff covering my jaw these days. This last week has been slow, and tedious without Vittoria. Work has been crazy, and the few hours that

I wasn't working, I wanted to be with her, but I gave her the space I promised her, and thankfully, she has decided to meet me here tonight.

I wanted to make love to her for the first time at my apartment, but I know that she needs this setting to solidify our relationship as Master and submissive. Instead, I had the room completely renovated. As a Master, I have had this playroom designated to me for almost five years now. No one is allowed access but me, and my submissives, but I didn't want to use the same equipment that I did with them, not for Vittoria. I had them rip everything out, paint the room a darker shade of purple, and replace all the apparatus. I had new toys shipped in and a closet of lingerie just for her.

I messaged her this week to ask what she likes, what she loves, what she isn't willing to do. I can't explain the pain I felt, knowing that her answers came from experience. I hate that another Dominant had his hands on her, that someone else trained her, and that she submitted to someone who wasn't me. I did it for her. I needed to know her hard limits, the stuff she wants to explore, the toys she enjoys, and her safe word.

I've been planning this all week, and I know exactly what I want to do with her tonight. I'm eager to see the new playroom... our playroom.

I don't even remember walking up the stairs, simply finding myself standing in front of the door with 'Master Fitzgerald' emblazoned on it in silver script, and underneath in bold lettering:

RESTRICTED ROOM. DO NOT ENTER.

"If you need anything at all this evening, Master Fitzgerald, just let me know."

"Thank you, Jacob."

I take a deep breath. Nerves and adrenaline fueling my every move as I turn the handle and open the door. I've never been nervous about my first time with a new sub, but my first time with Vittoria...

"Good evening, Nyx."

Holy Shit!

I take a moment to regroup. The sight of her, in here, in my space —the backdrop to this part of my life that I've kept hidden from everyone but her—completely fucking floors me. I want to be inside her more than I've ever wanted anything. I have to distract myself, taking in my new surroundings. The room looks phenomenal. There are pictures on the walls, various prints of a ballet dancer with leather restraints around her ankles, and one with her arms and legs tied using shibari, but neither picture shows a face. The only woman I want to see in here is Vittoria.

There is a new black St. Andrew's cross at the far end of the room, with silver shackles, top and bottom. There is a wall of floggers and paddles of various shapes and sizes. Spreader bars hanging from metal hooks, and a king size bed exactly like Vittoria's, and a couch at the foot of it. I requested one with adequate points to attach restraints and I can see lengths of purple rope resting on the arm. There is a cabinet next to the entrance of the room, housing all of the toys and restraints I could ever need, and a table in the center of the room, large enough to lay her out and tie her down, helpless and open to my every whim.

She is exactly where I requested her to be. She's wearing a black lace Basque and French knickers. She looks absolutely divine on her knees, her ass touching her heels, her hands gripped behind her back. Her head is bowed, eyes to the ground in a perfect submissive position facing the wall. I can't breathe taking in every single stunning detail of the way she looks tonight.

"Good evening, Master Fitzgerald."

I walk over to the far wall, perusing the collection of implements and choosing a particularly nice black leather flogger. I run it through my palm. This will do nicely.

I begin to ready myself, leaving Vittoria staring at the floor. Letting her anticipation grow and her mind wander to what I'm doing, what I have in store for her. I remove my iPod from my jacket and sync it to the sound system in the room. I haven't chosen romantic or soft music as the soundtrack to our evening. Instead,

Animals by Maroon 5, starts pulsing through the speakers with promises of primal pleasure, and I can see that she's affected by it.

I place the flogger down on the hard wood table and pull my t-shirt up and over my head, discarding it on the floor. I remove my shoes and socks and kick them under the table.

I watch the rapid rise and fall of her chest as her eagerness for my touch reaches a fever pitch, her eyes still trained on the wall four feet in front of her.

As I walk toward her, desire coils in every muscle of my body, threatening to spiral out of control. It takes me a moment to calm myself, to be the man I am, the man I hide from those around me. The darkest part of myself.

I stride over to her, stopping only an inch in front of her. I place my thumb and forefinger under her chin, tilting her head up, but she keeps her eyes lowered.

"You may look at me."

As she lifts her gaze and our eyes meet, the connection between us is more intense than it has ever been. A deeper understanding passes between us, a shared need for something more, something... darker. I feel my calm, controlled confidence return. My dick hardens in response to the power I wield over her. I was born to be a Dominant. I was destined to be *her* Dominant. It's all I know.

"Are you a submissive, Nyx?" The silence after those words leave my lips seems to span an eternity. My entire body vibrates from asking the question I haven't let her answer until now.

"Yes... Master Fitzgerald."

Her voice is like velvet, her words the greatest aphrodisiac. Even though I knew the answer, hearing her say it... out loud... is such a fucking turn on.

"How long have you been a submissive?"

I don't know if I want to know the answer. The thought of another Dom owning her, seeing to her every need—it kills me.

"Four years, Master Fitzgerald."

I am devastated by her revelation. I've wasted so much time avoiding her, shielding her from this side of myself. I clench my fist tighter around the flogger, knowing that I need to let this anger subside before I touch her.

Her eyes lift to mine, filled with a tender vulnerability, and everything else falls away. There is only us. Those who have gone before have been erased, and there will never be another.

I want her with a passion so fierce, so all-consuming, but before I touch her, I need her to spell it out for me. I need complete assurance that we want the same thing.

"And what is it that you want from me?"

"I want to be your submissive, Master Fitzgerald... if it pleases you. For as long as it pleases you."

Sweeter words have never been spoken. Words that bring light to my shadow of a soul.

"Stand up... let me look at you."

I take her hand and help her to her feet, leading her to the center of the room. Her body moves with fluid ease. Every step an elegant dance, a joy to behold. As she stands with her hands clasped behind her back, I walk around her, slowly memorizing the way she looks in this moment. Her legs, her tight little ass in those lace panties. The way her Basque pushes her breasts together, making them fuller and more curvaceous. Her hair cascades down her back, and there's a sweet flush on her cheeks.

"You look stunning this evening. Even more beautiful than I envisaged." I trail my fingers down her arm, goosebumps following in their wake.

"Are you nervous?"

"Not at all, Master Fitzgerald." The confidence I see reflected in her dark brown gaze is so fucking hot.

"You may simply call me Master, tonight." I lean in close to her ear, letting her scent me as I do the same, and I can't help darting my tongue out for one small lick of her neck. "Are you ready for me?"

I nibble at her earlobe, her body shuddering at my touch. Her reply is a broken, breathy plea. "Yes... oh God, yes, Master."

"Then I won't deny you any longer. Get on the table and lie on your back." Without hesitation, she climbs onto the table with feline grace. I place the flogger down beside her, freeing my hands to bind hers.

Soft leather cuffs have been anchored at each corner, easily adjustable so I can afford her as much or as little movement as possible. Tonight, I need her restricted. She needs to understand the full extent of how commanding I intend to be when it comes to her pleasure. Everything up until this point has been a drop in the ocean of what I want from her... *with* her.

I slowly run my fingertips from the top of her arm, down the inside of her elbow, watching her body react to this smallest of touches. When I reach her wrist, I grasp her tight and pull her arm up and into the restraint. The black leather and bright silver metal cuffs are stunning on her. I repeat the process with her other arm, her sensitivity to my touch making me hard as steel.

With her hands tethered tight above her head, I trail my fingers down the center of her chest, over her Basque, dipping them under the edge to feel her nipples turning to tight little rosebuds as I flick each one in turn, giving her just a taste of the attention she craves before making my way lower. I gently caress every inch of her body, except where she wants it most, before cuffing each of her ankles, spreading her legs wide, opening her to my gaze, my touch, and my every desire.

She looks so fucking beautiful in here. I take a step back to admire her, to stare in awe and wonder at the goddess before me. I have played this scenario over and over in my mind over the years. A fantasy that I never thought would become a reality.

She is completely at my mercy... willingly... freely.

Her eyes follow my every move as I make my way over to the cabinet by the door, removing a purple silk scarf from the top drawer and holding it up for her to see.

"This is all you're going to see for a while." I run the soft, delicate material from the tip of her toes, up the length of her body, letting it fall between her legs, teasing her, making her want it so badly that she'll do anything I ask of her.

"Lift your head." I place a tender kiss on her lips, holding her gaze before I cover her eyes. "Give yourself over to me tonight. Mind, body and soul. You won't regret it."

"Yes, Master."

I plunge her into darkness, heightening all of her other senses for what's to come.

I give her a moment to relax and enjoy this. I know that she'll relish this power play. She wants to submit, but sometimes her fierce nature gets in the way. I've removed that possibility tonight, and in doing so, have finally set her free. Free to explore her sexuality with me without responsibility, in a way she could never allow herself in any other situation. It will be my greatest pleasure to unleash her darkest desires and take her to her limits.

I pour a glass of champagne from the ice bucket I had Jacob set up for me earlier, and use the other glass to gather some ice, before placing both down on the table beside Vittoria's head. I want her to home in on the sound of the bubbles bursting against the side of the glass, tantalizing her senses with the possibilities.

I slowly and carefully open each and every clasp on the front of her Basque.

"You do look stunning in this, but you'll look even better when you're naked for me." With a flick of my fingers, the last clasp opens and I push the boned-lace lingerie away from her body, exposing her small, perky breasts.

"Lift."

She can only lift her body a centimeter or two off the table due to how tightly I fastened her restraints, but it's enough for me to pull the Basque from beneath her back and discard it on the floor. She is laid out with only her lace French knickers left to cover her nakedness. She looks so fucking hot, and I tease myself, and her, by leaving them on for a little while longer.

"What is your safe word, Nyx?"

"Hummingbird, Master."

"Good girl. Remember, as my submissive, you can say 'Humming-bird' at any time, and I will stop immediately. Tell me you understand."

"I understand, Master."

I take a sip of Champagne and hold it in my mouth, letting the bubbles fizz and explode on my tongue before dipping my head and clamping my mouth over her nipple, biting down ever so slightly as I let the liquid caress her skin, leaving it only a fraction of a second before I swallow and let the warmth of my tongue envelop her. Her body writhes beneath me, fighting against the restraints to push her breast further into my mouth.

The rush of power and adrenaline I feel is addictive. I want more. I lift my lips until they are a millimeter from her skin, and suck in a breath, causing a cold sensation on her nipple. Rewarded with a sharp inhale and her desperate groan for more, I smile against the heavy, soft, swell of her breast before turning my attention to the other nipple. I repeat the process, the constant change between hot and cold, wet and dry against her flesh, whipping her into a frenzy, tantalizing and teasing her until I can smell her arousal. I have to have a taste, even a small one... just for now.

I don't touch her, don't alert her to where my attention is drawn. I simply fill my mouth with Champagne, grab a cube of ice from the other glass and move down the table. I gently pull aside the lace of her panties, feeling how wet they are in anticipation of what I have planned. I run my nose up the length of her folds, scenting her, rock-fucking-hard in my pants at how phenomenal she is. I draw in a deep breath, eliciting a gasp from her before parting my lips, letting the crisp liquid bubble against her clit as I circle the tip of my tongue.

"Oh God... yes!"

I reluctantly lift my head.

"Did I say you could speak, Nyx?"

"No, Master." She can barely speak through her jagged breaths, and it is so fucking sexy.

"Well, I suggest you keep quiet then. I would really hate to have to deny you tonight. Your pussy is so damn sweet. I could eat you for hours, and if I have to deny myself that pleasure to punish you, then you'll most definitely regret it." I drag my tongue slowly from her soaking wet entrance, up through her folds and over her clit in one luscious lick. "Are you going to keep quiet until I tell you otherwise?"

"Yes. Yes, Master Fitzgerald."

"Good girl." I place the ice cube that's beginning to melt in my hand, into my mouth, before going down on her.

I hear her whimpers as she struggles to contain the screams my touch inspires, and it is so fucking hot. I glance up the length of her body, the contrast of hot and cold working to bring her to the edge of a mind-blowing orgasm. Her breasts are tight and her nipples hard. Her head is thrown back with the blindfold still in place. She's fighting against the restraints with her arms as she bites down hard on her lip.

I feel like my balls are going to explode when I pull away, leaving her frustrated and desperate for relief. So much of what gets me off is the anticipation. Of taking a woman's body to the point where she would beg for her release. With Vittoria, that feeling has only intensified. I've waited a very long time for tonight, and I plan to draw it out for as long as I can stand it, before I physically *need* to be inside her.

She writhes on the table as I walk over to the cabinet and quickly find what I'm looking for.

"Stop moving. I want you completely still for this next part." Her body relaxes immediately and I revel in how far she's come in the four weeks we've been together. Her submissive side is taking over again, and it's extremely satisfying to witness. It shows her growing level of trust.

I run my hand up the inside of her leg, letting the small length of metal in my hand graze her skin and pique her interest. When I reach the apex of her thighs, I grab hold of her over her pretty French knickers, cupping her tightly.

"This is mine now, to do with as I wish." As the last word leaves my lips, I rip her panties off and toss them aside, leaving her completely naked and on display. She is so fucking beautiful.

I spread her folds and tease her clit until its ready for the clamp I have resting in the palm of my hand. I lift it to my lips, coating it in saliva to help it slide over her tight little bud. Prying open the slim loop of metal, I feel the bite of it on my finger, sending a jolt straight to my dick, knowing how her body will react to this sensation. I position it carefully, making sure that I have it in just the right place to give her maximum pleasure. I let it go, both sides clamping together over her clit.

"Fuck!" She bucks off the table as much as her restraints will allow, unable to squeeze her legs together to alleviate the onslaught of sensation.

I pick up the flogger that rests beside her on the table and bring it down hard on her breasts. "I said don't move, and don't speak. You really are an unruly submissive, Nyx. I think you need a reminder of who is in control here." I bring the tight black leather down on her skin a second and third time, hitting her stomach and then her legs. "Are you going to behave?"

"Yes, Master."

"Good girl." I bring the flogger back down on her naked flesh, but this time I do it softly, trailing it over the areas that are red from her mild punishment.

She doesn't move, and she doesn't make a sound as I let the leather caress every inch of her skin. Every so often I hit her hard, watching as a contented look spreads across her features. I don't even need to see her eyes to know how much she loves this. It's written in every line, every curve, every muscle of her delectable body. She was born to be a submissive. I can see it now. She was born to be *my* submissive.

I want to climb on top of her and fuck her so hard she can't help but scream my name, but I'm not nearly done playing with her yet. I trail the flogger down between her legs, letting it move against her clamp, causing wave after wave of pleasure to course through her body. I can tell that she's close and I need to hear her scream in this room.

I crawl up onto the table between her legs, positioning myself so she can feel my breath against her skin as I speak.

"You can scream now. Let me hear you, baby."

I remove the clamp. "Oh my God, Master! Fuck!" I can't be gentle anymore.

I devour her pussy like a starving man, lapping up her juices, fucking her with my tongue, and it's only moments before she starts screaming my name.

"Master Fitzgerald! Yes... Yes... Master!" Her body pulls hard against the restraints as she finally finds her release, crashing over the edge into a euphoria that only an experienced Master can elicit. "Oh Fuck. Please... don't stop! Please... Master!" I couldn't stop if the room was on fire. The pulsing aftershocks of her orgasm, ripple against my tongue, making me harder than I've ever been.

I growl against her soft swollen flesh. "I'm just getting started."

I'm true to my word, kissing her, caressing her, letting her come down from her release, before I start working her back into a frenzy, and it doesn't take long. Her skin is sensitive to the slightest touch and her inability to curb the intensity of what she's feeling only quickens her release.

I don't stop until I feel that her body needs a rest to recover. I need her to come and come hard when I'm inside her. Her voice is hoarse and her body limp as I place a final kiss on her sweet little pussy, before looming over her body to begin loosening her cuffs.

My lips are almost touching hers as I speak. "Kiss me, Nyx. Taste how fucking beautiful you are."

She closes the gap, licking the seam of my lips before darting her tongue into my mouth. It's so sexy to hear her groans of satisfaction as she sucks on my tongue, relishing the taste of herself on my lips. I let her know exactly what she does to me, pressing my dick against her naked flesh, letting her feel how strained it is against the hard denim of my jeans.

I make short work of the cold metal buckles of her restraints against the warm leather. She doesn't move, letting me massage her wrists and ankles, taking my time with each one, enjoying the feel of her languid limbs under my fingertips.

I lift her from the table and walk over to the bed with her cradled in my arms, before slowly placing her on top of the covers. Her caramel skin is a stunning contrast to the deep purple sheets beneath her. I place a pillow underneath her head, positioning her at the right angle to see exactly what I'm doing.

I gently untie her blindfold and shove it in my pocket. It takes a moment for her to adjust to the dim lighting of the room, still too bright after an hour spent in complete darkness, but when her eyes find mine I am rendered speechless. I have never felt this way before, in this club… or ever when I'm with a woman. It excites me. It terrifies me.

I rip open the button-fly on my jeans, revealing the base of my cock, thick and straining to break free. I delight in the spark I see in her eyes at this mere glimpse. I don't take my eyes off of her as I slowly push the waistband down over my hips, letting them drop to the ground, leaving me completely naked and more than ready for her.

I kick my jeans to the side, taking my cock in hand. "Is this what you want, Nyx?"

"Yes, Master." The rapid rise and fall of her chest, and the breathy tone of her voice turns me on even more.

"Do you know why I removed your blindfold?"

"No, Master."

I crawl onto the bed, spreading her legs wide as I move between them, the realization of what is about to happen turning my adrenaline into an electrical current, fueling my desire to a level I've never experienced in my life. I take a deep breath before I speak, concerned that my authority is clouded by my need for her.

"I removed it because I want you to watch as I claim you. I want you to watch as I slide every hard inch of my cock inside you, making you mine. You will see our bodies join as one and remember how it makes you feel to see me pounding in and out of you. How I make your body sing with every sweet thrust of my cock inside your tight little pussy."

I kneel between her legs, taking my cock and guiding it to her slick entrance. The feel of her soft, warm skin against the tip of my dick is excruciatingly exquisite. "Do you want this, Nyx?"

"More than anything, Master."

I cover her body with my own, resting my elbows on either side of her. I can feel her heart beating wildly against my chest, her breasts pressed tightly against me as the length of our bodies connect. I slowly thrust the first few inches inside her, before pulling back and thrusting back in, but this time I make her take all of me until I'm seated to the hilt.

"Holy... Fuck! Jesus Christ, Vittoria. You feel so fucking good." I give her a moment to acclimate, to let her body adjust to being so completely filled by me before I begin to move. I lift my hand to cup her face, holding her gaze, showing her how significant this moment is. A moment that's been fated since the day we met, nine years ago.

"Who do you belong to?"

Her eyes are alight with love, devotion and submission as she responds. "You, Master Fitzgerald. I belong to you."

"That's right. Don't ever forget that *I'm* your Master. Your body is mine. Your pleasure is mine. Mine to give and mine to take away if you defy me. Do you understand?"

I hammer into her....

"Yes! Oh my God... yes!"

I thrust harder, lifting her legs onto my shoulders, allowing me to slide even deeper inside of her.

"Yes, who?"

I spank her ass so hard it makes my palm sting.

"Yes, Master."

I throw my head back in sheer animalistic lust and roar her name, before grabbing her hips and pounding into her.

"Vittoria... oh fuck... yes!"

With every circle of my hips and every thrust of my cock, she cries out, moaning my name as I take what is now mine.

She is mine. She will *always* be mine.

I can feel her walls tightening around me, and I know she won't be able to hold out much longer.

"Not yet. Your orgasm belongs to me."

I pick up the pace, slamming into her in a punishing rhythm, my balls slapping against her tight little ass,. When I feel the familiar pulse of my imminent release, I slip my hand down between our writhing bodies and circle her clit with my thumb.

"I want you to come with me. Let me feel how much you want it." I hammer into her, chasing my release, knowing that it's going to be so fucking intense. "Now, Vittoria. Come for me." She detonates like a bomb, an explosion of pure sensation. Her body tightens around me, milking my cock, catapulting me into my own release.

"Fuck! Holy shit! Yes... fuck! Vittoria!"

I ride it out, bucking wildly into her as she screams my name, her orgasm washing over her, again and again and again.

"Oh God... Master!"

I take her in a fierce kiss, swallowing her screams and keeping them for myself. She looks so fucking beautiful when she comes. To watch her climax while I'm inside of her is fucking transcendent.

We collapse in a heap, panting, caressing and kissing, completely sated. We lie in silence as I stroke her hair while she runs her fingers over the light dusting of hair on my chest.

"I love you, Master Fitzgerald."

"I love you, too, Nyx." She moves to pull the sheets over us.

"No. We're not staying here. I want you in my bed tonight."

Looking up at me, her eyes sparkle in the dim light of the play-room. "I've never been to your apartment."

I run my hand through her hair before grasping it tight and pulling her lips down to mine in a tender kiss. "Well it's time you get used to it. You'll be spending a lot of time there in the future. Now as reluctant as I am to say this... let's get you dressed."

She gives me a shy smile, which completely throws me off kilter. We've just shared something so amazing. She's given herself to me completely, and yet she can still be shy over something so seemingly inconsequential. "Yes, Master."

When we're dressed and ready to leave, I pull her into my arms, taking in the sight of the room around us. "Thank you."

"For what?"

"For tonight. For giving yourself to me. For letting me have the honor of being your Master."

I seal our departure with a kiss, take her hand in mine and leading her out into what feels like another world. The sights and sounds of Andromeda feel so different to me now. What we shared tonight went far beyond the reaches of this club, or my playroom. I contemplate that as we make our way to my apartment, my heart suddenly feeling heavy in my chest as I realize—Vittoria de Rossi has a power over me that no one in my life ever has. *She has the power to break me.*

This—us—just became something more. A living breathing entity that I don't have complete control over, and I never will....

CHAPTER 12

LOGAN

Six Weeks Later

I'VE KNOWN THIS DAY WAS COMING, BUT IN MY MIND I ENJOYED THE blissful ignorance of thinking we'd have longer together before this happened.

The past six weeks have been the most amazing of my life. Unfortunately, Vittoria had a set back with her injury, but the silver lining was that it gave her more time here with me, together with two weeks she already had scheduled off, and we've made the most of it. Three days after our first night in the playroom, Vittoria got a call from Lily. Carter and Addi decided to elope without telling anyone, and when Addi sent a message to Lily by accident, which was meant for Carter, it became a race against time for Xander and I to track them down and get our girls there in time for the ceremony. It was a crazy few days, exciting, comical, and hot as hell. We had so much fun together, and by the time we came home, she had a new sister-in-law. I'm so glad that I could be a part of it with her.

Watching Carter pledge himself to Addi, and seeing how happy they were, made me realize just how much I want it. Not necessarily marriage, I'm not even sure how Vittoria feels about that, but definitely the forever part. The highest honor a Dominant can bestow on his submissive, is to collar her. It's a definitive claim, a message to everyone else that she belongs to her Dominant, and more importantly, that he belongs to her. Vittoria's neck is far too elegant for a collar, and for me, it's not about showing everyone that she's mine. When the time comes, it will be about showing her how much she means to me, and my commitment to her—to us. I'll find another way to do it, without a collar—something for me to think about in the time we're apart.

Our relationship is stronger than ever, our bond as Master and sub, based on love, trust, and respect. The foundation of what we have, was built on a long history of friendship, and taking it slowly when we found each other again has been the best thing for us. At the time, I thought I might literally explode from the pent-up frustration that came from denying her. But, now I know that it was worthwhile. By the time we added sex to the mix, we were already past the point of no return. And the sex... holy fuck!

That first time in the playroom was unlike any other. Anyone will tell you that your first time with a new sexual partner is full of excitement, anticipation, lust and desire, and it's something I've always thrived on when training women to be submissives. Vittoria was something else entirely. Making love to her for the first time in there was... life-altering. Sex with her *means* something. It means everything. I now understand the phrase 'two become one.' Corny I know, but it's the truth. She is a part of me, and I carry her with me wherever I go. I thought that concept was a fairytale, an unrealistic expectation created by Disney to disappoint every girl in the world, when they grow up and realize it doesn't exist. But, I was wrong. It does exist, in the form of a tiny dancer, a fierce lover, my friend and submissive. I really am a lucky son of a bitch... although, it doesn't feel like it today.

Vittoria has been given the all-clear to start training, which is fantastic, but it also means she'll be flying out to rejoin the tour and start working with the physio to build her strength and get back to dancing full-time. I am so pleased for her, because I've seen the toll that this break has taken on her, and I know how much she loves ballet. It's her obsession—her addiction. But at the same time, I'm sad that the cocoon we've been living in for these past few months, this perfect life of a Master and his sub, is coming to an end. It won't be the same from now on, and it'll be months before we get to spend this length of time together again. It's been a gift and a curse. Knowing what I'm missing will make being on the road a lot harder.

I'll miss walking into the playroom at Andromeda to find her kneeling, ready and waiting for me. She is the perfect submissive in that room, she never falters, not even for a moment. She gives me her absolute trust and devotion, and I in turn reward her... over and over again, until she's limp in my arms, unable to walk out on her own two legs. I love the feel of her nestled in my arms, as I stride through the corridors, content that I've satisfied her in every way, before taking her home to the warmth and intimacy of my apartment. I'll miss lying down beside her and pulling her into my arms, listening to her breathing as it evens out and slows in peaceful slumber. I've become so accustomed to her. I don't know how I'll sleep without her beside me.

I'm supposed to start touring with the band next week, which I guess is a good thing. It's what I've been working toward for the past year of my life, and their new album is fantastic. They deserve this, and they deserve my full attention at such a crucial time in their career. I've been consumed with my desire for Vittoria over the past few months. Ever since she walked back into my life... she's become as necessary to me as the air I breathe. Our connection has become so much deeper, so much more profound. I've always loved her, but it's only now that I've really been able to spend time with her alone, and explore every facet of who she is, that I realize just how in love with her I really am.

She is everything to me, and the thought of us being on different continents for weeks or even months on end gives me a physical pain in my chest. How am I supposed to be a good Master when I'm not in the same country, when I can't adequately assess her wants and needs? She is so excited to get back to what she loves, what her body craves, but I can also see her internal struggle. She has the same concerns as I do. She's worried that the distance will tear us apart.

I've been wracking my brain over the past few days, thinking of ways to make this easier for her. I already know it's going to almost kill me being away from her for so long. Not being able to touch her, to feel her come apart beneath me... will be hell on earth. She's like a drug. The moment I got that first real taste of her in the playroom, my first real hit, I knew she would be a lifelong addiction for me.

It was hard when we first tried to stay in touch long distance, only talking via text and calls. FaceTime is great, but it doesn't even come close to being in the same room together. Something happens when we share the same space. The air around us becomes charged with lust, desire, love, and passion. It's an emotional and physical reaction that sparks inside of me.

I have a copy of her schedule over the next few months and have been trying to find days when I could visit her or have her flown out to see me, but it's not looking good. On paper, it looks like we're going to be missing each other by a day or so whenever I'm within traveling distance of her. I haven't told her yet, because I think it would be harder for her to say goodbye today if she knew that it might be months before we see each other again.

THE AIRPORT IS ALIVE WITH THE PEAKS AND TROUGHS OF TRAVEL. PEOPLE running into each other's arms as they're reunited after days, weeks, or months apart—family, friends, and lovers. The other side of the coin, the one that I'm on, are the people who cling to each other, taking one last embrace, one last kiss, remembering how it feels and holding onto it as their bodies part. Their fingers touch until the space between them is too great. The airport is a melting pot of emotion, and for me, it's becoming synonymous with Vittoria.

I wait as she checks her bags, drinking in every detail of the way she looks—her hair, her lips, her eyes fighting back tears as she walks over to me with her boarding pass in hand.

"I don't want to leave you." She wraps her arms around my neck, burying her head against my chest.

"I know. I don't want you to leave either, but this is what you've been working toward, what you've been desperate for. You need to dance. It's who you are, and I would never try to stop you or hold you back."

She lifts her head, looking up into my eyes with so much love. "And that's why I love you so much, Master Fitzgerald." A mischievous grin spreads across her face, and I know she's remembering what it felt like to scream my name in ecstasy before we left for the airport. Hogtied and spanked and loving every minute of it as she begged her Master for more. I can still taste her on my lips as we stand here in a sea of people, no one suspecting that her ass is a pretty shade of red right now. Her nipples are puckered with little plastic clamps I placed on them in the elevator of my building on the way here. I told her not to remove them until she gets to her hotel, and only when she has me on FaceTime to watch. It's a twisted kind of torture, for her and for me, but I wanted her to have a reminder as she travels so far from me today. I am her Master, and no matter where she is or how many miles are between us, I control her pleasure and her pain.

"Enjoying being a tease, Miss de Rossi? Two can play at this game. Remember that as you sit on the plane today, the engines vibrating through your body, sending sensual shocks to your beautifully pert... clamped nipples. Remember it when your panties become wet with your own arousal, and I'm not there to alleviate the discomfort." The groan my words elicit causes my pants to tighten and I thrust my groin against her thigh, letting her know exactly what her little noises do to me. I'll be dealing with my own discomfort while she's gone. "We better get you to where you need to be. As much as I would love for you to miss your flight and come home with me to my bed, I need to do what's best for you. Come on..." I grab her hand and navigate through the crowds, slowly making my way toward the security gate. The point of no return. and the moment when I have to watch her leave... again. At least this time, I know she's coming back to me, and that she is mine.

When the sign comes into view, I tighten my grip, my body reacting to our imminent separation, making me feel physically sick at the thought of it. My steps slow almost to a standstill, stalling for more time. I can't look at her, because if I do, I know what I'll see— tears, fears, and more emotion than I can handle. So I continue to walk, repeating the words over and over in my head, 'I am in control. I am her Master. Show no weakness, only strength.' I must have said it to myself twenty times when we find ourselves at the entrance to security, the board beside us mocking me.

PASSENGERS ONLY BEYOND THIS POINT

She turns in my arms, a quiet sob breaking free, causing my heart to fall into my stomach. I cup her face in my hands, wiping her tears as I lower my lips to hers. It's not a frantic kiss, but a gentle one, filled with passion and understanding. I savor the feel of her tongue caressing mine and the softness of her lips as they press against my own.

When I finally pull back, I'm fighting to keep my composure, forcing myself to remain strong for her. "Don't cry. We'll be together again soon. I promise. And, in the meantime, I want you to take it easy and do as the physio says. Don't push yourself too hard." I rain tiny kisses all over her face in my attempts to calm her. "Let yourself enjoy every minute. Don't be sad, and remember, no matter where you are. You. Are. My. Nyx. My goddess above all others. I am your Master, and I expect you to behave as such. You will obey my commands and know that you are always my priority." I hold her gaze, entreating her to understand the gravity of what I'm saying. "Do you understand?"

"Yes, Master Fitzgerald."

"I love you, Vittoria. More than life itself. I always have and I always will."

She holds me as tight as her arms will let her, leaving no space between us. "I love you, too. So much it hurts."

"No more tears. This is a good day. You're healed and ready to get back to what you love, what you were born to do. I'll see you soon. Now go, before I change my mind and take you home."

We share one last kiss, before she turns and walks through the gate, getting further and further away from me. I stand for a moment, watching her disappear from sight, feeling almost winded by her departure, like a part of me has gone with her—my heart.

After a few minutes, I pull myself together and start to weave my way through the crowds and out of the airport, heading home to my empty apartment. I need to get organized for my own departure next week. The Flaming Embers' debut tour.

Two Months Later

We've been on the road now for two months, and the boys are killing it night after night. The crowds love them, and they love the crowds. Word is spreading about how amazing they are live, especially for first timers. It's exactly what I was hoping for, and the media attention and interview requests are starting to roll in thick and fast. I've been preparing for this for months, and I'm ready to take them to the next level, but I'm not sure if all of them are quite ready for that leap. It's going to change their lives forever. What they have now is new and exciting, but it's theirs. This next step will take that away from them, and they'll have to share this success with the world, opening themselves up to scrutiny and judgment, and the pressures that come with it. I know they're going to be huge. I can feel it, and no one deserves it more than Campbell McCabe.

The show was amazing tonight, and as the backstage aftermath begins to calm, and the groupies leave with various band members, I find a quiet spot to sit with Campbell's guitar and play for a while. I'm nowhere near the player I used to be, but I'm good enough for my ears only. I'm tired of drunk girls trying to bed me, explaining night after night that I'm not interested because I have a girlfriend. Calling her that seems so trivial, and doesn't begin to describe what we are, but I'm not about to start explaining it to some slutty college girls. Instead, I politely decline their advances and go in search of somewhere quiet, which I've managed to find in this venue.

Since we started the tour, I've found myself becoming immersed in the music again, not just the managerial logistics of it all. The last time I picked up a guitar or wrote a song was years ago. I was too bitter back then to find enjoyment in it, but now that I'm in a better place in my life, I've started writing again. I can't play for long periods of time, but when I do, it's an amazing feeling, and right now I'm working on something I started writing for Vittoria.

As I sit with the guitar in my lap and a pencil in my hand, jotting down ideas and chord progressions, singing the lyrics I have so far, I sense movement behind me.

"Holy fuck, Logan! You kept that a secret."

I turn to see Campbell standing in the doorway with a shit-eating grin on his face. "No secret, just messing around."

"Bullshit! You're a talented bastard and you know it. You've got a better voice than me."

"Stop kissing my ass, I already got you a record deal. Are you drunk? Stupid question, of course you are. Great show tonight, you guys killed it."

He strides toward me with all the rock star swagger of a seasoned pro. "Aye, we were alright. I missed a few riffs here and there. Felt like a right bawbag. It was so fuckin' hot on stage, I was sweatin' like a rapist at confession."

"What the hell is a 'bawbag?'" I'm still getting used to his... way with words, but he makes me laugh on a daily basis.

"Sorry, mate. I keep forgettin' to cut out the slang. A bawbag is yer testicles. Sure, I'm a modern-day Shakespeare!" He grabs two beers from the mini fridge in the room and holds one out to me. "I dinnae want to drink alone. Join me?"

"Sure, why not. It's not like I have anywhere else to be." I take the bottle, twist off the cap, sending a shooting pain through my hand after only an hour of playing the guitar, which really pisses me off. I take a long swig of my beer before setting the guitar down and slumping back into my seat.

"So, what's your story, big man? You've got a voice any front man would kill for, an' you're flexin' yer hand wae a grimace on yer face. I'm no Sherlock Holmes, but I'm guessin' an old injury?"

"You're a perceptive guy, Campbell. Yeah, I injured it over a decade ago, and it ruined my chances of doing what you do."

"What happened? Tell me tae mind ma ain business if I'm bein' a nosey bastard, but you look like you could use a friend, and you might be our manager, but I consider us friends, too."

I don't know if it's his open personality, or the fact that I'm missing Vittoria so badly, but I find myself talking before it dawns on me—he's the first person I've ever told this story to.

"When I was eighteen, I had it all at my fingertips. I'd just finished school, with no intention of going to college. I had a band, guys I'd grown up with, who knew how much of an escape music was for me. I had an agent, Derek, who was in the process of finalizing the paper-work on a record deal for us, when he started dating my mom." I take another long swig before I continue. "My mom never did have great taste in guys. My dad was a deadbeat drug dealer, who skipped out on us when I was eight years old. We were better off without him, but he left behind some angry associates who came looking for him. Instead of getting rid of them, my mom started dating a long string of losers, each one worse than the last. I thought when she shacked up with Derek, that she'd finally found a decent guy. It wasn't ideal with him being my manager, but he assured me it wouldn't affect my deal."

My hands begin to shake as I relive what happened that night. The night that changed the course of my life.

"I came home one Friday night from a party at my girlfriend's house. Her parents were out of town for the weekend, and the drinks were flowing. I was more than a little drunk by the time I stumbled through the front door, into what looked like a war zone. The living room was completely trashed, and at first I thought we'd been robbed, until I heard them in the kitchen. My mom was screaming at Derek to calm down, and he was calling her every name under the sun. I ran through the living room ready for a fight, but nothing could have prepared me for what I found. Her face was black and blue down the right side, her eye almost entirely swollen shut."

"Fucking hell, man. That's brutal. I know... from experience." I can see that he's telling the truth, the same haunted look in his eyes.

"I saw red. Blind-fucking-fury. I tackled him to the ground, punching him square in the jaw before he even knew what was happening. I might have been taller than him, but he was twice my size and obviously had experience in beating the crap out of people, especially women. I was shouting at him to get the hell out of our house as we grappled on the kitchen floor, my mom screaming in the background that I should mind my own business. Can you believe that? I was the bad guy for defending her."

"I'm sorry, Logan. That's fucked up."

"Yeah, it is. I got distracted by her screaming, shocked that she was blaming me. I didn't see it coming. He was fast, and I was too dazed to notice that he was up on his feet, towering above me. He raised his dirty biker boot and slammed it down full force on my left hand, breaking twenty-two of the twenty-seven bones, and ending my career in a single blow." I can feel the bile rise in throat at the memory. "I'll never forget the pain, it was agonizing, and I knew immediately, that I'd never be able to play the same again. We didn't exactly have great health insurance. A basic fix was all I got, so now, I can barely play for an hour without my hand becoming sore. It's been years since I last played anything." I watch as Campbell rubs his hand, an unconscious response from one guitar player to another. He understands how soul destroying it would have been for me, but he doesn't speak, he just sits back and waits for me to finish. "He told me to kiss my deal goodbye, and that no one in the industry would touch me after I'd 'assaulted' him. That was the last time I saw him, and my mom never forgave me for it, for loving her enough to stand up for her. I lost everything I'd ever wanted, and for my troubles, I also lost my mom. These days we tolerate each other when necessary, but I moved out as soon as I got out of hospital, and I never looked back. She's had an endless stream of loser boyfriends, except now she's learned to prey on the rich and gullible. I paid my own way through college holding down three jobs at a time to pay my tuition. Eventually, I found my way back to the music business, even if it was in a different way than I'd hoped for. I get to be everything Derek should have been to me. I harness talent and *help* people like you to achieve the success you deserve. It took me a long time to come to terms with it, but now I love my job, and my life is pretty amazing, so I can't complain."

He blows out a long breath, scrubbing his hand over the scruff on his face. "I had nae fuckin' idea. I thought you were some rich kid who had it all. You're so... you've really got yer shit together, an' you're no' even thirty yet. It's amazin'. You're a fuckin' inspiration, man."

"Hardly. My 'shit' feels like it's all over the damn place. I like to be in control, and there are so many factors in my life that I seem to have zero control over. I've never missed someone the way I miss Vittoria. I know I sound like a pussy, but fuck it! I love her."

"The girlfriend?"

"Yeah."

"It's no' a pussy who admits to bein' in love. A man who ignores it an' denies it when he finds it is the real pussy. I want that. Tae love a lassie so much that I'd fuckin' die for her. Someone I'd gie it all up in a heartbeat for. I want a woman to write a song for, like the one you were playin' when I came in. I'm no' ashamed tae admit it, an' neither should you. Guys who cannae admit it are arseholes."

"How did you get so wise? You're only twenty-one."

He gives a hearty, raspy laugh before his face sobers and his tone becomes serious. "When you've seen what I've seen, you age well beyond yer years. Where I grew up, yer no' long a bairn. Childhood was a luxury in ma neck o' the woods. Music was my escape, an' turns out, it was ma savior."

"What happened?"

"That's a story for another night, an' a lot more booze. I think it's time we get the fuck out o' here an' get some shut-eye. The boys are off thinkin' wae their cocks the now, so I willnae be waitin' around for them."

"Tell me they're intelligent enough to be safe. We don't need to be dealing with an influx of Ember babies nine months from now."

"Aye, they're no' that daft. They're a shower o' clatty bastards, the lot o' them, but none o' them want to be raisin' weans any time soon. Cloak it before you poke it is our motto!"

"And you?"

"I've got ma sights set on other things in life at the minute. I'm no' interested it chasing tail the now. At least, no' the easy ones! Know what I mean? There's nae fun if there's nae chase!"

"I know *exactly* what you mean. Tori gave me a run for my money, and she was worth it, a thousand times over."

"Then, let's go back tae the hotel. A quick dram at the bar an' then you can call your girl an' tell her that."

"Sounds like a plan."

Campbell grabs his guitar and we head out to hail a cab to take us back to our hotel. He's quickly becoming a real friend, and someone I have the utmost respect for, even if I don't always understand what he's saying to me in his thick Scottish brogue.

When I finally get back to my room, I take his advice and call the girl of my dreams, her voice soothing the nightmares that threaten to envelop me. It's been a long time since I relived that night, and the pain in my hand is a reminder of what I lost. I drift into a fitful sleep with the dulcet tones of my submissive pledging her love to me fresh in my mind, and her love prevails. The nightmares of relived memories are kept at bay by a goddess who leads me to happier memories, an enchantress who soothes my soul... my Nyx.

PARIS

VITTORIA

Two Months Later

He's here.

My dressing room already feels smaller.

I could feel him tonight. I could sense him in the auditorium. Every move I made, every dance step—was for him. The pain was gone, for the first time in months. My focus was solely on the knowledge that his eyes were burning into me, watching me... loving me.

I've been aware of him at every performance he's ever attended, even when I didn't know he was coming. But now that my body is so attuned to his, it's a physical tether between us.

I drink in the sight of him after four months apart, and he looks even more handsome than I remember. My heart is pounding in my chest, my breath hitching at the sly grin that spreads across his deliciously full lips.

He stands in the doorway, his arm resting on the frame above him. He's wearing a three-piece suit—black with a pinstripe. The jacket is a perfect fit, the waistcoat clinging to his ripped physique, his shirt opened at the collar exposing just a smattering of hair. It's sexy as hell, and I let my eyes travel lower. I can feel my nipples pucker under my dressing gown at the sight of him, hard and straining against his pants. My core tightens at the memory of how phenomenal it feels when every long, thick, hard inch of him is inside me. The delirious, pleasurable pain that comes when he hits the very deepest parts of me.

"What's going on in that beautiful head of yours?"

My eyes dart up to meet his. He has the most stunning smile—sexy, smoldering, and dripping with the promise of the most divine sin. It touches his eyes, making them sparkle with an intensity unlike anything I've ever seen before. They are the deepest blue with a ring of green around the center, and they call to me on a molecular level, drawing me in, entreating me to see myself through them.

His hair is longer than the last time I saw him, styled to messy perfection, just screaming for me to grab hold and pull. He looks every inch the dark and dangerous Dominant I know him to be.

"I asked you a question, Nyx. Have you forgotten how this works? If I don't get an answer, you'll be bent over that vanity so fast it'll make your head spin, and I'll make sure your ass matches that sexy red lipstick you're wearing."

The sight of him has me in a trance, the edge in his voice snapping me out of it. "I'm sorry, Master Fitzgerald. I was thinking about how hot you look in that suit, and how badly I've missed feeling every glorious inch of you inside me, claiming me as yours."

"I'm glad to see you haven't lost your dirty little mouth. Don't worry, my sweet submissive, I'll make sure you get what you want. Now get over here and give your Master a kiss. It's been four months, and I don't think I can wait a moment longer."

"And why would I do that when you promise such fun if I refuse? The vanity sounds too enticing for words."

A sexy, mischievous grin spreads across his face and he's on me in seconds, his strong hands snaking around my waist, pulling me effort-lessly up and into his arms. Our lips collide in an earth-shattering kiss, his tongue forcing entry into my mouth, claiming me with primal desire. His touch is raw and rough, and yet he always handles me with such tenderness. It's a heady juxtaposition of sensations that drive me wild.

He spins us around, one arm holding me, the other sweeping everything off my vanity, clearing space for him to set me down. He breaks our kiss just long enough to rip my robe off my shoulders, exposing my naked flesh to his hungry gaze. "Fuck, I've missed you so goddamn much. I can't wait. I need you, now."

"I'm yours."

He bites down on my shoulder. "I know."

I loosen his belt and push his pants down just enough for him to spring free. His hands and lips are everywhere as he takes me with one hard thrust. It's euphoric! We lose ourselves in whispered words of love and screams of passion, bringing us back to each other after so long apart.

When we're sated and soothed, he pulls me close, holding me for the longest time. I savor the smell of him and how safe I feel in his arms. It's the first time in months that I've felt calm—like all is right in the world—in my world. "I'm so glad you're here. I can't even explain how much I've missed you."

"You don't have to explain. I feel the same way. I've never been so happy to see someone in my entire life!"

I chuckle, taking in the sight of my dressing room. "Yeah, I can see that by the carnage surrounding us." My makeup is all over the floor, broken and smeared on the carpet. The mirror is covered in Logan's handprints, and the imprint of my hair glitter from the performance is all over the glass.

He looks around, laughing along with me at how we've destroyed the room in our eagerness to reconnect. "Holy shit! What can I say? When I have to have you... I *have* to have you."

"You'll get no complaints from me, but dinner will have to wait until I've cleaned all of this up."

I drop to my knees, gathering all the items that were swept from my vanity in the heat of the moment, but Logan grabs my hand and pulls me to my feet. "As much as I love to see you naked on your knees, I don't want you doing it to clear up a mess I've made. There's only one reason to be on your knees in front of me, and now is not the time, unfortunately. I'll make sure this gets sorted, but for now, I want you to get dressed so I can take you out and feed you."

"Yes, Master Fitzgerald."

"God, you make me hard when you say that."

I lick my lips seductively, running my hands down my body as I turn to fetch my dress from the closet. It's like a red rag to a bull, and he takes me again, hard and fast and oh so delicious, before we finally get dressed and head out to dinner.

Logan's been here for half a day but has somehow managed to get us a reservation at one of the most prestigious restaurants in Paris. It's incredible—the food, the wine, and the company. I don't want to mention it, but my ankle is really hurting after tonight's performance. If I did, he would cancel dinner and have me resting back at the hotel. I won't let our small window of time be ruined by my stupid body refusing to heal. I'm managing to keep it under control with painkillers, and it'll have to do for now. I don't want Logan to find out, so I wait until he goes to the restroom to down a few tablets with my glass of wine. When he returns to the table, he has news.

"I have a surprise for you while I'm here in Paris."

"I love surprises! But I'm just so glad you're here, I don't care what we do or where we go."

He takes my hands in his across the table, sending a jolt of desire straight to my core. I've been starved of his touch for so long, even the smallest caress is like manna in the dessert.

"I've been asked to do a shibari Master class at Club Désir tomorrow night. I told them that I would have to confirm once I'd spoken to my submissive. What do you think? Would you like to be my muse and let me work you into a piece of art? More beautiful than anything in the Louvre."

His voice is so commanding and sincere, I couldn't possibly refuse him, even if I wanted to. It's an honor to have a Master such as Logan demonstrate something as intricate and specialized as shibari on me.

"I would love that. It's been so long since we've been to Andromeda together. I miss it."

He moves his thumbs across my knuckles, leaving a tingling sensation on my skin. "I'm glad. I've missed it, too. I've missed seeing you ready and waiting for me, and seeing you shackled in chains on my cross. I've arranged for us to have a private room after the demonstration, because I'm not sure I'll be able to wait to get you back to the hotel."

"Sounds perfect."

"You're perfect." He always says the sweetest things without making them sound clichéd or cheesy. Something in his voice makes it sound so sexy and... honest.

"And you're quite the smooth talker."

"Just being honest. Now enough about me, I want to know what's been going on with you. How is your ankle now that you're back dancing full-time?"

I don't want to lie to him, but I know he'll worry about me if I tell him how much it still hurts. I haven't told the physio either. He wouldn't let me dance if he knew how much pain I'm in every night. It almost killed me taking time away from it before. I can't do it again. I've been managing my own pain, visiting doctors in every city to get prescriptions for Vicodin. I can't let the ballet company doctor find out about it. He works closely with the physio and they would have me replaced in a heartbeat. If I time it properly, I can get through the full performance without any adverse effects on my dancing ability. But within an hour of the curtain going down, I can barely stand. I took a few extra pills tonight to make sure Logan doesn't see that happen. I should be able to make it back to the hotel and rest up for tomorrow without it becoming too much for me.

"Earth to Vittoria. Did you hear me? Or am I boring you already?"

I was so busy thinking about my deception, I forgot to answer the question. "Sorry. Of course you're not boring me. I'm just exhausted after the performance, followed by your... *performance* in my dressing room. Throw in some sparkling wine, and I'm feeling a little out of it."

"I'll get the check and we can go. My ballerina needs her rest, and as always, your wellbeing is my primary concern, my beautiful Nyx."

As promised, Logan settles the bill and leads me out of the restaurant to hail a cab back to the hotel. I must have misjudged my pills, or the alcohol is affecting me more because of them, because I barely make it out of the door before my ankle gives way and I lose my footing. Logan reacts at lightning speed, taking my weight and pulling me close. "Are you okay? Is it your ankle?" He scoops me up into his arms as we wait for the valet to get us a cab, and all I want to do is cry. I want to confess everything to him, but I can't.

"Just too much Champagne and heels that are way too high."

"Are you sure? You'd tell me if it was your ankle, wouldn't you?"

He looks at me, staring into my soul as I lie to his face. "Of course." My heart drops into my stomach as I nestle against his warm chest, hanging my head in shame. I haven't seen him in four months, my Master, the love of my life, and yet here I am lying to him. I'm a self-fulfilling prophecy. I've always known that I'm not good enough for him, that my darkness would taint his goodness. But instead of fighting it, I'm making it a reality and I hate myself for it.

He spends the rest of the night taking care of me. After lifting me in and out of the cab, he carries me up to our hotel room. He fills the tub, washing every inch of me with such sweet tenderness, before putting me to bed and crawling in beside me. I fall asleep content for the first time in months—four months to be exact. My nightmares subside, and the physical pain I feel in my waking hours fades into insignificance, wrapped in the arms of the man I love.

"Are you ready to leave for Désir?"

"Yeah. I'm a little nervous. I've never been outside of a playroom before."

Logan pulls me into his arms, his scent soothing my anxiety. "I spoke to the Master of the club last night. I laid down the ground rules for having us in the main hall. I told him that you will not be naked. I can show them everything they need to know without them seeing you like that. You're mine, and the thought of anyone seeing what's mine makes me so angry I can hardly breathe."

"Thank God! I would have done as you asked, but I really didn't want to be completely naked in front of all those people."

"Why didn't you tell me? Remember the rules. You need to let me know your limits. It's the only way I can protect you and make sure I'm not pushing you past what you can handle."

I plant a soft kiss on his lips. "I'm sorry. It's been so long since we've been together and I wanted to please you. We've had such a wonderful day today, talking and walking, and just being together. I didn't want to ruin it with a clinical discussion of hard limits."

He cups my face in his large, warm hands, forcing me to look at him. "*Nothing* between us is clinical, Nyx. Not ever."

"I love you."

"I love you, too." He holds me close, stroking his hands up and down my back until my body relaxes, melting into his strong, broad frame. I breathe in his masculine scent, letting it wash over me, giving me the confidence to go through with tonight. "I explicitly told the club that it is a view-only class. No one is allowed to touch you or participate in any way. It's just you and me. All you have to do is focus on me. My voice. My hands on your body." I let out a breath I didn't know I was holding, the tension leaving my body. "Vittoria." He pulls away, holding my shoulders with his hands, staring at me, looking for answers. "You've been worried about this. I can cancel. I don't want you doing anything that makes you uncomfortable. That's why I wanted to ask you first. You can't lie to me. I know it's been hard, us being apart, but I'm your Master, and you need to respect that at all times, distance or not. Do you understand me?"

"Yes, Master Fitzgerald."

"Good girl. So, what do you want to do? Do you want me to cancel? I can perform my Master class for your eyes only. It's well worth seeing!"

"I'm sure it is… and that's why I want to go with you. You're so talented. I've seen your work before. I stood in the back at one of your demonstrations in New York. It was breathtaking and heartbreaking. I wanted it to be me."

"I'm so sorry."

I caress his face with my hand, touched by his sentiments. "You have nothing to be sorry about. I chose not to tell you back then. I wanted to, but I was scared. Don't ever be sorry for who you are. I love everything about you, and without your past you wouldn't be the man standing before me. The man I've fallen head over heels in love with."

"What did I do to deserve you?"

I lower my gaze, uncomfortable at the thought of him putting me on a pedestal. "I'm the lucky one." His lips find mine, erasing all of my worries and insecurities, surrounding me with love and acceptance.

"Are you sure about this? About, the demonstration?"

"Yes. I'm sure. I trust you. Let's go. I'm desperate to be bound by you, Master Fitzgerald."

We leave for the club, hand in hand, full of anticipation for the night ahead. I'm still apprehensive about being so vulnerable in a room full of strangers, but I want to do this for him, and for myself. I won't live the rest of my life in the shadow of my own fear.

THE DÉCOR IS SUMPTUOUS AND INVITING, THE PRIVATE ROOMS FULLY equipped with everything a submissive could ever want for a night of extreme pleasure and pain at the hands of her Dom. The main hall has been set up for the demonstration with a leather table in the center and the ropes that will bind me, resting on top.

Seeing the way Logan commands the room is such a turn-on. Every nerve ending in my body is alive with desire, the anticipation of his touch causing butterflies to swarm in my stomach. He takes my hand in his, pulling me into his side.

"Are you ready, Nyx?"

"Yes, Master Fitzgerald. I'm ready."

He leads me through the crowd and over to the table. I can feel my hands shaking.

"Take off your robe." I do as he asks, the eyes of everyone around us focused on me. I drop the robe to the floor, letting it pool at my feet.

My Master has me dressed in a stunning outfit this evening, tailored specifically for me, and conducive to what he wants to do with the ropes. I'm wearing deep purple, satin ballet shoes, with jewel encrusted ribbons that he tied in the most intricate, striking knots, up over my ankles and twisting around my calves. They complement the deep purple lace panties I'm wearing, perfectly. I have a fitted minia-ture tutu, unlike anything I've ever worn before—sexy and sensual, and perfect for me. Instead of a bra, he has chosen a lace effect body art that covers my now tightly budded nipples, tapering off to the sides in an elegant swirling pattern. I catch a glimpse of myself in the mirrors on the far side of the room. I look... beautiful. I feel beautiful.

"You are stunning. Absolutely breathtaking." He places a gentle kiss on my lips, sending a shiver down my spine. "Will you dance for me while I prepare the ropes for you?"

"Yes, Master Fitzgerald." He nods in the direction of the DJ, and the music blaring through the speakers stops. Désir is momentarily plunged into silence, before something familiar starts playing. It's *Tempo di Valse* from Act One of *Swan Lake*.

He leans down, his lips brushing against my ear. "Don't look at anyone but me. You're mine, Nyx. Every magnificent inch of you is mine."

My breathing is heavy and erratic as he lifts the ropes in front of him, his eyes never leaving mine as I begin to dance for him... only for him.

I took enough painkillers to ensure that nothing we do tonight could hurt me, so I let myself go and enjoy the carefree feeling of dancing for my Master. I hear gasps in the crowd as I let the music guide me, but I don't see anyone but him. He's transfixed, his eyes hungry, brimming over with desire as he watches every move I make, his gaze lingering over my breasts as I caress my hands across my nipples. When the music fades, I bow before him and then assume my submissive position at his feet. The crowd is eerily silent, watching with bated breath.

"You may look at me." I am consumed with love for this man. He's everything to me. "Who do you dance for?"

"Only for you, Master Fitzgerald."

His hands are clasped behind his back. "I am honored. Truly." He slowly circles me, his familiar scent invading my senses. "Are you ready to be bound, Nyx?"

"Yes, Master Fitzgerald."

"What is your safe word?"

"Hummingbird, Master Fitzgerald."

"Good girl. Now stand up with your back facing me, and hold your arms outstretched behind you, crossed at the wrists." I follow his instructions, pressing my thighs together to alleviate the pressure of my own arousal. He reads even the subtlest movements of my body, speaking quietly enough that only I can hear him. "Your arousal is making me hard, little one. I can't wait any longer to get my hands on you." He grabs my hands and wraps the purple ropes around my wrists, rendering me helpless. The Master class begins.

His voice is bold and commanding as he addresses the crowd, who close in around us to better see my Master's work. "You should always begin your rope work by binding your submissive's wrists. That way, you have complete control over her body as you continue. Depending on their experience and level of discipline, you may also want to bind their feet. A simple line from the wrists down to the ankles would suffice, and repeat the knotting sequence I'm showing you now. The length of rope between can always be worked into the design. In this case, Nyx is a disciplined and obedient submissive, who does not require her feet to be bound at this early stage. Instead, I will incorporate that into my chosen design later in the demonstration."

The juxtaposition of the unforgiving rope and the gentle caress of his fingers on my skin as he works, has my senses at a fever pitch. I can feel my panties growing wet as he works the ropes around my breasts, tying the most beautiful and intricate knots, showcasing every line and curve to perfection. He frames the lace body art around my nipples, integrating them into the design. I know he can feel my breasts, heavy with desire and desperate for his touch.

I stand still, letting him work around me, his brow furrowed in concentration. He stands back to look at the design so far, advising the crowd that you need to check your design periodically for symmetry and aesthetics. He's sweating from the intensity of his work and the heat in here, unbuttoning his shirt and throwing it under the table. I can see the women in the crowd, greedily ogling his naked chest, his broad shoulders and exquisitely toned abs, tapering down to the most mouth-watering V that dips below the waist of his pants. I want to claw their eyes out, and I know he can sense my unease.

He closes the gap between us and whispers in my ear as he picks up the ropes. "It's all for you, Nyx. For your hands, your lips, and your pleasure. No one else's. Not ever."

I smile up at him, my heart swelling in my chest. I'm so proud to call him Master.

When he completes the knots on my chest, abdomen, and down my arms which are securely fixed behind my back, he lifts me up into his arms. I relish the momentary intimacy of our contact before he lowers me onto the table.

"Are you comfortable enough?"

"Yes, Master Fitzgerald."

"I'm going to turn you over onto your front in a moment but let me know if you get too sore lying on your hands. You have permission to interrupt me with your safe word if you need to. Understood?"

"Yes, Master Fitzgerald."

He returns his focus to the class. "Once you are done with the top half, it's best to lay your submissive down to finish working on their lower half. With their hands tied behind their back, they could become unsteady on their feet, and also, it gives you the freedom to position their legs to fit your design. For instance, hogtying allows for some very delicate and complex knots. That is how I'm going to bind my sub, this evening. It's one of the more difficult techniques, so I'll take it slow, but please come as close as you can and pay attention."

I feel slightly claustrophobic when everyone moves in to watch him work. He gently wraps his arms around me and flips me onto my front. "Pull your feet up to your hands." I do as he asks, enjoying the feel of his warm hands caressing the length of my legs.

"Most submissives are not as flexible as Nyx, so you will have to adjust your work to accommodate your own sub's physical limitations." He catches hold of the rope that hangs from a knot around my belly button and is currently resting between my legs. A jolt of electricity shoots to my core when he pulls it tight against my folds, the friction of my panties and the rope pushing me to the edge of orgasm. He adjusts the rope, making sure it's positioned properly, pressing his fingers underneath my panties and down on my clit. He can feel how wet I am, and I delight in his sharp intake of breath as he lifts his fingers to his lips, licking them clean.

He continues winding the ropes around my legs, constantly checking that I'm comfortable and that the ropes aren't too tight. When he's finished, he moves me onto my side and stands back to admire his work, a look of awe in his eyes as he drinks in the sight of me.

The crowd applauds him, their eyes fixed on the beauty he's created on my body. I am desperate to come apart for him, to feel his body pressing down on mine as he takes me to the peak of ecstasy and pushes me over the edge.

"I'll give you a few minutes to study the placement of the knots, and the different design options I've displayed for you this evening, before I take my leave and reward Nyx for her participation tonight." He takes a step back and is immediately accosted by at least half a dozen Dominants with questions about shibari. He keeps me in his sights the entire time, holding my gaze, reassuring me as some observers move closer to study his work. I can feel my heart racing at the proximity of men I don't know. I lock eyes with my Master and breathe through my fears… and that's when it happens.

First one, and then another, start touching me. One is running his hands over the ropes around my torso. The other tracing the ropes up my thighs. I'm frozen in fear. I try to shout for him, but it comes out as a whisper. "Hummingbird." I find his eyes in the crowd. He can't see what they're doing, he can only see my face. "Hummingbird." I can't move, I can't defend myself. I'm terrified. I don't think he can hear me, but he can see the terror on my face. He immediately starts pushing through the crowd, his eyes almost black with rage.

"Hummingbird... Master... please! Hummingbird... Logan!"

CHAPTER 13

LOGAN

"WHAT THE FUCK DO YOU THINK YOU'RE DOING?" MY FIST CONNECTS with his face, the sound of his jaw cracking resounding in my ear. I spin around and jab the other guy so hard in the stomach that he drops to the floor, gasping for breath. "What the fuck is wrong with you? I will rip your fucking head off!" I throw another punch, catching the first guy in the ribs this time.

"She's mine, you worthless motherfucker! Do you hear me? You're not worthy to fucking look at her! How dare you lay a fucking finger on her!" When he stumbles back, trying to scramble away from me like the pathetic asshole he is, I turn my attention back to the other guy. But before I do any more damage, there is one thing, one emotion that trumps the rage I'm feeling in this moment, bringing me back to what's important… my love for Vittoria. She needs me, more than I need to exact revenge.

She's helpless and sobbing, screaming her safe word over and over, shouting my name in a plea for help. I push everyone out of the way and lift her into my arms. "I'm here, Nyx." She's still screaming, unaware that it's me. "Nyx, listen to the sound of my voice. It's me, baby. It's Logan." I pull her tight against my chest, her body going limp in my arms. "Vittoria... try to focus on my voice. Nothing else. No one is going to touch you. You're safe. I've got you. I'm so sorry"

I turn to the Master in charge of this fiasco. "Show me to a private room, now!" I'm trying to contain my fury, afraid that it will only make this worse for Vittoria. By the time I get her into a quiet room, away from the shouting and fighting going on downstairs, she's hyperventilating.

I try to lay her down to check if she's hurt, but she won't let go of me. I cradle her in my arms, soothing her as best I can. "Take a deep breath for me, Vittoria. You need to calm your breathing. Breathe with me... in... and out... in... and out."

I turn my gaze to the sorry excuse for a Master standing in the doorway. "Don't just stand there, get me a fucking knife to cut her ropes, and bring me a glass of Scotch to calm her nerves." He turns to leave, and I shout after him. "And hurry the fuck up!"

I sit, rocking her back and forth, whispering soothing words of my love and devotion for her. Eventually the sobbing subsides and her breathing returns to normal. She doesn't speak, she just clings to me, like a baby to its mother.

When the incompetent Master returns, I quickly cut her free and throw the ropes at his feet. I grab the sheet off the bed in the room and wrap it around her, still cradled in my lap.

"What the *fuck* just happened down there? Was I not clear enough? I told you that *no one* touches her. SHE IS MINE, AND NO ONE FUCKING TOUCHES HER! What kind of sorry excuse for a club are you running here?"

He's full of apologies, both in French and English, but it's too late for that now. I want someone's head on a spike for this.

"Who the fuck were those men?"

His voice shakes as he tries to answer me. "Submissives. They are submissives in training. Their Mistresses were also in the crowd and they have been removed to their private rooms for punishment."

"Bring me their Mistresses, now."

"Master Fitzgerald, I understand you're upset, but they will be punished for their actions."

I'm seeing fucking red right now. "*Upset?* You think I'm upset? That doesn't begin to scratch the surface. I don't give a fuck what punishment those so-called Mistresses are giving them, it's not enough. Bring them to me, now, or I swear to God I will search every room in this place until I find them, and I will kill those motherfucking subs."

"As you wish, Master Fitzgerald." He scurries off with his tail between his legs, not a dominant bone in his body.

Alone in the silence, Vittoria finally speaks. "You're bleeding."

"Doesn't matter."

She sits up, taking my hand in hers, kissing my bloodstained knuckles. "You're bleeding. It matters to me."

I pull my hand from her grasp. I don't deserve her kindness. I let this happen. I should have been by her side the entire time. I shouldn't have let anyone distract me with their inane questions. "Well, it shouldn't. It's less than I deserve. I should be flogged for letting this happen to you. I'm so fucking sorry."

"It wasn't your fault. You're the one who saved me."

"Not my fault? You can't be serious. I'm supposed to be your Master. To protect you and keep you safe at all times. I failed you. You didn't even want to come here."

"I was apprehensive, but I came willingly." Her voice turns cold—void of feeling—and it chills me to the core.

"I shouldn't have pushed you. Can you ever forgive me?"

We're interrupted as the door opens and two French Mistresses walk in with their submissives on leashes behind them. I am so fucking livid at the sight of them, and I would be beating the ever-living shit out of both of those men if it weren't for Vittoria cowering in my arms. I can tell just from looking at them, that the woman on the left is the most aggressively dominant of the two. And sure enough, she steps up to speak to me. "We are so sorry, Master Fitzgerald. I am Mistress Giselle and this is Mistress Juliette. These are new submissives in training. They are boisterous and in need of severe and intensive training. We will make sure that they are punished for their actions. It was highly inappropriate and against our rules."

"With all due respect... Mistress..." I spit her title with all the vitriol and disdain that I feel for her in this moment. "I don't give a flying fuck about the rules here, and apparently neither do your submissives. I don't give a shit whether they are in training or not. Your job is to set the fucking boundaries. How can you stand here in front of me and call yourselves Mistress? I think you are both in need of some serious fucking training. My submissive is more dominant than you!"

"Well, maybe that's something *you* should be working on with her, instead of passing judgment on us."

She's really done it now.

"HOW DARE YOU QUESTION ME, OR MY SUBMISSIVE! She is worth a thousand of you. She is strong-willed, but obedient in every way. Don't even look in her direction. And as for questioning me, I'm not the one whose submissive was touching a helpless, vulnerable *fucking stranger*! It's beyond deplorable! What they did here tonight went against basic human decency. You do not touch anyone in that way, especially in her bound vulnerable state, without their express permission or that of their Master. There is something seriously fucking wrong with you if you think this is just a training issue. I'm disgusted and horrified that you would play this down as a simple lack of discipline. These men assaulted my submissive and should be caned until they bleed. I gave *strict* instructions that she must not be touched. You should be ashamed of yourselves, and this club. I'll make sure *none* of the Masters I know will ever set foot in here again."

"What can we do, Master Fitzgerald?"

"What you can do… Giselle," I refuse to call her Mistress, she doesn't deserve the title or the respect it commands, "is get those fuckers out of my sight before I kill them. The way I feel right now, I would literally rip their beating hearts from their chests and make them eat it."

"I am to be addressed as Mistress, *Master Fitzgerald*."

Her voice is dripping with disdain but shaking in fear. She should be afraid of me. I have never been so angry in my life.

"Well fucking earn it then, because from what I've seen here tonight, you're not fit to have the honor of the title. Now get the fuck out of my sight."

They look at each other, shocked, appalled, and scared, before making a quick exit without another word. The club Master remains, only long enough for me to tell him to call me a cab and get the fuck out.

My heart is racing, adrenaline coursing through me as I try to calm myself down, Vittoria still nestled quietly in my arms. All I can do is apologize to her, over and over, and it doesn't escape my attention that she never answers my question—*can you forgive me?* I don't blame her. I will never forgive myself.

IT'S NOT UNTIL WE'RE SAFELY ENSCONCED IN OUR HOTEL ROOM THAT Vittoria finally speaks to me. "I'm sorry."

"Don't ever apologize to me. You have *nothing* to be sorry for."

"I freaked out. Overreacted. It was a trigger for me... for my past."

I kneel in front of her as she sits perched on the end of the bed. "Do you want to talk about it?" I place my hands on her legs to offer comfort, but her body tenses underneath me, and it's a dagger to my heart.

"I... I can't. Not tonight. I'm exhausted. I just want to wash off this dirty feeling, and crawl into bed."

"Okay. I won't push you. Just know that I'm here when you're ready to talk to me. I'll go and fill the tub for you." She doesn't respond, lost in her own thoughts, so I leave her and head to the bathroom.

I stare at myself in the mirror while the taps are running, wondering who I am, and how I could have let Vittoria down so badly. I scrub my hands over my face and up into my hair, breathing deeply to try and calm the storm raging inside of me. I need to man the fuck up and be there for her. Whatever she needs from me, I'll give it to her. Whatever I need to do to make this right, I will.

She hasn't moved a muscle in the time I've been gone, staring blankly at the wall in front of her.

"The bath's ready." She doesn't move or react in any way. I don't want to startle her. "Vittoria, baby, I'm going to lift you into the bathroom now." Gently, I wrap my arms underneath her and carry her into the bathroom, carefully undressing her before doing the same myself. I pick her up and step into the tub, slowly lowering both of us down into the water. The silence is deafening, but after a few minutes, I feel her body relax against mine, her head resting on my chest. I grab the sponge from the side of the tub and tenderly lather her skin, washing away the dirt of our disastrous night.

"I love you, Logan."

Those four little words cut into the silence, causing my heart to swell in my chest, and my stomach to churn with guilt for what happened tonight. I tighten my grip, scared to let her go. "I love you, too, so much I can barely breathe. I... I'm so sorry."

"Me, too."

"Don't say..." She cuts me off.

"Listen to me. I am sorry, because if I could find a way to open up and tell you about my past, then this might not have happened. I know it's hard for you, when you don't know everything about me. You can't beat yourself up. It's not your fault. You couldn't have known something like this would happen, or how I would react to it. For that, I'm sorry, but I just can't... I'm not ready to talk about it."

She's right, but it doesn't make me feel any better when the sounds of her screaming for me are so fresh in my mind, tormenting me every second of every minute. If I had known a situation like that could be a trigger for her and cause some sort of panic attack, I never would have put her in that position. I don't know how to protect her when I don't know what I'm supposed to be protecting her from.

"I told you before. As long as you're working toward telling me, then I need to be okay with it. But Vittoria, don't *ever* do anything because you think it's what I want. Not if it puts you at risk for triggering bad memories. I don't want you to please me when it's detrimental to your wellbeing. I love you. Whether you say yes or no to something I ask of you, I will always love you. There is *nothing* on this earth that would make me stop loving you. You need to know that. Tell me you understand."

"I understand, Master."

I lift her chin, my lips finding hers in a plea for forgiveness—for redemption. "Please, call me Logan. I want to hear my name on your sweet lips."

"Make love to me, Logan. I need you tonight. I need to lose myself for a little while, and you're the only person who can help me do that. Please."

"I don't want to hurt you or take advantage of you when you're vulnerable."

She caresses my cheek with her bubble-soaked hand, her eyes soft and loving. "I'm not hurt. They didn't hurt me, and they weren't touching me in a sexual way. They were in awe of your work, which was truly stunning. Mine was an emotional response... to..." Her words trail off in strangled silence.

"To your past."

"Yes. You're not taking advantage of me. I'm asking you to love me. To show me how much you love me, and to help me chase away my nightmares. I want to fall asleep in your arms and enjoy the rest of our time together before we're separated by oceans and continents again. Please, Logan. Make love to me."

"I could never deny you, little one." I lift her out of the water and dry her off, before gathering her back up into my arms and out into the bedroom.

We make love into the early hours of the morning—no restraints, no rules, just us and the all-consuming love we share.

~

THREE MONTHS LATER

. . .

I EXTENDED MY TRIP TO PARIS, STAYING ANOTHER WEEK WITH VITTORIA. I couldn't bear the thought of leaving her after what happened, and I think she was relieved when I told her I wasn't heading back so soon, although she'd never admit it to me. She always puts up a strong front, very rarely letting her guard down. But when she does, it's like being given the key to heaven. A breathtaking sight to behold.

She only had a few days off between shows, but we made the most of them, taking in the sights of Paris. We've both travelled to the city before on numerous occasions, but there's something about sharing it with the person you love. It transforms into something magical, a true city of romance. We spent hours just walking and talking, holding hands and sipping coffee in the elegant cafés that can be found on every street. It took time, but we found our rhythm, the events at Club Désir, becoming a distant memory as we enjoyed each other as friends, and lovers.

I thoroughly enjoyed using my Boy Scout innovation skills to transform our hotel room into a temporary playroom, using the desk as a flogging table, the wrought iron artwork on the walls providing anchors for me to tether Vittoria with ties, creating a rudimentary form of a cross to restrain her in an upright position. In the end, I had to put the 'Do Not Disturb' sign on the door to stop housekeeping from walking in on the furniture moved, and makeshift restraints hanging from the walls! It was fantastic.

We ate in some of the most amazing restaurants, off the beaten track, not the usual tourist areas which are always bustling. We shared breakfast in bed, Vittoria providing a beautifully naked platter for me to eat from.

By the time I had to go back to reality, back to work, and out of Vittoria's orbit, I felt sick to my stomach. I didn't want her coming to the airport with me, leaving her to make her way back into Paris on her own. I made her promise to let me leave from the hotel, where we could say a proper goodbye. I got up early, ordered her favorite breakfast of blueberry pancakes, and wrote her a letter to open after I left, leaving it taped to the bathroom mirror so she would find it.

I gave her an intense pleasure spanking before breakfast, forcing her to stay completely naked, for my perusal, to see the blush of my handprint on her pretty little ass. She sat in my lap, feeding me as I reciprocated, making sure she ate every last bite, her satisfied moans making my cock twitch. Then, I took her back to bed and made love to her, until she was screaming my name, begging her Master for more, for harder, forever. She drifted off into a sated and peaceful sleep, nestled in my arms, before I slipped out of bed, dressed, and kissed her softly, drinking in her scent, memorizing it to tide me over until the next time she's in my arms.

I left her there three months ago, my sleeping beauty, and that's the image I hold in my thoughts, every night when I go to bed, alone, my heart heavy with the burden of distance between us.

The tour has been a major success, the guys have won over every city they've played in, the crowds growing as word spreads about the amazingly talented, Flaming Embers. We're about to start the final leg of the tour, hitting twenty-five major cities throughout America, and with the momentum behind them right now, we have offers coming in from radio stations and talk shows from all over the country, asking to interview the boys. It's going to be a grueling month, but at the end of it, I get to see Vittoria. I'm going to take a few months off and fly with her wherever she's traveling. I don't care if I have to live out of a suitcase again, I just want to be with her. It's been too long since we were last together.

I've been trying to make our schedules work, giving her numerous dates that I could have flown out for the weekend to be with her, but she always has something going on—promo, extra shows, or plans she can't get out of. At first I just put it down to bad luck and sucky timing, but as the weeks have gone by, she's becoming more withdrawn, her excuses seeming more and more implausible. I thought things were good with us when I left Paris, but now I'm beginning to wonder. She called me the second I landed to thank me for the letter I left her. We were on FaceTime with each other every day for those first few weeks, talking and laughing as if we were in the same room together, but then it stopped—like a switch being turned off. I couldn't get ahold of her on the phone for days. She would send me short text messages to say she was fine, and sorry that she missed my calls. I took solace in the fact that I knew she was safe, and that nothing had happened to her. If I hadn't heard from her, I would have been on the first plane out, to make sure she was okay.

It's been like this for a while now. She goes through phases of calling me, hyper and excited about the next time we'll be together, laughing and joking, and then, when I suggest some dates that I could make it happen, she shuts down. I've asked her on a few occasions if she's met someone, or if she's changed her mind about us and our long-distance relationship. I know how hard it is, and I wouldn't blame her if she wanted to find a Master who could be with her more often. What kind of Master can I really be to her when I'm thousands of miles away, for months at a time? I love her with everything that I am, but is it enough?

This past week she hasn't called me back, my only communication with her has been via text message, until tonight. It had been eight days since I'd last heard her voice, and I was really starting to worry about her. Speaking to her didn't allay those fears in any way, so I've decided I'm going to fly out to Italy. I have a few days off coming up, and I still have her schedule, which says she'll be there until next week. It should be easy enough to find her, all I need to do is go to the theater where she's performing. I'll worry about how pissed she's going to be, later. I'm past the point of giving her the benefit of the doubt. She's shutting me out again, and I don't know why.

Something's going on, and I intend to find out what.

BUDAPEST

VITTORIA

It needs to stop.

The pain, the nightmares, I need the agony to stop.

I need to make it all… just… stop.

I can't keep lying to everyone—to my family—to my friends—to Logan. He deserves so much better. I can't even look at him right now, and I know he's starting to get suspicious. It's been two months since I spoke to him on FaceTime. It's easy enough to do when he's on tour with the band, and I'm supposedly on tour with the ballet, but I'm running out of excuses.

It's getting hard to even hear his voice. The past two weeks, I've faked missing his calls, watching his handsome face flash on my screen until it goes to voicemail. I've become a master of deceit. I wait until it's late wherever he is, and then I text him to apologize for missing his call. Then, I promise that I'll speak to him the next day. Once or twice he's still been out partying with the guys, and I've been forced to speak to him, but I keep it brief. I feign rehearsals, or tiredness, or being out with Luca. None of it is true.

Without Logan, the nightmares are back, worse than ever. Since my injury in Prague, they've been happening more often, but now, after the shibari demonstration in Paris, it's every night, without fail. I wake up screaming, clawing at the man I believe is on top of me. The nightmares are becoming more intense, and it's not just reliving that awful memory. Now, I'm an adult in the dream, and I'm in a BDSM club, or I'm at rehearsals, or I'm alone in my apartment back in New York. He's everywhere, and I can never fight him off, no matter how hard I struggle. No one can hear me, because when I scream for help, scream for Logan, no sound comes out. Since the morning he left Paris, I've been plagued by what can only be described as night terrors.

It's terrifying, and horrific, and I can't escape it.

I don't eat, I don't sleep. I left my friends behind months ago. It's just me, in this hotel room, alone in my despair. I don't answer calls from Carter or my parents. I send them emails of my fake travels, saying I'll be in touch when my schedule calms down. I know if Carter heard my voice, he would know, he would come and get me, but I can't put him through that. I won't. He's done enough for me, given up so much for so long. His life is finally working out the way it should. He has the perfect family, and I won't be responsible for him having to choose between them and me. He's hardwired to protect me, and it almost broke him. It's for the best that he doesn't know.

I feel terrible for all the lies I've told Logan over the last two months. It kills me every time the words slip past my lips, but I can't see any other way to deal with it. The sexy, raspy tone of his voice, cuts deep into my soul, making me ache for him. I know that if I told him what happened, he'd be on the first flight out here, leaving behind everything he's worked so hard for, to be with me. I can't do that to him. I can't do it to me. I don't want to see the pity in his eyes. I thought I would get better, that I would get my shit together, and I would go home to him, to our life together. But that won't happen now. I can't see a way out anymore, at least, not one that will bring us back to each other. There's only one way out of this misery. For all intents and purposes, my life ended two months ago, and all that's left for me, is to complete the task.

TWO MONTHS AGO

"I'M SO SORRY, MISS DE ROSSI. THERE'S NOTHING MORE WE CAN DO."

Luca is by my side, squeezing my hand as the doctor delivers the news.

"I've repaired your ankle as best I could, enough to allow you to walk without a limp, but I'm afraid the injury was extensive. You won't be able to continue with ballet professionally. Dancing through the pain for so long has caused irreparable damage."

"Maybe if I take six months off? Then I could dance again?"

"You don't understand. If you continue to dance, you'll be in a wheelchair within a year. It's remarkable that you aren't already. You were very lucky."

I struggle out of Luca's embrace, the sight of his tears, a knife ripping through my insides.

"Lucky... you think I'm lucky? Ballet is all I care about. It's who I am. Without it, I'm nothing. Worthless."

"I know it feels like that now, but you're a young woman, with a lot to live for. When you come to terms with this, you'll realize that you are so much more than a dancer. I'm sure you have many people in your life who love you no matter what you do, including the man standing next to you. I'll leave you to digest all of this. A nurse will be in later to go over your rehabilitation program with you."

As the doctor closes the door behind him, my world falls apart. Everything I knew, gone. Just... gone. Luca tries to console me, but I can't bear to see him cry.

"Please go. I need some time."

"I'm not leaving you. Ballerina or not, you will always be my Vittoria bella. I love you, and I'm here for you." He moves to give me a hug, but the pity in his eyes is my undoing.

"Get the hell out. I don't want you here. You represent everything I can't have anymore. You're a bad reminder, and I can't even look at you. Get out... get out... get out!"

"Vittoria..."

"Please, if you care about me at all, just go."

He wipes the tears from his eyes, kisses me on the forehead and makes his *way to the door. "I'll call you tomorrow and see if you're up to having a visitor. I love you, bella. Always remember that." As the door closes, and I'm left alone in the silence and misery of my own mind, I give into the realization that my life as I know it, is over.*

I thought it couldn't get any darker than that day, but here I am two months later, and it's infinitely worse. I never did let Luca come back to see me. I went through physio by myself. Days and weeks of agonizing pain to get back on my feet. Nothing but darkness, loneliness, pain, and lies. So much time to sit and contemplate all of the bad in my life, and I've come to the only possible conclusion—I'm bad. I'm the poison in my own life. Without ballet to center me, to focus my energy, I've realized that it was all my fault. Marcus—my injury—Logan. It's all on me, and there's only one way to fix it.

I never open the curtains in my hotel room anymore, and I usually tell housekeeping to leave me alone. Today is no exception. The room is dark and quiet, only the sounds of my breathing to let me know that I can still hear, the feel of my heartbeat letting me know I'm still alive.

I am numb.

I feel... nothing.

It's the only way to cope with the pain, both mental and physical.

I've been taking pain meds for so long now, they have no effect on me anymore. They don't take away my pain, physical or emotional. I tried to stop taking them before the final injury that ended my career, but I couldn't get through a performance without them. They became part of my day, something I needed to get me through. I've scammed meds from doctors all over Europe, and now here I sit, with two bottles of pills, and a glass of wine from the mini-bar.

This is what my life has come to. I'm alone, in a hotel room, on the other side of the world from everyone I love. It's a sad way to end things, but it's a fitting one for me.

My phone begins to vibrate on the table in front of me. It's Logan. I debate whether or not to let it go to voicemail, but a part of me wants to talk to him one last time, to hear his commanding voice saying my name. To tell him I love him. I take a deep breath, before picking up the phone and pressing the answer button, ready to give the performance of my life.

"Hi, baby."

"Hey, little one. How's my girl? I feel like I never manage to catch you these days. I miss you so much. Only four weeks and we'll be together again. I'm counting the days."

I struggle to speak past the lump forming in my throat. "I miss you, too. More than I could ever explain."

"Are you okay? You don't sound too good, and it's not the first time. I'm worried about you. You would tell me if something was wrong, wouldn't you? We might not be in the same country, but you are always on my mind. I'm here for anything you need. That's what being your Master is all about, no matter how far apart we are. I love you. You know that, don't you?"

My heart is breaking, knowing what this will do to him, but I can't go on, it's too hard.

"I'm fine. Just tired. I love you so much, Logan. More than I've ever loved anyone."

"I know this is hard, but we'll get through it. We'll be together again soon, I promise."

I hold my hand over my mouth to hold in the cries that I know are fighting to break free.

"I need to go just now. Luca is hounding me to rehearse."

"Okay. I'll call you tomorrow. I love you."

"I... I love you... Master Fitzgerald."

I end the call and throw my cell phone across the room, watching it smash against the wall and fall to the floor in pieces. This isn't how my life was supposed to be. I wanted what every young girl dreams of.

I wanted to have a happy, innocent childhood.

I wanted to feel safe and secure.

I wanted to be a ballerina.

I wanted to meet a man, fall in love, and live happily ever after.

I wanted to have all of those things with Logan Fitzgerald. But life is cruel, and unfair, and I don't deserve any of that happiness.

I can hardly see the bottle of pills through the tears that are coursing down my cheeks, but I manage to get them open. I take three tablets at a time, placing them on my tongue, washing them down with a mouthful of wine—the sound of Logan's voice telling me we'll be together soon, haunting me.

I take another three, replaying over and over, the way he sounds when he tells me he loves me.

I keep taking the pills until the first bottle is empty, and then I pour myself another glass of wine, before starting in on the next bottle.

When I can't take anymore, I grab one of Logan's t-shirts that I brought on tour with me and the letter he left for me in Paris. I've read it every day, multiple times, memorizing every last word, but I still want to read it one last time—to run my fingers over his penmanship and remember the last time he made love to me. I curl up on the bed with his letter in one hand and his t-shirt clutched tightly to my chest. It still smells of him, and it gives me a twisted sort of comfort as I feel myself losing consciousness. I say goodbye to the pain, the hurt, and the guilt I've carried with me for so many years. I'm ready to let it all go, to let it all… stop.

He is the love of my life, even in death.

If only things could have been different.

If only *I* could have been different.

We could have been so happy… together.

CHAPTER 14

LOGAN

Today started like any other day. Mundane and ordinary. It's disturbing how quickly tragedy can throw your world into disarray. How a single moment can catapult you from monotonous to monstrous, temperate to terrified, in an instant.

When my alarm went off this morning, I hit the snooze button, like I do every morning. Then, after another nine minutes of pretending I could fall back to sleep, I grabbed my phone and checked to see if Vittoria had messaged me. It becomes a habit when you're constantly living in different time zones. A few months back, I would find a handful of messages in the morning. Sometimes funny, sometimes cute, and on a regular basis, downright filthy. Even now that the messages have become fewer and farther between, and the phone calls have all but stopped, I still find myself hoping. There were no messages, and as I dragged my sorry ass out of bed, exhausted from a late night with the band, I felt disappointed.

I'm doing my best in a bad situation.

It's difficult to exercise control over your submissive when you're on different continents, but she knows that I love her, and that I want to make it work. So why do I have this feeling in the pit of my stomach about her?

I've tried to ignore it, telling myself I'm just feeling a little overprotective of our relationship after speaking to her last night. She tried to sound upbeat, but something in her voice wasn't right. It's gnawing at me, and I just can't shake the feeling as I go through the motions of my day.

I'm sitting having lunch with Campbell and the boys when my phone rings. It's not a number I recognize. It's international.

"Logan Fitzgerald speaking."

"Mr. Fitzgerald, do you know a Miss Vittoria de Rossi?"

My heart begins to race and my stomach churns. "Yes. She's my girlfriend. Can I ask who I'm speaking to?"

"I'm a nurse. I'm calling from Kelen Hospital in Budapest. Your girlfriend was admitted to our emergency room today. Yours is the last number she spoke with on her phone."

"Hospital? Is she okay? What happened?" I can barely hear over the sound of my own heartbeat thundering in my ears.

"She was found in her hotel room by the housekeeping staff. It looks like she tried to commit suicide."

My mind starts racing. This can't be right. They must have the wrong person. Vittoria would never do that to herself, or to us.

"You must be mistaken. I spoke to her last night." Please be wrong. Please let it be someone else.

"I'm sorry, sir. There's no mistake. I've spoken with her. She advised me to call this number and no other contact in her phone."

"She's talking? Thank God. Is she going to be okay?"

"Yes. Physically she's going to be fine. Emotionally, she needs a lot of support."

"I'll fly out today, but it will be tomorrow before my flight arrives. Can I speak to her?"

"I'm sorry, but she's not well enough to use the phone at the moment. She's resting after the procedure."

"What procedure?"

"They had to pump her stomach. It was an overdose. Vicodin."

Holy fuck. *This can't be happening.* "Please, tell her that I'm on my way, and that I love her."

"I will, Mr. Fitzgerald."

I can't think straight, a thousand thoughts going around my head at a million miles a minute.

"Can you give me the address?"

"Of course."

She recites the address, and as I stare down at the napkin in front of me, my handwriting is almost illegible because my hands are shaking so badly. I realize she said Budapest.

"Budapest? She's supposed to be in Italy. She left Budapest months ago."

"I'm sorry. I know this must be a shock, and I don't know what she told you, but she is most definitely in Budapest."

"Fuck. I'm sorry, I didn't mean to curse."

"It's quite alright. It's a lot to take in. When you arrive tomorrow, give your name at reception and they will tell you where to go. I'll make sure they're expecting you."

"Thank you."

I hang up the phone, dazed, confused, and terrified beyond anything my brain can comprehend. It's a physical reaction. I feel like my life's blood has drained from my body, leaving only fear, coursing through my veins and straight to my heart. I forget where I am, until a thick Scottish brogue cuts through the fog.

Campbell and the boys excused themselves from the table when I answered the call, taking residence at the bar to give me some privacy. Only Campbell has returned.

"Are you alright, Logan? You look white as a fuckin' sheet. I dinnae mean to eavesdrop, but I heard you mention Vittoria before I left the table. Is she okay?"

I drop my head into my hands, unable to speak or to voice the horrific news I've just been given. If I say it out loud, it makes it real, and this... this cannot be real. Why would she do this? I spoke to her last night, and I asked her if she was okay. She told me she was just tired. She lied to me. I wasn't there for her when she needed me. I should have been there.

"Logan. Say somethin'. You're really fuckin' scarin' me. Is she okay?"

I take a deep, shaky breath, searching for the right words. "She's in hospital, in Budapest. She's going to be fine, I think, but it's serious. I need to go. I need to be with her."

"Fuckin' hell. I'm so sorry. What can I do to help?"

"I'm sorry, Campbell. I'll need to find someone to see out the rest of the tour with you. I hate to let you down." My thoughts are scattered, jumping from one thing to the next. "I need to call Carter. Wait… the nurse said Vittoria doesn't want anyone else to be notified. What the fuck do I do?" I start scrambling around on the table for my phone and the napkin with the hospital address, rambling like a madman about what I need to do in order to get to her.

Campbell pulls a chair up next to me, sits down calmly, and pulls me into a hug. He doesn't speak. He literally just holds me together, letting me gain whatever strength I can from him. I'm not one for hugging other guys, but in this moment I need it, and he knows it.

"Anythin' you need, Logan, I'm here for you. Don't gie us or the tour a second thought. We're big enough an' ugly enough to get on wi' it. There are much more important things in life. What matters is that Vittoria is goin' to be okay. She's goin' to get better. What we need to focus on right now, is gettin' you the fuck outta here and on a flight to Budapest." He lets go and moves back, giving me space, waiting for me to speak.

"Okay. I need to find out when the next flight is. I need to get back to the hotel and pack some clothes and get my passport."

"Right. I'll call the airline and see when the next flight leaves. You take a moment, take a breath, an' then we can go back to the hotel an' get yer gear." He turns toward the bar, signaling Rhuari over. "Get Logan a double Scotch, an' then take the lads an' make yerselves scarce. I'll meet up wi' you later at the hotel."

Rhuari gives me a sympathetic glance, obviously aware that something is wrong, even if he doesn't know what it is. He does as he's asked without question, and as soon as he sets my drink down, he squeezes my shoulder and leaves with the other boys. Each of them give me a subtle nod as they head out through the revolving glass doors of the restaurant.

I down the Scotch, needing something to take the edge off my utter despair. I feel helpless, lost, and completely disconnected from reality. Campbell is deep in conversation with the airline as I grab a passing waiter and ask for the check. When I turn my attention back to him, he swears at the person on the other end of the phone and slams it down on the table. "For fuck's sake!"

"When's the next flight, Cam?"

"The next flight out is tomorrow, an' it's fully booked. They said they could put you on standby, but failin' that, it would be Friday."

"It's Tuesday! They're saying I can't get to her until Friday? Which means I wouldn't arrive in Budapest until Saturday morning."

"That's no' fuckin' happenin'. I'll call every other airline there is until I find you a flight leaving today. Fuckin' ridiculous."

"Wait. I might have a way. Call the hotel and ask them to pack up my room right away and have the bags ready at the front desk."

"I'm on it."

I take out my phone and dial Xander. If there was ever a time to ask him for a huge favor, this is it.

He answers on the second ring. "Hey, bro. Where the hell are you? Jet-setting all over the place as usual?"

"Xander, I need your help."

He can tell by the tone of my voice that I'm not kidding around. "Anything. What do you need?"

"I need your plane. I need to get to Budapest right fucking now."

"What's wrong? What's happened? What's in Budapest?"

"Vittoria. She's in hospital."

"Where are you? I'll have it fueled and ready to come get you within the hour."

"I'm in LA. Fuck, Xander, I'm going out of my mind here."

"Have you called Carter?"

"She doesn't want anyone else there. I promise I'll call him as soon as I've seen her, but I need to respect her wishes. This is as serious as it gets."

"He has a right to know, but I'll let you be the one to tell him. Do you want me to come with you?"

"Thank you, but no. I need to do this on my own."

"Okay. There's no point in me getting my plane to come from New York to LA. That will just waste time. I'm going to organize a private jet to take you straight from LAX. I can have you in the air within the hour. I'll arrange transport for you when you get to Budapest and I'll make reservations for you at a hotel close to the hospital. You just get your passport and get to the airport."

"I don't know how to thank you. I'm losing it here. I spoke to her last night and she was fine."

"It's going to be okay. I'll go make some calls. You just go and look after her. She's family."

"She's my life, Xander. I don't know what I'd do without her."

"I know, man… I know."

I hang up the phone to see Campbell settling the bill.

"You don't have to do that."

"Shut the fuck up. Now, let's go an' get yer shit from the hotel. Are we goin' straight to the airport after that?"

"Yeah. Xander is arranging a plane to take me from LAX."

"He's a fuckin' stand-up guy. I like him a lot. Now let's get outta here. You've got a plane to catch."

We head back to the hotel, and as requested my bags are waiting at the front desk.

I'm so caught up in what I'm doing, trying to get to Vittoria, that it doesn't really hit me until I'm outside waiting on a cab to take me to the airport—*she tried to kill herself.*

I feel like I've been hit in the chest with a Mack truck, and my eyes fill with tears. I don't remember the last time I cried. I think it was the day my dad left when I was eight years old. The emotion is too much to bear, and my silent tears are the only release I allow myself. The only weakness I can show before I see her. I wipe my face, unwilling to let myself shed another tear.

Campbell is standing next to me. I don't know why, maybe it's because he's become one of my closest friends, or maybe it's because I just need to say the words out loud, but I tell him the truth.

"She tried to kill herself. I wasn't there for her when she needed me, and she tried to kill herself."

I can't even look him in the eye. I'm so ashamed of myself for letting her down.

"Holy fuckin' shit! I'm comin' wi' you, Logan. No man should have to deal wi' somethin' like this. It's too much for anyone to shoulder alone."

"She doesn't want anyone else to come, not even her brother Carter."

"Isn't he your best friend?"

"Yes. This will devastate him. How the hell do I tell him?"

"I know she dinnae want you to tell anyone, but she dinnae really know what's best for her right now. You'll hate yourself if you keep this from her family. She needs all the love and support she can get. Tell them they cannae visit her until she says so, but let them be there for her. You can explain everythin' to them face to face when you get there, but tell them to come. You need the support as much as she does, an' if you don't tell them, then I'm getting' on that plane wi' you."

"You can't do that. You have a tour to finish."

"Fuck the tour! I appreciate everythin' you've done for us, an' I'm lovin' every minute of it, but I learned at a very young age that people are what's important in life, Logan. I will walk away from it if you need me there wi' you. No questions asked."

"You're an amazing man, Campbell, and a really good friend. You're right. I need to tell Carter and the rest of her family. I'll call when I get to the airport."

My cab pulls up, and I breathe a sigh of relief, thankful that I'm finally on my way to her.

"Let me know how she's doin', and if you need anythin', just call me."

"Thanks." I throw my bags in the trunk and jump into the backseat, but just before I close the door, Campbell leans in.

"Just remember, none of this is your fault. She's in a bad place, an' only she can get herself out of it. You dinnae fail her. Sometimes life pulls people intae a darkness that no' even love can conquer. All you can do is focus on her. Be there to offer her the strength to fight and come out the other side."

"I should have been there."

"You cannae change it now. You have to move forward. Dinnae waste yer energy on the past. Now go and get yer lassie an' bring her home." He shuts the cab door, giving me a somber nod as I pull away into the LA traffic.

I take a few minutes to breathe, digesting everything he said to me. He's right. Vittoria doesn't know what's best for her right now, and I'm supposed to be her Master. My job is to act in her best interests, even if she hates me for it, and that's what I'm going to do.

I pull my phone from my pocket and dial Carter's number.

"Logan. How the fuck are you?"

"Carter. I need you to listen to me. I'm on my way to LAX, and I need you to call Xander and get on his plane."

"What the fuck?"

"Vittoria is in hospital in Budapest. It's serious, but she's going to be okay. I got a call less than an hour ago. I didn't get to speak to her, but the nurse assured me that she'll be okay. I can't go into the details just now, and honestly, I don't really know what happened or what's going on. She asked them not to call anyone else on her contacts list, but I know she's not thinking straight. She needs you, and so do I."

"Fuck! What the fuck happened? I'll call Xander and see if he can get me out there as soon as possible. Text me the hospital details and I'll meet you there."

"Carter, I know you want to see her, but I think that I should go and see her alone. She didn't want anyone else to come, and I need to prepare her for seeing you. From what the nurse told me, she's in a fragile state, and it could be worse for her if we both just show up and bombard her with questions."

"She's my fucking sister. If anyone should be going to see her, it should be me."

"Not happening. I'm sorry. I know it's shit, and I shouldn't be asking this of you, but remember that I didn't need to call you. She didn't want me to. I'm putting my foot down on this. I see her alone to tell her you're with me, or you don't come. Your choice."

"And who the fuck do you think you are?"

"I'm the guy who's going to be by her side, loving her until the day I fucking die. So back the fuck off. I know it's hard. I'm going out of my mind here, but we need to keep it together for Vittoria. She needs us. Both of us. And us fighting over who has more claim to her, isn't going to help her in the slightest. I'm going completely against her wishes here, so at least afford me the chance to speak to her and explain."

"Fine. If she doesn't… I can't believe she's there alone."

"I know, man. I know. Just get on the flight as soon as you can and we'll deal with everything else when we get there. I know it's easier said than done, but I'm fucking lost, and terrified, and I don't know what else to say."

"I'll meet you at whatever hotel we end up in. Keep in touch and let me know the minute you've seen her and know that she's going to be okay."

"Will do. Travel safe, brother."

"You, too. And Logan, thank you for calling me even though she asked you not to."

"See you in Budapest."

I hang up the phone, uncertain of whether or not I've just sealed my fate with Vittoria. She may never forgive me for this, but at the end of the day, it's a risk I have to take. I'm going to do what I think is right for her, whether she likes it or not. I feel so guilty for not telling Carter why she's in hospital, but it's not something anyone should hear over the phone. I can attest to that.

Xander is true to his word, as always, and as soon as I set foot inside the airport, I'm met by a representative who fast-tracks me through all the necessary checks and leads me out to a waiting jet. I will never be able to repay him for getting me to her as quickly as possible.

The staff are kind and attentive, but all I can think of is her. I'm consumed with thoughts of our interactions over the past few months, playing them over and over in my mind, kicking myself for not listening to the niggling feeling that something wasn't right with her. I brushed it off as par for the course in a long-distance relationship. It's hard to maintain intimacy when you're so far away from each other and have busy lives. I should have pushed her harder to talk to me, to share how she was feeling.

When I realize she's been lying to me for months, hiding where she was, pretending that she was still on tour, I'm so fucking angry with her. I have no idea who she is, or what's going on in her life. There are so many unanswered questions. Why isn't she with the rest of the ballet company? Why did she lie to me? Why did she feel she couldn't confide in me? And the one question playing on a loop in my mind, over and over again—why did she try to kill herself?

Time ticks by in slow motion as I stare out at the clouds, soaring thirty thousand feet above ground. I've always thought that there's something so beautiful and so serene about flying, like being given a glimpse of heaven. But today, it feels like the worst kind of hell. Every minute feels like an hour. Every hour feels like a day. I can't stand it. I can't stand not being by her side. I'm not there to tell her how much I love her, and to beg her to fight.

She can't give up. If she does, she won't just be ending her own life... she'll be ending mine, too.

CHAPTER 15

LOGAN

I DON'T KNOW WHAT I WAS EXPECTING TO SEE, OR HOW I EXPECTED HER to look when I finally got here. I had to come straight from the airport. I couldn't wait any longer, but I'm beyond exhausted. I didn't sleep at all on the flight here, too worried to find any respite.

She's sleeping when I arrive, but the nurses have been great, letting me sit with her, and filling me in on how she's been doing today. They said her vitals are good, her system is clear of drugs, and she managed to eat breakfast this morning. They also told me that she hasn't spoken, or even made eye contact with anyone. She's been staring out the window, clutching a piece of paper that she had in her hand when they found her. Apparently, she was screaming for it when she came around, and luckily, one of the nurses had kept it along with her personal effects.

I can see it crumpled loosely in her hand, and when I spy the Paris hotel emblem on one of the corners, I'm filled with... I don't even know what the word is for the way I feel. I'm overwhelmed with emotion. Love, fear, love, anger, and more love than I ever thought possible. She's holding onto the letter I wrote the last time we were together. She's holding onto... me. She looks so small and fragile, even thinner than before—frail. All I want to do is gather her up into my arms and never let go, but I'm afraid I would break her tiny frame. I remove my letter from her hand, careful not to wake her. She needs to rest, and I'm not sure I'm ready to talk to her yet. I don't want to say the wrong thing. I want to be everything that she needs me to be.

I sit back, my vision blurred from lack of sleep, but I push myself to focus on the piece of paper in front of me. Smoothing it out, I read the words she's been holding close. It's been so long since I wrote this, it feels like another lifetime. A happier one.

From a Master to his submissive,

My sweet and gentle Vittoria, my Nyx. As I write this letter to you, my beautiful submissive, I am filled with both pride, for the stunning woman that you are, inside and out, and sadness, that I must leave you today. When I'm with you, I'm drawn into your orbit, circling you, helpless to escape, and there is no place I'd rather be than by your side.

I never thought I'd be lucky enough to find love, and when I met you, I fell head over heels. I never in my wildest dreams thought that you could love me back. I fought it for so long, believing you couldn't possibly want the same life as I do. I knew then, that I wasn't good enough for you. And even now, I know it's true. But, the moment I let myself kiss you, the moment I felt your passion, I became selfish. You deserve so much better than me, but I can't stand the thought of giving you up, of letting another man make you happy. One thing I know with absolute certainty, is that no matter what my short-comings may be, no man will ever love you as much as I do.

When you trusted me enough to tell me about your lifestyle, I was astounded, and yet somehow, it made sense to me. You were made for me. Everything about you calls to me. I want every part of you. The first time I claimed you as my own in the playroom, I can't even describe to you how incredible that night was for me. To make you my submissive. To watch you give yourself over to me completely, was... magnificent.

You laugh that I call you Nyx, but to me, you are a goddess. My goddess.

Do you know why I asked you to dance to 'Tempo di Valse' at the club? It's because Swan Lake was the first ballet I ever saw you dance in. I was running late and missed the introduction, but when I set foot inside the audi-

torium, and saw you on stage, that music was playing in the background. I fell in love with you all over again. You didn't know I was there, but I stood in the back and watched you, captivated by your grace and beauty. Something happens when you dance, Vittoria, and it's an honor and a privilege to witness. You're not just a ballerina, you're an artist. Breathtaking and unique. Ethereal and yet more real than anyone I've ever known. You speak to me when you dance, your body communicating so much emotion, so much of your soul. I will never tire of watching you, worshiping you, in awe of your unparalleled talent.

I can never express to you how sorry I am for what happened here in Paris. I will never forgive myself for letting you down, and I promise you, I will never let anyone hurt you, ever again. I don't know what happened to you in the past, but know that I will always be here, ready to listen. I need you to be honest with me. What do we have, if we don't have trust?

You've changed my life. You breathe life into my mundane existence, and I'll spend the rest of my life protecting that. Protecting you.

I'm so proud of the woman you are. You're the most amazing, tender, and loving submissive, and I am humbled that you chose me as your Master. Know that I will never take this great honor for granted.

All my love, now and always
Your Master, lover, and friend
Logan x

I can't bear to look at it any longer. Folding it slowly, I place it on the table by her bedside. Why did she have this in her hand when they found her? As a reminder of how I broke my word? I promised her I would protect her, and yet, here we are. She's lying in a hospital, halfway across the world from where I was this time yesterday. This has been going on for months—months—and I had no idea. I'm supposed to know her better than anyone, and I have no idea what's going on in her life. I was too busy with the band, too busy with my label to notice what must have been right in front of me. I'm disgusted with myself.

I take her hand in mine and rest my head on the edge of her bed,

212 | EVA HAINING

emotionally and physically unable to function any longer. I'm here with her, and she's alive—that's enough for now.

∿

I WAKE UP TO THE SOFT, SOOTHING SOUNDS OF VITTORIA'S VOICE, HER fingers stroking through my hair. It feels like only moments since I closed my eyes, but the dim light in the room suggests otherwise. It's dark, the only light coming from a reading lamp above the bed. I struggle to open my eyes, and instead of fighting it, I take a moment to let them adjust, listening to her whispered words as she breaks my heart even further.

"I'm so sorry, Logan. I never wanted to hurt you. You're the best thing that's ever happened to me. The only person who truly knows me in any real way. I know I've disappointed you, that I've failed you. I've lied to you for so long. I don't expect you to forgive me. I broke your trust not only as your submissive, but as your friend. None of this was about you, or how well you love me. You have been... amazing. So much more than I deserve.

"This was about me. I'm lost, and I don't know how to fix it. I don't know if I'm strong enough. The only thing I do know, is that I love you, and I'm so, so sorry that you're here, dealing with my mess. I'm sorry... I'm sorry... I'm so sorry." She breaks down, sobbing softly, willing me to forgive her.

I squeeze her hand, warmly encased in mine for the past however many hours, and lift it to my lips, planting a gentle kiss. "I love you, Vittoria." My voice is rough from sleep, but also because there's a giant lump in my throat as I lift my gaze to meet hers. "I should have been here with you." I can barely lift my head up, so physically and emotionally drained by the past twenty-four hours. "When I got the call, and I couldn't get to you... fuck... I've never been so terrified."

She throws herself on me, begging for mercy. "Please forgive me, Master. You have to forgive me." I stroke my hand up and down her back, trying to calm her, but I'm devastatingly aware of how she's changed since the last time I touched her. I can feel her spine and her ribs protruding, her skin tight rather than soft. She never had an ounce of fat on her to start with, but now, she's almost emaciated. I can't believe I didn't know. I hold her, unable to speak. Can I forgive her for trying to end her own life? Her life means more to me than anything else in the vast universe that surrounds us, and she tried to end it, as if it meant nothing—less than nothing.

"Don't call me Master." It's all I can manage. I can't unburden my fears and concerns on her, she's not strong enough to handle it, and I wouldn't want her to hear the conflicting emotions that are battling in my head right now. I'm so relieved that she's here in my arms, and that she's still breathing. She's still part of this world. But, I'm so fucking angry with her, and I can't let her get even a hint that I feel this way. It would be selfish of me, and I won't make this any harder on her than it already is.

"Thank you for coming. I didn't know if you would."

I hold her tighter, wishing she could see what I see in her—what I love with every fiber of my being. "Don't you know by now? I would travel to the ends of the earth and beyond for you. When are you going to understand that I love you unconditionally? You're everything to me, and when I thought I might lose you... God, my world just fell apart. I can't lose you. It took me a lifetime to find you, and even longer to make you mine. Please don't give up on me."

She's crying uncontrollably now, as if she's in physical pain. All I can do is cling to her, hoping that my presence will bring her some small amount of comfort. I crawl up onto the bed beside her and lift her into my arms, cradling her in my lap as I've done so many times before. But this time it's different. It doesn't feel the same. *I don't feel the same.*

I've always felt like Vittoria's protector. Her guardian angel, although I couldn't be further from an angel. I've always believed that I could keep her safe from anything and anyone who might hurt her. Even when I let myself lose control with her, I was still in control of everything else around us. Now, I'm questioning everything we've ever shared together. I thought she trusted me. I thought she felt the same way about me as I do about her. I couldn't hurt her like that. I couldn't leave her behind to deal with such an insurmountable loss. I thought I knew her, but the last three months of our relationship has been a lie. Maybe longer. Every word spoken between us was... meaningless, and I didn't see it. I had no idea.

I'm ashamed to have ever called myself her Master. I knew she deserved better, and maybe if I had been selfless enough to let her go and find it, this wouldn't have happened. I've been lax with her because I love her so much, but in the end, I've hurt her more than any punishment ever could.

"Logan, I... I don't know what to say. No apology could ever be enough for what I've done."

"I have to know. Why didn't you talk to me? What's been going on with you? I thought you understood what I expected of you as my submissive. You should have come to me with whatever's been troubling you."

"I didn't know how to tell you. Telling you would have made it real."

"What? I need to know."

Tears begin to well in her eyes again as she finally opens up to me. "It started with my injury in Prague."

"Fucking hell, Vittoria! Has our entire relationship been a lie?" The shock on her face makes me realize what an asshole I'm being. "I'm sorry. I'm just scared and worried because I care. I won't interrupt you again. Go on."

She takes a deep breath before continuing.

"When I left you to go back on tour, my injury wasn't as healed as I hoped it would be. I couldn't bear to be away from dancing any longer than I'd already been, so I hid the pain from the physio and the doctor. I kept taking the painkillers to get me through each show. After a while, they stopped working so well, and I upped the number of pills I was taking. I started visiting doctors in every city we performed in, getting more and more pills to keep me going. At some point, I couldn't stop taking them. I danced through the pain, night after night, and by the time I got back to my hotel I was practically crawling to the bed, the pain was so bad. I couldn't give it up, Logan. Ballet is my life."

I grip her hand, horrified and heartbroken by her admission.

"Two weeks after you left Paris, I went on stage like any other night. I thought the painkillers were working. I leapt into the air, and when I landed on my ankle, the impact..." she struggles to say the words, "it ended my career."

"Vittoria..."

"I had surgery to repair the damage, but the best they could do was to make sure I don't walk with a limp. The doctor said if I continue to dance, I'll be in a wheelchair within a year."

I can't believe she's been dealing with this on her own. Her life has been crashing down around her, and she's been shouldering the burden by herself all this time.

"I was in the hospital physio facility for weeks after the operation, until I could walk well enough to look after myself. The ballet company had already left for the next city, and I was so lost, Logan. I was in denial. I didn't want to face up to what was happening to me. The longer it went on, the harder it became for me to tell you. The pain was crushing me, and to say it out loud... I just couldn't." She wipes her tears away with the back of her hand, her eyes bloodshot and swollen. "The pain in my ankle was excruciating, and I kept taking the pain meds, more often than I was supposed to. It got to the point where I couldn't leave my hotel room. I didn't want to face coming back to New York and explaining to everyone that my life-long dream has been burned to ash. In the end, I couldn't bear to hear your voice."

Her words cut me like a blade.

"It was just too painful. I love you so much, and I couldn't tell you. I didn't want to tell you. I felt like there was no way out, no way to get back to the life I had, the life we shared together. I took too many tablets. I didn't mean to. I wasn't trying to kill myself, Logan. It was a mistake. I'm so sorry."

I want to believe her. I want to believe her so badly. "Are you telling me the truth? I need to know. If you tried to end your life, I *need* to know."

She can't look me in the eye when she answers, "I'm telling the truth." There's my answer. She's still lying to me.

I hang my head, floundering in the dark, not knowing what to do or say for the best, and then Campbell's words replay in my head. Sometimes you need to do what's best for someone, even if they hate you for it.

"You're lying to me. You've *been* lying to me for months. I want to be with you, Vittoria, but if you refuse to be honest with me, to be honest with yourself, then we need to end this now." It seems like a heartless thing to say, but I'm clinging to the hope that her love for me is strong enough to force her to face up to what's happened—to what she did.

"I can't lose you."

"Then tell me the truth. Did you try to kill yourself?"

"Yes." That single, solitary word, destroys me, my soul shattering into a million pieces.

"Why?"

"Because without ballet, I'm nothing. I'm worthless."

"Don't *ever* say that to me again. I know you've lost something you love, something that's defined you up until this point in your life, but to say that you're nothing without it, that you're worthless, is an insult. I love you, Vittoria. More than I've ever loved anyone. Don't you see? You could never be worthless, when you're priceless to me. There are so many people who love you, who would have been devastated if you had succeeded in ending your life." Saying the words make me feel sick to my stomach. I can't even contemplate a reality in which she didn't survive.

"How can I make it right?"

"It's not about making it right. It's about learning your own worth. Learning to love yourself. Knowing that you are important, that you're loved. I would have been here in a heartbeat, if only you had let me in. You didn't have to go through this alone. No one should have to deal with what you've gone through in the past few months, completely alone. You're one of the strongest women I know, but everyone, and I mean *everyone*, including me, has their limits. You may see me as strong, but if I'd lost you, it would have been more than I could bear. I *need* you. If I haven't shown you that, then I am truly sorry, and I will spend every day of the rest of my life, making sure you know it in your heart and in your soul."

She moves to kiss me, but stops short, almost nervous of my reaction. "I need you, too. I'm so sorry I pushed you away."

"Promise me you'll talk to me from now on?"

"I promise."

I lower my lips to hers in a chaste kiss, filled with all of my love and devotion. "I love you, Vittoria. I love you. I love you." We stay in each other's arms, silently clinging to the hope that we can make it through this, together.

After a few hours, I tell her that Carter is here in Budapest, but that he doesn't know what happened. She's angry at first, but I know I did the right thing telling him to come. She's scared of how he'll react. How do you tell the brother you look up to, who you idolize, something like this? She's not strong enough to do it, and if I'm ever going to be worthy of the title 'Master' again, then I need to step up and do what needs to be done.

"I'm going to tell him tonight. Then, he can come and see you tomorrow and you can talk."

"What if he hates me when he finds out?"

"That will never happen. He loves you. He flew halfway around the world to be by your side. You need the love and support of your family. We have a long road ahead of us. You have to get through rehab and…"

She cuts me off. "I'm *not* going to rehab."

"It's not up for debate. The doctor says you need it, and I agree. You need counseling, and a chance at a clean slate. Whether you want to admit it or not, you're a drug addict." She starts to argue, but I'm not interested in her excuses. "Vittoria, this is a hard limit for me. You have to go to rehab. I'll take you back to the States, and you can go to a facility in New York where I can visit you every day.

I've seen firsthand what addiction does to people, and I vowed never to have that in my life. My dad was a dealer. There was a constant stream of junkies on our doorstep, looking for their next fix.

"I was six years old the first time I saw someone overdose. It was brutal, and sad, and I can't ever let that happen to you. My dad left when I was eight, and my mom ended up dating half his customers. The only saving grace was that she never started using. Addiction ruins people's lives. It ruined my childhood. I won't sit back and let it ruin your life. You're going to rehab and that's the end of it. Do you understand me?"

"Yes. I didn't know."

"How could you? I never told you. I've never told anyone. I just need you to know that I can't watch you destroy yourself like this."

"I'll go to rehab. I'll do anything to get my life back. To get back what we have."

"Good girl. I'll talk to the doctors and find out when I can take you home. In the meantime, you need to rest, and I need to go and speak to Carter. I'll bring him by in the morning." I kiss her forehead. "And, don't worry. He loves you, almost as much as I do. He just wants to see that you're okay and be here for you if you need him."

"Okay."

"I mean it, Tori. He loves you so much. He could never hate you. Now, get some rest, it's late. I'll be back first thing." I have to force myself to walk away, to leave her when everything inside of me wants to stay by her side—to never let her out of my sight again. But I need to go and speak to Carter, and I already know it's going to be one of the toughest conversations of my life.

"You're wrong. She would never do that. You must be mistaken."

He's distraught, devastated, and completely confused by my revelations.

"I wish I was wrong. I really fucking wish this was all a big mistake, but it's not. Vittoria tried to kill herself, Carter. She's been lying to everyone including me for months now."

I explain to him about her injury, the painkillers, the gradual addiction, and finally, the fall that ended her career. He breaks down, one of the strongest men I know. Absolutely crushed. Stricken with grief. It's hard to see him like this, but I'm right there with him, desperate to understand.

"Is she okay?"

"Physically, yes. They got to her in time. She'll need to go to rehab, which she's reluctant to do, but she needs it. I'm going to make a few calls tomorrow and arrange placement at a facility in New York for her, so that we can take her home and support her through this."

"Is it really necessary? Rehab?"

"Yes. It is. She's an addict. I know you don't want to hear that, neither did I. But she needs us to help her face it head on, not enable her to bury her head in the sand. If we don't help her now, we might not be so lucky next time. If housekeeping had gone in an hour later, she... I can't even say it. She needs to go to rehab, now, and we need to present a united front. I need to show her that we're here for her in any way she needs."

He grabs a drink from the mini bar, downing it in one before reaching for another. "I'm fucking terrified for her, man. How did it come to this? Why the fuck didn't you know what was going on with her? She's your fucking girlfriend."

"I'm going to let that slide, because you're in shock and you need to lash out at someone. You're her brother. She didn't come to either of us. She was really good at hiding it, and neither of us saw it coming. Believe me when I tell you, you couldn't hate me any more than I hate myself right now. You're right, I should have known something was wrong. Don't you think I'm asking myself the same question? How did I not see it? How could she have fooled me like that? Why would she go to such great lengths to lie to me? I didn't even know what fucking country my girlfriend was in. What kind of a waste of space asshole does that make me?"

"I'm sorry, Logan. I'm so fucking confused. I didn't mean to take it out on you. Vittoria's always been good at hiding her true feelings. Fake it until you make it has always been her mantra. I know this must be tearing you up. You don't need me adding to it. I just feel so helpless, like I've let her down. I'm her big brother, I'm supposed to protect her from the bad things in life, and I can't even protect her from herself. It's fucked up, and I don't know how to handle it. I'm so fucking angry at her, and at the same time, I just want to hug her and tell her how much I love her."

"I understand completely. I feel guilty for how angry I am about what she did, but I can't tell her, and it feels like a poison in my system, infecting everything it touches, rotting my fucking soul. How can I be angry at her when she's so vulnerable, and so obviously needs my unconditional love?"

"I guess we just suck it the fuck up and be there for her. And one day, the anger will subside. We focus on how fucking happy we are that she's alive, and that we have a second chance to help her." He stands and walks over to where I'm standing. "I know it took me a while to get on board with you guys dating, but I'm really fucking glad she has you. You're a good guy. You're my fucking brother. I can't think of anyone I'd rather have around to help her get through this and find happiness again."

"Thanks, Carter. That means a lot."

We sit in silence, staring out at the unfamiliar city, hauntingly beautiful and yet so tragic. I don't think either of us will be getting a good night's sleep, but at 1 a.m. I head back to my own room, agreeing to take him to the hospital first thing to see Vittoria.

I lie awake staring at the ceiling, wondering how the hell I'm going to do this. How I'm going to support her through rehab. How I'm going to piece together the broken shards of our shattered relationship. How we're ever going to move on from this.

Will I *ever* trust her again?

Will there come a time when I trust *myself*, and the decisions I make as her Master?

Can I even call myself her Master, and can she ever *really* be my submissive?

CHAPTER 16

LOGAN

One Month Later

EVERY NIGHT SINCE I ANSWERED THE CALL FROM KELEN HOSPITAL, I'VE been plagued by the same dream in the few hours I actually find sleep —a nightmare that could very well have been my reality. I decide to surprise Vittoria with a visit, and when I get there, I'm the one who finds her in her hotel room. But I'm too late. She's gone. Her body cold and lifeless as I cradle her in my arms, screaming my despair to a higher power I don't believe in, and that's when I wake up sweating, my heart pounding.

In the waking hours, things are slowly getting better, moving in the right direction, little by little.

We left Budapest three days after I arrived—Vittoria, Carter, and I, together. He was amazing with her when I took him to the hospital, but it wasn't a surprise to me. They've always been close, and he would do anything for her. It was tough to watch her break down in his arms, to sit idly by and let him comfort her in a way I'm not capable of right now. She doesn't have the same faith and trust in me that she has in her brother. I guess she still sees me as a fleeting presence in her life, rather than a fixture. I'm not family to her, and therein lies the difference. She *is* my family. She is the only person in my life I couldn't live without. Until she feels the same way about me, she won't be able to lean on me the way she needs to.

As soon as we touched down in New York, I took her to her apartment to pick up some clothes and then drove her to a rehab facility in the Hamptons. She begged me not to take her, and when we got there, she begged me not to leave her. It was excruciating, but it was a necessary evil. I didn't want to let her out of my sight, even if it was to help her get better, in a place where I knew she'd be safe.

Carter let me stay at his beach house for the duration of her thirty days in rehab, which allowed me to visit her every day. He and Addi came up on weekends with Verona, which was a great distraction for me, and I know it meant a lot to Vittoria. She wasn't ready to face her parents at first, but toward the end of her stay, she invited them to visit, and in the end it was cathartic for everyone. They gave her all the unconditional love and understanding that I knew they would. It was hard to see Mrs. de Rossi after her visit with Tori. She cried for close to an hour, from the moment she stepped out of the glass doors, and the whole car ride back to the beach house, before falling into Carter's open arms on the porch. Maria de Rossi has been like a mother to me for almost a decade, and more of a mother than mine has ever been. It was heartbreaking to see her so upset, and any words of comfort I could offer seemed so hollow in the face of what she's coming to terms with.

For me, it's been a rollercoaster of emotions over the past month. Two steps forward and one step back. Vittoria, being her usual stubborn self, has fought against any attempt on my behalf to act in her best interests. She shuts down whenever I broach the subject of why she kept what was happening from me. I understand better than most what losing the thing you're most passionate about can do to you. I know the feeling of being completely lost in your own life, when you can't do the one thing that gave you joy, that gave you an escape. The one thing in life that defined you.

I haven't told her what happened to me. She needs to focus on herself and work through her own grief. I hope at some point that my experiences will give her comfort and can help us to connect with each other again. But right now, all I'm doing is hanging on for dear life, refusing to give up on her—on us.

She's coming home today, and this is when the real hard work starts. It's easier to stay clean when you're in rehab, with round the clock support and understanding. The pressures of real life are left at the door when you sign in, but unfortunately, when you leave, you have to pick them back up and start dealing with them. She has agreed to come and stay at my apartment, at least for now. She's not ready to be alone, and I want her with me. I'm hoping it will become a permanent arrangement, but that's something to discuss at a later date.

As I lock up the beach house and load up the car, I have the same feeling in the pit of my stomach that I felt the day I got the call from Budapest. I try to shrug it off, but the last time I did that, it ended catastrophically.

"I've put your bags in the guest room. Make yourself at home, and I'll get to work on dinner. Anything you're in the mood to eat?" She looks confused, as if I'm speaking a foreign language. "Is everything okay? If you're not hungry just now, I'll hold off on dinner until later. It's no big deal."

"The guest room? I thought I'd be sharing your room. Your bed."

"I don't think that's such a good idea. At least, not yet. You're not ready."

"You mean you don't want me anymore." Her gaze drops to the floor. "I don't blame you. You didn't sign up for a suicidal, junkie submissive."

"Don't put words in my mouth, and don't ever fucking talk about yourself like that again, do you understand me?"

"Why? It's what everyone's thinking."

I close the distance between us, grabbing her by the shoulders. "Look at me." Her eyes meet mine, filled with tears. "No one thinks that. Everyone is worried about you. We all love you, and we want to be here for you, if you'll let us."

"I don't want your pity, Logan." She's angry. On edge. The pressure of leaving rehab is getting to her and she's lashing out at me, but I'll take whatever she throws my way. I'm in this for the long haul. "If you're going to look at me like that, then I may as well leave."

"Look at you like what? Like I give a shit about you? Like I *love* you? Like you scared the ever-living shit out of me when I was half the world away and couldn't get to you, and now I'm worried about you?"

She shoves against my chest, pushing me away. "Like I'm so fragile I might break at any moment."

"Give me a break. You tried to kill yourself a month ago. *One month ago.* You barely talk to me, and when you do open up in any way, the next day you treat me like shit. I can't turn off my feelings and pretend like I don't care. If I could switch off all the emotions I've been feeling lately, I would in a heartbeat, believe me. They're fucking crushing me! But I can't, so I apologize if me looking at you with concern and unconditional love bothers you, but you'll just have to suck it up and get used to it because I'm not going anywhere."

"I'm sorry."

"I don't want your apologies. I want you to stop treating me like I'm the enemy. I'm your biggest ally. We're supposed to be a team."

She runs into my arms, her small frame trembling. "I'm so sorry. I don't mean to be horrible, especially not to you. I love you. Tell me you know that."

I wrap my arms around her, holding her tight, afraid to let go. "I know... I know." As I stand here, clinging to the girl I love more than anything, I'm filled with dread for the days and weeks ahead. It's not going to be easy for her to put her life back together, or for us to get back to where we were what seems like a lifetime ago. Maybe we won't ever be the same again. Maybe all we can do is stumble forward, putting one foot in front of the other, and hope we can make a future together. What it will look like—I don't know—but what I *do* know, is that I want her to be in it. "Why don't you go and have a lie down? I'll come get you when dinner's ready."

Her body slumps against mine in defeat. "That actually sounds pretty good. I'm a little tired." She gives me a hesitant, soft kiss on the lips before heading for the guest room. I hate watching her go anywhere other than my bed, but it's too soon. If she's in my bed I'll make love to her, because I won't be able to stop myself. And if we make love, we'll ignore all the issues that we need to deal with, content to lose ourselves in each other for hours at a time, giving us a closeness and a connection we obviously lack in the rest of our relationship at the moment.

I want her so badly it hurts.

I want to worship every inch of her body, to show her what she means to me, to try and make her see herself through my eyes, but I'm concerned I'll do more harm than good. I thought I was a good Master—attentive to her wants and needs, emotionally available for her, and that we'd found a balance of discipline that worked for us. Now, looking back, it seems like it was all a lie. It's left me questioning every decision I make regarding her, and that in itself proves I can't be the Master she needs right now. Until I can find my own way back and feel confident in my abilities, I can't initiate anything physical with her.

I know her well enough to know my decision will make her angry, but I can't let that be a factor in this. She needs love, and discipline, and understanding, and I'm going to find a way to give her all of that. I can't lose her again. I won't.

∿

I HEAR HER SCREAMS FROM DOWN THE HALL. SHE'S HAVING A NIGHTMARE again.

I quickly turn off the heat on dinner and head for her room. It's become a routine now. I crawl onto the bed beside her, careful not to startle her, and then I stroke her hair, whispering words of comfort until she calms down and slowly comes around from her dream. It happened the first day she got home, and it's happened every day since, for the past two weeks. It's making her reluctant to take a nap at any time of day, but her body has been through so much in recent months, she can only fight it for so long before she has to give in and rest.

"It's okay, baby. I'm here. It was just a bad dream." She coils her body around me, burying her face in my chest. "Can you tell me about the dream?"

"I don't... I can't." She starts sobbing uncontrollably, and all I can do is hold her until it subsides. I'm treading water here until she opens up to me, but I feel like I'm drowning.

"Are you hungry? I've got loads of food, and Carter called to say they have a babysitter tonight, so I invited them over. I hope that's okay?"

"Yeah. It's fine. I'll freshen up and be out in a few minutes." I give her a tender kiss, which she tries to deepen, but I pull back, not trusting myself to stop.

"I better go and check nothing's burning." I make a quick exit, adjusting my pants to alleviate how tight they feel all of a sudden. One kiss and I'm like a horny teenager. It's been four and a half months since I made love to her in Paris, and I miss her more than I can put into words. *I miss the Vittoria I fell in love with.*

I distract myself by setting the table, and when the buzzer lets me know that Carter and Addi are here, it's a welcome relief. Being alone with Vittoria all the time is intense, and with no way to release the tension, it's becoming almost unbearable. I haven't made love to her, and I haven't punished her since she got home. I haven't treated her like my submissive, because I'm trying to give her space to rediscover who she is. It's torture, and there have been times when I've wanted to tie her up, punish her, and fuck her until she can't take anymore. I can tell she's frustrated too, but her frustration turns into anger, which inevitably gets directed at me. I'm hoping that tonight, she can find a way to relax and enjoy some time with Addi. I really need to chill and have a few beers with my friend—to just be *me* for a few hours.

When I open the door, I feel like a weight is lifted off my shoulders as they step inside.

"Hey, bro, smells fucking amazing in here. I'm starving."

"Good, it's ready."

I say a quick hello to Addi before shouting to Vittoria to let her know they're here. She comes bounding down the hallway, before jumping into Carter's arms. Her entire demeanor changes, a glimpse of her old self shining through. "It's so good to see you guys."

"It's nice to see you, too. You look amazing. How are you?"

"I'm good. Logan's taking great care of me."

Did I just hear her right? Fuck, she's like a different person. Not the girl I've been living with for the past few weeks. Maybe company is exactly what we needed to diffuse some of the tension around here.

We sit down to a great meal, Carter and I catching up on work and sports over a few beers while Addi very tactfully decided to make mocktails for her and Vittoria. Tori isn't supposed to drink alcohol right out of rehab, because they don't want addicts to replace one drug for another. Addi has this way of getting what she wants—she doesn't make it obvious, and she doesn't patronize. She sweeps you up into whatever she's doing, and all you can do is sit back and enjoy the ride. I can see why Carter is so besotted with her. They've been through so much, and it gives me hope that Vittoria and I can weather the storm and come out the other side stronger.

It's nice to see her laughing again. It's been so long since I've seen her smile a genuine, carefree, beautiful smile.

After dinner, we take up residence on the couch. Carter and I fire up the PS4 and decide to go old-school with some *Street Fighter*. It's a rare window of opportunity to relax and unwind. Addi is busy with Vittoria, and for a brief moment, I don't have to take full responsibility for her. Unfortunately, it doesn't last long. I should have known better than to let my guard down, even for a few minutes.

Vittoria starts stumbling around the living room, spilling her drink before tumbling headfirst into my lap.

"What the fuck? Are you okay?" I pause the game, throwing the controller down on the table, shifting her head back, away from my cock.

She looks up at me, her eyes glazed. "That's not the reaction I usually get when my lips land in your lap."

Carter grunts in disgust. "For fuck's sake! Brother in the room. Too much fucking information."

"Don't be such a prude! You've had more women suck your cock than I've had hot dinners."

"What the fuck is wrong with you tonight?"

"Nothing. I'm just telling you the truth. I'm not a little girl anymore. It can't be a shock to you that I suck my boyfriend's beautiful, big cock."

What the hell is she doing? I stand, pulling her up with me. "That's enough, Vittoria!"

"What are you going to do about it, L-o-g-a-n? Punish me?" She's up on her tiptoes an inch from my face, and that's when I smell it. *Alcohol.*

I turn to Addi. "I thought you said there was no alcohol in those drinks?"

She looks genuinely stunned. "There isn't. I didn't put any in them."

We all turn to Vittoria as one.

"What? So I spiced them up a bit. It's not like I'm underage! I can do what I like."

She is really pushing me now and I'm close to losing it. "No, you can't."

She slams her fists into my chest, struggling out of my grip. "Then punish for it. Tie me up, whip me, spank me, fuck me. Do something. Anything!"

"That's enough... Nyx! This isn't the time or the place to discuss this."

Carter steps up, his face stone-cold with rage. "What's she talking about, Logan?"

Vittoria is completely out of control, spinning around to start in on him. "It's none of your goddamn business. You're my brother, not my keeper. What I choose to do with him is none of your concern, so stay out of it."

"The fuck I will! What the hell is going on?"

"God! Don't be so naïve. You know exactly what's going on, you just don't want to see it. Whips, chains, clamps, collars, handcuffs, and canes. I love it all! I'm a fucking submissive. I'm Logan's submissive."

Who the hell is this person in front of me? My sweet, submissive Vittoria is gone, and this incarnation is spiteful and vindictive. "Enough! Nyx, you will assume the submissive position. Now! Not another word from you. I've let this go on long enough. I don't even recognize the person you've become, and I sure as hell don't like this version of you. You're cruel and spiteful and angry. Take it out on me, fine, but to treat your brother and your friend with such a lack of respect is fucking unacceptable. Now take your fucking position, and do *not* utter another word until I say otherwise. Understood?"

"Yes, Master Fitzgerald." She drops to her knees before me, her eyes lowered to the ground and her arms clasped behind her back. A surge of adrenaline courses through me, my confidence and control firmly back in place.

I hear Addi gasp as she watches the scene unfolding before her, making her way over to Carter as he stands frozen to the spot. His eyes are fixed on Vittoria, kneeling before me.

"Carter, let's just go. I think everyone needs time to calm down before we talk about this." She's trying to push him back toward the door, but it only serves to snap him out of his trance and focus his attention on me.

I step in front of Vittoria, making sure she won't get caught in the middle of what I know is about to happen.

"You've fucking brainwashed her. *You fucking bastard!* What have you done to my sister?" He lunges at me, but I block his punches.

"It's not what you think. You need to let me explain."

He takes another swing, this time catching my jaw. "Explain? Explain to me how you took advantage of my *little* sister? No wonder she tried to kill herself, being trapped in a relationship with a sick fucker like you."

Vittoria breaks her silence, screaming in my defense. "Don't you dare talk about him like that. I didn't do it to get away from him. I love him. He means more to me than anyone else in the world."

"Fucking brainwashed."

"You don't know what you're talking about."

It warms my heart that she wants to defend me, but yet again, she disobeys me.

"Silence! I told you to stay in position and be quiet until I tell you otherwise. Do it, now!"

"Yes, Master."

She returns her gaze to the floor and resumes her silence. I'm distracted by the simple beauty of it, and I don't see his punch coming, sending me crashing to ground with the force of his rage.

"You fucking bastard. I trusted you. I trusted you to look out for her. To love her. Not to fucking abuse her."

I jump to my feet, my own rage boiling over. "I'm not abusing her. I love her. She was a submissive before we got together. I didn't force this on her. I gave it up to be with her, but it wasn't what she wanted or needed."

"Bullshit. She would never willingly be such a pathetic doormat."

I throw a punch to his ribs, dropping him to the floor. "Don't fucking talk about her that way. You have no idea what you're talking about."

"I know you're twisted, and if she willingly does that shit, then so is she. You're fucking sick in the head."

"Get the fuck out of my house, Carter. I'll talk to you when you've calmed down and are willing to listen to what I have to say."

"I'm not going anywhere without her. Vittoria, get off the floor and come with me. You don't have to put up with this shit. It's not normal."

She doesn't move a muscle. She doesn't speak. She doesn't lift her eyes to acknowledge him.

"I said move, Tori. You're coming with me even if I have to carry you out of here."

She remains still, and I know it's hard for her, but she's letting me know she's all in—that she's mine—she wants to make this work. It's all I need.

I resume my stance in front of her. "You're not taking her, Carter. She's staying with me. I'm her Master, and whether you like it or not, she wants me. She wants to be my submissive. She was the one who pursued this, and thank fuck she did. She's the best thing that ever happened to me. I would *never* hurt her."

"You fucking punish her with whips and shit."

"You don't know what you're talking about. I don't hurt her. I never have, and I never would. That's not what this is about for us. She needs the boundaries, the structure, and the freedom of knowing I will always do what's best for her."

"Well, you're doing a great fucking job. She tried to kill herself. Explain to me how that's you being a good 'Master.' You're fucking deluded."

"I don't expect you to understand. Don't you think I hate myself for letting her down? For not being there when she needed me the most? I did the best I could. She chose to keep what was happening from me. She's a really good fucking liar, Carter. She lied to all of us. I'm no different than the rest of you. I believed what she told me, because I thought we didn't keep secrets from each other. For whatever reason, she didn't tell me, and she let it get so bad that she didn't know how to fix it.

"If I could go back and change it, I would. I would never have let us be apart for so long. I would have given up the tour to go and be with her. I would have done anything to make her happy, and to protect her from herself. I can't fucking change it, and I'll live with it for the rest of my fucking life. But, instead of doing the easy thing, and walking away, I'm here. I take shit from her every day, because she's angry at her own life. Not with me. She's heartbroken. Ballet was everything to her. I'm just trying to help her find her place in the world again.

"I'll take whatever she throws at me, and for however long it takes for her to realize that I'm not the enemy. But I suspect she already knows that. She knows I would walk through fire for her. I will *never* give up on her. If she chooses to leave, then that's her decision, and I won't force her to stay. One day, I'll explain all of this to you, and hopefully you'll see that all I've ever wanted to do is love her. I will *always* love her."

"You're kidding yourself if you think this is love."

Addi is by his side. "I think it's time to go." She turns to me with sympathy in her eyes. "We'll talk more when things have calmed down. Just look after her, Logan, or so help me God, you won't have to worry about Carter. I'll hunt you down myself."

"I'll look after her. I promise."

Carter walks over to her, dropping to his knees in front of her. "Look at me, Tori." She keeps her eyes to the ground. "Please, look at me. I love you."

I watch as his eyes fill with tears, afraid for his sister. "Nyx, you can look at him and answer him if he asks you a question."

He shoots me a venomous glare before returning his attention to Vittoria, who is now staring at him, tears coursing down her cheeks. "Come with me. I'll protect you. I know I've let you down so many times, but I won't do it again. Please, I can take you away from all of this. You don't have to let him hurt you, and you don't have to do as he says."

He didn't ask her a direct question, and so she just sits crying in silence. "Are you afraid of him?"

Her answer is immediate, and vehement. "No! He would never hurt me. He's telling you the truth."

"Why are you doing this? I don't understand."

"Because it's who I am. It's a part of me. I didn't change for him. He didn't corrupt me. He tried to push me away, but I wouldn't let him. I need this, and he's the only person who understands. He's unlike any Dominant I've ever had."

"There have been others? How many?"

"I'm not talking about this with you, and not in front of my Master. It's disrespectful."

"Why, Vittoria? Why do you need this?"

"I'll never be able to make you understand. I just do. I crave it, like air. I'm lost without it. Without him. I love him. Please, don't make me choose, because I love you, but I *will* choose him. I'll always choose him." My heart takes flight, fighting to break free.

Carter looks crushed, and I can't help but feel sympathy for him. Even if he hates me for this, I still care about him, I always will, but Vittoria is my priority. He doesn't say another word to her, raising himself to his feet and moving round to where I stand, squaring his shoulders. "You're fucking dead to me, Logan. This isn't over, not by a long fucking shot." He shoves past me, slamming his shoulder into mine as he makes his way over to Addi and heads for the door. As it slams behind them, I can hear him cursing in Italian, before an almighty thud reverberates throughout the room.

I wait until I know the elevator is gone before opening the front door and confirming my suspicions. There's a fist-sized hole in the wall outside my apartment, and blood dripping down the stone-colored paint. A stark and chilling contrast.

When I close the door, I'm met with the soft whimpering sounds of Vittoria. She's still in position, but unable to contain the grief that wracks her body. It's now or never. If I'm going to try and rebuild our relationship as Master and submissive, it needs to start now.

"Stand up, Nyx." She does as I ask, her sobs subsiding at the sound of my voice. "Go to the room at the end of the hall, strip, and wait for me in your position."

"Yes, Master Fitzgerald." She turns and makes her way down the hall, leaving me to catch my breath. After everything that just happened, I need a moment to process.

I slump down onto the couch, my jaw tender from Carter's punch. I grab a bottle of beer from the table and finish it in one gulp. This is not how I pictured finding my control again, and my confidence as her Master, but anger and my instinct to protect her always brings out this side of me. I guess I needed to be reminded of that.

The last time I was back in New York, I had my empty guest room turned into a playroom for Vittoria and me. I didn't know if she'd feel comfortable going to Andromeda after what happened in Paris, and I wanted us to have somewhere to express ourselves freely. She didn't know it was there until two minutes ago, when I sent her in. I can only imagine her surprise. I need to punish her for her behavior tonight. For her disobedience and lack of respect. She said it herself. She needs this. She craves it.

I make my way toward the door, discarding my t-shirt, and removing my watch, shoving it in my pocket. Adrenaline pumps hard and fast in my veins, my dick twitching at the thought of what I'm about to do. I turn the handle and enter the playroom—my domain. The fresh smell of paint is still in the air, and everything is in its rightful place. The couch, the bed, the table... and Vittoria.

"Good girl. Now, stand up and go to the wall behind you. Bring me the cat o' nine tails."

NEW YORK

VITTORIA

Six Weeks Later

LOGAN IS THE ONE GOOD THING IN MY LIFE. HE'S THE REASON I GET UP in the morning, and why I keep fighting against the darkness that threatens to pull me under on a daily basis.

Since the night he sent me to the playroom in the apartment, things have started getting better between us. The first few weeks were amazing. We reconnected through pleasure and punishment, and although things weren't perfect, they were so much better than before. For Logan and me, pleasure has always been at the center of our lifestyle, but lately, I've found that punishment gives me a release I can't get any other way. It lets me switch off in a way that dancing used to.

I can leave all the hurt, and pain, and emotion behind. I can find a quiet space in my mind, where feelings have no place. It's hard to explain, because of course, I feel the pain that's being inflicted on my body, but it somehow allows me to zero in on that one feeling—that one sensation—and it obliterates every other conflicting emotion I feel. It forces them not only into the background, but into a temporary oblivion. When I'm being whipped, or flogged, or spanked, I have a reprieve from my own self-loathing.

I used to cling to ballet. It was my saving grace. My redeeming quality. I've put my family through so much heartache over the years. I changed the course of Carter's life, and it's only through his own force of will and sheer determination to make things work when he met Addi, that he was able to turn it all around. It's given me some small comfort to see how happy he is now, but I can't forget the years I spent watching him push everyone away. I can't forgive myself for how he shoulders such a burden for protecting me. And now, I've broken his heart again.

I've tried not to dwell on his reaction to my choice of lifestyle. I still don't know why I told him. It's something that I've always considered extremely private—no one's business but my own. He confirmed my worst fears about myself. *There's something wrong with me.*

I love to be bound and vulnerable. I adore the feeling of being spanked and flogged and paddled. I have the most intense orgasms of my life after I've felt pain. Is that wrong? I crave the power that I hold. I make the decision of what my Master can and can't do to me in the playroom. I decide how much pain I can tolerate, and I can stop everything that's happening with a single word. I want to feel secure enough to give myself over completely to another person. I don't think I could cope with the intimacy any other way.

If there are no boundaries and no rules, then there are no limits to how much another human being can hurt me, and I can't deal with it.

As much as I love Logan, and as much as he wants to fulfill my needs, when it comes to pain, he's pulling back when I say harder. I know I'm not supposed to ask for more when I'm in the playroom, and initially it got me further punishment, which I relished. But Logan is an intelligent man. He realized weeks ago that I wanted him to punish me harder, and if I want it so badly, then it's not really serving its purpose. Logan uses painful punishments sparingly. He's never been a sadist. He enjoys giving pleasure, and if a little pain heightens the pleasure, then he's more than willing to inflict it. However, when pain is purely for painful ends, he's not willing to cross that line. More and more he's using pleasure as my punishment for disobedience. He withholds my release. He withholds his body from me. He won't let me touch him or allow me to give him any form of pleasure. When he pushes me to the edge of insanity, where I would do anything for that last caress to give me the most euphoric release imaginable, it's then that he pulls me back, leaving me frustrated and begging for mercy. That's a real punishment for me, and he knows it. I hate to be denied. I hate that I can't get my fill of him. Physical pain is nothing to me—I welcome it. But to have him stand in front of me, my God-like Master, so handsome and strong and virile, and have him withhold my orgasms... is excruciating.

With no pleasure release and no pain, I can feel the pressure building. All I want to do, is lose myself in a bottle of pills. It's all I can think about. Just a few to take the edge off, to give me some relief from the constant ache inside of me. A break from feeling every ounce of hatred toward myself that's always there, festering under the surface. I don't want to let him down, and I can't tell him about the one event that triggered all of the pain and suffering I've ever felt. He already looks at me differently—since Budapest. He doesn't have that same spark in his eyes when he holds my gaze. The adoration I once saw reflected back at me has dulled. It's still there, and I love him so much for that, but it's changed. I've changed. I can't go back to using. If I do, I might not survive it, but I feel like I'm fighting a losing battle and I'm terrified.

I want to talk to Logan about it, but instead, I find myself pulling away from him. I want to run into his arms, but instead I avoid them. I sit in silence when I'm screaming inside for him to help me. He can't help me now. He won't do what I need, and I'm angry. Some days I can rationalize and I know that he's acting in my best interests, but on days like today, when all I can think about is using, I can't be rational. I feel angry and hurt that he won't punish me. That he won't help me to find a moment of calm—the eye of the storm. Why doesn't he understand? I'm supposed to tell him when it's too much. I'm supposed to decide what I can handle. I'm supposed to be in control of how far is too far. He said he wants to make me happy, to give me what I need, and yet he's not giving me what I want *or* what I need.

I need drugs, or I need pain. It's one or the other. I don't have dance. I don't have my brother. I don't even have the escape of a peaceful night's sleep anymore. I'm plagued day and night by memories—by my failures. The longer I go without feeling the physical pain of my Master's punishment, the worse it gets, the growing distance between us seeming insurmountable.

I love him and hate him in equal measure.

Why can't he see that I need him to punish me so we can be together like we used to be? I can't love him the way he deserves when I hate myself so much. Those feelings that were pressing down on me in Budapest, crushing me from the inside out, are starting to fill my mind again. The darkness creeping in and consuming my every waking thought.

If he would just punish me like I deserve, then those feelings would go away. If I atone for what I've done, for being bad, then maybe God will let me be happy... with Logan. That can't happen until I'm properly punished.

It's the only way to save what Logan and I have.

CHAPTER 17

LOGAN

EVERY TIME I THINK THAT THINGS ARE GETTING BETTER WITH VITTORIA, we seem to have a setback. As soon as I let my guard down, even a little, I'm thrown back into the emotional turmoil that our relationship has become, and I'm so frustrated. I can't seem to find a way to maintain our connection when we find it.

After the mess with Carter, I knew that I wasn't helping by holding back as her Master. She needs control in her life, and when I walked into the playroom that night—fuck, she was so beautiful. I punished her for her disobedience, and it was fucking incredible for both of us. Then, we spent hours making love and fucking like our lives depended on it. We had been starved for each other, and the intensity of our bodies coming together again was beyond euphoric.

I realized after that night, I was still harboring so much anger and animosity toward her for having such a lack of regard for her own life. Punishing her like that again was a bad idea. I was harsh with her, probably more so than I've ever been, and it's not who I am. I won't be changed into someone and something that I'm not.

Soon after that, Vittoria started to act out in the playroom, which she's never done before. Sure, she has a fiery, headstrong personality, but that's never carried into a scene with us. She was always a perfect submissive in that setting, so I knew there was something wrong something different, when she started acting out, begging for more whipping, more paddling. Every time she wanted it harder and harder. Initially, my reaction was to really punish her for her disobedience, as a deterrent. I figured that when she felt the sting of a harsh punishment, she would change her behavior, but she didn't. She loved it. She thrived on it. Physical pain was no longer a punishment for her, so I decided that I would have to gain her obedience in other ways. She has always been fueled by pleasure, both giving and receiving it. It's what makes us so compatible. To deny her pleasure is the ultimate punishment. That has been my tactic with her over the past few weeks, but she's not responding in the way I had hoped she would.

I feel like I'm right back where I started when I arrived in Budapest. She won't talk to me about anything. She's withdrawn, and she doesn't react to me in the same way she used to. I can see in her eyes that she resents me, but I can't give in to her. I did that before, and she almost died.

A lot of Dominants would punish her, harder and harder until she bled, and they would continue to do so until she understood that pain isn't the answer. But I can't do that to her. She's been through so much in recent months, and to put her body through that, to intentionally cause her unbearable pain... I just can't.

Domination isn't about reveling in inflicting pain on a woman, at least, it never has been for me. My delight comes from walking the fine line between pleasure and pain with Vittoria. I want her to have complete faith in me, to trust that I will navigate the line with delicate precision. I would *never* hurt her. I want to help her push the boundaries, to explore the extreme heights of her own sexuality, which in turn fulfills my own desires.

What she's asking of me now is *not* what BDSM is about for me. She hates herself, for reasons I don't understand, and that she doesn't trust me enough to share. She wants me to punish her, to hurt her—really hurt her. Not in the pursuit of pleasure, but because she wants me to do her dirty work for her. She wants me to be the blade she uses to cut herself. To cause pain that will distract her from the real issues in her life. I refuse to be her tool of choice for self-harming, but I don't know how to move forward with her.

I have to go back to work today, and it'll be the first time I've left Vittoria since she got out of rehab. I'm apprehensive about leaving her, but at the same time, I'm relieved I have an excuse—a reason to take some time out and regroup. Work will be a welcome distraction from everything that's going on at home. The boys have finally finished up their tour and are back in New York, ready to start work on some new songs. I need to get their schedule organized and tie up all the loose ends from the tour, making sure that everything ran smoothly while I was gone. I feel terrible that I had to leave them on the final leg, but Vittoria is more important.

When I get to the office, not only do I have all the paperwork to deal with for Flaming Embers, but I now have a ton of demos from new bands to get through. Apparently, now that artists have heard I represent the boys, they're desperate to be my next signing. It's amazing for my relatively small label, but also a little overwhelming with everything else going on right now. But at least this is something I can control. So I throw myself into it, and barely stop to eat or drink all day.

It feels good to be back doing what I love, and I think I might have found my next band. They're currently out in LA but don't seem to have any luck meeting the right people, or having the right person see them perform. Hopefully, when things settle down here, I can make a trip out there to meet them and see if they'd be a good fit for the label.

Usually when I come across a great demo, I take it to Cube and get Carter to blast it through the sound system. It helps me visualize what I could do with them, and where I could help them improve. Plus, it's always good to have someone else listen to it and give an opinion. Considering Carter runs some of the best nightclubs in Manhattan, he tends to know what people are listening to.

Just another reminder of how fucked up my life is.

I've tried to get in touch with him, not for my sake, but for Vittoria's. She's hurting without him, and she really took his words to heart. I know that deep down, he doesn't really think she's sick or twisted. He just doesn't understand and he's fiercely protective of her. The problem is, she believes him. If he says she's wrong for wanting to submit to me, and for wanting to explore the boundaries of her sexuality, then on some level she believes it.

I'm going to have to make it right for her, but this time, I'm not walking away. If he thinks that's the solution, then he can fuck off. I've been through too much with her to walk away now. He's the one who should be ashamed of himself, the way he reacted. I know it's a shock, and if it was up to me, I wouldn't have told him, because it's none of his business. But it's out there now, and I'm the one who'll need to man up and get them talking again. I haven't figured out how I'm going to do that, and it's pretty low on my priority list right now, so he can stay mad, or disgusted, or whatever the hell he is, until I'm damn well ready to deal with him.

By seven o'clock, not only am I starving, but I'm really missing Vittoria. I thought I needed space when I left the apartment today, but turns out, she still enchants me, even when we're going through a tough time. I pull out my phone and try to call her, but it goes straight to voicemail. I decide to leave her a message, telling her exactly what I'm going to do to her when I get home.

I can't keep waiting for her to open up to me, because the longer I wait, the further away she seems to get. Tonight, I'm going to take back my submissive, in every way imaginable. I'm going to flog her, spank her, kiss every delectable inch of her body, and then I'm going to fuck her. It's not going to be gentle or filled with whispered sweet nothings. It'll be hard and raw, and she's going to feel it for days afterwards. There will be no holding back tonight. I need to see her falling apart for me, crashing over the edge into the blissful ecstasy of her release, over and over until she's hoarse from screaming my name.

I'm most definitely done working for the day. I need to get back to my apartment—to Vittoria, and to the playroom.

~

THE LIGHTS ARE OFF AND THE APARTMENT IS SILENT WHEN I GET HOME. I don't think anything of it at first, assuming that Vittoria is taking a nap in the bedroom. With my mind set on seducing her tonight, I kick off my shoes, throw my jacket over the back of the couch, and make my way down the hall to wake my girl in the most enticing way I can think off. But when I open the door to my room, a sliver of light streams in from the hall, and I can see straight away that she's not in here.

I check the bathroom before heading to the guest room. It's been a while since she slept in there, her nightmares getting the better of her when she sleeps alone. I couldn't stand knowing she was down the hall from me, and not in my bed where she belonged. It wasn't really a decision so much as a necessity when I lifted her from her bed and took her into my room. Ever since then, she sleeps with her body wrapped around mine, right where I need her to be.

When I find the guest room empty, an uneasy churning takes up residence in my stomach. I move from room to room, hoping to find her, but she's nowhere to be found. I pull my phone from my back pocket—no messages. I quickly dial her number and wait impatiently to hear her voice. She doesn't pick up, and I'm really starting to worry. The last time she stopped answering the phone to me, she—*I can't even think it*. She wouldn't do that to me. Not again. She's been making progress, no matter how small, and it's still a move in the right direction.

Carter wouldn't answer my calls even if I tried to speak to him, so I'm left with the prospect of calling her parents or calling Addi. I don't want to worry anyone if there's a simple explanation. She could have gone to the market to get food for dinner, or she could be meeting someone for coffee and she can't hear her phone. I'm sure she'll be back soon. I may as well grab a shower and wait for her.

I only last an hour before I'm really starting to worry. She never mentioned that she was going out, and she hasn't been out alone since she got back from rehab. I know she's a grown woman and can come and go as she pleases, but it's not like her. She would drop me a text to let me know where she is, and that she's okay. I guess nothing about her behavior has been 'like her' recently.

I pull on a pair of Cons, grab my keys, and head out to look for her, starting with the concierge downstairs.

"She left a couple of hours ago, Mr. Fitzgerald. She had a bag with her, big enough for a change of clothes, but no more. She didn't look very happy. I asked her if she was okay, but I don't think she even heard me. I'm sure the valet got her a cab, so you could ask him. He might know where she was headed."

I thank him for the suggestion and make my way outside to find the valet.

"I only started my shift an hour ago. The guy who was here already left for the night. Sorry."

Fuck. I have no idea where to begin. We've spent so little time together in New York, it's not like we have very many regular haunts I can check. The last time we spent a few weeks together here, she was injured. We basically moved between her place, mine, and Andromeda. I can't believe I never thought of it—she's probably at her place. She still has most of her clothes there, and all of her home comforts.

I jump in a cab and head for her apartment. I don't have a key, but her doorman knows me well enough to let me in without disturbing her. My phone starts ringing and I'm scrambling to get it out of my pocket, anxious to talk to Vittoria, but when I see the screen, I'm totally deflated. It's the club. I don't have time for them just now, I need to find Vittoria. I send it to voicemail just as the cab pulls up in front of her building. I throw some bills at the driver, my focus solely on getting to her as quickly as possible.

As I stride through the lobby toward the elevators, the doorman calls after me. "She's not here, Mr. Fitzgerald. She hasn't been here in months. I thought she was with you."

"Shit! Where the fuck is she?" I can feel the panic building as I contemplate numerous scenarios that involve her leaving me, or worse, trying to finish what she started in Budapest. I try calling again, but it goes straight to voicemail… again.

"Baby, when you get this call me back. I need to know you're safe."

As soon as I hang up, I decide it's time to call Addi.

"Hi, Logan. I'm sorry sweetie, but Carter doesn't want to speak to you."

"I don't give a fuck about him right now. I mean… fuck it. I don't have time for this. Have you seen Vittoria?"

"Not since we were at your apartment." And then it dawns on her. "What's going on?" Her voice sounds panicked. "What happened? Is she okay?" She loves Vittoria, and I know she's been worried about her.

"Honestly, Addi. I don't know. Things have been so strained between us ever since she got out of rehab. Even before that. From one day to the next I don't know whether she's happy or sad, or whether things are good between us or not. I thought we were moving forward, but I came home tonight and there's no sign of her. I've left her messages and had no reply. She wasn't at her apartment, and I don't know where to start looking."

"What about places she used to dance? Maybe she would go to one of them to think, to try and process everything?"

"Yeah, maybe. It's a start. I don't have any other ideas."

"Do you want us to help you look? I can call Carter. I know things are shit between you at the moment, but he still loves Vittoria… and you."

"Give me half an hour. If I haven't found her by then, I'll call Xander and you can get Carter involved. I don't want to worry everyone if she's just disappeared off shopping and got her phone on silent."

"Fair enough. Half an hour. Let me know the minute you find her."

"I will."

"And Logan…"

"Yeah?"

"For the record, I think you and Vittoria were made for each other. I know from experience that dating a de Rossi can be a roller coaster at times and comes with its fair share of heartache. But, I can also tell you, when everything finally falls into place and the drama subsides, it's so worth it. Hang in there. I don't care what you're into. I always knew you were a kinky bastard." I can hear the smile in her voice. "You're great for her... when she lets you in. You're a good man, and I love you to bits. So does my stubborn ass husband."

Her tender words are a much-needed balm, soothing my anguished crisis of confidence. "Thanks, Addi. I needed that."

"Thought you might. Now go find her and tell her I'm going to kick her ass for scaring the crap out of us!"

"It's a deal! And Addi..."

"Yeah."

"I love you, too. I hope you know that."

"I do, you big softy."

I hang up, feeling a little lighter. It's comforting to know that someone out there is championing me, willing Vittoria and I to succeed and find our own happy ending.

My phone goes off, and yet again, I'm disappointed. The club is calling. I ignore it and head off in the direction of Julliard. If Vittoria has gone anywhere to think about what she's lost in recent months, it's there. She lived and breathed that place for years, and it's where I first saw her perform.

I search every corridor, asking teachers if they've seen her, and every one of them wanted to stop and chat, desperate to hear how their favorite student is doing. I didn't have the heart to tell them that she can't dance anymore, and I didn't think she would want them to know. She's not ready for the barrage of sympathy she would inevitably encounter. She's so loved, by so many people. I wish she could see it.

I step back out onto the sidewalk, dejected and running out of ideas. Taking my phone out in defeat, I'm ready to ask everyone who loves her to help me find her and bring her home. Before I press the call button for Addi, I receive an incoming call from the club. Again? What the hell is going on there tonight? They're obviously not getting the hint that I'm not available.

"This better be fucking good. I'm busy and I don't have time for whatever shit you want me to do."

"Master Fitzgerald." It's Jacob, the chief of security for Andromeda. He doesn't sound good at all.

"Jacob. What's going on?"

"It's about Miss de Rossi."

"What about her?"

"She's here."

Thank God! She's okay. "Did she come looking for me? Show her to my playroom and I'll be there in ten minutes to pick her up."

"There's no easy way to say this. She's didn't come looking for you. She came looking for Master Liam. She's in his playroom..."

I cut him off before he says anything else. "Fuck!" I shove my phone in my pocket and start running in the direction of the club. "Fuck! Fuck! Fuck!" I'm smacking into people left and right, sprinting through crowds of angry New Yorkers, cursing and gesturing at me as I weave in and out, looking for any space to get me there quicker. My brain is going a mile a minute, unable to come up with any scenario where this isn't exactly what it seems like. *How the fuck could she do this to me?* After everything we've been through. She's my fucking submissive! *Mine!*

I run out in front of cars with no regard for my safety, taxis honking their horns at me to get out of the way, but I couldn't care less. There's only one feeling coursing through my veins right now—all-consuming rage. It fuels me, propelling me through the sea of people around me, my legs moving faster than ever before.

When I hit the block that houses Andromeda, I'm filled with dread at what I'm about to see, and what I'm about to do.

No submissive, not even Vittoria de Rossi can disrespect me like this and walk away unscathed. And as for Liam—he's a fucking dead man.

CHAPTER 18

LOGAN

I HAVE NEVER FELT SUCH ANGER IN ALL MY LIFE. NOT WHEN MY DREAM of getting a deal burned to ashes in front of my eyes. Not even in Paris. This is something completely different. This comes from somewhere much darker. I feel so overwhelmed by it, engulfed in it. I can't even see straight.

Cold, all-consuming, fury.

I slam open the doors and I can sense the change. This isn't my safe haven anymore.

"Where the fuck are they?"

Jacob speaks calmly, as if it will help me in the slightest. "Master Liam is in his room. She's in there with him."

I act on instinct, my fist connecting with his jaw. "Why the fuck would you let her go with him?"

He slowly wipes the blood from his lip before squaring his shoulders to stand a full four inches above me, but I'm not intimidated. He might be built like a wrestler, but the adrenaline fueling me right now would be more than enough to take him down. He shakes his head. "I'm going to let that one slide, Master Fitzgerald, but do it again, and I will take you out. You know I have no control over what happens in here, unless someone crosses the line. She came here looking for him.

She went willingly into that room. I'm sorry to be the one telling you this, but don't shoot the messenger."

"Fucking hell! I need to see her. I hope you're not going to try and stop me. She's mine. No one touches what's mine."

He steps out of my way, letting me pass without another word.

The music and the crowds are white noise in the background. A distant soundtrack to my life falling apart. I feel their eyes on me. They all know she's here. When I reach the door, I can feel the bile rise in my throat with the knowledge of what I'm about to see. I don't knock. I bust the door open and all of my worst fears are confirmed. Vittoria is here. My Nyx... with another Master.

"What the fuck is going on?"

Liam makes his way over to me, dressed in nothing but his loose-fitting pants. "It's not what it looks like, Logan. Let me explain." He tries to put his hand on my shoulder, but I dodge him and hit him with a jab to the stomach, winding him and knocking him to the floor.

"*Explain?* Explain the fact that you're in here with *my* submissive? How could you do this to me, Liam? I looked up to you. You're my mentor. You trained me to be a Master. You *know* what this means better than anyone. *She's mine. No one fucking touches her but me!*"

I turn to Vittoria. She's shackled to the St. Andrew's Cross at the far end of the room. Metal restraints holding her arms and legs spread wide... for *him*. She's dressed only in her underwear, her head hung in what I can only hope is shame. She's sobbing, and I want to comfort her, but the sight of her makes me feel physically sick.

I turn my attention back to Liam, who's picking himself up off the floor. "Why? She's mine."

He's angry that I got the best of him. I can see it in his eyes, and I watch as he changes into someone I don't even recognize. "She was mine first. Who do you think trained her to be a submissive?"

This can't be happening. Not Vittoria.

"That's right, Logan. I've claimed every single inch of that beautiful body of hers. You can't really blame me for wanting to revisit when she offered herself to me on a plate."

I hear Vittoria's voice slicing through the pain that's threatening to break me. "That's not what happened, Logan. Please. Let me explain."

I slowly turn my head toward her. My voice is cold, calm, and devoid of any emotion as I respond. "Do not... *ever*... address me as anything other than *Master Fitzgerald*. You do not *speak* unless I give you permission. You will not even so much as lay eyes on me until I tell you otherwise. I can't stand the sight of you. Do you understand me... Miss de Rossi?"

I can see how much my words are hurting her, but it's nothing compared to how I feel. She drops her head, her voice a broken whisper. "Yes, Master Fitzgerald." She continues to cry, tears streaming down her soft, flawless skin as I force myself to look away.

"I want the truth, Liam. Start talking now, or so help me God, I will drag you out of here by your balls and beat the shit out of you in front of every submissive in this place. No woman will ever want such a pathetic excuse for a Master.

"That'll make two of us."

"You're right. I probably can't show my face in here ever again, but the difference between us is that I don't give a shit. The woman you decided to chain up in here tonight is mine. She's the only woman who will ever be mine. I won't let you or anyone else take her away from me."

"Then you're a fool, Logan. Look at her. She came here willingly. You deserve better than this from your submissive."

"I know that." Vittoria's sobs intensify at my words, but I can't risk a glance in her direction. I failed her in some way, or she wouldn't be here. "The question is, do you want to suffer the same fate, Liam? Do you want to be able to show your face in here? If you do, then you better tell me the truth. What happened tonight?"

"Okay, okay." He sits down on the couch behind him, his head resting in his hands, deflated. "Firstly, let me start by saying, I consider you a friend, and I was planning to explain everything to you, until you punched me. I'm angry you did that in front of her. She was important to me once... she still is." I flinch at his admission. "She called me today and said she needed to talk. She sounded distraught. I was worried, so I told her to come. When she arrived, she was almost hysterical, begging me to punish her. Asking for the hard stuff."

I don't know how much more I can listen to.

"She said straight away that she didn't want anything sexual. That she belongs to you, and she would never have sex with another man. She kept saying repeatedly that her pleasure belongs to you. It was clear that she was unhinged. I told her she should be speaking to you. She started shaking, telling me you can't know about it, that she doesn't want you to know how bad she is. How broken and twisted she is. She wasn't making sense. I know she's been through a lot, but I also know you. You would never hold it against her. I can see how much you love her." He sees my confusion. "She hasn't told you, has she? What happened when she was young?"

She begins to thrash around, struggling against the restraints. "No! Don't. You can't. He can't know. I love him. I don't want him to look at me that way." I've never seen her like this before, so out of control—so scared.

"Logan, you need to talk to her. You need to know, otherwise you'll never be able to be the Master she needs." I don't know what to do with the anger coursing through my veins. It's suffocating me. "Nothing happened. I didn't touch her. I thought about it. I really fucking wanted to, and she really seemed like she needed the release. The pain. But, I saw the disgust in her eyes as I tightened the restraints and felt her flinch when my hands brushed against her skin. I knew it wasn't me she wanted. She wanted to hurt herself, and I was her way out. I couldn't do it. You're not the only one who fell in love with her. That's when I told Jacob to call you." His revelation hangs heavy in the air. "I never wanted her to leave. When she found out I was your mentor, that I trained you, she said she couldn't be my submissive anymore. That was two years ago. I never got over her. You know how easy she is to love. Problem is, she never loved me back. I was only ever a coping mechanism for her. I see now that she told me everything, not because she loved me, but because she didn't. She wasn't worried about how I'd look at her, or if my opinion would change."

Her cries are burning a hole in my chest. The howls of a broken, vulnerable, animal. A primal cry for help.

"She's different with you. You're good for her."

"Obviously not, or I wouldn't be standing in here with you."

"Logan. This isn't a reflection of your skill as a Master. She has chosen to hold back a major part of who she is. Until she relinquishes that, and lets you in, you can't help her. I know you're strong enough for this."

I hang my head, weak, broken, and completely lost. "I don't feel it."

"I'm not your mentor anymore. You surpassed me a long time ago. You were born to be a Master. Everyone at this club knows it. You need to own it. You're letting your feelings for Vittoria get in the way of your basic nature. And ironically, that instinct is exactly what she needs from you right now. You need to let go of the anger and talk to her."

"I'm sorry I punched you, Liam."

"Forgotten already. I would have done the same thing in your position. Punch first, ask questions later."

"I need some time alone with her, to get her down off that fucking cross, and out of here."

"Of course. I'll leave you. Take as long as you need."

He grabs his shirt and walks out, leaving me in the silence of my own despair. Vittoria's cries have subsided and she's completely motionless. I make my way over to her tentatively, my heart breaking at the sight of her, at what I've pushed her to.

I don't say a word. I can't.

I start working on her restraints, kneeling before her to remove the ones from her legs first, livid at the marks left on her skin where she struggled against the metal. When I stand to loosen the wrist restraints, I lift her chin with my finger, forcing her to look at me. I don't see hate, or regret, or love in her eyes. Her stare is blank, cold, and terrifying. She seems almost catatonic. I make short work of freeing her arms, her body slumping against mine for support. She can't stand on her own, she can't function. Panic rises inside of me. I don't know if I can do this—if I can pull her back from the brink. I hold her tight, fighting hard to suppress my anger and replace it with compassion.

I lift her up into my arms, her body limp, her head dropping down onto my chest. I lay her down on the bed and grab her clothes off the floor, a sharp pain stabbing at my heart. I dress her quickly, but she doesn't even look at me. Lifting her carefully back into my arms, I stride out into the hallway, and everyone stops to stare as I walk through the main room. It feels like every set of eyes is on us, but I have more important things to worry about. All I can think of is getting her out of here, getting her home. What happens then? I don't know.

SHE HASN'T SPOKEN SINCE WE GOT BACK TO MY APARTMENT. I THOUGHT it best that I give her some time to rest and regroup before I talk to her about all of this. In truth, *I* needed time, too. This is all so far beyond what I thought I was dealing with. I thought this was about the loss of her dancing career. I knew that someone had hurt her. I assumed a past boyfriend or Dom. I thought if I gave her time, she would open up to me. Hearing Liam say that whatever this is happened when she was young—I was so far off the mark. I should have insisted she told me from the start. I wanted to be with her so badly, I bent my own rules of full disclosure and afforded her the privacy that's now clearly destroying her.

It's been two hours since I brought her home, and as I creep into the bedroom, careful not to wake her, I find her in the exact position I left her, still staring at the same spot on the wall with a blank look on her face. I kneel at the side of the bed, directly in her line of sight. It's as if she's looking through me, as if I'm not even here.

"Talk to me, Vittoria. Look at me. Anything."

Nothing.

I'm not ashamed to admit that she's really scaring me. I don't know how to help her, but trying the soft approach hasn't worked, so I do the only thing I know.

"Look at me, Nyx… now." Her eyes come to life, darting up to meet mine.

"This is my fault. I've been too lax with you. Obviously, I was wrong."

"This isn't your fault, Logan. It's who I am. There's nothing you can do about it."

"Bullshit. For a start, do not call me Logan. I am your Master and you will afford me the respect I deserve after the stunt you pulled today. I may not have been the Master you need up until this point, but rest assured, I won't make the same mistake again. Sit up."

I watch the effort it takes for her to lift her small frame from the bed. She seems so defeated. It's devastating.

"Now, I need you to tell me what Liam was talking about. I've known for a long time that you've been keeping something from me. You were open about that fact. I thought if I gave you time, you would trust me enough to open up to me, but now I know this isn't about trust. This is about how you see yourself, about what you think is going to happen if you open up to me."

"I can't tell you."

I grab her by the shoulders, fighting the urge to shake her in my frustration.

"Enough! You *will* tell me, Nyx. I won't have a submissive who disrespects me. I can't protect you and care for you properly if you don't tell me what the hell is going on."

"You'll look at me differently. I don't want your pity. You won't think I'm perfect anymore. You'll think I'm dirty."

"Fucking hell! When are you going to understand? When are you going to grasp how much I love you? You're tearing us apart because of something you *think* is going to happen. Nothing can be worse than what I just witnessed, and I'm still fucking here. You're killing me."

I loosen my grip, caressing my hands up and over her shoulders, along her neck and onto her face, cupping her cheeks in my palms. My voice is soft but commanding, my gaze pinning her, entreating her to listen to me.

"I will make a promise to you here and now. Nothing you could ever say, nothing you could ever do, or that has ever been done to you, would make me love you any less. You're it for me, Vittoria. I don't think you're perfect, not by a long shot, but I love you, flaws and all. I love your strengths and your weaknesses. I love every part of you, the good, the bad, and the ugly. Please put your faith in that… in me. Let me help you. Please, Nyx… tell me why you hate yourself, when there is so much to love about you."

Her tears fall freely, drenching my hands. I pull her down onto the floor beside me, cradling her in my arms.

"You have to tell me, baby…"

Cries wrack her body, causing her to convulse in my arms. It breaks my heart to see her like this, but if she doesn't face it now, I fear she might never come back from this. I thought her overdose was a cry for help. That in her heart of hearts she didn't *really* want to die that day. I believed what I wanted to believe, because the alternative was too distressing, too awful to contemplate. I thought we were past the worst of it when she made it through rehab. But now I see, it was just the beginning. The end of her career was a catalyst for so much more. Ballet was her way of coping, and when that was lost, it all came crashing down around her. She overdosed… to end her own life. To end her perpetual suffering. How did I not see that? How could I have failed her so badly?

When her body settles and her cries diminish, I have to ask her again. I need to know.

"What happened to you?"

She lifts her gaze to mine, her eyes red and puffy, bloodshot from so many tears.

"I was ten years old when it happened."

Shit. I steel myself for what I fear is coming. I know I need to hold it together for her, to be strong enough for both of us.

"It was Carter's fourteenth birthday party and all of my parents' friends were there to help celebrate. People I had known my whole life. It was like any other day, any other party… until it wasn't. *I died that day.* The Vittoria I was… happy and carefree, trusting… just… died."

I pull her closer, wishing I could take this away for her, but I don't say a word, giving her the space she needs to continue.

"Marcus was one of my dad's best friends. He was like an uncle to me and Carter. We loved him. He was always the fun one, giving us treats, and getting my dad to cave if we really wanted something. Carter idolized him. I don't know how he managed to fool everyone for so many years. I don't know why he did it. I wasn't the only girl he…"

She starts to shake in my arms. "It's okay, Vittoria. I'm here with you. I won't let anyone hurt you ever again." I stroke her hair, trying to calm her rapid heartbeat. I can feel it pounding against my chest.

"He told me he had a surprise for me. That wasn't unusual, so I didn't think anything of it when he told me it was up in my bedroom waiting for me. He took my hand and led me upstairs, away from everyone. I knew something was different when he closed the door and turned the lock."

I don't know if I can hear this.

"He told me that if I screamed… he would hurt Carter. He knew Carter was everything to me. I was terrified of anything happening to him, so I kept quiet while he…" She breaks down. "I can't say it… please, don't make me say it."

"Shh. It's okay. I've got you." I need to know for certain. "Did he rape you?" It kills me to even say the words.

She nods her head, dropping her gaze to the floor.

The world crumbles around me. Everything I thought I knew, scatters into disarray. I am overcome with rage. I feel murderous, holding her broken, shaking body in my arms, and I need to take a moment to rein it in, because I can feel my own body beginning to shake. I try to breathe through the anger, my hands fisting so tight it hurts.

When I finally gain control of myself, I lift her chin, making sure she's looking into my eyes as I say these words. "Don't *ever* hang your head in shame, Vittoria. You did *nothing* wrong. You were a child. He was an evil son of a bitch, and that is no reflection on who you are." I wipe the tears from her eyes. "He took your innocence, and despite that, despite everything you've been through, you have grown into the most amazing, caring, loving, extraordinary woman I have ever met. I could never think less of you. I love you even more."

Her eyes search mine, looking for some hint that I'm not being truthful with her.

"Vittoria de Rossi, I love you. Understand this. Own it. Know that you deserve it." She tries to look away, but I won't let her. "No. You need to hear this. You need to stop hating yourself, punishing yourself for something that you had no control over. You are exceptional. You're breathtaking both inside and out. You are and will forever be... my Nyx. My goddess. My everything. Let me in, baby, please. I'm begging you."

She throws her arms around my neck, kissing me with everything she has, and I let her, giving her the connection she so desperately needs right now. That we both do.

When she finally breaks away, I know that we need to finish this discussion, because if we don't, one of two things will happen. Either, she'll close herself off from me again, and it will tear us apart. Or, we'll discuss it later, and I'll need to put her through this torment and despair all over again. I don't know if either of us can cope with that.

"Does Carter know?"

She lets out a sigh. "He was the one who found me." My heart breaks for them both. For the girl who idolized her big brother, and for him, my friend, having to deal with finding her, at the age of fourteen. I can't even begin to imagine how he was able to cope. "He made sure I was safe, before going to find Marcus. He attacked him in the middle of the party and that's when my parents found out. Marcus is still in prison to this day. My dad found out he'd done this to other girls and he made sure that he'll never see the outside of a cell."

"Good, because if he was out, I would fucking hunt him down and gut him like a pig."

"Carter feels the same way. Don't you see? I'm the reason Carter is the way he is. He always blamed himself for not being able to protect me. That stayed with him. It's why he never let any woman get close, it's why he's had such a hard time trying to make it work with Addi. It all comes back to him feeling like he can't protect the women he loves. It's my fault. It ruined his life. I hate seeing how it changed him."

Her tears begin to fall again, but this time they are for her brother. As always, she is thinking not of herself, but of everyone else around her.

"You can't shoulder that burden, Vittoria. It's all on Marcus. Carter loves you more than his own life, and that's his choice to make. It's understandable, you're very lovable." I get a hint of a smile from her. God, I miss her smile. "You can't feel guilty about him. He's doing just fine. Yes, he was a man-whore, but most guys our age are. Look at him now. He's making it work with Addi. He loves her something fierce. He's happy."

"Why are you being so nice to me?" I can't believe she's asking me this.

"Because I love you... more than anything or anyone in my life. You need to accept it and know it's a truth that will never change."

"I'll try." She looks so exhausted.

I know we need to talk about what happened at the club tonight, about what she did, but now isn't the time. She has trusted me with this huge secret, and if I push her as to why she felt she had to go to someone else, I'm concerned that it will push her over the edge. She needs to rest, and I need time to think. To process all of this and decide how we move forward from here.

"You need to sleep. We'll talk about Liam tomorrow."

It suddenly hits her.

"Oh my God. Oh my God! Logan... Master Fitzgerald. I'm so sorry, please forgive me, please. I can't live with myself if you don't forgive me. I can't believe I did that to you, after everything you've done for me. I wasn't thinking straight. You have to believe me. Fuck! Please."

I clutch her against me, forcing her to calm down.

"Slow down. Breathe. Stop. I told you, we will discuss this tomorrow. For now, I want you to rest. Do you understand me, Nyx?"

"Yes, Master Fitzgerald."

I press a tender kiss to her forehead. "Do you remember the

promise I made to you?" She doesn't respond. "I promised you I would *never* give up on you, that I *could* never give up on you. That hasn't changed. We have a long road ahead of us, but I'm here, and if you still want to be my submissive, then I *will* make this work."

I hate that I'm nervous of her answer. I hate that she has such a hold over me. I was so consumed with hate and anger tonight, and I know she has her reasons, and she's been through more than anyone ever should, but I would never let another submissive shame me like that and allow her to remain in my life. I worry that my love for her is making me weak, and if I'm weak, then how can I be the Master she needs to help her through this?

"I want to be with you, Master. It's all I've ever wanted. I will be better. I'll *do* better."

I'm overwhelmed by so many conflicting emotions, and I don't like it.

"You need to rest. Get some sleep. We'll talk tomorrow."

I lift her onto the bed, pull the covers over her, and turn to leave, but she grasps my hand.

"Please don't leave me, Master. Stay with me." I nod my head in defeat. She needs me, and her need to have me close comes before my own need for distance.

I lie down beside her and pull her against my chest.

"Goodnight."

"Goodnight, Master Fitzgerald."

It's not long before she falls asleep, her breathing becoming slow and even. It's then, in the darkness, that I become consumed by my own fear, and anger, and guilt. I don't know what the fuck I'm doing.

If I fail her again, it could be fatal... *for both of us.*

CHAPTER 19

LOGAN

I CAN'T EVEN LOOK AT HER.

How am I supposed to be there for her, to help her through this, if I can't look into her eyes without seeing the betrayal that's burned into my retinas, and seared into the walls of my heart?

Last night was one of the worst of my life. I can't say it was the worst, because that will forever be the day I got the call from Kelen Hospital—the day I found out that the love of my life tried to kill herself. That day has stayed with me, tormenting me, making it impossible for me to find my way back to her.

I want... I need to get us through this, because if I don't... well, the alternative is unspeakable.

I thought that we were slowly moving in the right direction. I knew we still had a long way to go, and that I couldn't hurt her in the way she wanted, but I thought removing physical punishment altogether for a while would give her time to understand where I was coming from. Now, I realize how wrong I've been. I still believe that hurting her to assuage her inner pain would have been unhealthy, but I think removing it completely, along with her pleasure, has only made her worse. Our physical chemistry has always been such a big part of how we communicate our feelings for one another, and the loss of it has been a huge roadblock for us finding our way back to each other.

I've tried so many times to get her to talk to me about it, about everything, but she just shuts down. Last night is the first time she's really opened up to me, about anything. I should have listened to my gut in the beginning. I convinced myself that whatever it was she was holding back, it couldn't have been that big a deal if she didn't feel the need to tell me. I was only lying to myself, and in the end, it hurt Vittoria more than I can handle. I was selfish, but that's no surprise. I've always been selfish with her. Since the first time I kissed her, I've been unforgivably selfish.

Last night forced me into action, and we need to build on that. She needs to talk to me now. If she doesn't, there's no hope left for us. She broke my heart, and my heart has been breaking for her every day since I got on that plane. It's almost more than I can bear. The only thing worse, would be to lose her altogether. Now that I know what she's been carrying around all this time, I hope I can be a better man for her. I need to find a way to move beyond her betrayal, and to help her deal with the loss of her career. She needs to talk to someone about what happened when she was young, to fully come to terms with it. If she'd worked through her emotions and her grief, I don't think we'd be in the situation we are now.

Dance gave her an escape, a way to cope, and that's been stripped away. She's lost. *We're lost.* But, I want to make it better. I want to keep my promise to her that I'll always be here, and that I will always love her, and protect her, even from herself.

I lie awake all night, staring at her, wondering what I'm going to say to her. I need to reinforce my place as her Master, because what she did with Liam can *never* happen again. I couldn't see that again and forgive her. I don't know if I can forgive her now. Logically, I understand why she did it—that she wasn't in a good place, and she didn't fully grasp what she was doing at the time. That was evident when I mentioned it. She was shocked and horrified with herself, and I'd love to say that I could put it behind me and move on, but I can't. Nevertheless, how can I punish her? How can I hold it against her after what she told me? It would make me the worst man in the world, to hear what she's been through and to punish her for reacting in the only way she felt she could.

I feel like I'm between a rock and a hard place. If I tell her it's okay, and that I forgive her, then my role as her Master is questionable at best. If I focus on what she did, rather than her subsequent revelations, I'm a dick. How do I navigate this? I usually excel when it comes to walking the fine line in life. It's where I feel most powerful, most like myself, but this is something else entirely.

I don't think I slept at all. I felt physically ill most of the night. I replayed the sight of her in his playroom, over and over in my mind, and when I managed to push it from the forefront of my thoughts, I was grief-stricken by what that monster did to her when she was a helpless, trusting girl. I had to jump out of bed at one point to throw up in the bathroom.

I'm weak, and pathetic, and I hate that I've let myself become this person.

I leave Vittoria to sleep while I take a shower and try to put the broken pieces of myself back together. I let the water cascade over my body, washing away my doubt and insecurity, steeling myself for the conversation I need to have with her. I stand under the shower head for at least fifteen minutes, my head pressed against the cold tiles, the water beating down on my back as I slowly regroup, remembering who I am and why she was drawn to me in the first place.

I stepped into the shower as Logan—battered and bruised by life. But, when I finally emerge, I feel stronger.

I control my surroundings.

I control my life.

I control my submissive.

I am Master Fitzgerald.

It's mid-afternoon by the time she wakes, and I listen to the sound of her cautious footsteps padding down the hallway and into the living room. She finds me pouring over contracts for work, distracting myself until she was ready to come to me.

Her demeanor is quiet, resigned. She knows what's coming. She stands at the end of the couch, her head bowed in a show of respect, her hands held behind her back. She doesn't attempt to speak, but instead waits patiently until I'm finished working on the papers in front of me. I make her wait, not to be cruel, but in gratitude of her willingness to submit to me. I know that opening up to me was hard for her, especially after what happened at the club. She knows that she betrayed my trust as my lover, as my friend, and as my submissive. This is her way of showing she's sorry. She doesn't try to force me to talk, she doesn't expect anything of me, and I acknowledge it with my silence. The way we interact as Dominant and submissive is a form of unspoken communication. It's part of who we are. This is her way of fighting for us.

When I'm done with my work, I clear the table, carefully and methodically filing the papers in my briefcase. I take my coffee cup to the sink and wash it out before getting to work preparing brunch for us in silence. She doesn't move a muscle or lift her head to see what I'm doing. She simply keeps her submissive stance until I'm ready.

When the dining table is set and the food is laid out, I cross the room, closing the distance between us. I drink in her scent as she stands before me, and in our silence, I hear her breath quicken at my proximity. It's a welcome response.

"Give me your hand, Nyx." She doesn't lift her head, but reaches out to me, her hands small and warm, her touch a sweet relief from the loneliness of the night. "Come with me." I lead her to the table and pull out the chair for her. "Sit. Eat." Her gaze remains lowered, careful not to meet mine until I say otherwise.

We eat in companionable silence, and I watch as she savors every last bite. She's always been slender, but recently, since Budapest, she's painfully thin, and it pleases me to see her devour her meal. Maybe it's because a weight has been lifted, now that I know what happened, or maybe she's eating because I told her to. Either way, I'll take it. I've wanted her to do things to make herself happy in recent weeks and months, but she's not ready for that, and if I can get her to treat her body with respect, even for my sake, then that will have to be enough until I get through to her.

When she's finished eating, she crosses her cutlery on the plate before clasping her hands in her lap and waiting. I take a moment to look at her, to really take in every aspect of her features—her long luscious hair scraped up into a messy bun, her skin, her stunning pouty lips, and her glasses framing beautiful brown eyes. The vibrancy that used to emanate from her is gone. She looks older than her years. Tired. Defenseless. It hurts to see her like this. I want to scoop her up into my arms and love her until she can love herself again, but I can't, because looking at her fragile features, I also see the look in her eyes when I walked into Liam's playroom. I can see the marks on her wrists from the metal restrains, and the same on her ankles. A reminder of how she gave herself over to another man.

"Look at me." She lifts her head slowly, and I can see that she doesn't want to meet my gaze. I see the reluctance in the clench of her jaw as our eyes finally find each other. "How are you feeling? Did you sleep well?" I'm trying not to let my voice sound cold, but it comes across that way.

"Yes, Master Fitzgerald. Considering how ashamed I feel, I slept relatively well, thank you." She shows her inner strength, holding my gaze as she confesses her guilt.

"You should feel ashamed of yourself. I'm ashamed of you for your behavior last night." She continues to stare straight into my eyes as tears begin to fall from hers. "What I'm about to say to you doesn't change anything that I said to you yesterday. I love you, and I will be here for you, for us. Nothing you told me has changed the way I feel about you. If anything, I love you more for trusting me with what happened."

I watch as her tears become a steady stream, dripping down her cheeks and into her lap. She makes no move to wipe them, holding her position with her hands tightly clasped. I want so badly to caress my thumbs across her soft cheeks, and kiss away every one of her tears, but I stop myself.

"Tell me you understand what I'm saying, Nyx. Whatever I say from here on out, whatever punishment I see fit, you must understand that I love you. I will always love you, and you are mine and only mine. Not out of obligation, but because I want you to be." She remains still. "Say the words. I want to hear you say them."

"I understand, Master Fitzgerald." Her words are broken, thick with tears, and I don't know if she believes a word I've said, but if I say it enough, I'm hoping it will sink in.

I stand from the table, leaving the empty plates behind and make my way over to the living room. "Come and assume your position at my feet."

She knows exactly what to do, and she does it with practiced elegance. She may not dance anymore, but to me, every move of her body is an ethereal dance—a joy to behold. The way her limbs glide across the floor with a flow and sensuality she can't even see—it's endearing. I sit back in the chair and watch as she stops in front of me, her toes mere inches from my own as she removes her top, folds it, and places it on the arm of the chair next to me. I usually reserve this position for the playroom, and ask that she wear only her bra and panties, but today, she isn't wearing a bra underneath the t-shirt she slept in. I watch her intently as she pulls down her shorts, revealing her lack of panties. There is nothing sexual in her movements, she is simply carrying out my request, folding the shorts and placing them carefully with her t-shirt.

I harden involuntarily at the sight of her. None of this is for my sexual gratification, or hers, but rather as an exercise in complete submission. For me, it will be a test of my willpower. Every inch of her flesh is on display, and I have to force myself to look away. I'm so conflicted by desire and disappointment. Images of her with me, tainted by the memory of her betrayal. She falls to her knees, clasping her hands behind her back and dropping her head. She has assumed her position at my feet. Submissive to her Master. I give her a moment to calm herself, to find her center before I speak.

"Now that you're ready, it's time to discuss what happened last night." I can see her body visibly react to my words. Her muscles tense and her jawline tightens. She's worried. "I am so angry, Nyx. I can't even begin to express the gravity of how I felt walking into Liam's playroom." I feel my own body tense at the memory, my fists tightening. "Look at me when I tell you this." Her gaze slowly lifts until our eyes meet. "You disrespected me in the worst possible way. You broke my trust. I have never had a submissive treat me with such contempt, and it will *never* happen again. If it were anyone but you, this relationship would be over. I need to know why. Why did you go to him? Why didn't you come to me?"

She sits for a moment before she gains the courage to speak, and I'm not sure if I'm ready to hear the answer. "Master Fitzgerald, I'm not sure if my explanation will make this any better, or if I really know the reason behind what happened. I've been feeling so lost in my own life. I hate that I can't dance anymore. I'm angry and sad, and depressed. I don't know how to channel what I'm feeling, and ever since my injury, I've had so much time to wallow in my own thoughts. It's all been coming back to me. The nightmares about what happened when I was younger are worse than ever. I don't know what to do. I thought that if I threw myself into our lifestyle, it would help alleviate it in some way."

She quietens down, and I know I have to ask the question again. "Why did you go to Liam?"

Her voice is barely a whisper as she speaks. "Because he knows what happened, and I knew he would give me what I asked for. I couldn't come to you. You didn't want to punish me hard, Master."

I can't even look at her. I'm seething with rage. "You never gave me the chance to understand, and to give you what you needed. You didn't trust that maybe, just maybe, I know what you need and that's why I *didn't* punish you to the extent you wanted. I'm the one who decides, me and only me. If you disagree with my decisions, then you speak to me. Under no circumstances do you ever go to another Dominant and ask them to touch you. Your body is mine and mine alone. It is for me to touch and taste and punish as I see fit. Seeing you like that... knowing that he restrained you..."

I need a moment to calm down, my anger threatening to overwhelm me.

"I'm so sorry, Master. I told him I wouldn't do anything sexual. Only the punishments."

"Don't you dare speak until I tell you to! You haven't earned the right. Do you understand me?"

"Yes, Master Fitzgerald."

"How dare you try and justify your actions. Every aspect of our lifestyle is sacred to me. Letting him touch you, even in punishment, is as bad as letting him fuck you. Confiding in him instead of me, and going behind my back, is as bad as fucking him. *You ripped my fucking heart out, Vittoria!*"

Her hands shoot up to cover her mouth and hold in the sobs that are wrestling to break free.

"Get your hands behind your back, now." My tone is cold, devoid of any emotion, because if I let myself feel, I'm going to explode.

I stand from the chair and walk around her, pacing the room as I decide what's next. Her eyes follow my every move, but I can't stand it.

"Don't look at me. I can't stand the sight of you, and I don't want your eyes on me. I don't want to see your shame." She sobs quietly as I continue to pace, trying to work off some of my pent-up aggression and frustration.

"Answer me this. If you walked into my playroom and found me whipping another submissive, would you be okay with it? Or would it feel like a betrayal? Think long and hard before you answer me, Nyx, because you obviously didn't think about it yesterday."

She answers immediately. "I would be devastated, Master. I would feel betrayed." Her words don't give me any comfort in my absolute despair.

"Devastated doesn't even come close to describing how I feel. I've loved you every day since the moment we met. I fought against it for as long as I could, and when I finally gave in, when I decided that I had to have you no matter the cost, I thought you felt the same. I thought that we were in this together. You're the love of my life, and I can't equate what happened with me being the love of yours. If I were, you never would have done it." The silence in the room is deafening as I struggle to put into words what I'm thinking and feeling. "I've lain awake more nights than I can count, asking myself if I'm worthy of you. If I'm man enough to be the Master that you want and that you need. Even before you... before Budapest. Every night since then, I've been questioning where I went wrong. What I could have done to help you, what I could have done to love you more, to show you, to make you understand that a world without you in it wouldn't be any kind of world for me. All this time, I knew you were holding back, but I never thought for a moment that you would hide something of this magnitude. Something so fundamental to the way I would have handled you as my submissive. I know you said you didn't want me to look at you differently, but that just shows your lack of faith in me, in us. If you don't know by now that I will love you, no matter what, until I take my last breath, then I haven't done a very good job of loving you. And I have most definitely failed you as your Master, in so many ways."

I scrub my hands over my face, my eyes tired and blurry from lack of sleep. I can barely see straight, and my limbs suddenly feel like lead as I walk across the room. I drop back down into the seat in front of Vittoria, defeated and exhausted, both emotionally and physically. I let myself sit for a few minutes, garnering whatever strength I can muster to finish our conversation.

"I won't walk away from you. I promised you I wouldn't, and I stand by that. But it's going to be a hard road back to having any form of trust in you. It's going to take time for me to be able to look at you and not see you shackled by him. We have so much to work through, so much we need to talk about, and if you can't do that, if you can't put your faith in me and let me work out a way to help you, and to help us, then you need to walk away. You need to stand up right now, get dressed, and leave. It's your decision. I love you. I always have, and I always will, but I can't fight for us on my own. You need to fight *with* me, and if you can't, if you can't promise me you will *never* try to find solace in another man's arms again, then we're done. There's no hope left. It's fight or flight, Nyx. Which will it be?"

"Fight. I want to fight for us, Master Fitzgerald. I love you, and I promise I will never let another man touch me. My body, my mind, my heart and soul, belong to you and only you. I will spend the rest of my life trying to make it up to you if you'll let me."

"Very well. I guess I'll have to take you at your word. Now, here are some new rules for you. If and when we return to the playroom, you will continue to present yourself as you did before, in your bra and panties. You are my gift to unwrap, and that is for my pleasure, not yours. If I ask you to assume your position anywhere outside of the playroom, then this is how you will present yourself to me. Naked. Not for my sexual pleasure, although I will never be able to look at your body without appreciating its beauty. You will be naked so you remember there can be nothing that you hide from me. You must be completely open and honest with me. Your nakedness will be an outward symbol of this. You will learn to be comfortable baring your-self to me in every way. Do you understand?"

"Yes, Master Fitzgerald."

"Also, you will not touch yourself unless I expressly tell you to. All of your pleasure is mine. I've been lenient up until now, my judge-ment clouded by my love and desire for you, but I see now that it wasn't good for you. You need to learn your place, and until you prove to me that I can trust you, until I feel you've earned your orgasm, I will not touch you, and you will not touch yourself. Understood?"

"Yes, Master Fitzgerald."

I couldn't touch her, even if I wanted to. The mere idea of it stirs up so much resentment inside of me. I want so badly to erase his touch from her skin, to stake my claim on every inch of her body, but I am repulsed at the thought of how freely she gave away what is mine and mine alone. I have to choke past the lump in my throat to get through the rest of our conversation.

"Do you have anything else you want to say at this point? Anything else I need to know?"

She reaches out to touch me, with tears in her eyes. "I'm sorry I hurt you. I was being selfish, and I'm so, so sorry."

I push her hand off my legs. "Don't touch me. Don't move your hands without permission, and always address me as Master Fitzgerald until you earn the right to call me anything else." I hate that her touch makes me angry. It's always been a soothing balm to my inner turmoil, but the moment her skin makes contact with mine, I see her with him. "You will remain naked until I tell you otherwise. You will remain here until I return. Maybe it will give you some time to really think about what I've said, and about the decision you made yesterday. I love you, but I can't be in the same room as you right now, because the disappointment is crushing me." I stand and leave her, naked, crying, and alone in the silence of the living room.

To an outsider looking in, I'm a total bastard for the way I've just treated her—the woman I love. But what they don't understand, is that Vittoria *needs* to be treated like this. She needs to feel punished, because it lets her know I care. It gives her structure, and rules, and boundaries. I thought that being lenient after rehab was the right thing to do, but I was wrong. That's when she needed me to step up and be her Master in every aspect of her life. This is all on me, and I hate myself for it. I let her down. I hate that I can't stand to look at her, and I hate that I can't pull her into my arms and make love to her, or tell her how sorry I am that I didn't know her when she was young. I couldn't be there to protect her from him. I hate that I have to be cold with her, but it's for her own good, and mine.

I'm so full of anger and rage and the deepest disappointment. I'm heartbroken. I need to work through it and find my way back to her, and hope that I can help her find her way back to me in the process.

CHAPTER 20

LOGAN

One Month Later

THE FIRST FEW DAYS AFTER MY DISCUSSION WITH VITTORIA, SHE SEEMED more like herself again. She was the perfect submissive, doing everything I asked of her without question, speaking only when spoken to, and always referring to me as her Master. The problem hasn't been her willingness to obey me, but rather my own reluctance to let her in.

It's been over a month since we last made love. I've continued to act as her Master, punishing her when necessary, but never excessively. I give her pleasure because I can't deny her, but it's infrequent, and I still can't bring myself to have sex with her. If I don't find a way to move past this soon, we may never find our way back to each other. Ever since that night at Andromeda, I haven't been able to connect with her in any sort of meaningful way. I know she needs the intense bond between Dom and sub, but I don't know how to recapture it. Every time I look at her, I see her restrained in Liam's playroom. I see how broken she was, and how badly I failed her. I'm broken, and I can't fix it.

Slowly, I can see her closing herself off from me again. She's becoming more and more introverted, protecting herself, her emotions all but switched off completely.

She's lost without ballet. She won't even listen to music anymore. She's withdrawn from everything she's ever loved, including me. She refuses to leave the house, she won't let her parents or her brother come to visit. She's becoming a shadow of the woman I fell in love with and slipping further from my grasp with every day that passes. She's not my Vittoria. She's lost inside the shell of a beautiful woman whose smile used to light up my soul.

Without ballet to help her cope, she needs the Master/sub dynamic now more than ever to help her deal with her emotions. She needs the intimacy that comes from entrusting her pleasure to me, and I want it, too, but I feel helpless, because I just can't give it to her right now.

Vittoria is a walking oxymoron—a dominant submissive. Being a submissive is a power play for her. She has absolute control over what a man can and can't do to her—what *I* can and can't do to her. She sees BDSM for what it really is, or at least she used to. The Dominant may only exercise complete control over his submissive within her parameters. She creates a framework which allows her to give herself over to me in safety. She will do whatever I ask of her, but only after setting the boundaries.

This is the way it should be for all submissives, and I've always tried to teach the women I've trained that submission to another human being is the ultimate act of strength.

There was a time when Vittoria understood that in its entirety, but she's lost her way, and I'm to blame. She's my responsibility, and in the time she's been mine, she's become an addict, lost her career, tried to commit suicide, and then turned to another Master for help.

If it was anyone else, I would walk away and let her find a Dominant who could help her find herself again, but I know that if I abandon her now, despite my failure, it could push her over the edge. I need to help her reconnect with her life. I owe her that. I want that for her, and at my core, I'm a selfish man. I can't give her up. I need her so much it hurts, even though I can't seem to get over what she did, and it's tearing me apart.

I am being crushed from the inside out by the guilt of how badly I've handled all of this. I should have seen it. I should have been with her. I'm supposed to know her better than anyone, but now, I feel like I don't know her at all, and yet I still crave her. She still calls to something deep inside of me.

I go in search of her, because I just need to be near her, and as I walk down the hallway and into our bedroom, I can hear crying coming from the bathroom. I run to the door and turn the knob, but it's locked.

"Baby, open the door."

"I can't." Her voice goes stone cold. "Go away, Logan. You can't help me." A chill runs through me. She doesn't sound like herself, and it terrifies me.

"If you don't open the door, I'm going to break it down."

Silence.

"Please, Nyx."

"Don't call me that. I'm not a goddess of any kind. I'm broken. I can't be fixed." I can tell by her voice that she's at the other end of the bathroom, so I take a step back and kick the door in. I can't take this distance between us anymore.

I stop dead in my tracks, the door broken and smashed, just like my heart.

I find her sitting on the floor with a pair of sharp, metal tweezers, scratching a line into her thigh. Her flawless skin now marred by three perfectly parallel deep red lines, each one around four inches long. She's staring at the floor as she carries out the repetitive motion, scratching her skin, over and over again until it bleeds.

I drop to the floor in front of her. Grabbing the tweezers out of her hand and scooping her up into my lap.

"What are you doing to yourself? Baby, this isn't the answer. Hurting yourself isn't the answer."

Her body is rigid in my arms.

"I'm bad, Logan. Bad things happen to bad people. I'm... he knew.

He knew I was bad. I can't dance anymore, its God's punishment. You don't want me anymore because you know. You know I'm right. I'm damaged, and bad, and you hate me now, just like I hate myself. That's why you can't look at me."

Her tone is so cold and yet her speech is frantic. I'm losing her. I stand up, still cradling her, and walk out into our bedroom. I lay her down on the bed and hold her face in my hands, forcing her to make eye contact with me, but she shuts them tight.

"Open your eyes, Nyx. Now." I know she'll respond to her submissive name. She craves my control. "You are *not* bad. There isn't a bad bone in your body." She tries to pull away. "Nyx. Look. At. Me." She obeys, her eyes glistening with unshed tears. "You... are the most amazing woman I have ever met. I knew the moment I saw you, that you were special. That you were too good for me." Her tears spill over and down her cheeks. "I have loved you since the moment I laid eyes on you. The moment I first tasted you, I knew I would never recover. I had tasted heaven. You need to hear me when I say this, God is *not* punishing you. Something terrible happened to you. Something that no little girl should ever have to deal with. You got through it, and grew up into this strong, confident woman. You became the most gifted dancer I've ever seen, and because it meant everything to you, you pushed through the pain. I can understand that. It's awful and so wrong that you had to give up what you love, but you have to keep living. You can't give up on yourself. You have so much to give. You are so much more to me than just a dancer. I don't love you any less because you're not a ballerina anymore. I know you're going to find another passion. Something you love, that brings joy back into your life."

Her sobs become uncontrollable, and I question if this is helping her, but I persevere. I finally tell her about my dream of becoming a musician—the deal, my mom, the anger I felt for such a long time. I explain to her how I found a way to still be a part of the industry I love, and how I've made peace with it. I know it's horrible that her career has been cut short, but she got the chance to live her dream for years, touring the world and performing with the best ballet company there is. Not everyone gets that kind of opportunity.

"You can't keep shutting it all out, Tori. You need to *feel*. You need to feel all of the hurt, pain, and loss. You have to grieve. Then, you find a way to let it go and move on with your life. You don't need to do it alone. I'm here for you every step of the way. Don't say that you're bad or that you're being punished, ever again. You are mine. You are worthy of love, and success. After everything you've overcome and achieved in the face of adversity, you deserve the best life has to offer, and if you'll let me in, I want to be the person to share all of that with you. I love you. You will always be mine. I'm sorry I haven't shown you that lately, but that's my issue, not yours. Please, Nyx. Please, don't hurt yourself."

I lie down on the bed beside her and pull her into my chest. Her tiny body shakes as she cries, strangled, anguished pleas for the pain to go away. It's heartbreaking to witness, but there is nowhere else I could ever be.

There are so many unanswered questions going around in my head, and I have to ask the most important one as I cradle her in my arms. "How long have you been hurting yourself, Tori?"

Her words are a whispered confession. "Since the night you found me in Liam's playroom. Never hard enough to draw blood before."

I pull her tighter. "Fuck. This is my fault. If I had been paying closer attention to you, I would have seen it, but instead I was pushing you away."

She lifts her head, her eyes finding mine. "This isn't your fault."

"Why, Nyx? Why would you hurt yourself? I don't understand."

It's a few minutes before she replies. "I feel like everything is boiling up inside of me all the time, and it's so overwhelming, and so painful. I have no way to let it out. But, there's something about that moment when I scratch into my skin, it's like releasing a valve. The pressure I feel inside dissipates, if only for a little while. I can switch it all off. Focus on that small patch of skin, that small, but intense amount of pain. Excruciating, but euphoric. It's not the same as the pain of a punishment. *I* control it. But, the elation is short-lived. Within minutes, I look at the mark that's left behind, reminding me of my weakness, and it's like an anvil slamming back down onto my chest. Does that make any sense?"

I've been holding my breath. Listening so intently to every word that she chooses to share with me.

"I don't know what to do with it, Logan. With all the pain, all the emotion, and all the grief." She starts sobbing uncontrollably, and all I can do is hold her. *I feel impotent.*

"Shh. It's going to be okay. I'm here. I'm going to help you. We'll figure it out... together."

She cries herself to sleep in my arms, whispering words of how dancing was her life, her soul, her everything. I lie with her for hours, cradling her, watching the rise and fall of her chest, trying to figure out a way to help.

I stare at her leg, the lines of dried blood ripping into my soul. It kills me to see how much she's hurting—to hear how she sees herself. I wish I could let her see herself through my eyes, even for a moment. She'd know how amazing she is, how loved and cherished she is, how her smile makes my pulse race even when I've been keeping her at arm's length.

I slowly extricate myself from her embrace, careful not to wake her, going in search of my first-aid kit. I'm sure there's one in here somewhere. When I find what I need, I quietly make my way back to our room and cautiously tend to her wounds. She moves around a little when I put some antiseptic cream over the cuts, but she doesn't wake. I place a small gauze pad over all three marks and tape it in place, before grabbing a blanket from the closet and covering her to let her rest.

That's when I realize... I know what I have to do.

"Logan? Where are you?"

I look at my watch. She's been asleep for almost four hours, and I've been in here most of that time, preparing. I quickly finish up and head out to find her. She sees me closing the door to my playroom.

"Hey. How are you feeling?"

She looks sheepish. Her hand moving over the small bandage on her leg. "I'm feeling a little better. Thank you for taking care of me. I know it's not easy."

I can't stand not being able to touch her, so I close the distance between us, wrapping my arms around her small frame. "It's my job to take care of you. Loving you is as effortless as breathing." I kiss the top of her head. "Do you trust me?"

She holds me tighter. "Yes."

"Then come with me." I lead her back to the playroom, opening the door to let her see what I've been doing.

The room is empty.

She turns, confusion etched on her flawless features. "What? Why? Don't you want to be my Master anymore?"

"No, no, no, baby. You've got it all wrong. I will always be your Master, and the playroom will be returned to its former glory, but I need you to do something for me first. It required the room to be cleared, and the mirrors to be rearranged along the back wall."

"I don't understand."

"I'm going to ask you again. Do you trust me?"

"Yes, Master Fitzgerald."

"Strip down to your underwear." Without hesitation, she removes her clothes leaving only a black lace bra and matching panties. "I want you to dance for me." I take the remote from my pocket and start the music. *Love Runs Out* by OneRepublic starts blaring through the speakers.

Vittoria drops to the floor, covering her ears.

"Make it stop. No. I can't do this. You know I can't dance anymore. Why would you do this to me?"

I stand over her. "Stand up, Nyx. Now!"

"No! You can't make me."

"You will stand up now and obey me. I am your Master, and if you don't do as I say, I will punish you. I will *not* tolerate an insubordinate submissive any longer. It stops now. I know what you need. You need to respect me, and if you can't do that, then go. I don't want you here."

Her eyes fly up to meet my gaze.

"You don't mean it."

I want to tell her that I could never leave her—that she's a part of me—but I don't.

"Try me."

She covers her mouth with her hand, holding in the sob I know is fighting to get out.

"*Stand up, now!* You dance, or you leave this room and don't return. Your decision."

"I can't dance." She stands up, her head lowered in defeat.

"You can't be a ballerina anymore. You can't push your body to dance professionally, but you can still dance. You can still feel the music and let it flow through you."

"I don't think I can."

"I'm telling you that you can. You need this. Let go. Take all of your hurt, pain, anger, and frustration, and let it out. Let the music in, and dance through the rage you're feeling. If you keep it inside, it *will* destroy you. You need to find yourself again."

I watch the tears as they fall silently down her cheeks, and my heart aches for her, but I need to push. She needs to do this.

"Dance or leave. What's it going to be?"

"I... I..."

She steps into me, punching me in the chest, slapping me, her breathing labored as she struggles to come to grips with what I'm asking of her. I just stand and take it, knowing that this is going to push her to face her feelings.

I put the song back to the beginning and turn up the volume until it consumes all of the air in the room, vibrating through our bodies. There's no escape.

"Feel, Nyx. Anything. Let yourself feel it."

She pushes me away and walks to the center of the room, dropping her head back, staring up at the ceiling.

I can see when it happens.

I watch the moment that she lets it take over. Her entire demeanor changes. It's thrilling and chilling to watch. The transformation is unmistakable.

She begins to run her hands over her skin, her body starting to move. Her long black hair sways as the music takes over. Anger emanates from every pore. Her movements are sharp and filled with frustration, her hands fisting in her hair as she thrashes her head in time with the beat.

Her feet start to move, gliding around the room with practiced elegance, and a freedom I've never seen from her. This isn't just ballet, this is a hybrid form of dance. The emotion she expresses is so raw and real and awe-inspiring. I stand frozen to the spot, transfixed by the beauty before me—around me.

I can tell that she's no longer aware of her surroundings. She's completely gone, lost to the rhythm, lost in the dance. It is unlike anything I've ever seen her do. She is so aggressive, pouring everything she has into this one song, this one dance.

It's amazing.

She's stunning.

I am in awe of her strength, her talent, her beauty, and her ability to speak to me through every move of her body.

She covers every inch of the floor, her legs carrying her to another plane.

She is fucking transcendent. She's my Nyx.

I see the woman I fell in love with. My Vittoria. She's right there. She's come back to me, and I have never wanted her more than I do in this moment.

When the song ends, she drops to the floor, breathing hard, her body glistening with a sheen of sweat.

I immediately go to her, unable to contain the desire coiling inside of me, coursing through my veins. I want her. I need her, and I can't wait any longer.

I lower my body down on top of hers, pulling her up by the back of her neck, our lips and tongues colliding in a frenzied fuck. I'm starved for the taste of her, and my hunger can't be sated. I can't get enough. She bites down hard on my bottom lip, a sharp pain and the familiar metallic taste of blood on my tongue. I take it and continue to give her everything I have, taking what I need in return.

She starts clawing at my back, pulling my t-shirt up and over my head, breaking our kiss just long enough to get it off and out of the way. I unclasp her bra and rip it off her, exposing her perfect breasts and tightly budded nipples. I take one and then the other into my mouth, nibbling, sucking, and flicking each one in turn, cupping the other with my hand. She feels so fucking amazing, and she tastes even better.

I kiss my way down her body, savoring every inch, every freckle, every line and curve. I want to take it slow, but I need her so badly, I can't hold back. I grasp the sides of her panties and rip, tearing them from her body. I bury my face in her pussy, licking and sucking her with a fierce intensity. Rough and hard, but with all the tenderness I can give. She's dripping with desire, and I lap up every last drop. It doesn't take her long to crash over the edge into a screaming orgasm, thrusting her hips, forcing me to take more of her. Hearing my name on her lips as she loses herself to the myriad of sensations is so fucking sexy. My dick is straining against the denim of my jeans, making it almost painful, but I need to hear her come, over and over again, until her body is limp and sated.

I flip her onto her front, lifting her ass in the air, forcing her to spread her legs wide for me. I continue to lick and suck, pulling her tight against my face as I kneel behind her, thrusting my fingers inside of her, delighting in the moans of pleasure she can't contain. I'm harder than steel, and her final cries of ecstasy are my undoing.

I stand, pulling her up with me.

"Take off my pants." She rips open the button-fly of my jeans, tugging the waistband down together with my boxers, licking her lips, her eyes focused on my erection. "Do you want it? Tell me how badly you want to feel me inside you."

Her eyes lift to meet mine as she speaks. "It's a physical ache. I miss how you feel as you thrust every... hard... inch..." Her hand travels up my thigh and fists around the base of my cock. "I miss the feeling of your warm come spilling inside of me." She kneels before me, and I feel like I'm about to shoot my load at the sight of her—naked, willing, and sexy as hell. "I miss the taste of you on my tongue." She darts it out and licks a drop of pre-come from the head, before taking me fully into her mouth, her warmth and wet surrounding me. It's fucking amazing.

"Fuck! Vittoria... I've missed this. You look so stunning on your knees." I take a moment to look across at the mirror, at the sight of her with my cock in her mouth, her head moving back and forth, her breasts bouncing with every thrust. It's so fucking hot.

I'd love to let her continue, but I need to be inside her... now.

I take a step back, the loss of her mouth leaving me momentarily bereft. I grab her by the ass and pull her up and into my arms. My lips crash down on hers, our juices mingle as our tongues tangle and twist in an all-consuming dance of desire. I stride across the room with her small frame wrapped around me, pressing her back against the wall. I quickly position myself, and drive my cock into her, in one sharp, hard thrust.

It's a cataclysmic event. Not only a physical connection, but the deepest emotional connection we've ever shared. I hold her gaze for just a second, so many unspoken words passing between us before I devour her mouth, fucking it as I hammer into her. She's screaming my name, begging me for more. Harder. Faster.

I press into her, my hands against the wall on either side of her head as I continue to fuck her hard, making love to her with all that I have and all that I am.

"Come with me, Vittoria. I want to hear how much you love me."

She lets go, her walls tightening around me, forcing me to give into my own release. It's intense and so fucking good to finally let myself reclaim her. I love the sound of her voice, hoarse from screaming as she pants and moans, telling me how I make her feel. It pushes me over the edge as I pound into her, feeling each hot spurt of come fill her.

"Fuck... Vittoria... you're mine. You'll always be mine. Say it. I need to hear you say it."

"I'm yours... Logan. I'll always be yours."

I ride out the aftershocks of my release, kissing and nibbling her lips, letting her do the same.

Music is still blaring through the speakers as I lower myself to the floor, her limbs wrapped around me, our bodies still joined in the most intimate of ways. We stay like this for a while before either one of us speaks.

"Vittoria, please don't hurt yourself. I can't bear to see you treating your body this way."

"I'm sorry. I just felt so lost and alone."

"I know, baby. I wish you had been able to come and talk to me about it. I thought I was doing the right thing after Budapest, not pushing you too much, and then Liam happened."

"I can never apologize enough for what I did. I promise, I'll spend the rest of my life trying to make it up to you."

I smooth her hair with my hands. "Stop apologizing. We've talked about it. I forgive you. I know I've been struggling to come to terms with it, but most of that has been because I felt like I was losing you. You haven't seemed like my Vittoria for such a long time. I should have listened to what you wanted from me. It's just... I didn't want to hurt you, especially when you felt you *deserved* to be so harshly punished. BDSM has always been about pleasure for us. The thought of hurting you in any real way is abhorrent to me."

"Logan, you don't have to justify yourself. You were right. I see that now. I should have trusted you, as my Master, and as my best friend. I thought I knew better, and I made it worse. I felt like I'd lost everything that ever meant anything to me. You forcing me to dance tonight... I felt like myself again for those few short minutes. I still have a lot to work through, but you were right, I need ballet in my life. Maybe not as a career, but in some way. I love it too much. It's a huge part of who I am, and how I manage everything else in my life. There has been a huge, gaping hole in my life, and tonight, for the first time is a long time, it feels... smaller."

"Have you ever spoken to anyone about what happened with Marcus?"

"I did in the beginning, but it was too hard to keep going over and over that day. I shut it out and threw myself into ballet. I guess it all came crashing back into my life when I had to quit."

"Please tell me that you know, none of it was your fault. There was nothing you could have done."

"I know… on a good day, when I'm rational. I know it was him and not me. He was bad. But on the tough days, I just hate myself, and I don't know how to fix it. I thought I could fix it with pain, but it's a fleeting moment of relief and then it all comes flooding back."

"You need to talk to someone. You can't keep feeling like this. It breaks my heart. You're the most amazing woman. You're intelligent, beautiful, loving, and talented in so many ways. You have to learn to love yourself."

"Will you help me?"

I tighten my embrace. "Of course. I'm here for whatever you need. If you want me to find someone for you to talk to, then I will. I'll do anything and everything I can to make you believe just how precious you are to me."

She nestles her head against my chest. "Thank you. I don't deserve you. You're an amazing man."

I lift her chin, looking down into her stunning, troubled eyes. "You do deserve me. You deserve whatever you desire in life. I. Am. Yours. For as long as you want me." I dip my head down and capture her lips in a soft kiss.

I feel myself hardening inside of her, and she responds, gently swiveling her hips on my lap, taking the lead as we make love—slow, sensual, and spiritual. It's late by the time I carry her out of the play-room. She's asleep by the time I lay her down on the bed and pull the covers over her. I lie beside her, awake for hours, just staring at her in peaceful slumber, more in love with her than I ever dreamed possible. She's been through so much, and yet she still shows strength in her weakest moments, love in her darkest hours, and trust in me, when I've failed her more times than I could ever forgive myself for.

CHAPTER 21

LOGAN

Five Months Later

I never thought I would say this, but I really am the luckiest guy on the planet. I have the girl of my dreams, a job I love, good friends, and a future ahead of me that I never thought possible. Flaming Embers are topping the charts, taking America by storm. Carter and I are talking after months of fighting and misunderstandings. In the end, it wasn't me, but Vittoria, who bridged the gap, and explained our lifestyle to him in a way that he could understand and accept. She's a force to be reckoned with when she puts her mind to it, and when she decided she'd had enough of his bullshit and ignorance, she let him know it! I'm so goddamn proud of her.

Looking back now, I don't know why I didn't figure it out sooner. Maybe the timing had to be right, but the moment it all fell into place, it felt like the most natural thing in the world.

Dance.

Dancing saved the love of my life so many years ago, long before I knew her. Then, when I finally found her, it broke her. The logical conclusion should always have been that dance would bring her back to me. And it did.

In the months following our breakthrough in the playroom, our relationship has gone from strength to strength. I'm not going to lie and say it was all moonlight and roses, whips and nipple clamps. That night was a new beginning for us, but we still had to fight every single day for what we have, and it was and is totally worth it.

Vittoria has been clean for nine months, which is an amazing milestone for her. She started seeing a therapist, finally letting herself feel all of the pain and sadness in her life. She's finally grieving the loss of her childhood innocence, the loss of ballet, and her suicide attempt. It's been rough on her, but together, we're working through it. After every session with her therapist, we sit down to dinner and discuss what she was talking about. Sometimes there are tears, but mostly these days, there's joy. Joy in rediscovering who she is, what she loves, and where she's heading.

It's been such a privilege for me to witness her transformation these past months. She hasn't self-harmed again, although I know the temptation is still there on the bad days. The difference now, is that she comes and talks to me when she feels the urge to hurt herself, and we work through it together. She's been wrapped up in a cocoon of self-loathing and fear for so long. It's hard to break free of that, but, seeing her emerge as a happy, healthy, strong woman, has been such an honor.

As a submissive, she's wonderful. Knowing her better, knowing what fuels her, what has shaped her into the person I fell in love with, has really deepened our relationship. I'm better able to anticipate her needs, knowing what her triggers are. She's more trusting of my decisions, and I'm learning to trust her again. There had been so many lies between us—so much deception. It's taken me a long time to get over that and take her at her word. Trust is a gift, and when it's lost, it's difficult to regain. I have to give her credit where it's due. She's never questioned me or been bitter when I've struggled to trust her. I think she understands what she put me through, and she knows that it took a lot for me, as a Master, to move past some of the things she's done.

The incident with Liam, which still makes me feel sick to my stomach, should have been the end of our relationship. I don't know another Master who would forgive such a transgression, but in the end, it was my decision to stay and fight for her—for us. I can't hold her mistake against her for the rest of her life, so I guess, it's not just her who's been on a journey of self-discovery.

I've spent so much of my relationship with Vittoria questioning myself, my decisions, and my place as her Master. Control has always defined me, and the loss of it threw me into a spiral of doubt. It's taken me a while to realize that loving her isn't a weakness. It's a strength. She challenges me in ways that no one else ever has, forcing me outside of my comfort zone, which is exactly where I'm going to be this time next week.

Next Saturday is Vittoria's birthday, and I have a few surprises up my sleeve for her. We've been living together at my apartment since she got out of rehab, but it was never a conscious decision It was more necessity than anything else, and that's not really the way I wanted to begin our life together. I've been looking at apartments with my realtor over the past few weeks, and I've narrowed it down to three that I think Vittoria will love. I'm going to take her to see them when we get back from LA, and whichever one she chooses will be our first real home together. It's been hard keeping it a secret, but it's a huge step for us, and I want it to be perfect.

I've been talking to Xander about one of my plans for the last few weeks, and he's been a huge help getting it all set up. I've been looking for a space for Vittoria. Somewhere to call her own, and somewhere to find her passion for dance again. I don't know what she wants to do, but she would make an amazing teacher, or choreographer. I wanted a blank canvas for her to explore her options, and Xander had just the place. He recently bought a building on the Upper East Side, that has a great space on the first floor. Perfect for a dance studio— hardwood floors, wide open and spacious. I've had mirrors installed along one wall, and ballet barres fitted. I got Carter to organize a top-of-the-line sound system through his club contacts, and I hooked it up with a new iPod fully loaded with music from every ballet I've ever heard of, and all the contemporary bands and artists she likes. I even added in a sneak peek of the new Flaming Embers album, which I know she'll get a kick out of.

My last surprise for her will be asking her to wear my collar. For a Master to collar his submissive, is tantamount to marriage. It's a big deal, and I know Vittoria will appreciate the significance of it for us. I didn't want to go with the cliché of an actual collar. She has the most stunning neck, and I like it naked and open to the caress of my lips. Plus, I don't need for everyone to see it. It's for Vittoria and me. No one else. I decided on understated elegance. A perfect match for my stunning submissive. I had a set of custom-made platinum bracelets made for her. Each is padlocked, and they can be connected to restrain her at any time. She won't be able to take them off without the key, which I will keep possession of. To anyone else, they will look like delicate, beautiful, intricately designed bracelets. Only we will know their true meaning. I'm having the inside of each bracelet engraved. The first one will read:

To my darling Nyx, you are mine
The second bracelet reads:
And I am yours. Always, Master Fitzgerald

They should be ready when we get back to New York next week, and I'm planning to give them to her on her birthday. I think she'll love them, and I can't wait to see what they look like on her dainty little wrists. I also plan on testing them out at her birthday party, seeing how well they work when they're joined together, restraining her. It makes me hard just thinking about it.

Vittoria appears in the doorway looking breathtaking in a simple fitted white t-shirt and jeans. The picture of subtle sophistication. "What are you thinking about? You have that look in your eye."

"And what look would that be?"

She slinks toward me, mischief in her eyes. "The one that says you're thinking very naughty… very dirty things about me."

"You know me too well, Nyx. Clearly, I need a better poker face."

She makes herself comfortable in my lap, wriggling around, well aware of what she's doing to me. "I like that I know when your filthy mind is at work. It'll make it all the sweeter on our flight today. Especially, as I'm not wearing any underwear. Something to think about."

She moves to stand up, but I pull her back down against me. "You realize that I didn't give you permission to go out in public without any panties on? That means I'll have to punish you." Her breath hitches and I know she's aroused at the idea. "So, now I have a dilemma. Do I bend you over my desk right now, spank your naked little ass, and enjoy the fact that you won't be sitting comfortably on our flight? *Or*, do I leave you sans panties, and let you travel with the anticipation of how I'm going to tie you up and punish you in our hotel room in LA? Decisions, decisions." She's squirming now, and I know exactly what she wants, and I'm more than happy to oblige. "LA it is. Just know, that whatever your dirty little mind can come up with today, it's going to pale in comparison to what I'm actually going to do to you tonight. Now go and grab your bag. We need to get going."

She has a smug grin on her face, getting exactly what she wants. She loves the anticipation, the sweet torture of it all. It makes the final release all the more intense. She stands to leave, but I hold her in place. "Stand still." I dip my hand down the front of her jeans, feeling her smooth, soft, warm skin, pushing my fingers against her folds. "You're wet, Nyx. Why are you so wet?"

I remove my hand, leaving her wanting more when she pulls my fingers up and into her mouth, tasting her own arousal. "Mmm. Because everything about you turns me on, Master Fitzgerald. Your body, your face, your voice, the way you smell, the way you make me come, and the way you punish me in such... delicious ways."

I slap her on the ass and send her on her way, looking forward to five days of sun, sex, and sounds. If everything goes well with the band we're going to see, they'll be the support act for Flaming Embers' next tour.

Before we leave, I make a point of going to the playroom and packing a little something extra for our trip. After all, I have a punishment to administer tonight. This is going to be an unforgettable trip.

~

"THEY TOTALLY KILLED IT! THAT WAS AMAZING. YOU *HAVE* TO SIGN them."

"They were pretty great, and they're keen to work with me, so it could be a good fit all round. But, before I do anything, I want to go and hang out backstage with them. Get a feel for their dynamic, and their lead singer, Josh. They'll be going on tour with Campbell and the boys next year if this works out, and I want to make sure that there won't be a clash of personalities."

"Then let's go and meet them!" She's almost giddy with excitement tonight, her earlier exhaustion from our afternoon... activities, a distant memory.

As soon as Josh sees us, he excuses himself from the throng of women that surround him, wannabe groupies of a potential rock star in the making. He extends his hand to me. "You must be Logan Fitzgerald. We're psyched that you're here. Thanks for giving us a chance. And who is your beautiful guest?" I squeeze his hand a little harder than necessary, letting him know that she's off limits.

"This is my girlfriend, Vittoria. I'm aware that she's beautiful. I don't need or want your comments on the subject." I can see she's amused by me, trying not to all-out laugh at me right now, but she knows I would most definitely punish her for it, and not in a fun way.

She holds out her hand, and when he takes it, she diffuses the tension in seconds. "Hi, Josh. I'm Vittoria. Logan's girlfriend, possession, and sex slave. Pleased to meet you. You guys were awesome tonight, really amazing." He starts laughing and misses her nudging me in the ribs. She was dangerously close to the truth and if anyone else had said it, it would have made the situation awkward, but not her. She has this way about her that people respond to. An air of innocence and a warmth of personality that's so endearing, and impossible to ignore. Everyone loves her, which pisses me off, and it makes me so damn proud. I want her all to myself, and I can't fault people for finding her as magnetic as I do, but I still want to throat punch any man who looks at her.

290 | EVA HAINING

"Thanks. I was feeling the pressure with this guy in crowd, possibly deciding my future."

I bring his focus back to me, and away from Vittoria. "Well, let's go and talk somewhere a little quieter. Dinner?"

"Sounds perfect. Can you give us half an hour to pack up and get our stuff back to my apartment? I don't want to leave it here."

"Sure. We can wait."

"Cool."

He disappears to find the rest of the band and I take the opportunity to sneak us into a quiet room backstage. There are a few couches and a guitar in the corner that she spies immediately. "Will you play something for me?" She picks up the guitar and brings it over to me, thrusting it into my hand. "Please? Campbell told me you have the best voice he's ever heard, and that you're a great player, too."

"I'm not the player I used to be. My hand doesn't move the same way on the strings anymore."

"I'm not going to be judging you on technique, Logan. I just find it weird that I've never heard you play or sing a single note. It's been such a huge part of your life, of your story. I want to hear you."

I take the guitar and sit down on the closest couch. The feel of the wood and strings is so familiar to me. It's comforting, and a little sad. I decide to play the song I wrote for her when I was on tour with the boys, but I don't tell her that. The room seems eerily quiet as I begin to sing, strumming my fingers over the strings, and losing myself in the lyrics. They seem even more poignant to me after everything we've been through since I wrote it. Almost like a premonition of what was to come. I forgot how caught up I could get, everything around me fading away, leaving just me and the guitar, and the music. I really miss it, and as the song comes to an end, I'm bereaved. I lost my chance before it began. I feel Vittoria's loss all over again. Devastated for her, I remember the way she used to command the stage, taking the music and the audience with her on an enchanting adventure.

I set the guitar down and turn to see tears streaming down her sweet face. "What's wrong? Are you okay?"

"That was... God, Logan, your voice is stunning. And the emotion you put into it... it was like listening to your soul. You're so talented. I can't believe you never told me."

"What would I say? I never tell anyone about it. It's in the past, and it was over before it started. I told you what happened. It is what it is."

"I was so wrapped up in my own heartbreak at the time, I never fully appreciated what you've been through. Logan, I rarely see anyone who feels music the way I do, who channels it through their own body. You do that! You understand it in ways that no one else can. I can't imagine how difficult it must have been for you to go through losing that alone. I had you, and it still almost broke me. You're amazing."

"I had no choice. My mom didn't want to know. She thought I ruined her life. So, I got on with it, not because I'm some remarkable guy, but because I just had to. There was no other option for me."

"Is that why things are still bad between you and your mom?"

"Yeah. She never once saw it from my point of view. That I lost everything trying to defend her. All she saw was me getting in the way of what she thought her life should be. I was an inconvenience to her, and I still am."

"Have you ever told her how you feel?"

"No. It wouldn't do any good. She's fundamentally selfish, she always has been. She's incapable of seeing anything from someone else's perspective, how her actions might affect them. Her number one priority is herself, and that's never going to change."

"But, maybe it would help *you*. Let you get it off your chest?"

"Let's not waste our night talking about my mom."

"Okay, if that's what you want."

I pull her into my arms, seeking comfort in her warm embrace. "It is. Please change the subject."

She starts stroking my hair, twisting it in her fingers. "I loved the song you were singing. So haunting. Who's it by? I don't think I've heard it before."

"I wrote it... for you." She stops dead, her body frozen for a moment before she pulls me in, her lips finding mine in a fierce and passionate kiss.

"I love you so much, Logan Fitzgerald. What did I ever do to deserve you?"

"You're… you. You're mine. You're everything."

She quickly straddles me, her legs coiling around my waist as she deepens our kiss, desperate for more, and I'm about to oblige her when there's a knock at the open door. Josh is standing waiting with his eyes cast to the floor. "We're good to go when you are."

I'm beginning to dislike this guy already. First he hits on my girl, and then he cock blocks me. He's lucky I'm a professional, and that I believe I can help his band to take it to the next level.

I pull Vittoria close, leaning in to whisper in her ear. "We'll continue this later."

"Yes, Master Fitzgerald." Fuck, it's hot when she calls me that in public, even if it's in whispers, and it makes me want her even more than I already do.

All through dinner, all I can think about is her. I can't concentrate on the meeting, or the band. My mind replays those three simple words, over and over again, 'Yes, Master Fitzgerald,' and it has me straining against my jeans. Her blatant public submission is such a turn-on. I'm really looking forward to hearing her say those words to me while she's wearing my bracelets.

I can't wait to get her back to New York—to our future.

LOS ANGELES

VITTORIA

I NEVER THOUGHT I WOULD FEEL THIS WAY AGAIN. I NEVER THOUGHT I would be truly happy and content. It's been nine months since I left rehab, and true to his word as always, Logan has been by my side, loving me, and saving me from myself. The day after we made love in the playroom, he arranged an appointment for me with one of the best therapists in New York, and I've been seeing her twice a week ever since.

Within two sessions, I was diagnosed with depression brought on by PTSD, and I've been learning how to read my moods, and to recognize when I'm going through a rough patch. I can recognize my triggers and my coping mechanisms. Ballet has been my way of coping with everything since I was ten years old, and it worked to an extent, but I never really dealt with the root of the problem.

I feel like I've been reborn these past months. Like I can look at the world through fresh eyes and see my life for what it is. It's not perfect, but it's pretty damn close, and who can ask for more than that? Logan has been so attentive, loving, and commanding. Anticipating my needs and acting only in my best interests at all times. He's never selfish and is always so understanding and patient with me. I couldn't ask for a better Master, lover, and friend. He's the whole package, and

I wake up every morning wondering how I'm lucky enough to be loved by such an amazing man.

We're in LA this week. Logan's meeting with a new band, and he didn't want to leave me behind. It's still a sore point for him that I lied to him when we were apart before. I don't think it's that he doesn't trust me. I've done my best to earn back his trust over the past few months. I think he's just worried about me more than anything. It's been hard on him, and I've hurt him in ways I can't even begin to fathom, but he's been so gracious and loving. I would do anything he asked of me, and coming here wasn't exactly a chore. I want to be with him, and we've been having the most wonderful time together.

Last night I heard him play the guitar and sing for the first time. I knew he had aspirations that were dashed when he was a teenager, but I never grasped the gravity of his loss until now. His voice is phenomenal, and the touch he has when he plays, is so natural—so effortless. There are technically brilliant dancers and musicians, but you can always tell a truly gifted artist. They have an edge you can't teach, that you can never replicate. I had it, and so does Logan. I'm sad for the eighteen-year-old boy who never got to live out his dream, the one he was born for. It puts my own story in perspective. I thought my life was over because my career ended prematurely, but watching him last night, I realized how lucky I've been. I got to live what I love. I got to know what it felt like to do everything I dreamed of since I was a kid. No one can ever take that away from me.

I'm in awe of Logan. He found a way to harness what he loves and carve a successful career for himself. He gives me hope for the future. I want that—to find a way to marry my love for dance with a fruitful career and a future I can be excited about. Don't get me wrong, life is great right now, but I can't live off of Logan forever, it's not who I am. I can't define myself by my relationship with him. I'm his submissive, and I love it. I love him, but I want to find a new identity for myself, something that's just for me. I want to be a person he can be proud of.

∾

WE'VE HAD A GREAT TIME WHILE WE'VE BEEN HERE IN LA. ENJOYING great food, great music, and great company. Our nights have been spent making love, and my Master has come out to play and punish on several occasions. It's been the perfect break.

Today is our last day, and Logan finished with all his meetings yesterday, so we're going out exploring. I get a full day with him, all to myself, and LA is ours for the taking! First stop is going to be Griffith Observatory. I love anything and everything to do with the stars. There's something about staring up into the sky above and contemplating just how small and insignificant you are in the scheme of things. Our lives are a blink of an eye, a single grain in the sands of time.

You can't see much through the telescopes in the observatory, the LA skies are too smoggy. But, the exhibits are mind-blowing. We spend hours just walking around, talking and taking in every detail. It's so calm and serene, and I love every second of it.

When we finally head out into the California sunshine, ready for lunch, my phone starts ringing in my pocket. Logan pulls me close, scrambling my thoughts with his exquisite kiss. "Ignore it. Today is our day. No interruptions. Just us, remember?"

"I remember. Just let me check who it is." He starts kissing my neck, and behind my ear, right where he knows he'll drive me wild. He doesn't play fair. "Oh shit! It's Luca. I haven't spoken to him in at least six months. I really need to take this. Sorry. I promise I'll be quick."

He reluctantly lets go of me, promising some wonderful form of punishment for my disobedience.

"Hey, Luca. How are you?"

"Vittoria bella. How I've missed your sweet voice."

"I've missed you, too."

"I'm sorry to call you out of the blue like this, but I have some major news."

"Don't apologize. I'm thrilled that you called. So, what's the big news?"

"I've been asked to take a position as a choreographer at the Joffrey Ballet Institute in Florence."

"Holy Shit, Luca! Congratulations. That's amazing. What an honor." The Joffrey Ballet is one of the most prestigious ballet schools in the world, and their program in Florence is one of the best. It's a real honor to be headhunted by a school of that caliber.

"There's more." He pauses, gauging my reaction, but I just wait for him to continue. "They want you."

"What do you mean they want me?" I can see the anguished look in Logan's eyes as he puts the pieces of my conversation together in his mind.

"They need a choreography team. Several of the faculty members have seen us perform together over the years, and they thought you were astounding. They're right, Vittoria. There was no one better than you."

"*Was*, Luca. I can't dance anymore."

"You won't need to. Don't you see? This is a way to be a part of what you love. To create art and beauty, and ballet. You can do this. They want you, and so do I. This is a once in a lifetime opportunity."

"When do they want you... us, to start?"

"Next week."

"*Next week?* That's impossible. I have a life here, Luca. I can't just leave it all behind."

"I know it's a lot to take in, but will you at least take a day to think it over before you say no? This is huge, and you can't just dismiss it without even thinking about it."

"I know it's a once in a lifetime opportunity, Luca. I mean, the Joffrey Ballet doesn't come knocking every day, but I..."

"Just think it over. Talk to Logan. Call me tomorrow. Okay?"

"Okay."

I hang up the phone, stunned and confused, and shaking like a leaf. Ten minutes ago, everything was clear to me. Now, I feel—I don't know what I feel.

"Vittoria? You look pale. Do you want to sit down? What's going on?" I look up into the eyes of the man I love, and I can see that he's worried. "Talk to me."

I take a deep breath, trying to compose myself.

I go on to relay my conversation with Luca, word for word. The job, the opportunity, the honor of being asked, and also, the fact that I can't accept the offer.

"You're taking the job. No arguments." His voice is cold, lacking any emotion.

"You want me to go?"

"Fuck! Of course I don't want to lose you, Tori, but like Luca said, this is a once in a lifetime offer. You can't just turn your back on it. You know in your heart that he's right. That I'm right."

"What about us?" My heart is racing, dread filling my stomach as I await his answer.

"You're the love of my life, my soulmate. What kind of man would I be if I held you back? If I made you choose between me and a career you love? I can't be that selfish with you. You need to do this."

"You didn't answer the question, Logan. What about us?"

"We... we'll have to say goodbye. I can't be your Master across continents again. It didn't work the first time, and the consequences were too much to bear. I won't risk that again. You need a clean break. A chance to find... love, happiness, and everything your heart desires."

"*You* are what my heart desires, above all else. Even ballet."

He walks us over to a bench and sits me down, dropping to his knees in front of me. The resignation in his eyes has me struggling to breathe. "You can't give this up for me. You would hate me for it in years to come, and I couldn't live with that. If you don't at least try, you'll always wonder. I can't be the reason you miss out on such an amazing chance. I could never forgive myself."

"So you just want me to leave in a week, and that's us done? After everything we've been through and how hard we've fought to be together? You just want to throw it all away? Don't I mean anything to you?"

"You think this is easy for me to say this to you, to contemplate you leaving? You mean everything to me, and you fucking well know it, so don't say shit like that. I love you, and I will always fight for you, for what's best for you. This is what's best. I'm telling you, as your Master, that you need to do this."

I can't believe he's saying these things to me. That he's not fighting for me to stay with him. My head is spinning, my world turned upside down. "But, I can't leave you."

"Just for a minute, don't think about me. There is only one question that you need to answer, and the rest we can deal with later." I can't stand to see the pained look in his eyes as he forces himself to say the words. "If I wasn't a factor, and you were offered this job, would you take it?" I don't want to answer him, because I know what he'll make me do, but I can't lie to him. We agreed on complete honesty a long time ago. "Answer me, Nyx."

"Yes. I would take the job in a heartbeat. It's the nearest I will ever come to dancing again, and it's with one of the best schools in the world."

"Then you have your answer."

"It's not that simple. You *are* a factor in this, in my life. You are the *only* factor that matters." I can't hold back the tears, letting them roll down my cheeks as I fight to make sense of this.

"Let me take you back to the hotel. This isn't the place to be talking about life changing decisions, and I think we could both use a minute to process all of this." He takes my hand and leads me in the direction of our hotel. The silence between us is deafening, but I can't speak past the lump in my throat, and I can see that Logan is struggling to maintain his calm bravado. A sick feeling settles in the pit of my stomach. I know what he's going to say, what he's going to do. He's my Master. He always has been, and always will be, selfless when it comes to my happiness.

I don't know if I could be happy in Florence, without Logan. What I *do* know, is that he's going to take the decision out of my hands—the impossible choice between the love of my life, and the one thing I've loved my whole life.

He's going to make me leave him.

CHAPTER 22

LOGAN

I can't believe how quickly all of this has happened. A week ago, I was planning to buy a house with Vittoria. I was going to give her my version of a submissive collar, and we were going to live happily ever after. Now, seven days later, I'm standing in my closet, picking out a shirt to wear to her leaving party. I can't even begin to process all of this.

After the initial shock, Vittoria is slowly becoming excited about the opportunity to work with Luca at the Joffrey Ballet, and what better place for her to start over than Italy. She has family there to help her get settled, and she'll being doing something that she loves, at one of the most prestigious schools in the world. It's a once in a life-time opportunity and she knows it. That's why I insisted that she take it.

She agonized over the decision for days, back and forth as if it were a real choice, but in the end, she realized that I wasn't going to back down. I couldn't bear for her to live a life here with me, always regretting what might have been. I know how much she misses ballet, and this is her way to reconnect with that part of herself. I understand the need for that better than most. I managed to find a way to channel my passion for music, and it changed my life. I want that for her, and I know she'll never be truly happy without it.

I decide on a black shirt and charcoal pants—dark—just like my mood. Carter has organized an amazing party, with all of Vittoria's friends and family, and it's the last place I want to be tonight. Her flight leaves first thing tomorrow morning, and all I want to do is steal her away, and not share her with anyone. I want to take her into our playroom one last time and worship every inch of her until it's time to say goodbye.

As I stand, staring at the mirror and beyond it into empty space, Vittoria creeps up behind me, snaking her arms around my waist.

"I could stare at you all day long. I don't blame you for doing it, too!"

I twist around to see her mischievous grin shining up at me. "If you must know, I was thinking about all the things I'm going to do you after the party. I hope you don't plan on getting any sleep tonight."

Her smile drops, her mood turning somber. "I don't have time for sleep. I need to spend every minute I have left with you." Her arms tighten around me. "I can't bear even thinking about tomorrow. I don't think I can leave you. I love you too much."

"And I love you too much to make you stay. You need this. I've seen what losing your career did to you, and I've been through it myself. You need this chance to forge a new path for yourself that brings you joy and contentment in your life. A way to express your beautifully artistic soul."

"You've been where I am, so why can't you see that I choose you over dance?"

"Because it took me years to come to terms with what happened to me. There were ups and downs along the way, frustration and elation. You need to experience all of those things. You need to know in your heart that you tried. If you find yourself years from now, feeling like you don't need it the same way you do now, then come back to me. I'm always going to be here, Vittoria, but you can't put your life on hold for me. You can't stop living. You need to go to Italy, immerse yourself in your work, and your new home. You can't be looking to the past all the time. If you do, I'll be holding you back, even when I'm no longer with you."

"But..."

"No buts. I'm still your Master, at least until you step on that plane tomorrow." The lump that's forming in my throat is making it difficult for me to keep talking. The thought of not being her Dominant by this time tomorrow, is soul destroying. "And, as your Master, I'm telling you that this is what's best for you."

"I... I..." Tears begin to fall from her beautiful brown eyes, breaking my heart, making me want to drop to my knees and beg her to stay. I know she'd say yes, and that's exactly why I can't do it.

"Let's try to enjoy tonight. Your friends and family all want to wish you well, and when the party's over, you're mine for one last night." I pull her close, my lips finding hers in a tender kiss. "Now go and get dressed before I ditch the party and take you to the playroom."

"Sounds perfect to me." I give her a warning look and a sharp slap on the ass, telling her to get a move on. This is already becoming more of a struggle than I can handle, and I need the distraction of everyone else if I'm going to get through this and let her go.

By the time we need to leave, I'm pacing the floor, her gift burning a hole in my pocket. I was going to give her the bracelets I bought, but I thought it would be too hard for her, knowing what I had planned. Instead, I had the key to the padlock put onto a platinum necklace for her. She'll never know what it unlocks, but I need her to have it anyway. She doesn't know about the apartments or the ballet studio either, and that's the way it has to stay.

When she steps out into the living room, I feel like I've been punched in the chest, my heart aching at the sight of her. She looks absolutely stunning in a deep purple lace dress. I know she's chosen the color carefully, an exact match to our playroom and the ropes I used on her the first time I tied her up. It hugs every curve of her body to perfection, with a split up to her thigh, exposing her exquisite legs. Fuck, I'm going to miss her.

"You look... it should be illegal to look as good as you do. You are absolutely stunning, Miss de Rossi."

"Why, thank you, Master Fitzgerald." *She's killing me.*

"I bought you a gift. Something to remember me by."

"I could never forget you. Not ever."

I take the box from my pocket and place it in her small palm. "I hope you like it."

She slowly unwraps it, her eyes darting up to meet mine as she opens the box and sees the key nestled inside. "Oh my God. Logan, it's so beautiful."

I take it from her, the sweet scent of her perfume enveloping me, and I can't resist a kiss as I fasten my key around her neck. "This way, you'll always have a part of me with you."

Her eyes fill with tears as she runs her fingers over the intricate design. "I love it, but I didn't get you anything."

I turn her in my arms, placing my hand over her heart. "Vittoria, you've already given me everything I ever wanted. I don't need a gift to know that." I give her a soft kiss, licking the seam of her lips, begging entrance, which she willingly gives.

"Shall we?" She takes my hand, and just this smallest of touches has me fighting to keep my composure. As I lock the apartment behind us, I feel like the countdown has begun. The beginning of the end.

CARTER HAS REALLY OUTDONE HIMSELF. HIS NEWEST NIGHTCLUB, Vortex, looks phenomenal. He shut the place down for the night, so that the party is all about Vittoria. The DJ is amazing, and the boys from Flaming Embers have flown in to do a short set for her. She's become close with them over the past six months and I know that they're all going to miss her. I also know that Campbell is going to be checking on me every five seconds after she gets on the plane tomorrow. He's become as close to me as Xander and Carter, and he's really been there for me throughout my relationship with Vittoria. He's seen the best and the worst of me during all of this, and I think he probably understands more than most, how utterly devastating this is for me.

It's a joy to watch Vittoria as she interacts with friends, old and new, laughing, crying, and dancing. I'm overwhelmed to see her so happy and watching her move on the floor is such a privilege. She may not be a ballet dancer anymore, but she still commands the room, the music flowing through her like it always has, and she's completely lost in it, until *Love Runs Out* starts playing. Her eyes search the crowd until she finds me, our shared memory of the moment we found our way back to each other, heavy in the air between us. It's our secret, and as she begins to move, I know that it's for me. Everything and everyone around us fades into the background. I'm mesmerized by her—besotted—and I'm struck by how empty my life will be without her.

When the music fades and the spell is broken, Carter takes to the stage.

"Hey, everyone. I just wanted to take a few moments of your time to honor the woman we're all here for tonight. My baby sister." She makes her way through the crowd, burying her head against my chest as tears well in her eyes. "Vittoria is without a doubt, one of the strongest women I know. She's a force to be reckoned with, and I know that she'll do amazing things at the Joffrey Ballet. They'll be lucky to have you, Tori, and I'm so happy for you, but I'm also really going to miss you. I know we've had our differences, especially about your taste in men." The crowd gives a collective chuckle, and for some of them, a knowing nod. "I never thought that any man would be good enough for you, and when Logan came to me, telling me that he was in love with you... well, I punched him in the face... on several occasions." Vittoria shakes her head, laughing and crying at the same time. "I wasted a lot of time being angry and ignorant, and just plain wrong about you two. Standing here tonight, celebrating your impending adventures, it's clear to me that you *did* make the right choice when it came to Logan. Any man who puts the needs of my sister above his own and loves her enough to let her go... is worthy of her love. I'm sorry that it took me so long to see it, but better late than never, right? Logan, you've always been like a brother to me, and I can't thank you enough for everything you've done for Vittoria over the past year. You've been there for her in the good and the bad, stuck by her when most men couldn't handle the pressure. I've watched her turn into this formidable, confident, amazing woman while she's been with you, and I just want to thank you. You've given me back my sister. The one I used to play hide-and-seek with as a kid. The one who used to jump on my bed on Christmas morning to tell me Santa had been." I can see he's struggling to hold it together. Vittoria is a mess in my arms at this point, and I'm not far behind, my throat burning from holding it all in. "So, thank you. I love you, bro. And, Tori, no matter how far apart we are, you will always be my baby sister, and I will always be here for you. Ti amerò sempre. Everyone, please raise your glasses, to an amazing sister, daughter, aunt, and friend. To Vittoria."

I hold tight as she crumples in my arms, her body shaking as she sobs uncontrollably. I want to tell her that it's all going to be okay, that it will get easier, but I can't even speak. I just cling to her, battling my own grief, staving off the overwhelming emotions that are fighting their way to the surface. I have to keep it together until she leaves. I can't and I won't make this any harder on her.

Carter steps down off the stage and into Addi's arms, obviously upset, but trying to keep Vittoria from seeing just how devastated he is. The DJ restarts the music with something a little slower, the tone of the party calling for something more sedate. *Thinking Out Loud* by Ed Sheeran comes over the speakers, and I can't imagine there being a more perfect song for us to share a last dance together.

"Dance with me." She doesn't speak, she simply takes my hand and lets me lead her onto the dance floor, snaking her arms up around my neck, her head resting against my chest.

As we sway to the music, I find myself singing the words to her—a declaration of my undying love,. But as the lyrics sink in, and the gravity of the situation hits home, I can't... I can't keep singing. It seems fitting, that we are right back where we started, so long ago. Dancing to a song that speaks volumes of my feelings for the girl in my arms. Knowing that I'll need to let her go when the night is over. We've come full circle. From a stolen first kiss, to a heartbreaking last.

"Take me home, Logan. Make love to me."

I have no words, but she doesn't need them. She knows how I feel, and as I take her hand in mine and lead her out of the club and back to our apartment, the air between us crackles with electricity. The unspoken promise of an unforgettable final night together.

I DIDN'T SLEEP AT ALL LAST NIGHT, AND VITTORIA ONLY SUCCUMBED TO her own exhaustion three hours ago. I know that she wanted to stay awake, to spend every possible moment with me, but in the end, it was too overwhelming.

I thought our final night together would be frenzied, and fierce, but the reality was something so much more than that. When I brought her home from the party, we didn't talk, we didn't need to. I led her down the hallway of my apartment and into the playroom—our playroom. I watched as she stripped off her clothes, removing all barriers between us, before she did the same to me. It was slow, and sensual, and sexy as hell. I used every surface, every restraint, every toy in that room, teasing her, pleasing her, navigating that fine line between pleasure and pain with her, one last time. We made love, we fucked, we worshipped each other for hours, and it was the most amazing night of my life.

It was everything you could ever want in a goodbye, but I can't believe it's actually here. That it's happening. We have to leave for the airport in five minutes, and I'm just not ready to say goodbye. How do you say goodbye to the love of your life? Your reason for being?

I grab her suitcases and watch as she takes in everything around her, memorizing every little detail of my apartment, of what has been our home together for the past nine months. Everywhere I look, I see her. Little touches that turned my house into a home. Things that will remind me of her. She wipes the tears from her eyes, leaves her key on the table by the door, and walks out, unable to look back, overcome with emotion.

It feels like a death march as we make our way to the car in silence, and the drive to the airport is so devastatingly quiet,. Vittoria clings to my hand, her knuckles protruding with the force she's exerting, and I drive slower than I ever have before, just trying to delay the inevitable. The mood is somber, a physical weight bearing down on us, around us, between us. I've never felt so helpless, and hopeless.

When we reach the airport, I park in the furthest away lot, giving myself every possible minute I can get with her. I keep her tucked under my arm, pressed close to my side as we slowly make our way into the terminal. I have to let her go to the desk for check in, and as I wait for her, my mind is racing to find any way out of this. Could I just leave my life behind, my business, all of the bands who depend on me for their livelihood? Could I be that selfish, and follow my heart to wherever Vittoria is? Even if I could, it would take at least a year for me to get all my affairs in order, and then what would I do? We've tried the long-distance thing in the past, and it didn't work. It almost tore us apart, and it almost killed Vittoria. I couldn't risk that again. I know she's much stronger now, and she doesn't need me the way she used to, but she deserves someone who can be there for her, and as much as it kills me to think of her with another Dom, I can't expect her to wait around on the off chance that we could make it work in a year, maybe longer. She's already put her life on hold in so many ways over the years. Now is her time, to live life to the fullest, and only for herself.

I'm lost in my own thoughts when her hand brushes my arm. "That's me checked in. They told me I need to go through to the gate now, they're going to start boarding in twenty minutes." Her voice is strained, her eyes welling with tears. "I thought I would have more time… that we would have more time. I'm not ready. I can't do this."

I clasp her delicate, flawless face in my hands, willing myself to remember every single detail of her exquisite features. The way her eyelashes kiss her cheeks when she blinks, the warm velvet brown of her eyes, and the way her full lips twitch when I'm near. "Vittoria, listen to me. You *can* do this. You're the strongest woman I know. You've been through so much; and you're still one of the sweetest, most caring, giving, and loving people I've ever met. The way you feel everything with such intensity, isn't a flaw or a weakness. It's your greatest strength. Never forget that."

"But what if the depression comes back? I'll be alone, and what if I can't cope?"

"Take a deep breath." She does as I ask, my obedient submissive until the very end. "You know that the depression is something you might have to fight for the rest of your life. There are going to be highs and lows, and you have the tools to deal with it. That's what we've been working toward all these months. You know that hurting yourself, or using, will never be the answer." I lean in and give her the lightest of kisses before I continue. "And you won't be alone, baby. You have Luca, and you have family there. You'll make friends quickly, because to know you is to love you. And Vittoria... it's really important that you remember this... if you feel like you can't cope, and that you have no one to turn to who understands... I will *always* be here for you. I will always love you, and no matter what happens, and how much time passes, in my heart, you will *always* be mine. You're the love of my life, and you will forever be, my Nyx."

She throws herself into my arms, crawling up my body as if she can somehow attach herself to me. "I don't want this, Logan. I don't want to go. I want to stay here with you."

It takes every ounce of strength I have not to agree with her. Not to walk out of here with her in my arms. "I know it feels like that now, but you need to remember how excited you felt when this opportunity was offered to you. It's a once in a lifetime chance, and you have to take it."

"You're a once in a lifetime chance, Logan. We're a once in a lifetime kind of love."

She's breaking my heart, and I'll never recover. "I will never be a once in a lifetime chance for you, Vittoria. You have my heart, today, tomorrow, forty years from now. It's yours. I love you with everything that I have, and everything that I am, and that's why I need to let you go. You need to do this, or you'll always look back with regret, wondering what your life could have been like if you'd been brave enough to grab it with both hands."

"But I love you."

"I love you, too." I claim her lips one last time, pouring all the love I feel for her into this kiss. Our final goodbye. The taste of her lips and the feel of her tongue caressing mine, will forever be ingrained in my memory. "You're going to miss your flight if you don't go now."

Her eyes are red, tears coursing down her cheeks as she struggles to regain composure. "I can't walk away from you."

"Then, I'll do it for you. As much as I don't want to. It will be the last thing I do for you as your Master. Turn around, and don't look back. I'm going to leave now, and you are going to get on that plane, and go and start a new amazing life, full of all the happiness and love that you deserve. I'm so honored to have been your Dominant, Vittoria de Rossi, but I need to let you go now. Goodbye, Nyx." I give her one last kiss, one final embrace, before turning her to face the gate And then I do the hardest thing I've ever done. I put one foot in front of the other, and I walk away, her sobs echoing in my ears, her words ripping my heart open.

"I love you, Master Fitzgerald. I always have, and I always will."

I feel the distance growing between us, like a physical tether being stretched to its limit, before it finally snaps, and it's gone. She's gone, and my life is destroyed. I am a man set adrift, lost and alone in a sea of thousands. Turning around, I torture myself with one last glimpse of her, and as I see her disappear around the corner into the departure gates, I can't hold back anymore. I let all of the emotion I've been holding inside, come flooding out.

"Fuck!" My eyes are clouded with unshed tears as I shove my way through the crowds. "What the fuck have I done?" I pick up the pace, fighting to outrun my desolation, feeling claustrophobic all of a sudden, and unable to catch my breath. When I finally burst through the doors, out into the fresh air, I struggle to draw breath, gasping to try and fill my lungs. And when it finally comes, it's painful. Every inch of my body hurts. Craving her, needing her, wanting her so badly I feel like my heart has been torn from my chest. I need a way to release at least some of this all-consuming despair. I start punching the pillar in front of me, over and over until my knuckles bleed, shouting until my voice is hoarse. "Fuck! Fuck! Fuck!"

"Logan Fitzgerald. What the hell are you doing?"

I turn to face her, stunned and defeated. "You have got to be fucking kidding me!" I'm yelling to the heavens, to the universe, to give me a fucking break. She's the last person I want to see.

"Well, that's a lovely way to greet your mother. The airport seems to be the only place I run into you these days. I see your temper is as fierce as ever." She's staring down at my blood-soaked hand, and that's when it dawns on me. I'm not angry at her anymore.

"You know what, Mom? Yes, I'm upset and I lashed out. I've just put the woman I love on a plane, and she's never coming back. But, you know what, she taught me something. A lot of things actually."

"And what would that be?"

Her dismissive tone and snide sneer don't deter me. Not today. If I keep anything else bottled up right now, I'm pretty sure I'll have a heart attack, or a stroke. "I don't blame you for what happened to me. I made a decision to protect you, because I love you. You hate me for loving you too much? That's your issue, not mine. I've spent years being angry with you for ruining my chance at a career in music, but it wasn't your fault. You were dealt a shitty hand in life, and you coped the only way you knew how. If I could go back, I would do it again. I would defend you, because no woman deserves to be treated that way. You're my mom, and I love you. I always will. So, if you want to stay angry at me for what you believe I did wrong, I can't change that, but I'm not going to waste any more of my time hating you. I found a way to move past it and still be involved in music. I love what I do, and I'm really fucking good at it."

"Logan. I don't... I never..." She doesn't deal well with emotions. "You're rambling like a crazy person in public, dear." She fidgets with her purse, unable to have a real, honest moment with her own son. I shouldn't have expected anything less.

"I need to get out of here, Mom. I'm sorry you can't see what's right in front of you. But, I'm done feeling bad about it. Love me, don't love me. Hate me, don't hate me. I'm done. Goodbye."

I walk away, and she doesn't try to stop me. She doesn't say a word, but as I make my way to my car, I feel like a weight has been lifted off my shoulders. I've watched Vittoria face her fears and her demons over the past nine months, but never once have I faced my own. She's the reason I was able to do it today. To say how I felt, and let it go, once and for all. I guess it should give me some small comfort, but it only highlights what I've lost—the one person in the world who truly understood me, and who loved me anyway.

I never thought that my life would take this turn. I thought we would spend the rest of our lives together. I pictured the white picket fence, a ring on her finger, maybe even kids one day. Things I never thought I wanted, until her. Things I'll never have without her.

I've heard the saying, 'sometimes love just isn't enough,' so many times, in movies, in books, in life. But, I don't know if I agree with that. After everything I went through with Vittoria, I firmly believe that love is enough. I also believe that life is full of twists and turns and curveballs, and sometimes when you love someone with every fiber of your being... you need to let them go and find what makes them happy, even if it makes you unhappy. I will always love Vittoria. I will always be in love with her, and I'll always do what's best for her, even when it takes her away from me.

I guess the clichéd saying that I can relate to is, 'better to have loved and lost, than never to have loved at all.' Loving Vittoria de Rossi and being loved by her even for a short time, was worth the pain I feel, and will continue to feel at her loss. I hope she finds happiness in her new life—that she finds love and passion and adventure. I only wish that I could have been a part of it.

As I drive out of the airport, the smell of Vittoria's perfume lingering in the air around me, I don't know where I'm going. I can't go back to my apartment. Everything in it reminds me of her, so I decide to just keep driving. I don't know what the future holds for me, but wherever it takes me, I know that no matter where she is, and no matter how much time passes, my heart will always lie with her, my goddess... my Nyx.

EPILOGUE

LOGAN

It's been a year since Vittoria left for Florence, and nothing has been the same since I convinced her to take a chance and follow a new dream. I know I did the right thing for her, but I've regretted it every moment of every day since. I miss her more than words could express, and I've questioned my decision every night as I lie awake, alone in the silence of my empty apartment. My empty life.

We kept in touch for the first few months, emailing and texting, and the occasional phone call. She needed some guidance on the tough days. A stern voice to assure her that she was strong enough to adjust and learn to love her new life. It broke my heart to hear her doubting herself, telling me how much she missed me, how much she still loved me. But, as the weeks went by and she settled into a routine, our communication became less and less, until it stopped altogether. Not because we cared any less, but because the distance between us hadn't altered our feelings for each other in the slightest. They were stronger than ever, and it made it almost unbearable to function so far apart.

I remember the day it happened, when we both came to the realization that we could never move on with our lives if we continued to rely on each other across the continents. I want her to be happy, and I was holding her back. I am her past, and she had to start focusing on her future, no matter how much it pained me. We were talking on the phone that night, and I could hear it in her voice, in the way she said goodbye—defeated and deflated, she knew I had to let her go. That she had to let *me* go. To allow her to spread her wings and fly again. She lost so much of herself when she injured her ankle, and I know that I helped her find her way back. I forced her to fight for her life, to face her demons and let go of the past. To be happy again. But, I knew there was a void I could never fill. I just hope beyond hope, that she found what she needed—what she craved.

I often hear Carter and Addi talking about how she's doing, and the projects she's working on. They try to minimize what they say in front of me, but she's a huge part of their lives, and I told them a long time ago that I don't want them to censor anything around me. I want to know about her, even if it throws me right back to the moment that she left—the moment I sent her away. I hope that by now she's moved on, because I know firsthand how devastating it is when you can't. I haven't, and I feel like a little piece of me dies with every day that passes. As my life twists and turns in the opposite direction to hers, I spiral further and further out of control. I don't want that for her.

From the little I know, she seems to be getting closer to Luca. It's good for her to have someone who obviously loves and understands her, but I can't say it makes me happy. It devastates me. I can't imagine her ever being with someone else and having what we shared. It was so profound. I have to believe that our type of love only comes along once. That maybe she can find happiness with him, but that some small part of her will always belong to me. I hope she will always keep a little piece of me in her heart.

Carter and Xander have been on me since the moment she left, to give up the studio space I rented for her in Xander's building, but I just can't. I'm not ready to let it go. If I do, it's like I'm letting go of her. They finally convinced me last week to at least sublet the space, so I've hired a realtor to find someone, but I don't want to think about it being used for something and someone other than Vittoria. When I first saw it, I felt like it was meant for her, for our future together. It just goes to show how life can throw you for a loop. Maybe at some point, I'll be able to let it go completely, but for now, subletting is the best solution.

I went ahead with buying one of the new apartments I'd looked at for Vittoria and me. I couldn't stay in my apartment. Everywhere I turned, I saw her. Everything reminded me of her. It was too hard, so within a month, I boxed up my life and moved to my new place. I like it, but it's always felt like it's missing something. It's missing her. Even though she never saw it, I know she would've loved it. I guess in time, I'll make it my own. I'll find a way to fill the empty space. Someday, it will feel like my home. I'm just not there yet.

Liam has been a good friend over these last few months, which came as a surprise. I never thought I would confide in him again after what happened, but in a strange way, he's the only person who understands even a fraction of what I'm going through. He loved her once, and I think on some level, he still does. She's not an easy girl to get over.

He's been trying to get me back to Andromeda, and to the lifestyle. They never replaced me, so they've been lacking a Master to demonstrate, and to train new submissives. It seems strange to me now, that training subs used to be my life. I was happy back then, at least I thought I was. It's easy to believe you're happy when you don't have any concept of how much better your life could be, but once you cross that line, there's no going back. You can't *unknow*.

I need to get a grip and start making changes in my life, to start moving on, and tonight I'm taking the first step. I've debated it with Liam for weeks, and now it's time. Time to start training again.

I've got a busy day to keep my mind off of how difficult this is going to be. I'm meeting with Campbell and the guys to discuss their upcoming world tour. They really hit it big with their last record, going triple platinum. Their success is stratospheric, and through it all, they've remained humble and hardworking.

I won't be going on this tour, due to another big decision in my life. I've hired a new manager to take over the bands, and I'm branching out into producing. I've opened up a recording studio on the Upper West Side, with the best equipment money can buy, and some great people to work alongside me. Flaming Embers will be cutting their next record in there after the tour, and I have a new band lined up to start laying tracks for their debut album next week. Seeing Vittoria find a new dream, pushed me to re-examine my own life. I love what I do, but I wanted more. I wanted to *create* music again, and this new venture lets me do that. It's a major step for me, and I'm really excited about it.

After my meeting with the guys, I'll swing by the studio for a couple of hours before I head to the club. I'm going to meet a potential submissive to train. I told Liam I would only agree to it if he ensures that none of the girls he brings me look anything like Vittoria. It was always a rule of mine, but it's even more imperative to enforce it now. It would be a betrayal of what we had. Liam thinks this girl will be a good first step back into the scene. I can only stay for a few hours to meet her, and possibly run through the basics of hard and soft limits.

Later, I need to go over to Xander and Lily's place. I've been summoned, along with Carter and Addi. Apparently, they have some big news they want to discuss with us. I don't really want to spend my evening with two happy couples, especially after going to meet a new sub. Seeing all of them, and what I could have had, will be a tough blow on an already rough day.

I head out the door with a weight on my chest, and an unsettling feeling in the pit of my stomach. I just need to push through it and come out the other side. It *will* get better eventually.

∾

As I step inside the doors of Andromeda, everything is just as I left it. Jacob stands guard at the entrance, making sure that only members are granted access. He greets me with a smile and a nod. "It's good to see you back, Master Fitzgerald. Place hasn't been the same without you."

"Thanks, Jacob. It's good to be back." If I say it enough, maybe I'll start to believe it.

The main hall hasn't changed in the year I've been gone. I see the same faces, their surprise evident as I make my way through the crowd. The familiar smell of leather that permeates the space is strangely comforting. Maybe I can learn to be this person again. To be happy with what I know, what I'm good at. I am the best Master Dominant in New York. There is no one who can train new submissives better than me. It's who I am, and I need to find a way to be content with it.

I asked that my playroom redecorated. I had everything replaced for Vittoria, and I can't work in there with the ghost of the time we spent together, haunting me. I requested that I be moved to a different room entirely, but he said it was too much disruption for the other Dominants, so I opted for everything to be changed. The walls will no longer be the sumptuous deep purple. Instead, they will be red. It's a standard color for a playroom. Dark, sexy, and it's visually stimulating for a submissive. Red signals danger—the forbidden. I don't know why, but it works. I'm not looking to make my playroom personal. I just need the necessary equipment to train with, and a door that can be locked.

The night Vittoria left for Florence, was the last time I set foot in that room. I took the submissive bracelets I bought for her and left them in my cabinet. I couldn't bear to have them in the apartment, and I didn't want to get rid of them. I made sure they were left alone. Everything else in the cabinet has been replaced, but that box should be sitting right where I left it a year ago.

When I reach my playroom, I run my hand over the name emblazoned on the door. *Master Fitzgerald.* I haven't been called that in such a long time. I don't feel like I deserve the title anymore. And, I hate the idea of another woman saying it to me. It'll never be the same. I think I'll have my new sub address me simply as Master.

I open the door, and all the memories come rushing back to me. I want to turn and leave, but I wouldn't show such a lack of respect for the submissive I'm here to meet.

"Fuck!"

They haven't changed the room at all. It was supposed to be done two days ago. Liam should have told me. I don't want anyone in here when it looks like this. *I* don't want to be in here when it looks like this.

The lights are dim, but I can see my new trainee, sitting in the submissive position in the darkest corner of the room. I can only see her silhouette from where I stand, but I'm not impressed that she's choosing to hide in the shadows. I'd almost forgotten how timid and shy new subs can be.

"I can't do this."

I make my way across the room to where she sits on her heels, her hands clasped behind her back. A box on the table catches my eye. It's Vittoria's box. Her bracelets. Anger swells inside of me. I need to get this stranger out of here as quickly as possible.

I immediately head over to the table to remove the box and can see that it's open. The bracelets are gone. In their place is a note, together with the key I gave Vittoria when she left.

From a submissive to her Master
This is the last time I will ever defy you, Master Fitzgerald. You were wrong. Nothing in life can compare to how I feel when I'm in your arms. Your love is the music that flows through me, giving my life beauty and meaning. The only dance I want, or need, is the one that we perform, every time you make love to me. I want forever, and I want it with you... if you'll still have me.
All my love, now and always,
Your submissive
Nyx x

My heart is racing as realization dawns, and I slowly turn to face the corner, but she's not there. She's kneeling on the floor two feet in front of me, dressed in nothing but a deep purple lace bra and panties. Her hands are clasped in the front, showing me her wrists, glistening with two platinum bracelets, padlocked shut. The ones I had engraved for her over a year ago. Her eyes are lowered to the floor, awaiting my instruction.

She has never looked more beautiful than she does in this moment, and I'm struggling to catch my breath, my heart ricocheting off my ribcage, ready to burst out of my chest. I can't believe she's really here. She's right where she's supposed to be, where she was always meant to be. I let her go, and it was the biggest mistake I ever made, but she's come back to me. She's always been mine, and she always will be.

A love like ours is written in the stars, fated from the beginning of time. *It's endless.* She is my goddess in the shadows. An enchanting beauty, too lovely for this world. The missing piece of my soul, we are bound together for all eternity. I was born to be her Master. She was destined to be my submissive.

"Nyx?"

"Yes… Master Fitzgerald."

THE END

ABOUT THE AUTHOR

I'm happiest when wandering through the uncharted territory of my imagination. You'll find me curled up with my laptop, browsing the books at the local library, or enjoying the smell of a new book, taking great delight in cracking the spine and writing in the margins!

Eva is a native Scot, but lives in Texas with her husband, two kids, and a whizzy little fur baby with the most ridiculous ears. She first fell in love with British Literature while majoring in Linguistics, 17th Century Poetry, and Shakespeare at University. She is an avid reader and lifelong notebook hoarder. In 2014, she finally put her extensive collection to good use and started writing her first novel. Previously published with Prism Heart Press under the pen name *Sienna Parks*, Eva decided to branch out on her own and lend her name to her full back catalogue! She is currently working on some exciting new projects.

ACKNOWLEDGMENTS

First and foremost, the biggest thank you I could ever give, is to my amazing husband. You took supportive to a whole new level with this book. You lived through the tears and self-doubt, the moments when I threw in the towel and you picked it back up and shoved it in my face. You forced me to find myself again, and to give my all to these characters. Bribing me with watching an episode of *Outlander* every day in exchange for a chapter was a stroke of genius on the homestretch! You've given up your weekends with me, to allow me to focus on my writing, and you let me talk incessantly about my characters as if they were our friends. Venting my frustration when they didn't want to talk to me, and jumping around, rambling when they finally did! You took it all in your stride, the way you do with everything. You continue to teach me what true love is, on a daily basis.

It's been a rollercoaster couple of years for us. We uprooted our life in Scotland and moved to the U.S., taking on the greatest adventure and the most grueling challenge of our marriage. You soared through with flying colors, dragging my sorry ass with you. You are my home, my calm. Your arms are the one place on Earth that I feel at peace, completely loved and cherished, and for that, I will never be able thank you enough. You are part of me, the better part, and you will always have my heart. I love you.

Now for the amazing people that have helped get this book across the finish line in style!

Sharron — Where do I begin? I'm in tears just thinking of how much I want to say to you, to thank you for everything that you are to me. To have such amazing support from a family member means more than I can ever express. You have become such a close friend, and I feel blessed every day to have you in my life. You've kept me going with your words of encouragement, and a good Scottish kick up the backside when I needed it. I love you to the moon and back.

Ria — The girl who made me a published author! How many meltdowns have you suffered through? You've seen the worst of me, and the best of me throughout this process, and you always gave me love in return. We understand the ups and downs in each other's lives in a way that strengthens us both. You have championed me, but also, Logan and Vittoria, from the start. You loved their characters, even when I couldn't. You believed in me, when I didn't, and you always knew that I would find their story inside of myself. That I would be able to use my own emotion and despair, and channel it into this book. You never gave up on me, and for that, I will always be grateful. Your red pen skills are wicked, and I'm excited to see what's next for you. I love you so much.

Megan Davis — My HTML savior! You have saved my ass so many times girl, and you always rock it! I was honored to have you come on board as a beta on this book, and your reaction — well, we were both exhausted by the end of that day! Your reaction to Logan made all the blood, sweat, and tears that went into writing him, worthwhile. There are always a few people who make a book memorable when they read it and message me, and you are that person for this book, so thank you so much. You're a great friend and I love your guts!

Diane, Diane, Diane — Logan is all for you, baby! I don't think I would have finished this book if I didn't know how desperately you wanted to know Logan Fitzgerald. You are by far, his number one fan, and I love you for it. You made me strive to make him the best that he could be, and I can never thank you enough for that. And the fact that you wrote a line in the epilogue kinda rocks! Thank you so much for sticking with me through thick and thin. Love you, girl.

Leslie — Here we are at the end of the series... for now! It's been the never-ending story at times, but I want to thank you for giving me the confidence and courage to tell Xander and Lily's story. If you hadn't, Logan and Vittoria's story would never have been written. Thank you so much. You are a testament to true friendship and strength. I love you.

Noemi — You have championed me from the start, and loved my characters as much as I do. You stood by me through all of my ups and downs. Thank you so much for all you do to promote me. You're a beautiful friend. I love you.

To my editor Jaye Hart — Where to start? Master Fitzgerald would never have found his way back out into the world without you. Your appreciation of Vittoria's connection to ballet, fills my heart with joy! I'm sorry your MacBook overheated on this one! Thank you for being so easy to work with, and understanding of my particular brand of cray-cray. You're a kickass editor and an even better friend. Love you, bud.

To my anonymous Dominant and submissive — Thank you so much for letting me pick your brains throughout this process! Your willingness to help me portray a realistic, emotional relationship between a Master and his very much loved submissive, was invaluable. I wanted to do justice to how beautiful, tender, and real a BDSM relationship can be, and you helped me achieve that. You are a wonderful couple, and true friends. Thank you.

And last, but by no means least: To my readers. My eyes are filling with tears as I try to think of a way to convey how deeply you have touched my heart. When I started this journey, I didn't think anyone was going to take notice of my books, but you took a chance on a new author, and gave me a dream come true. There are no words that could ever do justice to how truly grateful I am. Thank you so much for taking this journey with me. I have cherished every minute of it.

SOCIAL MEDIA

www.instagram.com/evahainingauthor

www.facebook.com/evahainingauthor

www.twitter.com/evahaining

www.amazon.com/author/evahaining

www.bookbub.com/profile/eva-haining

https://www.goodreads.com/author/show/20271110.Eva_Haining

www.evahaining.com

Made in United States
North Haven, CT
04 September 2023

41125670R00180